ABOUT THE AUTHOR

Chris Street spent her childhood in Surrey and studied English at the University of York before forging a successful career in leadership development. After more than two decades working at senior level for major corporates and international consulting organisations, she and her husband bought a hotel, a boat, three horses and two cats, and moved their young family to the west country.

Today she pursues her passion for writing from a village west of Truro, just a few minutes from her creative inspiration – the magnificent coast of Cornwall, and the sea.

THE
LOOKOUT
BOY

CHRISTINE STREET

Troubador Publishing Ltd
Unit E2 Airfield Business Park,
Harrison Road, Market Harborough,
Leicestershire LE16 7UL
Tel: 0116 279 2299
Email: books@troubador.co.uk
Web: www.troubador.co.uk

ISBN 978 1 805143 54 3

British Library Cataloguing in Publication Data.
A catalogue record for this book is available from the British Library.

Printed and bound in Great Britain by CMP
Typeset in 10.5pt Adobe Garamond Pro by Troubador Publishing Ltd, Leicester, UK

for Georgia, Loz and Alan:
my own steadfast navigators

Canary Wharf
November

The moment she opened her door, Joss knew they'd found him. Two grim faces, a flash of police ID, a soft 'Mrs. Jocelyn Harris?' and something peeled away from her like a layer of skin. She closed her eyes and took a breath.

This is it. This is when everything changes.

'DI Preston, Mrs. Harris,' announced the older of the two, a whey-faced man in a tired car coat. He gestured towards his companion. 'And PC Alison Harvey. May we come in?'

They followed her into the vast lounge, the pallid inspector and his silent colleague, visibly disconcerted to find a thin blond boy watching their approach with saucer-eyed anguish.

'*Mum?*' Ollie pushed the knuckles of one hand between his teeth as Joss scooped him against herself, burying her face in his hair to inhale his sweetly familiar scent.

Don't say anything.

'No school today, son?' the DI asked gently, and she looked up in shock.

The clock was showing 0845. Dear God, how could that be? Beneath an oversized sweatshirt Ollie was still in his Iron Man pyjamas, and her own damp nightdress was adhering like clingfilm, thankfully screened by the kimono she'd thrown on in an effort to stop shivering hours ago. Only now did she become aware of traffic noise, the distant clatter of a train, weak winter sunshine struggling through the panoramic east-facing windows.

'Perhaps your son might leave us for a moment?'

Ollie's arms compressed her ribs, fingers clawing at her back as he shook his head.

'It's alright. Best if we're not separated.' She pressed him close. 'He's strong.' *They've no idea how strong.* 'We'll be strong for each other.'

The policeman pursed his lips. 'How old are you then, young man?'

Joss felt the tug as Ollie tightened his grip on her robe – the only sign he'd heard the question. 'Twelve,' she answered for him.

'Well. If that's what you think best.' Preston frowned, but conceded with a brief nod. 'Please sit down, Mrs. Harris. I'm afraid it's bad news.'

'It's Felix then.' Her voice cracked, and she turned away. The wary compassion in their eyes was unbearable.

Her husband's body had been pulled from the Thames shortly before dawn, the DI told her. In spite of the cold he'd abandoned his scarf and coat on the quay at St. Katherine's Dock a short walk away, his wallet untouched in an inside pocket.

His beautiful cashmere coat; the Burberry scarf I bought him... Imagining these items strewn on a riverbank, marking the spot where he must have plunged into freezing darkness, triggered a silent howl in her brain. They'd need to confirm the cause of death, the inspector went on, and unfortunately she'd be required to identify the body. There'd be an inquest, toxicology reports and so on; standard procedure, he was sure she'd understand. 'But on the face of it... '

She covered Ollie's ears with flattened hands. 'You think he meant to do it.'

'It looks that way, Mrs. Harris. I'm very sorry.'

'Perhaps I can put the kettle on.' The uniformed PC moved into the kitchen area and began casting about for the mugs, teabags and sugar Felix always tidied scrupulously away behind its sleek cupboard doors. Joss watched with a kind of dazed embarrassment as the young woman eyed the ultramodern boiler tap, realising there *was* no kettle. 'Please don't worry,' she murmured, and the officer re-joined her colleague, cheeks blotching pink.

They settled on opposite sofas, the visitors perched beside each other at the edge of the largest, Joss cradling Ollie on the other. 'Obviously this is a dreadful shock,' the DI ventured. 'If you'd like a few minutes… perhaps to get dressed…'

Ollie shook his head again, enormous eyes imploring her, *Stay.*

'Maybe in a minute.'

'Of course.' Preston exchanged glances with his partner. 'As you can imagine, Mrs. Harris, we'll need your help with a few questions. When you feel up to it.' He cleared his throat. 'Anything you can tell us about your husband's circumstances, his state of mind over the last few days…'

As he spoke, Joss watched his eyes flicker round the room. His PC's curiosity was more overt – she'd begun twisting in her seat, her expression increasingly troubled. Joss chewed her lip while the woman scanned the photos displayed across every wall: their first wedding anniversary, Felix bending to kiss the top of her head; Ollie aged four, laughing on Felix's shoulders in the grounds of Wheal Blazey, her parents' Cornish guest house; Felix receiving his company's *Man of the Moment* award just two years ago. Instagrammable perfection, all of it.

Then both officers turned their attention to the curtain heaped on the floor beside a cracked hurricane lamp, its wax and candle-sand sullying an area eight feet square. On a coffee table near the window, the remains of a tumbler of scotch squatted by an overturned glass of red. Across the room, through the doorway to Felix's office, papers littered every surface. Joss averted her eyes from the chaos of gaping drawers and cabinets, dangling chargers and laptop cables unconnected to any devices.

'Mrs. Harris,' the DI said carefully. 'Forgive me for asking. Did you and your husband have some sort of… domestic last night?'

You could say that.

As Ollie convulsed against her, she stroked ribbons of hair from his forehead and murmured, 'It's OK, sweetheart, it's OK.' But her hand had begun to shake. Bile rose in her throat, constricting her breath. The sound that emerged was pitifully inarticulate.

'Mrs. Harris?' The inspector's face was taut. 'Is there someone we should call?'

She shifted her gaze to the window, where a pewter sky filled the narrow gaps between towering financial citadels and glass-balconied apartments just like this one, flanking the river. 'My mother,' she said at last. 'Annie Livesey. Her number's in the phone.'

'On it,' said Alison.

While the officer dialled and spoke in hushed tones ten feet away, Joss rocked Ollie in her arms and stared at the images of his singular, clever, photogenic father. *The Godball*, his colleagues called him. He'd always liked that. *Used to* like that.

Privately she suspected it was never meant as a compliment.

Alison put the phone into her hand.

'Oh my darling,' Annie wailed. 'My poor girl.'

Then she started to cry in earnest, scalding tears coursing down her face and neck to mingle with those of her son. 'I don't know what to do, Mum. What should I do?'

'Bring Ollie. Come back to Wheal Blazey,' her mother said. 'Come home.'

ONE

Wheal Blazey
Six months later

Returning designer socks to a forgetful guest gave Joss an excuse to walk Ollie to school. The post office was just around the corner.

The air along the coast path plucked at her senses, clean and fresh as new paper. Spring in Cornwall was so luminous – every year it surprised her all over again. Scents of gorse and wild garlic filled her nose, sharpened as ever by green base-notes rising from the sea. 'I've always loved this view,' she told him. 'You can see the whole town from up here.'

He lifted his head and grunted.

Joss gave him a sideways look. 'You'll be brown as a berry by the end of the summer, Ol.'

'Whatever.'

She shook her head at him, biting her lip.

They continued down into St Roslyn – still a working port, unspoiled but not too chocolate-boxy, with pleasant streets, a busy harbour, two or three pubs and a good school. The school where Ollie was about to complete his first term.

'I want to stay with *you*.' Paused at the entrance, he gave the gatepost a half-hearted kick. 'I wish we were home.'

Home? A loaded word. She was afraid to ask what he meant. 'Only one more week till the Easter break, sweetheart.'

Not an entirely comfortable prospect, she thought. Her parents' guesthouse was filling up, and it was worryingly clear they needed help. Time alone with Ollie was likely to prove a challenge. But she managed a smile, gripped him by the shoulders and said, 'Courage, *mon brave*.'

Big, sky-blue eyes in a flawless face looked dolefully up at her. Felix's mini-me. He wiped his nose on a cuff and hoisted his schoolbag resignedly over one shoulder as she watched him to the door, little flames igniting in her heart. Love was such a mighty thing, she reflected. But it could weigh you down like lead.

From the post office, she headed back the way she'd come. Tucked beneath imposing cliffs was a crescent of sand with pungent rockpools at one end and a simple café at the other: Little Roslyn Beach. As a child, and during many grown-up visits since, this had been her favourite place to sit and think. Or just sit. She glanced at her watch. Her mother was handling breakfasts and check-outs this morning – no tricky customers this week, nothing too complicated. Maybe she could snatch half an hour to herself and – *yes!* – the café was open. Five minutes later she was settled on a flat rock clutching a latte, gazing out at the incoming tide.

The breeze from the sea had a real bite to it. It was too early for most tourists, but a lone jogger had stopped to throw lumps of bladderwrack for his dog, while a pair of teenagers with rolled-up jeans and pipe-cleaner shins poked about in the rockpools. Overhead, herring gulls cackled and swooped. She followed the birds' progress across the vast expanse of blue and wondered how they could possibly be related to the scabby vandals who'd pillaged their London bins on a regular basis.

God, London. It was beginning to feel like someone else's life. *If only.*

Even on this beach, the past had left its footprints. They'd picnicked here, just the two of them, the August weekend she'd brought Felix to Wheal Blazey for the first time. She could still picture him too far out in the water, performing ridiculous acrobatics for her benefit while other beachgoers looked on, transfixed. She remembered him charging up to her while she sunbathed, depositing wet seaweed on her bare stomach, chortling when she shrieked. *You refuse to go in the sea, Miss Cowardy Custard, so I've brought the sea to you.* The way he'd taken control of her parents' barbecue, astonishing them by making a pepper sauce and garlic mayo from scratch. The nights he'd left her breathless, wasted with pleasure in the wreckage of her mother's best bedlinen.

He's quite... *imposing,* Annie had said cautiously when pressed. Joss had taken the comment positively. *He's someone who makes things happen, Mum,* she'd enthused, *and it's me he wants with him.*

What had he seen in her? In honesty, she'd never really known. But being without him these last few months had been like stumbling through the aftermath of a tornado. A landscape of mangled, broken things.

And now her cheeks were wet and she'd let her coffee get cold. *Dammit.*

She retraced her steps, ascending towards Wheal Blazey's slate roofs and mellow rubble-stone walls as the building emerged, bit by bit, between land and sky. The remains of its old engine house were just visible above encroaching heather on the western boundary. Romantic, handsome, iconic – Joss had come across those words many times over in the visitors' book. But it was an insatiable creature, her childhood home. Since she'd been back she'd noticed tell-tale signs of rot in its ocean-facing casements, timbers beginning to buckle, faded paintwork, roof tiles urgently in need of replacement. *It's eating money.*

A vibrant show of pink beside the entrance steps caught her eye: the huge camellia, a glamorous old stalwart that had resurged in that same place every Spring since she was knee-high, clinging to her mother's skirts.

'I see Elsie's still going strong,' she remarked as she joined Annie in the kitchen. Sun through the old sash windows was turning its limed walls the colour of clotted cream.

'Elsie? Oh, the camellia! Probably the most dependable thing around here.'

Milk jugs and ketchup bottles were assembled in battalions on the oak dresser. Her mother was swabbing them with ferocious energy, as if they were mucky children.

'Have I missed something?'

'Well, for starters,' Annie muttered, not looking up, 'It seems we've got mice.'

'Mice?'

'The couple who checked out of *Puffins* this morning said they'd been kept awake by overhead scrabbling. It has to be mice. Fields all around us... and of course we insulated the rafters properly last year. Perfect conditions to breed in.'

'Oh, we'll sort it out.' Joss reached for a dishcloth. 'It can't be that big a deal.'

'Unless TripAdvisor make it one, God forbid. I might ask Ollie to put bait trays up there – do you think he would?'

'I'm sure he would. He needs things to do, Mum.'

She gravitated to a breakfast table, where Annie had organised the day's post into bundles: trade flyers, guest confirmations, general correspondence, and what looked like an alarming pile of supplier invoices. She peered curiously at her mother. The air around Annie seemed to be crackling with tension.

'Any CVs yet?' Recently she'd persuaded Annie to consider part-time holiday help.

'One the agency says looks promising. A sixteen-year-old spending Easter down here, hoping to earn some extra cash.'

'Ideal. So... Anything else?'

Annie cleared her throat and concentrated hard on a cruet she'd already thoroughly buffed. 'There was a call.'

'A call?'

'From Felix's lawyer. *Your* lawyer, I should say. He said there was something in the post for you, and he's available today if you want to talk about it.'

Icy fingers clamped themselves around every organ in Joss's body and squeezed. She looked again at the stack of 'general correspondence'. Protruding from beneath a hotchpotch of enquiries, parish notices and thank-you cards was the pristine corner of a white A4 envelope. Her mother had buried it at the bottom, she realised – endearingly protective. Or, more likely, trying to deny its existence.

She pursed her lips while she teased out the contents. *Here we go then. Big girl pants on.* 'We know what it will be,' she said. 'They've had the hearing. They've told me all along what to expect.' Flashing Annie a brave half-smile, she unfolded a formal-looking paper.

Dear Mrs Harris

We write to notify you of the outcome...

It didn't matter that she'd seen it coming. In black and white, the terminology was a punch to the gut.

...conclusion of internal investigations, independently audited... determination of the court... sequestration of assets... proceeds of crime...

She scanned it four times before she began to shake.

Annie folded her into a tight embrace as her legs gave way, then steered her onto a chair. 'Oh, my darling.' Her voice was frayed with anguish. 'It's over now, all over. What's done is done. You can move on.'

Joss gazed up, leaking tears. 'Move on? To *what?*' She pushed the notice out of reach as if it might burn her fingers.

'No money left at all? No assets?'

She raised her palms, communicating weary impotence. 'The flat, cars, investments, savings, pension funds… everything was in Felix's name, *everything*. And in terms of their total value – it doesn't come anywhere near the shortfall. I've been made insolvent, Mum. And they think they've been generous.' She winced at the bitterness in her own voice – but it was entirely self-directed. Final confirmation of her own stupidity. *As if I needed evidence.*

Annie slammed the nearest ketchup bottle onto a tabletop and glared at it, her face and ears flushing scarlet. 'That treacherous weasel of a man! If he were standing in front of me now instead of lying cold in his grave, I'd wring his *bloody neck.*'

Perversely, the tangled logic of this made Joss laugh. Knots that for months had been calcifying inside her like rock seemed, for a fleeting moment, to ease. Annie was right of course. There was nothing she could do now; no more waiting, no more subjugation to false hope. The slow-moving juggernaut of legal process had prostrated her – but at last it was trundling off down the road. She blew her nose. 'You'd have to stand on a chair to do that,' she retorted, and Annie rolled her eyes.

But the light relief was short. She took her mother's hand, lightly tracing its prominent veins, thin bones betraying tiny distortions of early arthritis, skin roughened by years of hard work with little respite, and felt a twist in her heart. Annie was ageing by the day. 'I hate this whole dreadful business for making you so angry and unhappy,' she said. 'But things weren't always—' She tossed her head. 'I mean – if Felix were here now, he'd probably convince you—' Of *what*? she stopped to ask herself. That he *meant* well?

'I'm sorry, sweetheart. You're going to have to forgive an occasional rant.' With a sigh Annie patted the fingers wrapped around hers. 'In spite of everything, I know you must have loved him.'

Joss closed her eyes, feeling slightly sick. There he was again, cruelly vivid in her mind's eye, braced against the curved glass of their stylish balcony while he toasted the river and the twilit city below. Lord of all he surveyed. As if he owned the air.

Look what you've done to us. Bastard.

'Anyway,' she rallied, 'I may now officially be broke, but I'm grateful to be home while I try to figure things out. What we both need going forward – Ollie most of all – is stability and routine. Family. People around him he can trust.'

'Poor mite,' her mother said. 'He's so quiet these days. Will you tell him about the judgement?'

'I don't think I need to. He's not silly.'

'I can't help wondering what's going on in his mind.' Annie frowned at her hands. 'I mean, what he really thinks about his dad. They seemed so close. Does he ever talk to you about him?'

Joss picked up a sauce bottle. Her thumb found a tiny blister in the neck, and she worked at it with a fingernail. 'Sometimes,' she said. 'If he needs to.'

The lie made heat rise in her face. *No* would have been the honest answer.

While Annie's hand moved soothingly across her back, words she'd used on that last night echoed in her brain. *We won't tell anyone what happened here, Ol. People don't need to know. It won't help.*

She gathered herself. 'I bought him a notebook a few days ago,' she added. 'A journal. Somewhere he can log his private thoughts, if he ever needs an outlet other than me. I got the idea from a feature on mental health in one of last week's supplements.'

'A kind of safety valve?'

'Exactly. For his eyes only. Though I don't know if it's really his thing.' She retrieved the polishing cloth and pulled a face at the sticky rim of the jar she was holding.

'Well, between us we must give him what he needs. Restore his faith in things. In *people*.' Annie pulled herself determinedly upright, swept up the document and shuffled it back into the pile. 'Stability for you *and* for Wheal Blazey is something I pray for every night. As for family—' She paused, and Joss saw her eyes fill. 'I'm only sorry your father can't play more of a part. But the way things are with him now…'

'I know, Mum.'

Beyond the window, the familiar white-haired figure sat swaddled in blankets on his favourite bench between two enormous rhododendrons. He'd once tipped Ollie upside down on the lawn in that same spot, making the toddler shriek with laughter as he growled in his best evil-pirate voice, *I'll have to shake the doubloons out of your breeches to buy ice-cream and grog if we're headed for the beach today, matey.*

Ollie had adored his grandad. Surely still did? Two losses to come to terms with; a double portion of grief. *That*, as Felix himself would have said, *is a bloody crap gig.*

'I'll take a sandwich out to him,' she offered. 'Then I'll come back and help you with the accounts.'

Jack Livesey's bird-bright eyes and wide smile greeted her as she lowered herself beside him and manoeuvred the plate securely into the centre of his lap. 'Hallo, Dad,' she said.

'Hallo, dear.' He examined her face with interest, then

picked up his sandwich and peeled back the upper slice. 'Cheese and pickle? My favourite.'

'It *is*!' Joss pressed his arm. 'Medlar pickle from the deli in St. Roslyn. You've always liked it.'

He blinked at her. 'Have I?'

'Well, yes. Or… Maybe that was Mum.' *Never mind.* She sat back slowly, watching him eat.

A few bites in, he waved a shaky hand towards the house. 'It's so nice out here. The place is looking glorious. And Annie's hellebores are out, do you see?'

'They love this soil.' The gallant white roses tumbled like surf along the perimeter of the main building as far as the two-up, two-down keeper's cottage nestling behind it. Unavailable to paying guests – it needed too much TLC – this cottage was, for the moment, her sanctuary. 'It's pretty fresh out here though, Dad. Wouldn't you rather come inside for a cuppa? I don't want you to get cold.'

He coughed politely. 'Are you down here on holiday?'

'On holiday? Dad, I've been living here since Christmas!'

For an instant he seemed completely dumbfounded. Then he peered more closely into her face, brows drooping over narrowed eyes. 'You were in London before?'

'That's right.' She nodded and smiled. *Keep going, Dad.*

'But don't you miss your friends there? Your work?'

This brought her up short. Friends? Well… Felix had had friends: marketeers and traders, people he played squash with, people he networked with at the sailing club. Drinking buddies. For a while she'd kept up with a couple of girls from uni, at least until his sniping about them got too much. But work? 'I haven't had a job in years,' she sighed. 'Not since Ollie came along. And not before then, if I'm honest.'

Jack looked bewildered. 'But you're such a lovely girl. And you have a good brain. It seems a waste.'

She smacked his wrist. 'Good brain? If only you knew. It's a rats' nest in there!'

He chuckled at that, and returned to his sandwich.

But she'd have to find a proper job at some point. Dear Lord, what could she even *do*? She had no experience in anything, no professional skills or qualifications. The world had moved on while she'd been playing house, bringing up her son, supporting her smoking-hot husband... And what was she left with? Ash.

There'd been a time she could have said to her father, *I feel lost, help me, I need your advice.* Jack had always been her rock. Once when she was five, a freak wave had sucked her from the shallows of a local beach, submerging her in a terrifying series of cartwheels until he'd hurled himself fully clothed into the water to wrestle her out of its clutches. He'd called her his 'fearless, feisty girl.' He'd made her feel safe. *Never forget, that husband of yours is lucky to have you*, he told her every time they visited. Two years ago she'd shown him bank statements she couldn't understand, transactions and accounts she didn't recognize, sneaked out of Felix's office. *No need to tell your mother*, he'd counselled her then – *she'd only worry.* Now, she just wanted to clasp his hand and say, *I've screwed up, Dad. My life is a mess. I'm frightened of the future and I don't know how to get Ollie through this.*

She studied his profile intently until he looked round again, fixing shining eyes on hers. Had he read her mind? For just a second, it seemed miraculously possible. Then he nodded and said, 'My daughter lives in London too – I think.'

There was no time to deal with the pain that sliced into her at that moment. Her mother had appeared on the steps and was frantically waving the house phone.

'It's Ollie's form tutor!' Annie was shouting. 'He's not at school. They don't know where he is!'

TWO

'I'm sorry, Mrs. Harris. Ollie went to sick bay feeling poorly this morning, and we agreed he could call home and arrange to be picked up. The nurse left him for just a minute, but when she got back he'd gone. So we thought it wise to check. But from what you say, he hasn't called?'

'No, he hasn't.' A cold fog thickened in her head while she tried to make sense of this. Perhaps he'd tried her and got voicemail? Perhaps he was on his way right now, doggedly plodding up the coast path while they were speaking. She asked herself whether the landline in the main house had been busy that morning and she'd left her mobile out of earshot. Neither, of course, was the case.

'How long since you discovered he wasn't there?' As a rule it took him fifteen minutes to walk home – twenty if the weather was fine and there were seals in the bay.

Audible seconds of pondering followed – prevarication, she was certain – before the teacher replied, 'An hour or so?'

'An *hour*! How on *earth*— ?' She reached for her jacket.

'I'm sure he won't be far away, Mrs. Harris. St. Roslyn is a nice little town, very safe.' He oozed complacent reassurance, which she found deeply irritating. There was such a thing as being *too Cornish*.

'If he's taken a detour on the way home, it will probably be to the marina. It's been a magnet for the boys these last few weeks. Some of them – including Ollie, as I'm sure you know – have been sneaking down there during break times, watching all the yachts come out of winter storage—'

'I certainly *didn't* know that,' she fumed. 'He hasn't said anything. Someone from the school should have told me.'

'Well. We'd appreciate you getting back to us, Mrs. Harris once you've—' But she'd already handed the phone to Annie and was making for the gate.

Circling seagulls miaowed like cats as she hurried into town, the noise feeding her anxiety. *Today of all days…* Why did troubles always arrive together, like proverbial London buses? Everything felt off.

There was no sign of Ollie on the coast path, nor the quay. Was he poorly? She doubted it, he'd been fine that morning. She tried his mobile as she advanced, but phone coverage in the bay was – she already knew – worse than dire. One thing his teacher might be right about, though. She clung to the thought. Ollie *did* like boats.

St. Roslyn had a large, busy marina thanks to its well-protected harbour and deep-water approach. The sea was usually benign between the port and the outer margins of Chy Head, the monumental granite mass where weekend sailors tended to get caught out. Joss passed jauntily painted trawlers and a handful of crabbers moored on the quayside as she hurried towards the boatyard. Then she saw it: the red and grey of a St. Roslyn school blazer, haphazardly slung over one shoulder. *Thank God.* Her slender blond boy, with his back towards her.

Two things struck her as she drew near. The first was the beauty of the dark green hull Ollie seemed preoccupied with, clamped securely in position by a sturdy trestle five feet from the ground. Joss knew nothing about yachts, but even she could tell there was something different about this one. It was wholly constructed of wood, bowsprit to stern, and its mast – one gigantic piece of timber – towered majestically over its fibre-glass and aluminium neighbours. The second was the realisation that Ollie was steadying a ladder propped against the hull, his free hand nursing an open can of Tribute.

'*Ollie?*'

'Mum!'

For a moment they stared at each other. Then Joss heard the loud thwack of a hammer from the cockpit above their heads, followed by a clatter of metal and an indignant roar. '*Ow*! *Sod* this *fucking thing*!'

Ollie gulped down a giggle as she lifted a warning finger and glared in the direction of the voice. '*Excuse* me?'

'Ollie,' the voice continued obliviously, 'Hand me the jib track, will you?'

Joss stepped forward to grasp her son's wrist as he set down the can and selected a length of metal from a toolbox by his feet. 'What are you *doing*, Ol?'

Sensing movement, she squinted upwards. A pair of dark eyes connected with hers, brows arched in enquiry. Their owner, she noticed, sported a tangled mat of black hair, smears of grease down one side of a wind-burnt nose, and a chin that hadn't seen a razor in days. A faint west-country burr inflected a voice that observed, 'I see you've got company, Ollie.'

Ollie fidgeted with the steel in his hand, his eyes darting from one adult to the other. 'It's my mum,' he said. 'This is Mr. McCalvey, Mum, and this is his boat, *Kara*. She's going in the water next week. He wants to sail her down to the Med one day.'

Joss heard a throaty chuckle as the man stood up, stretched, tore a square from a roll of paper at the edge of the deck, and proceeded to clean his hands. 'Well, that's an introduction and a half,' he grinned. 'But unless I get this rigging fixed I won't be going much further than Mousehole. Hallo, Ollie's mum. It's just Cal, by the way.'

Joss stiffened and planted her feet a little wider, hoping he'd understand the posture as indignation. Or confidence, at least. 'My son should be in *school*,' she said. 'His form teacher called me half an hour ago.' She tightened her grip on Ollie's arm. 'He bunked off this morning, and I gather it's not the first time.'

'Ah. I did wonder.'

The yachtsman swung himself onto the ladder and dropped with easy grace onto the tarmac. Close up, he was younger than he'd first appeared – early thirties, she guessed, like herself. *Good.* She felt more equal to him.

'In that case you should have *challenged* him. Before you got him doing odd jobs.'

He tilted his head, looked at her and shrugged. 'I didn't think to give him the third degree. And it's only been a couple of times.'

A couple of times? She gaped at him, nonplussed, as he glanced backwards to brush a splatter of mud from the hull with his fingertips. 'Working on this temperamental old lady is an education in itself, frankly – no chalk and talk required. Though a textbook might have helped me avoid making such a dog's breakfast of all the string.'

Was his mouth curling at the corners just a bit? His eyes were shining with what Joss could only assume was suppressed amusement. *Cheeky sod.* She pointed at the beer can, her temperature rising. 'Is that part of his education too? He's only twelve, for heaven's sake.'

'Nearly thirteen,' Ollie offered.

'Oh, that's mine,' McCalvey explained cheerfully. 'I did let him have a taste, I'm afraid. His share of a proper drink, for a proper job.'

This rendered her momentarily speechless. As she continued to stare, McCalvey extended a hand. 'Nice to meet you anyway, Mrs. Ollie,' he said.

She couldn't bring herself to take it – not least because, despite his efforts, McCalvey's fingers were liberally spotted with resin. Unfazed, he took a step back and smiled. 'Ollie tells me his dad used to take him dinghy sailing on the Thames.'

'At weekends, yes. He wanted—' but she stopped herself, absurdly wrong-footed. Why should she explain anything to this man? There was no way she'd reveal to a stranger that Felix had wanted to make his son more robust, more independent. *I don't want him growing up a mummy's boy.* Words from a man who hadn't spoken to his own mother in fifteen years.

'You don't sail yourself?' McCalvey's voice cut into her thoughts.

'No.'

'Mum's frightened of the water,' Ollie chipped in. 'When she was little, my grandad once had to—'

'Ollie!' Joss silenced him with a look.

Something shifted in McCalvey's expression. 'Better that than overly confident,' he said.

'Yes. Well.' She yanked the blazer over her son's shoulders, gripping the collar while he wriggled himself inside it like a netted fish. 'We should get back.'

Ollie scanned her face, then flung himself against her, tucking his arms into her jacket as he pressed his forehead to her chest. Cuddling him, she was conscious of McCalvey taking them both in, his lips settling into a grim line.

'I apologise,' she heard him murmur. 'I shouldn't have let him hang out here so long. But to be honest, it seemed like... he needed a change of scene.'

Adrenaline drained out of her like water from a cracked jug. She felt utterly exhausted. Was she overreacting? She opened her mouth to offer something more conciliatory – but then the world exploded.

At the far end of the harbour where the sea wall yielded to rock, the doors of the lifeboat station were opening, its siren wailing a galvanizing call to arms. Another noise – much closer – assaulted their ears; McCalvey had ripped a pager from an inside pocket and snapped to attention, focusing on its pulsating lights. He glanced up – 'I'm on call, sorry' – turned on his heel, and ran.

The door of the chandlery thirty feet away burst open and an older, stockier man in a yellow RNLI waterproof set off in pursuit, shouting, '*Capsize by the Head, Cal! We'll need to launch the inshore.*'

'He's a lifeboat volunteer!' Joss watched with startled interest as the men accelerated towards the rumbling steel-grey ocean, the granite bulk of Chy Head looming on the horizon like an ominous Sphinx.

Ollie pulled at her sleeve. 'Maybe,' he said. 'Dunno. I just like his boat. Can we go?'

They headed back, heavy-footed and twice as slow as Joss's dash to the port in the previous half hour. For a while she let him trudge along in silence, acutely sensitive to his shuttered face, the way he clenched and unclenched his fists with every step. *It seemed like he needed a change of scene,* that man – McCalvey – had remarked. Annoyingly presumptuous, now she thought about it. What would *he* know?

'So, talk to me, Ol,' she said eventually.

He dropped his head. 'I had gut ache.'

'Really?'

'Only because those morons Finch and Davis made me want to throw up.'

She touched his shoulder. 'What happened?'

'It doesn't matter,' he said, but dark red patches were blooming in his cheeks.

'It clearly does.'

He stooped to grab a cane splinter from an abandoned trawler basket, and began to rake the sea wall with it. 'They just *say* things,' he grunted. 'Stupid things. About… girls. Other kids' sisters. Mums they see at the school gate. They've made a list.'

'What sort of list?'

But she could hazard a guess. She knew those boys; swaggering bullies in the year above Ollie, each of them fuelled by burgeoning testosterone vastly greater than their emotional maturity. Finch in particular was trouble. It was in the genes. His father was Annie's nearest and most problematic neighbour.

'Like – a scorecard.' He thrashed at the old stones with a violence that made her reach for his arm to still it.

'I suppose I'm on it?'

Abruptly, he stopped walking. 'At the top. They said that because Dad's not around any more, you must be desperate for a proper… that what you really need is a good…'

'Oh, *Ollie*.' Joss tipped her head back and groaned.

'I told them to shut up,' he hissed. 'I wanted to punch them. I went to sick bay just to be on my own. So I wouldn't end up smashing a rock in their idiot faces.'

He was rigid from head to foot, though his fingers continued to curl into fists, then uncurl again. She could almost see the fault lines fracturing his skinny body; heartache manifesting itself like blisters on his skin. 'Well, that wouldn't have helped anyone,' she said quietly. 'You did the right thing. But why didn't you *call* me?'

He scowled at his feet. 'You're always working during the day now, doing check-ins, helping Gran. I was planning to get back at the normal time, so you wouldn't know and you wouldn't have to worry.'

'But Ol—'

'I never want to make you sad.'

She grasped his shoulders. His whole face seemed closed, sewn up tight by invisible little stitches. 'It's my job to worry about you, silly. It's what mums do.' She raised his chin with her fingertips to make him look at her. 'And I'd have told you those boys aren't worth a second of your time and energy. It's only words. They're just showing off.'

'Well I *hate* how they are. They think they're so cool, but they don't know anything about me, or you, or Dad. As if we could forget everything, just like that. As if someone else could just come along and—' He was breathing hard now, and his voice was hoarse.

'What they think doesn't matter, sweetheart. But Ollie… we *should* talk about Dad. There are things it might help you to understand—'

'*I don't need to talk about Dad.*' A clenched fist beat the air with every syllable. 'I understand *enough*.'

'Calm down, hon. Just listen for a minute—'

'There's no point.' He tore himself away from her, slamming his palms against his ears. 'Everything in our lives has gone to shit.'

'Ollie!'

'There's only me and you now, Mum. That's it. Nothing else matters. We don't need anyone else. And I'm *not* going to talk about it any more.'

His ferocity was a shock. She reclaimed his hand and turned him in the direction of home, clutching her jacket tight as if the breakers beyond the harbour wall had spattered her with grit.

THREE

My name is Oliver Harris.

My mum says writing stuff in this book might help me sort my head out. So here goes.

We're staying in Cornwall at my Grans because my dad is dead and all our money is gone. Meaning I go to a rubbish school, live in a scabby old cottage, and wait hours every day for Mum to get a break because there's too much for my Gran to do and my Grandad is sick.

But at least we're near the sea.

So today is Day 1 of the Easter holidays. This morning I polished cutlery and did filing, then Gran asked me to put traps down for the mice. She made me wear rubber gloves and double-lock the shed where she keeps weedkiller and poison in case my Grandad finds them. It sucks that she can't trust him any more.

After that I stayed in my room. There were photos we still hadn't unpacked. The one I like best is of Mum and Dad's first anniversary when she was pregnant with me. She's in a red silk dress and Dad's *kissing the top of her head. She looks happy, really happy.*

It's down to me now to make her feel like that again.

I won't let anyone else hurt her, ever.

I'm going to keep her safe.

He was their last departure of the day: Guy Tremain, the land agent who'd booked himself into Wheal Blazey's priciest sea-view room on three previous occasions to Joss's knowledge. Pouring his coffee at breakfast, she couldn't help noticing the expertly undercut hair, the Tag Heuer on his wrist, the natty linen suit. He reminded her of a poster she'd had as a student: vintage Bowie as the 'Thin White Duke' – urbane, ironic, impeccably elegant. As he waited in reception for his bill, she realised she'd been examining his business card for a stupidly long time, just to avoid the appraising eyes behind his trendy aviators.

'I'm not sure I know what a land agent is,' she told him.

'Well then you haven't lived, Mrs. Harris. Or… can I call you Jocelyn?'

She fussed with the stapler. 'I think that's allowed, as you seem to be a regular.'

'And I'll be back again in a week,' he said. 'Things are pretty lively on the property front down here at the moment. Farmers with acres they don't use, developers wanting sites for new builds. My job is to value land assets, then bring people together and help maximise their potential.'

'Some of the locals must think you're their fairy godmother then,' she said. *God, that sounded facetious.* 'Sorry, I didn't mean —'

'No no, you're spot on.' He grinned. 'A good deal on a piece of estate that's been languishing in the same family for years can be transformational. Though heritage and tradition are important, of course. I never forget that.'

'Good *morning*, Mr. Tremain.' Annie arrived in reception. Her greeting was cordial but, Joss intuited, the tiniest bit cagey. 'I'm guessing you're off to Roslyn Glynn?'

It was up for development, Roslyn Glynn. *Acquired for clients: proposed site of 90 stunning new homes, to include luxury senior living.* She'd seen the hoardings in fields five miles east of town.

'The artist's impressions are terrific,' Guy said. 'You probably know that outline planning's been granted. The next phase is consultation. That's why I'm back next week. There's a meeting with the developers in the town hall, Wednesday evening. Open forum.'

Annie tutted. 'You'll find the townspeople have strong views,' she said.

'Of course they do. And it would be very helpful to have you both there.' He fixed gleaming eyes on Joss. 'Come with me. Ask questions. See for yourself. I think you'll end up agreeing it's a positive move for St. Roslyn. Enhanced transport services, twenty affordable homes within the plan, retail units. And the council have some very progressive ideas, like commissioning an arts centre to enhance the town's profile, with workshops and event spaces. I understand they're looking for lottery funding to make that happen.'

'*You* go, Jocelyn,' Annie said. 'One of us should. I'm more than happy to keep an eye on Ollie and your father for a few hours.'

Joss glanced from her mother to Guy, feeling oddly rattled. 'Well, I suppose—'

'Excellent!' Guy exclaimed. 'So it's a date!'

A *date*? Now, *there's* a troubling word, she reflected; far too open to interpretation. She dropped her eyes, handed back his credit card and said levelly, 'I suppose it might be useful to find out more.'

'I'll look forward to it,' he beamed. They nodded their goodbyes, and Annie accompanied him to the door.

Her mother, she noticed on her return, had acquired a light blush.

'What?'

'Oh, nothing,' Annie said. 'Except…'

Joss glared at her. '*What?*'

'He obviously likes you,' Annie said. 'And he's pleasant, don't you think? Clearly good at his job. Straightforward.'

'Stop it, Mum.'

They were interrupted by the change-over team clattering into the hall: Tegen, a curvy, flame-haired Madonna, closely followed by her placid alter-ego, Bridget. Local girls who'd come looking for work within hours of leaving school almost four years ago. 'OK if we have our break now, Mrs. L?'

'Fine,' Annie said. 'But don't forget, Tegen – we've a student coming for interview in half an hour. You're still OK to show her the ropes?'

'Course!'

Joss watched the pair sail into the kitchen and start rummaging for mugs. Every time she encountered them they seemed to be in fits of giggles – whispering, elbowing each other in the ribs, then giggling some more. Both of them pretty as peaches. How lovely to be so light-hearted, she thought; so *free*. She clawed a tendril of hair back into place behind an ear and frowned at the desktop. 'We'd better get a few questions ready.'

Annie found her glasses and leafed through the paperwork in her tray. 'Here's the profile,' she said. 'Katie McCalvey. Sixteen years old, living in Bristol.'

McCalvey? The second time in a week she'd heard that name. As she took the sheet from her mother, she realised the banter in the kitchen had stopped. Tegen appeared in the doorway. '*What* did you say this girl's name was?' she asked, and Annie repeated it.

'But she's not local?'

'Apparently not.'

Bridget arrived at her friend's side, and they shared a look. 'Only, *we* know a McCalvey,' Tegen said. 'Works down the marina, restores yachts. Volunteers on the lifeboats too. He comes in the Ship for a drink sometimes.' She slapped Bridget's hand as the other girl gave her a mysteriously hard poke. 'Maybe they're related?'

Joss re-read the CV. Good exam results, a decent school attended for the last five years, form prefect, Duke of Edinburgh award, weekend jobs in fashion retail… 'Unlikely,' she concluded.

But half an hour later – preceded by a teenage girl with spectacularly unnatural fuchsia hair – he strolled into the hall.

'Cal McCalvey!' Tegen's shriek was triumphant.

Beneath her vivid thatch, the schoolgirl's expression remained coolly neutral, though her companion visibly started. 'Well, yes – hallo, ladies – it's me.' That same low voice with the soft burr, though this time distinctly more cautious. 'And this is my…'

He hesitated. Joss took in the watchful dark eyes underscored with a crackle of fine lines; the tanned face framed by unruly black hair; chafed fingers; a faint tang of engine oil. She risked a quick, covert glance at her mother's pristine sofa cushions just across the corridor.

'This is… Katie.'

Annie extended a hand, which the teenager eagerly shook. 'I'm pleased you contacted us about holiday work, Katie. Tegen and Bridget can show you round and describe what they do, and we'll chat afterwards. Does that sound OK?'

'Sounds good.' Katie surveyed the reception area with interest. 'This is obviously where people check in and out. I like it.'

'And thank you so much for bringing her along, Mr.… McCalvey is it?'

'Oh, no problem. McCalvey, yes. But – it's just *Cal.*'

Tegen and Bridget watched him fidget in the tight space, grinning like Cheshire cats. If McCalvey's regular job was at the marina, Joss speculated, he'd probably interrupted his morning schedule to deliver their interviewee. She began to discern a subtle resemblance between the two of them; not just in the eyes – dark and slightly feline – but in the air of defiant self-reliance each seemed to give off like a fine dust. Whatever relationship linked the personable teenager to this unsettled, unsettling man, she'd put good money on it being complicated.

Scraping hair away from his forehead, McCalvey appeared to register her presence for the first time. 'Mrs. Ollie!'

'Jocelyn, actually.' Everyone turned towards her. She heard Tegen's *eh?* and caught her startled, wordless exchange with Bridget. 'Though most people call me Joss. That goes for you too, Katie, if you're OK with that.'

An appreciative smile brightened McCalvey's expression. '*Joss,*' he repeated softly.

For a second she held his gaze, her skin stippling with tiny, inexplicable goosebumps. Then she noticed Tegen inclining towards him with big, hungry eyes. *Oh, I get it.* Joss glowered at the floor, scolding herself. *The man is obviously St. Roslyn's answer to Don Juan. Six inches closer and she'll be licking his ears.*

Tegen stretched an arm towards Katie. 'Don't tell me Cal here is actually your *dad?*' she squawked. And with a brief backward glance, the teenager replied, 'Yep, that's him. My dad Cal.'

'Well I'm buggered!'

'*Tegen!*' Annie hissed, and the girls laughed.

McCalvey's comically rueful grin made Joss snort and fold her arms. Not so much Don Juan as the Artful Dodger, she thought wryly – caught with his hand in a jar of sweets.

'Well – Cal,' Annie said, 'Can we interest you in a coffee while Katie looks round?'

Immediately, he stepped back. 'Oh, no thanks, I'm good. I need to organise a few things while I'm waiting for this one.' He patted Katie's shoulder – a gesture she ignored – then moved to the door. 'I'll be out by the pick-up, Katie.' And he sauntered off into the sunshine.

'Sorry.' Katie waved towards the exit. 'He always prefers being outside, to be honest.'

'*Well*,' Tegen remarked, 'I didn't even know he was ever *married*.' She swivelled searchlight eyes back to the teenager. 'He looks bloody young to be your dad, though, don't mind me saying.'

'Oh, I live with my mum now,' Katie replied evenly. But the look she returned was icy.

Once Annie had shooed the girls out of reception, calm efficiency descended. 'Seems a bright spark,' Joss said. 'Friendly and polite.'

'And what interesting hair! It probably costs a fortune to achieve a look as – *arresting* as that.'

'Makes me wish I'd gone pink myself when I was younger,' Joss remarked. She grinned at her mother's beady look.

They spent a few minutes rehearsing their questions; then Annie gazed through the window and sighed. Jack was slowly levering himself out of his garden chair. 'I think your father might be wanting his lunch,' she said. 'We should probably settle him in his den while we do the interview.' But when he failed to appear in the hallway, they headed for the entrance steps.

Jack had stopped halfway across the car park and was resting against a large white pick-up bearing the logo of St. Roslyn Marina, while McCalvey reorganised hardware in the load area behind the cab. The younger man was evidently explaining something, and Jack, they could hear, was responding with interest. 'My word, is that right? Such a clever piece of kit... Locally made?'

'Gadget talk,' Annie surmised. 'Should we go and get him? Mr. McCalvey might appreciate the interruption.'

Joss touched her mother's sleeve to signal *wait*.

Though his hands fluttered and the tremor in his voice was heart-wrenchingly audible, her father was clearly an enthusiastic contributor to the conversation. He looked, in fact, remarkably happy. She noticed that McCalvey – *Cal*, as he preferred to call himself – was careful to face him whenever he spoke, pausing every now and then to gauge the elderly man's reaction and listen. *Properly* listen, she understood with surprise. From the obscurity of the doorway she watched McCalvey reach for some kind of winch, which he laid in her father's frail hands, supporting them gently with his own. Jack said something she didn't quite catch, but she saw McCalvey smile. 'I agree with you, it's not exactly sophisticated,' she heard him say. And as he reclaimed his piece of kit, he touched her father's arm.

'You know, I think they're absolutely fine,' she said.

But a short, heavyset figure was striding towards them through Wheal Blazey's open gate – steel-capped boots crunching on the gravel, a large Alsatian-type dog straining ahead of him on a short leash. From a hundred yards away, the visitor's dour expression was all too evident. 'Hell's bells. It's Finch.' Annie pulled herself determinedly straight. 'What's he after, I wonder?'

Joss squinted at the man's approach. 'Well I'd hazard a guess it's not a cream tea.'

Finch marched past the pick-up, ignoring Jack's smile and

McCalvey's brief, quizzical nod, and ascended the steps. He grunted at Joss before halting abruptly in front of her mother, wrenching the dog onto its haunches and declaring, 'Annie, I'd like a word.'

'Bill!' Annie offered her hand. 'Nice to see you.'

Joss glanced towards the pick-up. Her father seemed agitated now, his eyes flicking between the vehicle and the doorway. By now the girls would be touring the upstairs bedrooms – safely out of the way. 'Let's go inside for a minute,' she suggested. 'At least into the hall. If you wouldn't mind keeping your dog—'

'Yes, *alright*.' Finch snatched at the dog's lead and barged past them.

Once through the door, he leaned heavily against the counter by the desk and waited, scrubbing irritably at his chin, until Joss and her mother assumed expectant positions against the opposite wall.

'What can I do for you, Bill?' Annie asked.

Finch noisily sucked his teeth. 'I can't stay long, Annie. I just want you to be aware – I think your tank and soakaway's failing. I've been all round my fields today and there's a smell, plus foul water backing up. I've had to move my animals.'

'Oh dear.' Annie sounded sympathetic but unmistakeably nervous. 'Sorry about that, Bill. Are you sure we're the cause?'

'Of *course* I'm sure,' he snapped. 'I've been saying for years the drains you've got aren't right for a property the size of this, not when you get busy. The system's worn out, Annie, it's not doing its job any more. You need it sorted.'

To emphasise the point, he lifted the arm still connected to the dog and aimed his index finger at the centre of Annie's face. Clearly spooked, the dog leapt to its feet with a thunderous bark, baring huge yellow teeth – stopped in mid-air by the choke of its collar. Instinctively Joss flung an arm sideways in her mother's defence, exclaiming, 'Careful!'

'*Mum!*' The shriek was Ollie's.

She spun towards him. He'd entered from the back of the house and was hovering in the corridor, just outside the kitchen. And now, in the other direction, her father was making his ponderous way up the entrance steps. *Bloody Nora* – this wasn't good.

'Ollie – sit Grandpa down behind reception for a minute, would you?'

Ollie shuffled past the visitor to take his grandfather's hand and lead him behind the counter to the swivel chair. Once seated, Jack gazed ahead in passive bewilderment while Ollie stood at his shoulder staring grimly at the dog.

'Right. Well thank you, Bill, for the information.' Annie had maintained a dignified posture throughout, but Joss saw her fingers shake as she raised a hand to fidget with her collar. 'I'll get someone to take a look.'

'Do that,' Finch said rudely. 'And soon.'

A pulse in Joss's temple began to thump. 'My mother has *told* you we'll look into it,' she said. 'You don't have to bully us.'

He fixed her with a dead-eyed stare and leered, showing tobacco-stained teeth. '*Bully* you? I don't think you know what bullying is, girlie.'

Oh, I think I do. 'Please take your dog outside now, Mr. Finch. It's making my son and father very nervous. So, if that's all you came here to say—'

'I'll be saying a damn sight more if this doesn't get sorted,' he snarled.

Ollie was looking ashen. Jack had rotated his chair towards the window and was conducting a one-way conversation with the outside world, plainly disengaging from the scene. One small mercy, Joss thought. Her heart was really pounding now.

Wires in her brain seemed suddenly to connect in a flash of white heat. 'We've heard you. So please *leave.*' She stepped forward and jerked a thumb towards the door. 'Leave *now.*'

The next second, she took in Finch's bloated, enraged face as he shouted 'Caesar! *Down!*', the leash in his hand unravelling. A horrendous bark was followed by a yell of '*No!*' from Ollie, while a searing bracelet of pain encircled her wrist. The animal had her arm in its teeth.

Finch delivered two hard punches in quick succession and the dog relaxed its jaws with a resentful whine. A momentary hiatus followed – everyone deathly still, rigid with shock – before he grumbled, 'He felt threatened. You shouldn't have come at me like that.'

Joss stared at him, the storm in her head stripping away all possibility of speech. His eyes flickered to where her mother had taken hold of her wrist and was bending to inspect the damage: two red welts between visible puncture marks. 'He's torn the skin,' Annie blazed. 'Thank God he didn't have time to go deeper. Never, *never* come near us with that monstrous creature again, or we'll get the police out.'

Finch gathered the leash and glared at her. 'I can see this place is too much for you.' He tipped his head in Jack's direction. 'Two women on their own… It's a massive undertaking, this. And the problems will only get bigger.' At last he pulled the dog aggressively to heel and headed for the door.

Joss watched him stomp down the steps, shivering as her rage collapsed into cold, debilitating anguish. 'I've probably made it worse, I'm so sorry,' she said wretchedly. 'A bomb went off inside, I just saw red, I couldn't help myself—'

'*Rules!*' Jack's roar cut her off. He was facing them once again, his eyes flaming with affront. 'We have strict rules about dogs, don't we Annie? They're not welcome at Wheal Blazey. Well done, girl. Good thing to send him packing.'

'Quite right, dear,' Annie agreed, her tone simultaneously consoling and defeated. Jack gave a decisive *there we are then* nod and swivelled backwards to resume his scrutiny of the garden.

'Repellent little man.' Annie turned back to Joss. 'There's always a problem. As if we had the money to throw at it every time. Let's get you into the kitchen and bind this up with antiseptic, just in case. Perhaps Ollie can put the kettle on for us, will you do that, Ollie love? If we weren't about to do an interview, I'd suggest something stronger.'

Joss looked into her son's white face and forced a smile. 'Drama over,' she said. 'The evil troll of St. Roslyn and his canine sidekick have left the building. We can all breathe out.'

Ollie's eyes were glistening, enormous. 'Are you really, *really* OK, Mum?'

'I really, really am.' She held out her free arm. 'Come and have a hug.'

He relaxed his fist two inches above the counter, and something tumbled out of it. Joss saw what it was and let out an astonished 'Oh!' It was a paper knife, gifted to Annie years ago by an appreciative guest: a long, silver-plated blade with an ornate ivory handle. As Ollie moved in for a hug she ruffled his hair, pointed at the elegant object and said, 'What were you going to do with that, might I ask? Poke the dog in the ear with it?'

He fixed his eyes on her injured wrist with offended gravity. 'I'd have stopped him,' he said.

'Well, *that* was a funny old day.' Joss shrugged as she tucked the duvet around him later that night.

'Are you taking on that girl? The one you interviewed?'

'Your friend Cal's daughter, yes.'

Ollie kneaded his pillow into shape. 'He's *not* my friend. It's his boat I like.'

'OK.' She shook her head and sighed. Sometimes her son cuddled loneliness to himself like a security blanket.

'If I spend tomorrow morning doing Katie's induction, maybe we can go to the beach later?' she suggested. His enthusiastic *yes!* put the smile back on her face. 'So, what will you do with yourself until then?'

He reached for her bandaged hand, tenderly arranging his fingers alongside hers before responding, 'I thought I might go for a bike ride.'

'Good idea.' Half a dozen bikes were available for guests to borrow on a first-come-first-served basis. 'Take one with a saddlebag and we'll pack it with Coke and biscuits.' *That's another day sorted.* She glanced around the room. 'You've done a super job in here, Ol, it's looking really homely. And you found more photos!'

Her eyes lingered on the one he'd awarded pride of place, on top of his chest of drawers: their first wedding anniversary. *Such a handsome couple*, people used to say. She leaned closer to examine those rosy, oblivious faces, struggling to reconnect with her twenty-one-year-old self. 'That's my favourite,' she heard him murmur, and she nodded. 'It's a great photo.'

He wriggled straight. 'Do you remember that night?'

Joss sat back and took a deep breath. 'Every minute,' she answered.

'God, you look stunning.' Felix had always loved her in that red silk dress. He retrieved his phone from the waiter he'd commandeered to take the photograph, checked the result, and raised his glass. 'Here's to my miraculous wife, who's given me the best anniversary gift any man could have.'

Once the second blue line had confirmed it, he'd insisted they go for dinner to an appallingly expensive Thai restaurant in Covent Garden, where he decided his recent promotion and the conception of their (obviously) very special first child should be solemnly marked with champagne. 'No more than an inch for you, though,' he instructed, confiscating her glass with a theatrical sweep of his arm.

'But it's happened so quickly,' she sighed. 'We were going to wait.'

'Oh, why hang about?' He was exultant, a victor celebrating his spoils. Other diners turned their heads to look at him. 'It's serendipity, Joss. Great events coming together. Fate – and my talent, ahem, not to blow my own trumpet – have intervened to fast-forward us in life. We'll be the perfect family unit.'

For Felix, nothing was ever unmanageable. Everything was an opportunity; everything had some kind of payoff, if you only looked at it the right way. While she lurched between excitement at the thought of a baby and concern for its impact on her own prospects – however slender – he was standing triumphantly in the future as usual, celebrating.

But he was brilliant, her husband, she had to admit. At twenty-nine he was already being rewarded with the most lucrative clients, huge commissions, bonuses twice the size of her parents' annual earnings at Wheal Blazey. And he worked like a dog – schmoozing, strategizing, negotiating. The greater the challenge, the brighter Felix seemed to burn.

'I feel bad, though,' she told him. 'I'm only months from starting the course I want to do, and now I'm going to be asking for a deferral. Not to mention having to sort out something temporary to tide me over till then.'

'Joss!' He looked aghast. 'You don't have to do any of that. You don't have to go after any qualifications, or even work at all.'

'But I *do*, Felix.'

'You absolutely do not. What for?'

'I've applied to train as a teacher,' she said. 'You know that. I want to use my brain. I can't just… sit around.'

He stared as if she were mad. '*Sit around*? Don't be ridiculous. You'll always be using your brain. You'll be educating our little ones, besides anything else.'

'Felix – you don't want me to be a stay-at-home mum, surely? That was never the plan.' But then she wondered, *was there ever a plan?*

'Joss,' he continued, patiently authoritative. 'It would *never* have been the plan to contract out the care of our children to someone who won't give them one hundred and ten percent, in the way that *we* would.'

She studied his handsome face – the face of a deft tactician. It was hard not to concede to that brook-no-argument smile. 'Well. I guess we need to see how it all turns out.'

He grasped her hand too tightly, pressure from his thumb unwittingly hurting her wrist. 'I can't imagine anything better than coming home to find my beautiful wife and adorable baby waiting to greet me.'

'With vomit on the matching designer T-shirts you'll have bought us?' she teased. 'Continuous loops of Trumpton and Sesame Street on our state-of-the-art home cinema?'

'Don't be funny,' he scolded. 'I just don't want you away from home, I don't want my child being under-stimulated in strange hands.'

At times she had a discomforting sense of being ambushed, *unglued*, by the express train that was Felix, hurtling along tracks with no regard for how soundly – or otherwise – they might be embedded. She tried to imagine herself alone with a baby, unemployed, her own family three hundred miles away. 'You know, sweetheart,' she ventured, 'a baby may give you the chance to reconcile with your own mum. Grandparents are so important. Don't you think you could—'

'Don't go there, Joss.' It startled her, the speed with which his relentless positivity could morph into something dark. She knew from experience the suggestion might make him angry – at first anyway. But he looked devastated by the idea; *cowed*, like a kicked dog. 'I will *never* let that woman anywhere near a child of mine.'

'But Felix—'

'She walked out on my father. Left him to rot. Abandoned us both for an easy life with a millionaire slimeball and didn't look back. I will *never* forgive the selfish, callous bitch. She tore him apart and I was left with the broken pieces of him. I've *told* you this.'

'I know.' She touched his sleeve. 'But it was a long time ago, and—'

'That's enough!' he hissed. 'There's only me and you now. Me, you and our baby. That's it. No-one and nothing else matters.' She shrank before the laser-beam purity of his resolve, the steel in his eyes. 'I am *not* talking about this again.'

In bed that night he'd been earnest and attentive, cradling her face as he eased himself inside her with slow, solicitous care. 'Promise me,' he whispered. 'Promise you'll always be here for me. I *need* you, Joss.' The desperation she saw in his eyes, the pleading in his voice, made her wonder and worry. 'Whatever happens in the future, it's me and you. We're a team. Me and you against the world. You'll always love me, won't you? Promise me you'll never leave?'

She noticed the bruise on her wrist was still vivid three days later.

FOUR

McCalvey had called into the mini-market for provisions on his way home and on impulse bought prosecco. Not really his thing, but he'd taken a punt Katie would appreciate it – the end of her first week's work, after all.

Outside his rental above the chandlery's metal steps, he dug down for his key and took a deep breath, picturing the flinty eyes that would measure him up the moment he walked through the door. He glanced behind him at the ocean. Kara was peacefully afloat out there, secure on a swinging mooring under clouds the colour of lilac.

Just get in there, for Christ's sake.

Katie stood back, hands in her pockets, as he unloaded the groceries on his narrow kitchen counter and asked, 'Had a good day?'

'Yeah, alright.'

He emptied his old string bag and looked at her properly. She was reviewing his expenditure: a fat wedge of local cheese, a cooked ham, bread and pickles, the fizz, and a tin of cat food.

'You're feeding that mangy old stray!'

McCalvey shrugged. 'Poor little bugger's had a lean few months.'

She grunted and picked up the prosecco. 'You remember I'm staying over in St. Ives tonight?'

Crap. A doorstep remark from that morning came back to him. 'Your schoolmate. The one whose folks have a holiday cottage.'

'That's the one. The 'Tinner' leaves on the hour, I checked the timetable. Can I take this?'

'It's yours. But don't you need something to eat first?'

She gave him a look of mild irritation mixed with a kind of stoical amusement. 'We'll be eating when I get there.'

'It'll be dark by then.' He narrowed his eyes. 'You'll watch yourself, won't you?'

'Oh My God. Please stop trying to act like a dad! It's a *bus*! Nothing will happen to me *on a bus*.'

McCalvey leaned heavily over the worktop while he mutely counted to five. 'Come on, cut me some slack, Katie – I don't get much practice at the dad thing.'

There was a lot she could say to that. He held his breath and waited. But she just looked at him for a long moment, muttered 'I'd better get changed,' and disappeared into the bedroom.

He stacked the fridge, consoled by the sight of an unopened six-pack of Doom Bar on the top shelf, silently promising it, *I'll get to you later*. Or maybe he'd go to The Ship for a pint. Or possibly both.

They'd been guardedly polite since her arrival. Katie's stay with him was expedient, they both knew it. Her mother Lisa had a new man – a *lifestyle consultant*, whatever the hell that involved – who'd invited both women to spend Easter with him in his native Sicily. Katie had been quick to decline. McCalvey had burst out laughing when she told him that while it was fine having a smouldering Latino boyfriend round the house most evenings, she wasn't up for being the third wheel in a middle-aged holiday '*schmoochfest.*'

'So,' Lisa had challenged him during a subsequent phone call, 'we agreed it was time to activate her father's sense of responsibility. Can you remember where you left it, Cal?'

Then, deal done, Katie had googled herself the guesthouse job.

He hadn't been sold on the idea. From the door of his apartment the view was glorious; you could see right across the bay to Chy Head, and the nearest beach was only five minutes' walk away. But she wanted money – she was saving for driving lessons – and she wanted distraction. 'You're the boat nerd, Dad, not me,' she'd retorted when he questioned her about it. 'I'm not fussed about the wet stuff. Don't take it personally.' But he couldn't help it. He did.

She re-emerged to scrutinize herself in the only mirror he possessed, a plain rectangle above the shower-room washbasin. The person reflected there was glossy, considerably older, her gothic eyeliner and extravagant lashes colour-coordinated with a purple satin biker jacket and eye-wateringly tight jeans.

He hovered behind her, taut with discomfort. 'You look… different,' he said; then after a minute, 'Nice.'

'Thanks!' She executed a graceful half rotation. 'Alvaro picked this jacket out for me at London Fashion Week, actually. He gets to know lots of designers in his line of work.'

'Terrific.' Even to his own ears, the word sounded deeply ironic.

'He's a very considerate person in fact, Dad,' she flared. 'He knows what will suit me, and he sources really good stuff at discount rates.'

'Everything a teenage girl could wish for then.' An inner voice taunted him, *you are way out of your depth here, McCalvey.*

'It's not about me *being a teenage girl*,' she fired back. 'It's a very adult market and big business globally. You have absolutely no clue what would suit me, or what I want in my life. I happen to be really lucky that Mum's found someone who… Oh, *forget it*.' She tossed her head. 'I need to go.'

She stomped back into the bedroom to grab an overnight bag while he tinkered with the jars and tins on his cupboard shelves. As she swept past the kitchen counter on her way to the door, he glanced up. 'Got your key?'

She stopped and they eyed each other. Then she took a step towards him, picked up the prosecco and murmured, 'Cheers for this, Dad.'

They exchanged small, forgiving smiles.

He followed her outside, leaning over the rail to watch her go. As she descended the steps and swung away in the direction of the town's one bus stop, he lifted his eyes to the sky and groaned.

She had a point. He had absolutely no clue. The *Dad* role was foreign territory, and the workings of a pink-haired sixteen-year-old's mind were as impenetrable to him as quantum theory. But she had his genes, like it or not. In her case, he suspected, *not*.

Distracted by a sinuous movement at his ankles, he looked down to see the familiar black and white battle-scarred tom gazing balefully up at him. He bent to scratch a torn ear. 'Sorry, buddy,' he muttered. 'She's not into cats. But don't feel bad about it – you're not the only one round here she thinks is a waste of space.'

'It's a beautiful car,' Joss said, once Guy had claimed a parking bay by the town hall and helped her uncurl from the roadster's leather seat. 'Very classy.'

'German engineering, Italian bodywork,' he grinned. 'I do have a planet-friendly Japanese job, but this one comes out for special occasions.' He wiggled his eyebrows in a way that made her search intently for something in her handbag.

The hall was filling up as they took their seats. Half a dozen hard chairs were assembled on the platform, occupied by what Joss took to be a combination of planners, builders and local dignitaries behind a scale model of the proposed development, Roslyn Glynn. To be fair, the mock-up revealed generous plots, a variety of architectural styles and plenty of appealing greenery. Play areas, access to the beach, walking distance to town... there'd be worse places to raise a family, she thought. It would be a safe, settled, regular little community. The insight jabbed her with a sharp little needle of longing. She twisted in her seat to avoid looking at it.

She recognised a number of faces – suppliers, retailers, friends of her parents, people she'd known since childhood; Lorcyn the bank manager, who'd given her a rabbit on her sixth birthday and asked to be her boyfriend (he must have been eight at the time.) And Morwenna, her best friend from junior school, now the proprietor of *Wenna's Antiques*, a quirky browser's paradise in an arcade behind the harbour. They spotted each other at the same moment, and the pleasantly freckled redhead scrambled through the coalescing masses towards her.

'*Joss*! How are you doing?' Joss caught the gleam of curiosity her old friend flashed at the well-dressed man on her right, and smiled.

'I'm good, Wen.'

'Honestly?'

'Getting there.' Though Morwenna only had the bare bones of her story, Joss knew she wouldn't hassle her for updates, especially in this public place. 'Wenna, this is Guy Tremain, a land agent staying with us at the moment. He thought someone from Wheal Blazey should come tonight to hear what's being proposed.' *That*, she decided, *should head any misconceptions off at the pass.* She turned back to Guy, who extended a hand and beamed. 'Delighted.'

Morwenna helped herself to the adjacent chair and indicated left with her thumb. 'Watch out for old man Finch. He's collaring everyone tonight about his bloody dog.'

'His dog?' Joss peered into the crowd and soon identified her problem neighbour, evidently haranguing a knot of fellow farmers in the process of taking their seats. She looked quickly away as he registered her presence with a scowl. 'What's the problem with it?'

Morwenna shrugged. 'He thinks someone put rat poison by its kennel.'

'No!' Her jaw dropped. 'Is it alright?'

'He's going on about his vet's bills, so I don't think it's popped its clogs yet.'

Joss squinted at the man again, part of her transmitting sympathy while a less charitable part was tempted – just a little – to gloat. So someone else had reason to hate Finch's horrible beast. But rat poison? That was disturbing.

An official called the meeting to order, and the hubbub began to subside. Before she sat back, Morwenna glanced from Joss to Guy and said, 'Quick drink in the Ship afterwards?'

Joss looked regretfully at her watch, preparing to decline just as Guy replied, 'Great idea.'

The saloon was heaving with early-evening drinkers as the three of them manoeuvred their way to a free table. Guy immediately produced his wallet, but Morwenna put a hand on his arm and said, 'First one's on me. I need to say hallo to someone at the bar anyway.' She winked at Joss and set off before he could argue.

'Lovely girl,' Guy remarked. He arranged himself gingerly against the chair's sticky upholstery. 'So what did you think?'

'About the development? Overall, I guess I'm pleasantly surprised,' Joss admitted. 'It did seem a shame to lose a piece of land so close to the coast – but from what I gather, those fields have never been especially productive. Let's just hope the place isn't overrun with second homers.'

Guy pursed his lips. 'Oh, I think there'll be a balance. Of course we have to look after local families. But I wouldn't be too quick to dismiss the benefits of incomers' spending power in this community.'

Joss opened her mouth and closed it again, her mind scrabbling to formulate a response of any significance. She frowned at the crush of drinkers vying for attention at the counter. When had she last been able to hold her own in an economic or political discussion? Sometimes she felt like an imposter in her own county, emerging half-blind from her marital cocoon. Naïve and irrelevant.

In a softer voice, Guy said, 'Your own paying guests contribute something positive to the area, after all, Joss. If you really thought about it, you'd see there's massive unexplored potential in Wheal Blazey. Perhaps more than you allow yourself to imagine right now.'

'You're going to have to explain that to me.'

'Well, it's a beautiful place, and I know it's been in your family forever. But the upkeep must be enormous.' Briefly, he toyed with a coaster. 'Forgive me if I'm speaking out of turn – but I strongly suspect it's not delivering much of a profit. And I can't see your folks having the stamina to run it for many more years.'

A scaly little bug of worry unfolded its wings and rattled in her brain. For weeks she'd been trying to squash it. 'Please don't tell me we should turn it into flats,' she cautioned him.

He dismissed the suggestion with a wave of his hand. 'No-one in their right minds would alter Wheal Blazey's character.

Any developer worth their salt would want to preserve the history and integrity of the building. Trust me, though – as a residential project with planning permission, it would achieve six figures on the open market. Easily.'

She shook her head. 'We're fine at the moment, thanks.'

'I'm just shooting the breeze, Joss – but it must be worth considering, surely?' He put a hand over hers. 'One day when you have five minutes to spare, take a look at some of the fine old country houses people like me have helped re-purpose in the last few years. I could take you to see some of them, if you like. Raven House, for example, thirty miles up the north coast – look at its website. Neglected for decades, but a real landmark now: lived in, well-managed, well cared for. Restored to its former glory.'

It was exhausting, the thought of jumping from one sinking ship to another. The prospect of more change was too big. She wasn't ready for it, she wasn't *equipped* at any level – rationally, financially or emotionally. 'I appreciate the thought, Guy,' she managed to say. Glumly she scanned the bar again, hoping to spot Morwenna returning with their drinks. A large glass of white would help her feel more sanguine about things, she decided. Not quite so useless. So *feeble*.

In fact Morwenna was in conversation with someone she recognised. Lounging on a bar stool, one hand nursing the scant remains of a pint and the other lightly touching Morwenna's sleeve, was Cal McCalvey. Taken aback, Joss watched her friend nod goodbye to him as another figure – curvy and porcelain-skinned, even more familiar – inveigled her way into the gap and placed a proprietorial hand on McCalvey's shoulder. *Tegen*.

She was still gaping at them when Morwenna arrived at the table and unloaded the drinks. Guy raised his gin and tonic in appreciative thanks before saying, 'Back in a tick, ladies – I'm off to find the facilities,' and gliding away.

Morwenna tracked Joss's sightline. 'That girl works at Wheal Blazey, doesn't she?'

'Tegen. Yes.'

'Look at the pair of them.' Morwenna shook her head and sighed. 'The *Virgin and the Gypsy*. Though I'm probably well short of the mark on the first bit. He's on his own tonight – nowhere to go, drunker than he thinks, and she's completely besotted. What could possibly go wrong?'

'You know him? Cal McCalvey?' Joss was finding it hard to drag her eyes away. As far as she could tell, Tegen was oozing into McCalvey's personal space with limpet-like persistence, while he sat back looking genially quizzical. Was he being polite? Did he actually find Tegen *attractive*? Bizarrely, she hoped he didn't. *As if it's any of my business.*

'Oh, I know him,' Morwenna replied. 'As well as anyone does, I guess. We had a thing for a while.'

'A *thing*?' Too big a gulp of wine scoured Joss' throat and fizzed in her nose. 'When was this?'

'Three or four years ago, when he came to St. Roslyn to buy his boat. We met here in this pub actually. He spent a few nights at mine before he got the marina job and moved in above the chandlery.'

Joss twisted in her seat to study the seated figure again, recalibrating. With his tousled hair, five o'clock shadow, rumpled jacket and jeans, he looked as if a typhoon had blown him through the door. The man obviously had zero interest in his own appearance, she decided – or zero vanity, to put it more generously. But as she watched him talk, she had to concede, albeit grudgingly, there *was* something disarming about the faintly ironic smile and caramel skin, even with its tell-tale beery glow. *I bet he scrubs up well.* For a brief, subversive second, she pictured him as Morwenna's lover, and blushed to the roots of her hair.

God, how she missed sex – the thrill of fierce, full-on, the-world-can-go-to-hell physical congress. Sometimes she *ached* for it, alone in her room at night: the way Felix had once made her feel, a lifetime ago, when things were good. When she thought he was everything she wanted. When she trusted him.

She swallowed more wine. 'So... you decided he wasn't your type?'

Morwenna returned a wistful smile. 'Jesus, I was mad about him. I mean, those *eyes*. But in the end it was a passion killer, realising he always had one eye on the door.'

She tried to resist a second glass, but they easily won her over. Evenings like this in the last six months – sociable, cheerful, child-free – were rare; she could count them on the fingers of one hand. The saloon was warm, the wine was cold, and little by little her internal stays had begun to work loose.

Guy took her arm companionably as they made their way back to his car, then helped her buckle up. As he started the engine he said, 'I was sorry to hear about your husband. It must be hard.' His eyes were solemn.

Unwelcome clammy heat washed over her face. She remembered he'd only ordered a lime and soda for himself when it came to the second round. So *now* he wants a sensible conversation, she grumbled inwardly – just when her brain had turned to mush.

'Will you stay in Cornwall, Joss?'

'I don't know.' She wanted to hang on to the luxury of forgetfulness. If only for one night.

As they drove out of town to pick up the coast road, her eyes skimmed the ragged hedges, splashes of cow parsley and campion flaring every now and then in the car's lights, the sea a sleeping giant under a powdering of stars. 'It's hard to see how I could go back to London – financially, apart from anything else,' she told him. 'I'm in a bind, to be honest with you. Ollie needs a life. But Wheal Blazey is… well…'

'A burden?'

Home, she wanted to say. *The vision my parents always had. Their dream.* But a burden, yes. She didn't need accounting experience to understand a balance sheet. At full occupancy, they might just break even this year. And if they were to need capital…

'I can help you, Joss,' he said.

She caught her top lip in her teeth, frowning through the windscreen as the noble old house materialised ahead of them beneath a rising moon. 'I'm really not much more than a lodger at the moment, Guy,' she told him. 'I'm the prodigal daughter returning empty-handed to the fold, lending a hand while I consider my options. It's not mine to sell.' *Maybe that will shut him up.*

He stole a sideways glance. 'You're probably sick of people telling you you're still young with lots going for you. Lots of life ahead. Something better *will* come along, Joss. When you're ready.'

She pulled a face and found a thread in her sleeve to pick at.

'Think about it, though,' he added. 'Your parents are sitting on a potential goldmine. A retirement fund, at any rate. You should talk to them. Or let me.'

She took in his expensive watch, beautifully tailored suit, the way he smiled approvingly at the noise of his car's powerful engine as he revved it in the car park before turning it off, and decided she'd had enough. One day, she thought, men would stop telling her what she should think and do, when really it was all about *them*.

She'd already opened the door and put a foot on the gravel when he appeared by the car's front wing, offering his hand. Wincing at her expression, he said, 'You think I'm putting pressure on you.'

'Well you are, Guy. A bit.'

He helped her out of the car but kept hold of her wrist.

'Honestly Joss, I have your interests at heart.' He sounded genuinely affronted. 'But maybe I *am* the best person to talk to your parents.'

'Don't! *Please* don't.' Two big glasses of wine and her brain cells seemed to be tumbling about like bees in a bucket. *I don't need this.*

'But—'

'It's too soon. We need time as a family to sort things out. *I* need more time. There's… a lot to work through.'

'Joss—'

'Please *leave it*, Guy.' Her attempt to snatch back her hand had the reverse effect of making him tighten his grasp, clumsily pulling her nearer. 'Look, I'm sorry, Joss, I just want to—'

'*Stop!*'

A bigger, angrier woman seemed to have invaded her body. Shocked at her own vehemence, she closed her eyes and took a deep breath. 'I'm sorry,' she said more quietly. 'I'm not thinking straight. I know you mean well.'

He relaxed his grip, patted her hand and smiled. 'No offence intended.'

The man seemed wholly unembarrassable. Not someone to be fazed by dissent or anyone else's discomfort, she understood. Felix would have liked him.

'None taken,' she said.

'Goodnight then, Joss. Sleep well.'

She set off down the narrow path connecting the main house to her cottage. The mottled old porch with its swags of clematis and honeysuckle was clearly visible from where he'd parked his car. After one final wave, Joss delved for her key and realised her front door was open. Annie was waiting on the step.

'Are you alright, darling? I heard the car. I thought I heard raised voices.'

Joss rolled her eyes. 'Just a stupid tipsy discussion on the local economy, Mum. Sorry it's so late. Morwenna persuaded us to go for a drink.'

'Oh!' This noticeably cheered her mother. 'Well, good. You can debrief me in the morning.'

'Everything OK?'

'Ollie turned in twenty minutes ago – I suspect he's asleep by now. Your father and I wore him out after dinner with a few rounds of Old Maid, bless him.'

Joss squeezed her arm. 'Thanks a million, Mum. Tea? Coffee?' But Annie shook her head. 'I don't like to leave your father too long.'

They parted with a hug. Joss closed the door softly, simultaneously peering into the darkness of the stairwell. All quiet.

She checked her watch. Ten o'clock, and her head was beginning to pound. *What a lightweight.* Closing time was still an hour away, and the Ship would be getting rammed.

The evening, she reflected, had been a decidedly mixed bag – convivial and discomfiting at the same time. First there'd been the creepy news about Finch's dog; then the sight of Tegen cosying up to Cal McCalvey… The image of the two of them at the bar returned to nag at her. She hoped McCalvey had managed to extricate himself. A lovesick chambermaid working alongside the object of her obsession's teenage daughter was *not* a prospect to be relished. And now she had Guy's ruminations on Wheal Blazey to reckon with too, *dammit*. If she went to bed, she knew she wouldn't sleep.

Her kitchen, with its faithful old range, farmhouse table and mismatched chair cushions, was just off to the right. She'd made it her own in these last few months, enhancing its rustic vibe with colourful fabrics, mugs, bits of pottery, wild flowers and shells from local beaches that she'd collected, scrubbed and dried. She'd made it pretty. Not a word she'd ever have used to describe their docklands apartment. Probably someone else's apartment by now. Realising how little she missed it surprised her.

She drifted towards the kettle, filled it from the tap and set it to boil, but sat at the table long after the switch had clicked to *off*.

Maybe Guy was right. Maybe they'd be foolish to ignore Wheal Blazey's potential in a rising market. It had everything: a romantic setting, gracious architecture, history, views...

What was the project he'd mentioned? Raven House, she seemed to remember, somewhere up on the north coast. She took out her phone and found the website, stubbornly hoping not to be impressed. But the home page showed a collection of elegant buildings sympathetically designed as extensions to a carefully reconstructed nineteenth-century manor. '*A prestigious development of spacious apartments and town houses complementing the meticulous restoration of this fine country house and former children's home after extensive fire damage* '... And – bloody hell – the selling prices of the few available apartments were *insane*.

She put down her phone and slumped in the chair.

Would her parents seriously ever consider selling Wheal Blazey? Guy had made the point they were likely to be able to retire on the proceeds. But then what? The place was part of them. It was part of them all.

Closing her eyes, she pictured herself with her father, rock pooling in the coves below the house, where tiny crabs had tickled her fingers before she set them free. Tracing the imprint of centuries of human and animal traffic across their hall's gleaming flagstones with chubby toddler toes. Listening to her bedroom rafters creak on summer nights when soft rain from the fields cooled the house.

An owl hooted from a nearby tree. Joss shook herself slightly and moved to open a window. Above Wheal Blazey, the sky was the colour of seawater trapped between rocks: clear, deep and dark.

This is where I've always felt safe.

The only place, she realised. Nothing else compared.

I saw the way he grabbed her from the window. She was really upset. She told him to stop. Dickhead.

My dad would have wiped that smug smile off his face.

He's not around any more, so he can't.

But I can.

FIVE

'One for the road?' Tegen gave his hand an encouraging squeeze.

'Thanks, lovely, but I think I've had more than—'

'Ah go on. You look like you've lost a tenner and found fivepence. I'll join you.' She gestured around the emptying saloon. 'Fill the tank before disappearing into the night, eh?'

'OK then. If you're twisting my arm.' McCalvey stretched, yawned, and shook his head, mourning the last dregs of his willpower. 'I'll buy.'

With a measure of tequila in front of her, Tegen poked him in the chest and said, 'You're a dark horse, McCalvey. A wife and a teenage kid! What's the story?'

He rubbed the side of his face, thinking he should really go home and sleep the evening off. Why should his *story* matter, for Pete's sake? But the girl was friendly, and she seemed to like his company. He was flattered. And he didn't want Katie interrogated in the morning.

'Her mother and I split up a long time ago,' he mumbled eventually.

'No shit! Call me Sherlock, but I think I guessed.'

That made him laugh. She grinned, pleased with herself. 'You were young, though, to have a kid.'

He examined his drink. 'We were just kids ourselves.'

'So what happened?'

He downed the rest of his beer. 'We grew up.' *One of us did anyway. And it wasn't me.*

'You're still in touch with her, though?'

'Oh sure. Christmas and birthdays. We're very… civilised.' He shut his eyes, visualising Lisa's pale, pretty face. Every so often she reached out to him, suggesting he spend a couple of days with them in Bristol. *You're her dad, after all. Why not?*

He never had.

'What's she like?' Tegen persisted.

'Who?'

'Betty Boo, o' course. *Duh.* Katie's mum.'

'Lovely. She's lovely.' His head felt clogged with mud. 'Most of the women I've known have been lovely.'

'Yeah?' She made a duck face.

But he believed it was true. A lot of women had come and gone in his life. Many of them had shared his bed. None of them had ever been a problem. *The problem is me,* he thought wearily. *The problem is always me.*

He looked morosely into his empty glass. *Jesus, McCalvey, listen to yourself – you are totally, comprehensively, pissed.*

Shuffling straight, he gave Tegen a *don't take me too seriously* wink. In return, she grinned and arched an eyebrow.

That wink might have been a mistake, he reflected.

She eyed him a few more seconds, then changed tack. 'She's great, though, your Katie. I like her.'

'That's good to hear,' he said. 'So what's it like, working up at the Livesey's?'

'It's alright. Hard work. Mrs L's OK, she leaves us alone.

But it's changed a bit with the old man getting sick and widow-daughter being around.'

'Widow daughter?'

'Her husband drowned in the Thames last year, didn't you hear about that?'

McCalvey blinked at her. 'Bloody hell. No, I didn't.' He'd never paid much attention to onshore talk. He'd glimpsed Joss across the pub earlier – hazel-eyed and nice-looking, now he thought about it. Even if she did act as if she had a poker up her backside. But who was he to judge?

'She's young,' he said. 'That's terrible.'

'Then there's her son. Moody little so-and-so. Pain in the arse.'

Her son. Of course – Ollie. *Christ*, poor kid. Suddenly he felt slightly sick.

'I think I should make tracks, Tegen.' He fumbled with the collar of his jacket and wobbled to his feet.

Immediately, she reached for her coat. 'You live above the chandlery, right? My place is on the way. You can walk me home.'

He knew, of course, what she had in mind.

On the steps of her rented caravan in a park behind the marina, she hesitated for the briefest moment before saying 'I could make us a coffee?'

He took a step back. 'Thanks, my lovely… but I should really… ' For crucial seconds he wavered, swaying slightly, while he pictured the lumpy sofa-bed waiting in his tiny flat and gazed at her hopeful face. Half of him wanted her to make the decision for him. The other half was telling him *just turn around and go.*

'Katie told us she was off to St. Ives tonight, so I'm guessing you have a late pass,' she said.

'Even so – you must have work in the morning.'

'Oh, for fuck's sake. It's not brain surgery.' She tugged his sleeve. 'Come in for a coffee.'

He felt pleasantly stupid, as if a friendly alien had pasted a smile across his mouth and whispered *she really likes you* in his ear. What on God's earth did she see in him? What did *any* woman ever see in him? One of life's great mysteries. It never ceased to amaze him.

Her caravan was cluttered and too warm. Once she'd closed the door, he felt rapidly in need of better air. Small spaces had always made him anxious.

She pointed to a couch randomly heaped with throws and cushions, and said, 'Have a seat. I'll sort us out a drink,' before disappearing behind a partition he assumed hid a kitchenette. 'I think I've got more wine somewhere.'

'Oh God, no,' he called after her. 'Wine would finish me off. In fact – if you can do me a cold glass of water—'

'I can manage that.' She reappeared briefly, then said 'What the *eff* are you doin'?'

Without much forethought, he'd started to push out the van's perspex panes as far as their rusty hinges allowed, pausing only to inspect the worn stretch of carpet between the largest window and the only door.

'Sorting out an escape route?'

He looked up, flustered. 'Sorry. I just—'

Just what? Sometimes his own behaviour mystified him.

He rubbed his nose and took a breath. 'I just wanted… to feel the breeze.' With a contrite smile, he collapsed onto her couch.

She shook her head and snorted. 'OK, Sailor Sam. Anyway. I'm getting myself a nice glass of red.'

McCalvey scanned the girl's untidy living quarters and felt deeply tired, as if he'd been submerged, sharp edges all worn away. He came to himself abruptly when she landed heavily beside him.

'You *really* need caffeine,' she scolded. 'But here's your water – have this first.'

She was very close, one hip pressing against his, and he was only mildly surprised when she leaned over to hold the tumbler to his lips. A moment later she substituted her own glass, smiling with indulgent triumph as he took a sip.

After that, things happened quickly.

She held her palm against his cheek until he'd swallowed, then set the glass down to take his head between her hands. Just before she bent to kiss him on the mouth for the first time, he looked hard into her eyes and thought he saw a tiny flicker of unease. He gripped her by both wrists. 'I'm not sure you want to do this.'

'Oh?' She shook her arms free. 'So what will it take to *make* you sure?' Wriggling forward she kissed him again, her lush red hair sweeping his face.

'Tegen—'

Her breath was warm on his neck; she began to massage the rise of his jeans and *shit*, he was already hard – things were moving faster than he knew was wise. Grazing his ear with her tongue, she closed her eyes and murmured, 'I've been wanting to get with you a long time, Cal McCalvey. Whenever I see you, I think, I bet I can put a sparkle in those big brown eyes.'

She's just a kid, he tried to tell himself – but God, she was precocious. *She knows exactly what she's doing,* a silky voice cooed in his head, trampling down his fuzzy misgivings.

He knew then that he'd follow it through. It was like sleepwalking. It was like drowning. *She likes you,* the voice persisted. *She wants you. Why not give her what she wants?*

He started to return her kisses, blood heat rising, surrendering himself to the sweet unravelling of everything coiled inside. She loosened his belt to insinuate teasing fingers, exclaiming *my, my – you* are *pleased to see me*; and when he grabbed her arm, she took his hand and guided it between her legs. Seconds later she'd pulled the sweater over her head and unhooked her bra.

She made it so easy.

He took his cues from her squeals of delight, the way her ample, creamy body responded to every touch. The sex, when they got to it, was fierce. She came within a couple of minutes, exuberantly loud.

The act brought him temporary oblivion. No complications, no baggage, no noise in his head – just a liberating abandonment. Peace, of a kind.

They dozed for a while, entangled in a stew of rumpled fabric and discarded clothes.

He broke back into consciousness with a start.

There was an acrid smell in his nose. *Smoke?* He couldn't place any windows, only yellow walls enclosing an oppressively small space, growing smaller by the second. He scanned the room urgently for the source of his fear, his stomach cramping badly. The door… he had to get to the door…

Then he heard it – a frightened child, screaming in the dark.

What's happening? Where is he? Is he safe?

He fought his way out of the covers as pain knifed his temples.

'Hey there, sailor. You OK?'

Tegen's sleepy voice changed everything. He twisted 180 degrees, checking every cavity and corner, before subsiding groggily back into the cushions.

Christ – not again.

Nothing was wrong. The windows were open, chilly air was wafting in, and there were no imprisoning walls – just the curves of her shabby caravan. And he could see the door.

'Bad dream?'

He pressed his thumbs into his eyes and nodded, all at once self-conscious that his entire upper body was slick with sweat. She handed him what remained in the water glass. 'Alright now?'

'Tegen – I have to go.'

'Why? You don't need to.' But he'd already pulled on his jeans and was re-threading his belt.

'Stay! I can make you breakfast.' She licked her lips, inclined her head and grinned. 'We can work up an appetite if you like.' But as she scrutinized him more closely, her smile mutated into a hard line of concern. 'You *like* me, don't you? No regrets?'

He stared at the floor. 'Of course I like you. And no, no regrets.'

'I like you too,' she said, shuffling closer. 'A lot.'

The neediness in her tone dismayed him. *I shouldn't be here. This is all wrong.* He forced himself to meet her wide, mascara-smudged eyes. 'It's just – Katie will wonder what's happened to me.'

'She's in St. Ives, remember?' There was a flinty new edge to her voice now.

'Yes but… she said she might get a lift back.'

The lie hung between them, poisoning the air. Tegen snatched the blanket to her chin and glared, her body language unambiguous. *This meant nothing to you.*

It wasn't what he'd intended. He glanced helplessly between the window, the couch, the floor and her face, wishing he could make it right. But he couldn't stay in that room. 'Look, Tegen, I'm sorry. It's just me. I don't really…'

'…do this sort of thing?' she finished for him. Her voice was heavy with sarcasm.

He touched her cheek and placed a sad, chaste kiss on her forehead, sensing her anger ebb to a thin-lipped sulk as he slowly detached himself.

'You said you *liked* me.'

'I do like you.' What else could he say?

'So… you want to do this again?'

Fuck. He covered his confusion with an awkward smile as her expression changed to something flirtatious and more assured. She touched his hip with an extended finger, then traced a winding passage to his crotch, pouting when he stopped her with a firm hand.

'OK,' she murmured. 'But tomorrow's another day. You'll be back.'

As she pitched herself into the disordered cushions, he heard a low moan of frustration. But he was already moving through her door.

The speckled sky elevated his spirits a little as he trudged through the park. For him, nothing could ever match the quality of this air. Everything in these silent early hours was sharply defined in silver and black; everything was fresh, and smelt of the sea.

He glanced briefly in the direction of the chandlery but turned instead towards the harbour. A stone ramp led him onto the hard, where dozens of working boats and weekend yachts had been hauled beyond the reach of the morning tide. Safely stashed against the harbour wall, oars neatly stowed, was Kara's tender. He released the line and dragged the dinghy to the water's edge, immersing his canvas shoes in the process. Soon he was rowing quietly into deeper darkness.

He might have been the only person in the world. The sea was black silk, the sky a velvet cloth stippled with crystal, and the only sound was the skilful, steady *plash* of his blades.

Stroke by stroke, Kara came towards him in the moonlight.

As he let the dinghy drift towards the stern, he greeted the smooth hull with his fingertips. *It's me, girl.* At the rear, he secured the tender and released the steps that would take him into the cockpit. He checked the lines. Everything was stable.

Stretched out on cushions retrieved from the locker, he gazed up at the stars and pinched the bridge of his nose until it hurt.

Outstanding evening, McCalvey. What a class act you are. Another bloody car crash. He should have trusted his instincts and taken himself off before things went as far as they did. Though that, he muttered aloud, would be a first.

What the hell was he thinking? Tegen was so young, so pretty, so *needy*… he hadn't been in his right mind. He'd been cruel. And why, for fuck's sake, did these toxic, scary dreams keep tormenting him? The one tonight was unpleasantly familiar: the suffocating, windowless room; a caustic smell that nearly choked him; the screams of a terrified child…

He had to find a way to make it stop. Eliminate the triggers, whatever was playing with his brain and activating these grisly dramas. Food? Beer? Boats? Women? Any of those, he grumbled to himself, and he was *really* in trouble.

Anyway. In the morning he'd be sober, the memory would fade, and there was a good chance Tegen would look back on this grubby little episode and realise he wasn't worth her energy.

The lapping of water in the spangled dark gradually began to ease the racket in his head. Finally he tumbled into fractured sleep, while Kara rocked him gently towards dawn.

SIX

'Excellent breakfast as always, Mrs. L.' Guy passed his key across the counter to Annie, but his eyes were on Joss as she arranged flowers and newspapers on the console nearby. 'A satisfying end to a fruitful week. I'd say *thank God it's Friday*, but in your line of business I'm sure that would be an annoyingly fatuous comment.'

Annie laughed. 'Yes, the weekend hordes will be with us very shortly,' she said. 'But where would we be without them?'

'Putting your slippered feet up in front of *Love Island*, maybe?'

Joss chided him with a look, and he winked. 'I'll be back around midday to pick up my bags and check out.'

'Meetings this morning?' Annie asked.

'Walking the Roslyn Glynn site with the developers.' He extracted his car keys, checked the contents of a chic leather document wallet, and made his exit. The noise of a vigorously revved car engine assaulted their ears less than a minute later, as Ollie arrived through the door.

Annie shook her head. 'That man's remarkably comfortable in his own skin.'

'Good for him,' Joss muttered darkly. She turned to greet her son. 'Hey, squirt. What are you up to?'

'I wanted to borrow a bike again. OK, Gran?'

'Of course, love. Keys and padlocks are under the desk with the toolbox.'

'*Helmet,*' Joss instructed automatically. She made some final adjustments to her floral display while he rummaged through bits of hardware, squirrelling accessories inside his anorak before heading for the coat cupboard. She waved him cheerfully away.

'Well.' She wiped her hands. 'If Ollie's occupied and you're holding the fort here, I'll take Dad his breakfast.'

She knew every square inch of her father's den. He'd taken possession of the little study years ago, nabbing himself a couple of hours' downtime on quiet afternoons to read, catalogue his photos, or tinker with his model aircraft and tall ship collection. They'd even found a door sign for him a few birthdays ago – *Jack's Nest* – which served to keep inquisitive guests at bay.

'What do you *do* in here, Grandad?' Ollie once asked him, and he'd replied, 'I *think.*'

'What about?'

He'd ruffled Ollie's hair and smiled. 'About my good luck.'

Now he sat inert in his comfy old chair, oblivious to the products of his skilled fingers gathering dust on the shelves, and gazed at the TV. A million miles away, Joss thought sadly. As if he'd veered off the tracks of his own life.

She glanced at the photos on her left as she set down his tray. In a prominent one, Ollie was a giggling, sand-speckled toddler, hanging on to his grandad as if they were mismatched best mates. In another, he was transfixed by the replica of a biplane her father was varnishing with meticulous care. A washed-out wedding photo in an old bronze frame captured two delighted lovers with toothy smiles and unrecognisably thick wavy hair.

Ollie hated looking at these pictures now. They gave him an achy, hollow feeling in his stomach, he'd told her – as if something special that belonged to him had accidently been thrown out with the rubbish.

She adjusted the blind to prevent sunlight blurring the TV screen. Someone was reading the news. There were live reports of forest fires in a distant country, images of helicopters swooping low to douse the flames, a sombre voice chronicling heatwaves and cyclones. Jack's posture was rigid.

'Let me find you something more entertaining, Dad.'

She knelt in front of the box, scrolling through the channels until she recognised the calming tones of a familiar gardening journalist. 'That's more like it,' she said. 'Keep your ears open for any tips on salt-resistant planting.'

She watched him toy anxiously with his poached egg. 'Are you OK, Dad?'

He gave a curt nod.

She tucked the remote beside him on the chair. 'Turn it off if it gets too boring – the red button,' she told him. 'And the paper's just here.' She kissed his dry cheek and studied him for a minute. 'I'll be back as soon as the last couple leave. Are you *sure* you're OK?'

'I'm perfectly alright,' he said irritably. She'd become, she realised, an irrelevant stranger.

He'll be fine, she persuaded herself. He was comfortable, he had his tray, and familiar things were just an arm's length from the chair. If she could free herself up for a couple of hours later, maybe she'd walk him down to the beach with Ollie.

Reception was busy; she had to go. But she left the room with a heavy heart.

McCalvey had just attached a trailer to the pick-up to tow a damaged yacht from the shallows onto shingle when horns started to blare above the slipway. He glanced up, expecting to see the usual 4 x 4s competing for a parking space – then the shouting started.

He climbed onto the footplate to take a better look. Within seconds he was jogging up the slope to where a small crowd had gathered.

Stock-still in the middle of the road, Joss's father was offering muddled responses to the exhortations of concerned onlookers who'd formed a loose circle around him.

'*You need to get out of the way, old feller…*'

'*Where are you supposed to be?*'

'*You'll get yourself run over, mate…*'

McCalvey scanned the immediate area for any sign of Joss, her mother or Ollie, without success. He stepped forward and put a hand on Jack's arm. 'Mr. Livesey? Jack?'

The circle began to fragment as its members sensed resolution. Jack's eyes slid towards McCalvey. 'Who are you?'

'I'm Cal. You probably don't remember me. I'm… an acquaintance of your daughter.'

'You know my Jocelyn?'

He exhaled with relief as memory flickered in the old man's eyes. 'Yes, Jack, I do. Now, how about we step out of the way of these good people and this traffic, eh?' He grasped Jack's arm more firmly and guided him to the wall, where he released his hold and peered into the drawn face. 'Are you on your own, Jack?'

'I'm on my way home,' Jack replied. He waved vaguely at the row of shops on the opposite side. 'It's over there I think, my home.'

'Is anyone with you?'

Jack smiled vacantly. 'Do I know you?'

McCalvey took another good look round. The gaggle

had dispersed, and none of Jack's family appeared to have accompanied him to the seafront. At this hour he was pretty sure they'd be tied up anyway, with breakfasts and check-outs to do. He glanced at the yacht he'd been planning to assess for repairs, resting on its trailer. Safe to leave for an hour or so.

'Jack – I can take you home if you'd like me to.'

'Home?'

'Home to Wheal Blazey. Would that be alright?'

Jack faltered, his eyes darting along the street, lips trembling. 'I don't know,' he said. 'I want Annie. I think I had an egg on a tray.'

Right. Not many options here. 'My car's on the beach, just below the slipway,' McCalvey said. 'Let's get you back to your breakfast.'

He held out an arm, and after a brief hesitation Jack shuffled forward. They descended slowly towards the pick-up, where McCalvey propped open the passenger door. Jack stopped beside it, watching with interest as McCalvey uncoupled the trailer; then his filmy gaze travelled a few yards further, taking in the yacht.

'My son-in-law sails a boat like that. Do you know him?'

'What?' *The dead husband?* After an uncomfortable double-take, McCalvey beckoned him towards the step. 'I don't think so, Jack.'

Jack tossed his head. 'Of course not, of course not, I'm such an old fool. He sails on the Thames. Takes the boy with him sometimes. But then…' All at once his voice rattled with annoyance. 'I think he went away. Is that right? He went away, didn't he?'

Bloody hellfire. 'I really don't know.'

Jack stood cogitating, his eyes fixed on the water. Then McCalvey heard a low growl. 'I'm sure he did. He's gone now. Gone, and *good riddance.*'

'Sorry?'

'I've always wondered about him. Tricky so-and-so. But what can I say? She's my daughter.'

McCalvey stared at him, perplexed. Talk about a curved ball… *Tricky?* He thought of Joss and suppressed a jab of curiosity. *Nothing to do with me.* If he'd learned any lessons during the last few years, the need to steer well clear of other people's entanglements was a big one. He patted the grab handle. 'Up you get then, Jack.'

Jack pulled himself into the cab and onto the passenger seat. McCalvey closed the door after him, resumed his place behind the wheel, and leaned across to fasten the belt.

'What are you doing?' Jack asked, suddenly sharp.

'Just buckling us both in, nice and safe. It's only a short journey.'

McCalvey started the engine and drove up onto the tarmac, turning left to join the coast road. Within minutes the town had dropped behind them, the outlook widening to a pleasant vista of colourful shrubs, lushly curving fields, and a glittering expanse of ocean growing larger on the car's near side under a cloudless sky.

At first Jack sat quietly, eyes forward, stiffly resistant to McCalvey's efforts to make small talk as they climbed. Then in an affronted voice he said, 'Where are you taking me?'

'I'm taking you home.'

'No, you're not!' Jack exclaimed. 'My home is back down there. You're heading in the wrong direction.'

'No really, it's fine, Jack, I know where you live.'

'*Who are you?*' Jack shouted. He turned sideways to glare at McCalvey, distress contorting his face. 'I don't know you.'

McCalvey put his hand on Jack's arm.

'Don't you touch me!' Jack batted the hand away. A split second later he'd leaned across to grab the steering wheel, causing the car to swerve left. The vehicle bounced wildly as its huge wheels struck the lumpy buffer of rough grass, lurching to an abrupt stop as McCalvey pounded the brakes.

'Calm down, Jack. It's only a bit further—'

But Jack had begun to howl, beating on the windscreen and the side panel with tightly closed fists. 'I want to get home. I need Annie. Where's Annie?'

McCalvey unbuckled himself and tried to steady the other man by placing both arms firmly round his shoulders, but Jack lashed out in fear, catching him violently on the chin. In the brief time it took him to recoil from the blow and lose his hold, Jack yanked the door open and threw himself out of the car, bellyflopping to the ground.

He turned onto his side, moaning pitifully as McCalvey jumped down after him.

'Are you OK? Can I give you a hand up?'

Jack had started to shiver. Wary of reaching out to him again, McCalvey lowered himself until he was balanced on his haunches two feet away. For a moment he waited in silence, steadying his own nerves. Then he tried again. 'Jack?'

The elderly man turned desperate eyes towards him. 'I don't know where I am,' he said shakily. 'I thought I knew the way, but I've got myself completely lost.'

A damp stain was beginning to spread across the front of his trousers. McCalvey caught a whiff of urine, and his own anxiety melted into quiet sadness.

'If you'd let me help you, Jack,' he said, 'I can take you back to Annie. I promise I'll take you home.'

Wordless minutes ticked by. Eventually Jack hauled himself to his elbows to gaze down through lanky fuchsias and clumps of gorse at gleaming ribbons of silver blue. One or two cars passed by, but McCalvey had managed to stop the pick-up yards from the road and they weren't disturbed. The air was warm; wheeling gulls harangued each other in the distance. *We could be out for a picnic*, he thought wryly.

'It's a great view from up here,' he said.

'It is.' Jack pointed a tremulous finger at the water. 'There's a natural jetty down there. Fallen rock, granite, that's made a horizontal wall. Mussel Cove. My father used to keep a boat there.'

'Really? I know Mussel Cove.' McCalvey shuffled nearer. 'It's deep. Deep enough for a keel.'

Jack nodded. His lips worked silently for a moment. 'I used to sit on that jetty as a boy and look up at Wheal Blazey. It was a mine captain's house, you know. So beautiful. One day, I said. One day I'm going to live in that house.'

'You made it happen, Jack.'

Filmy grey eyes turned towards him. 'Did you say you know my daughter?'

'Yes I do. And your wife, Annie.'

Jack looked at the car. 'Where were we going?'

'Home. To Wheal Blazey. I expect they'll have kept breakfast for you.'

'You think so?' The expression on Jack's face lightened and he waved at the road. 'Will you take me there now, then?'

'If you're sure that's fine with you.'

'So... what did you say your name was?'

McCalvey smiled and offered his hand. 'It's Cal,' he said. 'Just Cal.'

When the pick-up rumbled into the car park and halted by the entrance steps, Joss and Annie came running.

Annie reached the vehicle first, wrenching open the door to grasp her husband firmly by the arm and help him clamber out, her voice a frayed combination of reproach and relief. 'Oh, Jack, thank heavens! Where *on earth* have you been?'

Heart thumping, Joss bent to clasp her knees and regain control of her breath. *This was all my fault.* She raised her head to take in her father's grass-stained shirt and sodden trousers, then noticed McCalvey approaching her mother from the other side of the car. *Damn.*

Her poor, vulnerable Dad… She'd made a stupid mistake leaving him alone too long, and he'd ended up having to be rescued. By *this* man, of all people. What must McCalvey think of them? Though from what she'd seen, she wouldn't describe him as a beacon of responsibility either.

She chanced a sideways look and caught him frowning at Wheal Blazey's open door. Wondering what his daughter was up to, maybe? Or hoping to run into his buxom young admirer. Ha! Out of luck on both counts, she thought; the girls were stripping beds in the upstairs rooms.

But then, he'd been a good Samaritan. If he hadn't spotted her dad…

Jenny was effusive as she brushed twigs and foliage from her husband's clothes. 'Thank you so much, Mr. McCalvey. *Cal.* Thank you for bringing him home. I only hope he wasn't too… challenging.'

'Glad to help.'

'Did he get into some sort of scrape? It looks as if he's been in the wars.'

'He did startle me a bit, to be honest.' McCalvey covered his jaw with one hand, seeming self-conscious. The skin beneath his fingers, Joss realised, was red. 'Are *you* alright?' she asked. 'Looks like you've had a scrape yourself.'

His eyes met hers for the first time. 'Oh, I'm OK. But I'll tell you something for nothing – he'd be a real bugger to kidnap.' And then he smiled – a twinkly, good-natured smile she couldn't help returning.

The sound of squealing disc brakes and churning gravel

heralded Ollie's arrival. Seeing the state of his grandfather, Ollie dumped the bicycle behind the car and ran forward, his face creasing with concern. 'What's happened?' He grabbed Jack's muddy sleeve as Annie reached for his.

'Your Grandad went walkabout this morning,' Annie said. 'But he's alright now.'

'Oh *Grandad!*' The high-pitched wail prompted Joss to move nearer, murmuring, 'He's fine, sweetheart, shush now, let's not get dramatic—' but Jack had already recoiled in alarm.

'You should have stayed here, Grandad, you mustn't go wandering.' Ollie curled his fingers tightly around Jack's wrist and gave it a vigorous shake.

'Get *off* me. Who do you think you are?' Jack immediately snatched his arm away, and Ollie froze.

'He worries about you, Dad,' Joss intervened. 'He just wants you to be safe.' She pressed Ollie's shoulder, willing him to step back, and heard the beginning of a sob.

'Hot drink and a change of clothes,' Annie commanded, gripping Jack's arm. 'We're all feeling a bit fraught, I think.' She nodded at her daughter, grandson and McCalvey in turn, then smiled determinedly into her husband's eyes. 'Come along, Jack. Let's say goodbye to everyone and get you sorted out.'

'Annie?'

'Yes, love.'

'What's going on? I don't think... I don't...' All at once Jack seemed heart-wrenchingly frail. He stared back at the group, then said querulously, 'I don't know all these people. Do I?'

Joss exchanged a desperate glance with her mother. 'Of course you do, Dad,' she said. 'Ollie's your grandson. Your *favourite* grandson, you always joke.'

Jack examined Ollie's appalled face, then turned back to

Annie with baffled impatience. 'Not *him*,' he said. 'That rude boy should go away.'

As Annie guided him towards the entrance, she glanced at Ollie over her shoulder and mouthed, *Don't worry. Very tired. See him later.*

Everything went quiet. For surreal, terrible seconds Joss couldn't even hear the birds, the sea, or the hissing of trees. She felt desiccated, as if all the oxygen and moisture had been sucked out of her body. When Ollie turned back, she saw that his face was awash with tears.

She pulled him tightly against herself. What was there to say? Nothing that wouldn't sound glib. Nothing that would amplify or explain what he already understood too well.

From just beside her, McCalvey's soft voice broke the silence. '*Shit*, Joss. This is awful. I'm sorry.'

She responded with a shrug. There was no point trying to make light of it, waving him out of their gate with blithe assurances: *it's nothing, it happens, we'll be fine.*

It would never be fine.

'I wish I could do something to help.'

'You've done plenty,' she told him. 'You found him and brought him home safe.'

McCalvey pursed his lips, and his eyes searched her face. His distress floored her for a moment. 'You seem to have a lot to cope with, Joss,' he said. 'Ollie too.'

She peered at him. Did he just mean her father? The challenges of Wheal Blazey? Or... had someone given him the lowdown on her own recent history? *If he thinks I'd share any of that, he has another think coming.*

She fixed her eyes on the doorway, visualising Annie peeling off her father's soiled clothes while the kettle boiled. Reality drenched her like cold rain, inescapable and bleakly depressing. They'd have to get help. Somehow they'd have to find the money for regular care, or they'd all go under. *I'll sit mum down tonight, and we'll talk.*

'We keep each other going, one way or another,' she told him. 'My dad still loves us, I really believe that. And Ollie needs him.'

Ollie's weeping was audible now, though his gulps and grunts betrayed strenuous efforts to hide it. McCalvey's brow was furrowed. 'Why don't I take him sailing?' he said.

'Sorry?'

'I could take him out on Kara for an hour or two. How about it? He'd love it.'

Joss felt Ollie straighten up a little. He wiped his eyes and turned his face to McCalvey, who tilted his head and smiled. 'What do you think, Ollie?'

'Hang *on* a minute!' she exclaimed. This had come right out of left field. *Kara?* The boat she'd seen had seemed built for speed, and they didn't know this man from Adam…

But the whimpering had stopped.

'Yeah,' Ollie murmured. 'That would be good.'

She narrowed her eyes at McCalvey. 'Look, I'm sorry. With respect, we hardly know you and Ollie's only twelve. It's kind of you to offer, but I can't let him go out to sea unsupervised on a strange boat with—'

'Come with us then,' he said.

'Me? No!' *God, no.*

'We'll pick a calm day. It'll be an experience.'

How *dare* he put her in this position! The suggestion was mad. Maybe even dangerous. But Ollie had grabbed her hand and was gazing up with big damp eyes, newly bright with hope. So now she was the bad guy. *Thanks a bunch, Cal.*

'Maybe another day,' she sniffed. 'When we've had a chance to talk about it. Properly.'

'But *Mum*—'

The roar of a finely tuned engine preceded the appearance of a familiar wine-red sports car through Wheal Blazey's main gate. Joss didn't know whether to feel relieved at the imminent interruption or overwhelmed by another complicating presence in what was turning out to be a pretty terrible day.

As Guy drew up, McCalvey touched her arm. 'Two hours, max,' he persisted. 'Just give it a try. Next Saturday maybe, if the weather's good.'

She was struggling to frame a decisive rebuttal, when something about the roadster's bonnet stopped her in her tracks.

A significant area of the front bodywork had been brutally disfigured by a network of jagged scratches, many of them deep enough to expose the car's metal carcass. The damage was shocking. Joss stared at it open-mouthed as Guy climbed out and slammed the door. His face was scarlet.

'Guy – my God – did you collide with something? Trees?'

He responded with a bitter laugh. '*Trees*? Are you kidding?'

McCalvey looked grimly from one to the other, then down at the car. He gave a low whistle. 'Bloody hell,' he said. 'That looks deliberate. And expensive.'

Guy scowled. 'I left it near Roslyn Glynn this morning, on the perimeter track. It's still just fields round there, they haven't broken ground yet, you have to walk to the portacabins. I couldn't have been more than an hour.' He thumped the car's roof with a fist. 'Some bastard must have seen me park up.'

'So, no CCTV?' McCalvey asked. 'No witnesses?'

Guy shook his head. 'I've taken photos and reported it, but I'm not holding my breath. I'll get the assessors out over the weekend when I'm home.' He looked at Joss. He was trembling with rage. 'I'll just settle up and go.'

'Of course,' she said. 'I'm so sorry, Guy.'

She hadn't noticed Ollie slip away to retrieve his discarded bike, but as Guy vanished inside the house he wheeled it towards her, one hand on the handlebars, the other holding the saddlebag in place. 'I'll put this back in the bike shed,' he said. 'But *Mum*—'

'Ollie, just let me sort out Mr. Tremain's bill.' She glanced at McCalvey, who'd opened the pick-up's offside door and was readying himself to leave.

'*Mum!*' Ollie lodged himself in front of her. 'I *really* want to go out on Kara. *Please.*'

His desperate entreaty charged the air between them. Joss groaned, pulled a tissue out of her pocket, and smartly wiped his nose.

'Call it maritime therapy,' she heard McCalvey say. 'What about a week tomorrow, before term starts? I could meet you both at midday, outside the chandlery.'

'*Mum?*'

'Oh for God's sake! OK,' she muttered. 'OK.' She shook her head, glared at them both, then hurried away to the steps.

SEVEN

She won't admit it, but she's dead nervous.

I don't think she & Cal like each other much, but that's OK. They don't have to be friends. It's all about the boat.

She's doing something that scares her, for my sake. That's such a great thing.

She already knows I'd do the same for her.

Outside the chandlery, they paused to take in the spectacle of St. Roslyn in early summer. For the last two nights Joss had checked every online weather station, guiltily praying for adverse conditions – a blast of unseasonal rain at least. But this morning the water was marbled with sunshine; gulls bickered in the clear air, and vapour trails scribbled their way across a sky the colour of cornflowers. She had to resign herself. There was no escape. She was going out on McCalvey's boat.

A dozen sails glimmered in the bay, all of them travelling a bit too fast for her liking, some heeling at impossible angles. She took Ollie's hand as they crossed the threshold, and squeezed hard. He squeezed back. 'You'll be fine, Mum.' She was already perspiring inside her showerproof, and her underused trainers were pinching her toes.

The emporium was a marine Aladdin's cave. Joss moved past cabinets loaded with brass weights, gleaming instruments, fiendish-looking toolkits and huge, laminated maps next to rails hung with wetsuits and storm jackets – a whole other world. She watched Ollie examine everything intently, item by item. *Maritime therapy* was the phrase McCalvey had used. Maybe he was on to something.

As a family they'd been somewhere like this before, shopping for bodyboards. She remembered Felix's voice as he threw his arms wide in front of a packed display, declaring, *Feels like an adventure could start in here, eh, Ol?* Together, father and son had explored every corner, lingering over the most intriguing or most beautiful objects. Ollie had squealed with pleasure at finding a compass small enough to examine with childish fingers but surprisingly heavy – set in brass with a hinged lid, a jewelled bearing at the centre of a bevelled face, and a needle that sparkled in his palm like a shard of uncut diamond.

Look at this, he'd whispered, holding it up for her to see. He'd turned to his father with real yearning. *Can we buy it?*

Felix had laughed. *No point,* he'd said. *Something like that needs a boat. But don't worry, kiddo – I'll always make sure you're heading in the right direction.*

It came back to her with an unpleasant jolt. They'd argued in that shop.

Someone had dropped a crumpled pamphlet on the floor. Ollie had scooped it up and discovered a twenty-pound note underneath. 'Nice one! Finders keepers,' Felix had chuckled. 'Enough for a mask and snorkel.'

'Absolutely *not*!' she'd exclaimed. 'Take it to the counter, Ol – they'll be back for it when they realise it's gone.'

'Oh come on Goody-Two-Shoes,' Felix had mocked her. 'Whoever's daft enough to let it fall out of a pocket deserves to lose it. Fair do's.'

'Fair do's?' She'd stared at him open-mouthed while Ollie glanced anxiously from one to the other, paralysed between his desire and his conscience. 'Twenty pounds is a lot of money, Felix. What if someone needs it for lunch? Or they've promised their kids ice-creams?'

She could still remember the exasperation she'd seen in his eyes. The coldness. 'This is why, my darling, you'd never make it as a businesswoman.'

'This isn't about *business*,' she'd flared back. 'It's about *integrity*.'

Eventually he'd shrugged and wandered off as Ollie took the note to the cashier – but not before she'd heard him hiss, *Mother Bloody Superior* under his breath.

Dear God. Hadn't she heard alarm bells, even then?

'Hallo there!' a cheerful voice boomed, making her jump. 'You must be our Wheal Blazey punters.'

He filled the space in front of them, the big bear of a man Joss recognised from her visit to the marina, when he'd chased after McCalvey in response to the lifeboat summons. 'I'm Marty,' he announced. 'I run this place. Cal's fetching Kara to the pontoon, he won't be long. He's asked me to fit you up with lifejackets.'

Lifejackets! Oh Lord. In case they ended up in the briny, of course. 'Joss,' she said faintly. 'And this is Ollie.'

He beckoned them to the back of the store where racks of vests and flotation devices covered most of the wall.

'I think this one will do you.' Marty held out an orange vest. Her anxious 'Oh... Right then' made him grin. 'Don't worry,' he said. 'You'll be in safe hands. If there's one thing Cal's careful about, it's what happens on his boat.' He gave a good-humoured snort. 'The only thing, probably.'

Ollie was already buckling himself into a smaller version.

'You can leave your showerproof here,' Marty said. 'You won't need it, you've got yourselves a perfect day. I won't sell it, I promise. Or if I do, I'll go halves.'

His teasing relaxed her a little. Once he'd helped her tighten the straps, the jacket felt reassuringly comfortable. 'All sorted, buddy?' she heard him say, and she turned to see McCalvey quietly taking stock of them from the open door.

Kara's cockpit was flawlessly varnished and surprisingly elegant, her neat lockers integrated with sickle-shaped benches that made Joss think of church pews. At McCalvey's suggestion she tucked herself against one corner of the stern, the guardrail supporting her back and a stanchion within easy reach of her left hand. Immediately, McCalvey turned his attention to Ollie – 'Up for giving me a hand, Ollie?' – and she understood with relief that she was peripheral to this whole arrangement. 'I'll use the engine to get us off the quay. Once we're moving you can slip the lines, forward and aft – OK?'

Ollie nodded, wide-eyed and tense.

McCalvey let the motor idle while Ollie acquainted himself with the deck's fixtures, fittings and overall layout. Joss noticed he was watching Ollie like a hawk. *Safe hands*, Marty had told them. She sensed he was right.

'Ready?' As McCalvey put Kara into reverse, Ollie sprang to free the mooring ropes before bundling them on deck. 'Extra points for tidying them out of the way,' McCalvey said, and Ollie promptly set about looping them into orderly figures-of-eight.

The sea was millpond calm. Even so, the sensation of the liberated hull drifting gently backwards from the pontoon brought goose bumps to Joss's skin. She flashed McCalvey a tight smile that signalled *OK, we're in your hands. Look after us.*

Then she fixed her gaze on the horizon, and prayed to God she wouldn't be sick.

'It's safe to get the mainsail up now, without using the motor,' McCalvey said. 'Still OK to lend a hand, Ollie?'

Ollie jumped to the front of the cockpit, where McCalvey had started to feed the halyard into the teeth of its cleat. 'Here you go,' he said, passing Ollie the rope. 'See if you can get the main up. Give it some welly.'

Ollie began to haul. Realising within seconds the weight and resistance he was dealing with, he gritted his teeth and stabilised himself by wedging one foot against a locker, his expression fierce. Inch by inch, the canvas ascended Kara's mighty mast. McCalvey stood close behind, helping with the last half metre. 'Right, cleat it off now, nice and tight.'

Ollie did as he was told. Then he turned to Joss with a smile that made her heart brim with love. This beautiful boat, his part in setting her up, McCalvey's trust – it all seemed to be feeding something inside him that was *hungry*.

'Take the helm for a minute, Ollie,' McCalvey said, 'And point her over there, towards the little beach at the tip of Chy Head, will you?'

Ollie scrambled to the tiller and fixed his eyes on the landmark. A narrow bank of sand and shingle was just visible where the granite monolith plunged into the sea.

McCalvey moved forward to release the furling line and free the jib. As the boat slipped towards open water, he played with the sheet, adjusting and readjusting the tension until the foresail billowed into a gratifyingly smooth crescent. Like a big cat finally released into her natural territory, Kara began to heel to port and rapidly pick up speed.

'Still OK, Ollie?' Beaming, Ollie gave him a thumbs-up.

God Almighty. Joss hooked her arms round the guardrail as the boat tipped. The sea was level with her hips, nerve-wrackingly close, the huge mainsail looming on her right like a giant wing. Oddly weightless, almost horizontal, she realised she'd lost control of her feet and legs, and there was precious little she could do about it. But she saw Ollie's eyes glitter with exhilaration as he pushed the tiller forward and away in small experimental movements; then McCalvey overlaid his own hand, nudging things back a little until their trajectory stabilised. 'Good job, shipmate,' she heard him say. 'There's a lot of canvas on this boat to manage. I expect she's more responsive than anything you're used to.' He patted Ollie's shoulder, then looked at her and winked.

For a moment the expressions on their faces, man and boy, were strikingly similar – focused, purposeful, totally absorbed. It had been months since she'd seen enthusiasm like that on her son's face. *Go on,* she wanted to encourage him, *enjoy this moment.* He'd forgotten that life could be good. Perhaps they both had.

There were no obstacles ahead and the breeze was constant as Kara cleaved her way into deeper water. Guided by McCalvey, Ollie held the boat steady as the coastline dropped behind them, the wash from the stern creating a sparkling train of lace. A dozen gulls arrived to ride the swell, squawking and dipping in expectation of snatching a meal.

Joss turned to the sun, her face damp with spume but deliciously warm. She closed her eyes, finally surrendering to the radiance of the day as salt dried on her skin.

The route McCalvey had chosen took them eastwards, away from the promontory past ribbons of sand interspersed with picturesque little coves. 'Less challenging, less bumpy,' he told them. 'It's beautiful round the Head, but the rocks on its fringes can be treacherous. I've been involved in too many rescues there.'

The view from the sea was breath-taking: the coastline lush, the water serene and astonishingly clear – almost inviting. Joss took a moment to assess the state of her own nerves. Amazingly, their anxious jangle had subsided to a bearable hum. *If Felix could see me now...*

'Refreshments?' With a theatrical flourish, McCalvey reached into a locker and produced a shopping bag. Cheese straws, peanuts and crisp packets appeared on a side bench, followed by a 4-pack of Tribute, two cans of Sauvignon Blanc and a bottle of Coke. 'Awesome!' Ollie exclaimed, and Joss laughed.

'I thought you might be a white wine kind of woman.' McCalvey surveyed his offerings and shrugged. 'Sorry – this is about as good as it gets when I put a picnic together. Not very creative.'

'Unexpected,' she said. 'But brilliant.' She returned his smile.

They zig-zagged parallel to the coast for the best part of an hour, McCalvey taking control of the tiller at key moments, beer in hand, guiding them to more comfortable positions in the cockpit when a shift in the breeze required a jibe. He was vigilant and careful, reining things in to limit any pitch and roll, manually wresting the hefty boom from one side to the other to avoid the risk of heads connecting with it during changes of tack.

Ollie gulped down his Coke – *'no beer for you today, you've got your L-plates on,'* McCalvey teased – while interrogating him about sheets, travellers, jammers and winches. Meanwhile Joss savoured her wine and watched her bare arms turn pink.

'Have you sailed all your life, Cal?' she asked.

'Long as I can remember.'

'Do your folks sail?'

He seemed not to hear, preoccupying himself with something in the distance. She took a sip and tried again. 'You're not from round here originally?'

'Not really.'

A full minute passed with no further elaboration. She raised her eyebrows at Ollie. *Did I say something?* He shook his head.

But confined together in this little space, small talk felt important. And she appreciated the effort McCalvey had made. He'd been thoughtful. He'd surprised her. He *interested* her.

'So, where's home for you, Cal?'

The look he gave her was somewhere between irritation and unease. 'I couldn't really say.'

She gaped at him. Was the question so hard? 'What brought you to St. Roslyn then?'

'A job.'

This, she thought, was like pulling teeth. Clearly he wasn't comfortable with the personal stuff. Well, OK. She could relate to that.

He finished his beer, crumpled the can in one hand and lobbed it with impressive precision into the empty bag. Then he rubbed his nose, returned her gaze, and said, 'The marina job. And Kara. I came across her a few years ago when she was just a shell, neglected in someone's barn. Sooner or later I knew she'd be up for auction. She was a steal, to be honest.'

Joss breathed out. This was safer ground. 'How old is she?'

He examined her face for a moment, wordlessly asking, *You really want to know?*

She really did.

'Constructed in the 1940s, most likely. My guess is she was privately commissioned to race.' His gaze shifted to the narrow deck, then upwards to the masthead. 'She's mahogany, over oak and elm. I've tried to stay faithful to the original build. It's taken me four years to get her back into this condition.'

'You've done a wonderful job.' Joss followed his eyes along the edge of the canvas. 'Where did you get the skill?'

There was a small beat before he responded. 'Plymouth. I was apprenticed to a shipwright there. It's... what I do.'

Hallelujah. He'd shared something significant. She inclined her head and smiled. 'Sounds like she was lucky you found her in that barn.'

'We were both lucky,' he said.

When she blinked inquiringly at him, he gave a small, dismissive huff. 'Probably should head back.'

Subject closed. She watched him push the tiller away, executing a wide, controlled circle to point Kara's nose in the direction of home. 'You can helm us back if you want, Ollie.'

Ollie eagerly repositioned himself centre-stern. McCalvey climbed onto the coach roof, swinging both sails forward into a goosewing to collect what little breeze remained. Satisfied, he re-joined Joss on the bench.

'Thank you.' She touched his arm. 'Look at him. You were right, this is as good as any therapy. You've completely made his day.'

'He's fine,' he said. 'His instincts are good. He knows what he's doing.'

Mellowed by warmth and wine, she twisted in each direction to absorb the vastness of sky and sea, delighting in the boat's peaceful motion, the gorgeous landscape, the look of joyful concentration on Ollie's face. 'We should be playing some inspiring seagoing music,' she said. 'Sea shanties, or Vaughn Williams. Or yacht rock – that's a genre, isn't it? Christopher Cross or Rod Stewart – you know, *We are Sailing* – that kind of thing.'

'I have music!' McCalvey got to his feet.

'You do?'

Within seconds he'd descended into the tiny cabin, reappearing with a battered CD player. Joss caught Ollie's look of sceptical astonishment: *What the hell's that?*

'I bought this years ago, when I was spending the winter in dry dock,' he said. 'I've got some old CDs in a box down there somewhere. What kind of stuff do you like?'

She hesitated. 'Oh, I don't know…' His approval suddenly felt ridiculously important. 'I'm a bit of a dinosaur really.'

'Try me.'

'Well… I love Springsteen. The Stones. The Faces, Eagles. Queen, Foo Fighters, Roxy Music, U2…'

He laughed out loud, which made her laugh too.

'I blame my mum and dad,' she explained, shaking her head. 'When I was small they had a real thing for 70s and 80s rock bands – and, oh my word, you should have seen the way they *danced…*'

It was a vivid, technicolour memory – her parents in workmen's overalls, jiving to music thumping out of old-fashioned speakers while their paintbrushes dripped emulsion onto dustsheets in the hall. It was just before they opened Wheal Blazey to guests for the very first time; she must have been about four. And her dad, God bless him, had grabbed her hands and made her twirl with him to *Bohemian Rhapsody…*

She shook herself, aware of a soft gleam in McCalvey's eyes. 'They had good taste, your mum and dad,' he said.

'To go with their good genes, obviously.'

'Obviously.'

She raised an instructive finger. 'And of course there's Bowie.'

'Yes, Bowie!' He looked pleased. 'Heroes, Jean Genie, Rebel Rebel. You are *definitely* my kind of woman!'

He turned away immediately – but not before she'd caught a roguish grin that meant *oops*. Her face flamed as she stared at his averted head, then she looked at the floor. Two tins of wine were rolling in the corner by her feet. Both empty.

'All OK, Ol?' She glanced anxiously at her son. His eyes

were fixed intently on the horizon, his face a taut mask, hands gripping the tiller with ferocious determination. It seemed he hadn't heard a word.

'I think I can at least find some Springsteen,' she heard McCalvey say. '*Born to Run?*'

'Oh no. It has to be *Dancing in the Dark.*'

'Hang on.'

He disappeared below for several minutes, then climbed slowly back into the fresh air, a disc in each hand. Joss noticed him taking sharp, shallow breaths, beads of perspiration on his forehead. 'Cal – are you alright?'

He waved a hand towards the cabin's interior. 'It's a bit tight down there.'

'You're claustrophobic?'

He filled his lungs and blew hard. 'Catches me out sometimes. No big deal.'

No wonder he prefers to be outdoors. 'Ollie!' She took hold of Ollie's wrist and shook it. 'Help Cal out, lovey. Go and grab some CDs. I can steer for a minute. We're only going in a straight line, after all.' She pulled herself upright, set her jaw, and took hold of the tiller.

With a sigh Ollie relinquished his post. Making his way past McCalvey, he asked, 'Got any Jay-Z? Dua Lipa?'

'Sorry, buddy.' McCalvey shook his head.

'Drake? Stormzy?'

McCalvey and Joss exchanged helpless looks. *See?* she mouthed. *Dinosaurs.*

Ollie descended the cabin steps while McCalvey climbed back into the cockpit, moving behind Joss to lay a supportive hand on the tiller. 'Enjoying yourself more than you expected?'

'I *am*,' she told him. 'It's fabulous.'

'As good as dancing with your dad?'

'Almost.'

He squeezed her arm. She put a hand on his in reflexive acknowledgement, just as Ollie reappeared. He paused in the hatchway, apparently engrossed in something between his hands. By the time he glanced up at them, McCalvey and Joss had jerked apart.

'What have you got there, Ol?' Joss asked, her voice a little too bright.

Ollie extended an open palm. He was holding a compact compass, testing its weight, letting his thumbs trace the perfect curvature of glass. Darts of light played around the needle as he lifted the instrument into the sunshine.

'They're lovely things, aren't they?' McCalvey said. Ollie nodded. 'I found it by the chart table.' His tone was curiously petulant, Joss thought; almost accusatory.

'One of these days I'll find a way to fix it permanently. It needs to be screwed into a proper plate, and I'm nervous about drilling into the old wood. So it sits in a side pocket most of the time.'

'Don't you *use* it, then?' Ollie's fingers tightened round the object in a gesture that seemed provocative, even proprietorial. For a tense moment Joss thought he was going to ask, *Can I have it?*

'Oh, I use it often enough. When I'm beyond sight of land.'

For a few more seconds Ollie stood between the darkness of the cabin and the sunny cockpit, glancing between McCalvey and the treasure he'd found. The air around him seemed to bristle with inarticulate challenge.

'We won't need it today, though,' McCalvey said levelly. 'Today I can see exactly where we're going.'

'Ollie – *put it back*.' Joss's voice was firm.

Compressing his lips, Ollie reversed down the steps. McCalvey gave Joss a quizzical look and she shook her head.

'He loves everything about this boat.'

'Ah well,' he said, 'They get you like that. If I hadn't had Kara these last few years I'd be a basket case by now.'

The remark intrigued her, but she had no time to respond. Ollie had re-emerged, this time clutching a CD. 'I've found some Abba!' he told them, evidently much cheered.

McCalvey's groan made them both laugh. 'God, I've been rumbled. OK – let's have it.'

Ollie reclaimed the tiller as McCalvey took charge of the disc. Moments later, the pounding bass notes of *Does Your Mother Know?* tore into the air.

Joss wiggled her eyebrows at Ollie and grinned. This had been one of their secret party-pieces, a celebration of Friday afternoons when homework was done and the weekend beckoned. McCalvey watched, mesmerised, as they leaned into each other to belt out the chorus, Ollie's voice growing louder with every note, inhibitions vanishing as his mother fixed gleaming eyes on his and drummed on his shoulder.

'*Right* then,' McCalvey said when the track finished. 'Make way for some ancient classics.' He replaced the disc with the Springsteen one he'd sourced, stepping back in triumph as the strains of *Dancing in the Dark* reverberated across the deck.

'Yes!' Joss breathed approval, closed her eyes and began to sway to the rhythm. As Kara continued her oblivious, stately progress across the flat water of the bay, she joined her voice to McCalvey's, the two of them shattering the silence as they gripped invisible microphones to accompany each verse, heads back and knees bent, owning an imaginary stage.

A glorious playfulness, full of nostalgia for simpler, freer times, caught hold of them like flames in a wind. McCalvey quickly replaced the Springsteen track with Bowie's *Rebel Rebel*, cranking up the volume of the raucous riff as they planted themselves against the lockers to play air guitar. By the time the track ended they were both convulsed with laughter, surprised and delighted with themselves, and unaccustomed tears of merriment had started to tip down Joss's pink cheeks.

Ollie surveyed them with disgust. 'That was *terrible*,' he said. His glowering disapproval reduced Joss to a poorly suppressed fit of further giggling that threatened to double her up.

Then McCalvey pointed to the boat's port side.

Dolphins!

There were at least half a dozen of them, apparently curious to see what all the noise was about, and eager to play.

'Shit! They're *huge*!' Ollie gasped. Joss bit back an automatic rebuke.

The creatures took it in turns to break the surface, shiny grey bodies flashing white underbellies as they arced with magical, muscular elegance either side of the prow.

'Go say hallo, Ollie,' said McCalvey, and he took back the tiller.

Ollie ran forward and threw himself onto his stomach, stretching both arms over the water in an effort to reach the visitors. One of them tucked itself alongside the hull, carving a fluent, agile passage that mirrored the boat's progress, avoiding collision by a hair's breadth. Mischievous eyes sized up the straining fingers; a slender nose nodded up and down in a chipper greeting.

Joss lifted both hands to her mouth. 'I can't believe it,' she breathed. 'If I could have designed the perfect day for him – for us – it would be this.'

'I'm glad.'

She fixed him with a bright, knowing look. '*Now* I get it,' she told him. 'When I asked you where your home is… it's *here*. Out here, on Kara. Am I right?'

The question briefly seemed to confound him. 'At sea, you

mean?' He grimaced at the horizon. 'Not exactly a place to put down roots.' Then he turned back with an enigmatic smile. 'But maybe that's the appeal.'

Put down roots.

That was it, in a nutshell.

He might be allergic to the concept – but it was a phrase that captured everything she wanted, if she could only find fertile ground. The words lingered in her mind as St. Roslyn's safe little harbour finally came back into view.

'Just look at me!' she shrieked at her reflection in the hall mirror. 'Face like a tomato and hair like a Cornish hedge!' Ollie grinned up at her, similarly rosy-cheeked. 'I can see you've been sailing, Mum,' he said. But the sight of Annie slumped in her chair behind reception instantly dampened their spirits.

'What is it?' Joss asked. 'Has something happened?'

Her mother glanced up, her eyes red-rimmed in a chalk-white face. 'We've had a visit from The Environment Agency.' She stabbed a pencil into a desktop jar. 'Bill Finch has reported us. Or at least, told them his land is being contaminated by what he's decided is our non-compliant soakaway.'

'The *toad*!' Joss growled. 'That's a bugger. Sorry, Ol.'

'Quite.' Annie pulled a face. 'Nothing we can do, for the moment. They have to undertake a full investigation, probably in the next couple of weeks. His best guess is that we'll need to install a treatment plant. I've been researching the cost. Horrendous, as you can imagine.'

Joss had recently helped Annie with a set of spreadsheets, trying to get a fix on cash flow, forecast outgoings, projected revenues and available reserves. One thing she could thank Felix for at least, she thought bitterly: he'd been a stickler when it came to domestic budgeting, insisting she knew the basics of financial management. A deeply ironic parting gift.

And the figures had confirmed it: Wheal Blazey was only just scraping by. She examined her mother's gaunt face with concern.

'Let's wait and see,' she said. 'There may be a straightforward solution. The culprit might not even be us.' *Of course it's us,* the rational part of her brain retorted. *This is the biggest house for miles, and Finch's fields are right below our run-off.*

'A treatment plant will cost thousands,' Annie groaned. 'And we've just agreed to fund a carer for your father. I don't see how we can possibly afford—' She caught sight of Ollie's huge, unblinking eyes and abruptly stopped.

'We'll sort it out,' Joss told her, projecting a conviction she didn't feel. 'If it comes to it, we'll talk to the bank.'

What *on earth* had she been doing, messing about on McCalvey's boat for most of the afternoon? She should have been here, addressing these problems, dealing with real life.

'Ollie and I will grab a shower, then he can start getting ready for school next week and I'll come back and help. We've got paying guests to check in, Mum. Money will come. There'll be things we can do.'

Annie managed a wan smile. But all Joss saw in her eyes was defeat.

EIGHT

I hit a boy today.

It was during break. I knocked him over and kicked him in the face.

Mum had to come in and see the Head.

I don't care. I'd do it again.

She knows why.

Mr. Bingham's office had a restrained, wood-panelled air of officialdom that made Joss defensive from the moment he asked her to sit down.

She was already flustered. A prospective carer for her father was due in less than an hour. Now Annie would probably have to interview the woman on her own. The timing was terrible, and the call – *there's been an unfortunate incident involving Oliver this morning* – had made her sick with anxiety.

Ollie was fidgeting on a hard chair to her left, grim-faced and pale against a sunless background of framed certificates, class photos and academic books. To right, a tiny girl with a waist-length pony tail sat framed in the window, hands clasped in her lap. Through the glass Joss could see the playground, netball posts, the science block and the annexe that housed the dining hall. Cabbage and mince today, her nose told her. Twenty-five years ago she'd been a pupil here herself. Sitting here in front of the headmaster, it was hard not to regress to the child she'd been then – bright, but full of self-doubt. Painfully eager to please.

'Thank you so much for coming in, Mrs. Harris. As mentioned on the phone, Ollie has been involved in what might best be described as a *fracas*, as has Millie here. One of our teachers, Mr. Hatfield, was on break duty at the time. I'll ask him to join us now.'

He buzzed through to his secretary, and two minutes later Mr. Hatfield arrived – nervous-looking and young. He failed to meet her eyes as he cast about for a chair. Probably still a probationer, she thought. Once upon a time, that might have been *her*.

'Perhaps you can summarise what happened for us, Mr. Hatfield.'

'Of course.'

He'd spotted two clusters of children at the far end of the recreation area, he told them – boys and girls in what seemed to be opposing ranks. 'Not unusual in itself,' he added, 'but there was an obvious tension, a bit of jostling between the groups.'

Most of the boys were in Ollie's year, he continued. Some of them spiralled away at his approach, but not before he'd seen one of the bigger lads, Craig, pull Millie towards him 'rather roughly.'

'There was an altercation,' he said. 'And Ollie pushed Craig to the ground.'

'An altercation?' Joss glanced at Ollie, who widened his eyes as if to say *this whole thing is stupid*. 'Was he provoked?'

'Possibly.' The teacher looked at her for the first time. 'But when the other boy was down, Ollie kicked him, with some force, on the chin. He's actually in sick bay now, having his jaw examined. It might be broken.'

'I see.' *Oh God.*

'The thing is – Craig was in no position to defend himself at the time,' he said. 'Ollie's reaction was unnecessary, to say the least, and violent in the extreme.'

Mr. Bingham leaned forward. 'We want to be fair, Mrs. Harris, and Craig's parents will want the full story, as I'm sure you do. So I've asked Millie here to give us her account of what happened, and why she thinks Ollie intervened as he did.'

The girl's eyes flicked from the adult members of her audience to Ollie. 'He was trying to defend me,' she said quietly.

'Please explain, Millie,' Mr. Bingham encouraged her. 'Take your time.'

She hesitated, a blush creeping upwards from her neck. Then she said, 'All the boys were jeering. Saying things about how frigid and… and… *unshaggable* all of us are, that we've probably never been kissed. Someone said Craig thought I was hot, and then they started chanting.'

'Chanting?'

She nodded and lowered her eyes. 'Just do it,' they kept saying. 'Just do it. And Craig came right up close and said, *Come on, darlin', you know you want to.*'

All three adults shuffled uncomfortably in their seats. Joss swallowed hard.

'What happened then?' Mr. Bingham asked.

'He… he grabbed me round the neck and tried to kiss me. And… and…' She shook her head. Tears welled in her eyes, and she thumbed them away. 'He put his hand up my jumper. He… got into my *bra.*'

Joss stared into Millie's enormous eyes and felt the girl's fear, her acute humiliation. The impact was physical and profound, as if her own body had been violated. She heard the headmaster's voice, weirdly distant, saying, 'It's very brave of you to share this with us Millie. Are you able to tell us what happened next?'

'I said *don't*,' she told him. '*Don't.*'

In appalled silence, Joss pulled a tissue from her sleeve and passed it across. Millie blew her nose, adding, 'He's a lot bigger than me.'

'And what did Ollie do?' Mr. Bingham asked.

'He launched himself at Craig and shouted at him to get off me.' She glanced at Ollie, offering a tentative smile.

'Did Ollie hit Craig, Millie?'

'I don't think so, not right then. He just kind of torpedoed him, and then Craig let go of me and fell over.'

'So Craig ended up on the ground,' the headmaster summarised. 'But Mr. Hatfield says he saw Ollie kick him after that. Is that what happened?'

Millie looked at her lap. 'Yes.'

'Do you think he actually meant to hurt Craig?'

'I don't know. I suppose so. There was blood, and Craig was howling.' A moment's silence followed – a sense that everyone was silently gathering themselves. Then she looked straight at Mr. Hatfield and said, 'Craig is *horrible.*'

Mr. Bingham sat back slowly, exhaling through pursed lips. 'Well. Thank you Millie. You've been extremely helpful. Are you OK to return to class?'

She jumped up and made for the door, flashing Ollie one last look that Joss interpreted as apologetically grateful.

'Some might take the view,' the headmaster solemnly intoned once she'd left the room, 'that there was an element of gallantry in your response, Ollie, prompted by a desire to protect a smaller schoolmate. Be assured, the school will be dealing separately and severely with Craig's wholly unacceptable behaviour. But your action in attacking him with such ferocity, even though you'd separated him from Millie, seems vindictive and potentially dangerous. What do you say to that?'

Ollie glanced from Mr. Bingham to his mother, chewing his lip. His expression had collapsed, Joss thought, from stolid defiance into something much more complicated. He rubbed his nose and said, 'I just lost it. I can't explain.'

'You just lost it,' Bingham repeated.

Ollie's head dropped.

The headmaster turned his attention to Joss. 'My proposal, Mrs. Harris, is that Ollie meets with Craig and his parents to apologise. You may feel it appropriate to attend with him. It seems fair, however, that we ask Millie to repeat her testimony at that meeting, in the hope it offers some mitigation.'

Joss nodded, lost for words. Her head had begun to throb, and her eyes felt hot.

'In the meantime I believe I have no choice but to suspend you, Ollie. You may think you had just cause to behave in the way you did, but that would be a mistake. Inflicting grievous injury on a boy you'd already rendered powerless is savage and cowardly. You must learn to manage your anger. Am I clear?'

'Oh *Ollie.*' Joss addressed the back of his head as he dejectedly unhooked his bag and blazer from the cloakroom peg. 'This is serious. Mr. Bingham is right. You *have* to learn to manage your anger.'

Maybe she should be angry too, she pondered – read him the riot act, punish him with her own disappointment. But how could she blame him? He'd surrendered to a violent impulse, fired by another boy's cruelty. Surely it wasn't all bad?

Even so, the act of apparent brutality had shocked her. He'd told the headmaster he'd 'lost it.' Did her sensitive, clever, moody boy really have it in him to do something so vindictive? So mindless?

'He'd already let go of her,' she challenged him quietly. 'You didn't have to kick him in the face. What were you *thinking?*'

He pulled himself straight. For a few seconds he faced the wall, saying nothing. Then he turned to meet her eyes. 'He might have done it again, Mum. Or something worse. I couldn't let him.'

She'd seen that look before. It broke her heart.

The woman descending Wheal Blazey's front steps – arm in arm with her father, Joss was startled to notice – was silver-haired and petite in a neat blue twinset. Annie was a step behind, smiling at a genial exchange between the two: *Such a beautiful garden, Mr. Livesey, let's get you to your favourite bench...*

'Ah, here she is now – Jocelyn, my daughter,' Annie said, 'With my grandson Ollie.' Her smile wavered. 'Home early, from the look of things.'

Before Joss could prepare the ground, Ollie mumbled, 'Got suspended,' and the stranger looked up with interest.

Joss took in a pair of bright eyes in a fine-boned, pleasant face. Combined with a small, beaky nose, the overall effect made her think of a garden bird – chirpy and keenly alert. A former nurse with a breadth of care experience, she recalled from the agency's profile: early sixties, recently retired, wanting to move back to her home county after two decades away.

Joss extended a hand. 'He was standing up to a classroom bully,' she elaborated. 'Hallo. You must be Eva.'

'Eva Sibbert,' the woman nodded. She shook hands while managing to keep one arm tucked companionably into her father's. Jack was gazing indulgently at her as if she were a cherished long-lost friend, and her mother looked delighted. *This is a done deal*, Joss realised.

'Good to meet you both,' Eva continued. 'Your parents have been telling me all about you.' She leaned closer to Jack and smiled up at him. 'It's your lovely daughter Jocelyn and her son Ollie, Mr. Livesey.'

'Yes,' he said. 'I'm very proud of them. And please call me Jack.' A spring that had been coiled tight in Joss's stomach began to unwind. *This woman makes him feel safe.*

Eva turned to Ollie. 'I'm sorry you've been suspended. I hope you're alright?' She transferred her gaze to Joss as she added, 'At least your mum is here to support you. That makes you a lucky boy. Don't ever forget it.' The smile she offered them before turning back to Jack was warm and unpretentious.

Joss blanched as if she'd seen a ghost. She exchanged a look with her mother. Annie's eyes widened with understanding.

Your mum is here to support you. Don't ever forget how lucky you are. Another woman had once used those words – a woman who'd pressed Ollie's shoulder outside the London church where they'd said their farewells as a sad confetti of snow wilted to nothing on a wet pavement. Felix's mother.

Elegant and forlorn, Eleanor Harris had slipped quietly into the obscurity of a seat at the very back, only identifying herself to Joss once the last mourners had exited through the porch. While Annie took Ollie to one side, wiping his eyes and tidying his hair, she'd stepped forward to introduce herself and murmur, *I saw the notices. I'm sorry. I had to come. But I won't stay.*

Stay, please, Joss had begged. *Tell me what happened between you and Felix.*

And at last it had come out. Eleanor Harris had faced a terrible choice – to remain with her controlling, alcoholic, abusive husband, or leave him for a better man. Over the years she'd reached out to the son she'd left behind; written letters, left messages, even waited outside Felix's office. 'I thought he'd forgive me. That one day he'd let me find him again,' she said. 'But he was too attached to his father. Brainwashed by him, really. His father was obsessively proud of him – and increasingly dependent, as things soured between us, on his uncritical love. However bad things got, I knew my husband would never hurt Felix.'

'You tried to reconcile with him? I never knew.' Joss was aghast.

Eleanor had shrugged. 'They were peas in a pod, the two of them,' she sighed. 'Stubborn, volatile, difficult. Needlessly cruel sometimes. There was only so much energy I could give them, only so much heartache I could bear. But what about you? Did my son turn out to be a good husband? A good father? Did he… did he make you happy?'

Joss detected the question's nervous undercurrent. 'We had our moments,' she said.

Then Ollie and Annie had joined them, and Eleanor had knelt beside her unfamiliar grandson and spoken those words.

Joss watched Eva settle her father onto the bench, take his hand and point to an agapanthus beginning to unfold its stunning trumpets of sky-blue. She felt a violent tug as Ollie yanked her sleeve. 'I'm starving,' he muttered. 'I'll be inside when you're done sorting Grandad out. And you're right, by the way, Mum. I *was* standing up to a bully. I know I'll end up telling everyone I'm sorry about it. But it'll be a lie.'

He flashed the group a bitter look and stomped into the house.

Beyond the gate, white horses were breaking in the distance on a restive ocean. Joss closed her eyes, clenched her teeth, and took a steadying breath.

Peas in a pod.

NINE

When had Felix suggested it would make sense to revert to separate bank accounts? It must have been around the time he was promoted to Partner. Their finances were about to get complicated – that was his rationale. There'd be share options, dividends and commissions to factor in on top of his regular salary. They could keep a joint account for capital expenditure, he said – cars, holidays, artwork, furniture – and he'd set up a personal one for her, to make sure she was always 'comfortable.'

'Ooh, I've always fancied being a kept woman,' she'd teased him.

God, her naivety had been breath-taking.

It was when an IT supplier she'd never heard of called during the day to confirm a large payment to Felix – intended, she initially suspected, for someone else with similar bank details – that she first rooted among his papers. That night, she poured him a large Scotch and asked him about the holding company she'd seen in his statements.

The glass stilled in mid-air. 'You went through my accounts?'

'The guy on the line sounded pretty anxious, and you're

so scrupulous about these things. I thought it would be easy enough to check.'

He set down the whisky untasted, his face hardening to stone. 'You went through *my accounts?* What made you think you had the right?'

'The *right?*' She blinked at him in amazement. 'I'm your wife! We're supposed to be a team!'

He scowled at her. *Scowled.* 'Teams work on trust,' he said. 'But clearly you have a problem with that, or you wouldn't be sneaking around, poking into arrangements that are nothing to do with you.'

'*Felix!*'

A muscle in his jaw twitched. 'I should have locked the bloody desk.'

Had he come home already drunk, she wondered? Had something happened at work? 'You're acting as if you have a secret,' she said. As the words left her mouth, she realised it might be true.

Briefly, he seemed to recover. He tossed his head, dismissing the previous remark. 'I didn't mean to snap at you, sweetheart,' he said more gently. 'There's nothing to worry about. I've dealt with that payment. A few wires got crossed, that's all. And the name you saw – it looks like a holding company, but it's a mistake, a mix up. Someone transferred money to my account in error, and I transferred it back.'

'OK.'

She could have left it there. But if she had, a pernicious little worm of doubt would have burrowed further into her brain until it festered. 'The transferee has your initials, though. And from what I saw, it wasn't just one payment. There were four or five of them. For a shedload of money, Felix. So… I admit, I'm interested to know what that's all about.'

He gave a melodramatic sigh, heaved himself to his feet,

and made for the kitchen. 'It's just work stuff,' he muttered over his shoulder. 'To do with a couple of new suppliers.'

'So – why didn't you *say* that?'

He shrugged. 'Don't like talking about work. Anyway, I'm starving.'

She followed him to the fridge, something unpleasant fermenting in her gut. 'So why would a new supplier have your personal bank details? Not to mention money from them going into a different account.'

'You're trying to be clever.' He turned to face her. 'It doesn't suit you.'

'Hey! This is *me*, for God's sake.' His tone made her instantly furious, then fearful. 'Promise me you're not involved in anything shady. Felix? Promise me!'

His hand shot up to grip her jaw, compressing her cheeks, tipping her head violently backwards. She whimpered as her eyes goggled and watered. Leaning in very close – so close she could feel the damp heat of his sweat, the sourness of his breath – he hissed, 'Don't. Fucking. Meddle.'

For seconds they stood locked together. In her peripheral vision Joss saw he'd raised his free hand. She knew then, with terrifying certainty, that he wanted to hit her.

'Don't you dare!'

She watched him deflate like a punctured balloon. He stared at the hand that had clamped her chin as if he didn't recognise it, and stepped away.

'Shit. *Shit.* I'm so sorry Joss. I don't know what the hell came over me.'

She stared at him open-mouthed. Her own hand moved to touch the tender side of her face as tectonic plates of awareness shifted in her brain, plunging her into a black crevasse.

'Joss. Oh my *darling…*' He took her into his arms and buried his face in her hair. 'I'm so, so sorry. I'm a fool… it's been insane at work and I haven't been handling it well.'

She let him nuzzle her neck and kiss her cheeks, nose and chin while her hands hung limply at her sides. When he finally looked into her eyes he was tearful. 'I couldn't bear it if you didn't trust me. The idea of it makes me crazy, turns me into a stupid mad bastard. I just… I just flipped. I love you so, so much, Joss. And you love me too, don't you? You know you can trust me. Everything will be fine. The two of us are fine. We're good together.'

'Are we?' She pushed him backwards. 'This isn't you. You're not the man I know. The man I know – or thought I did – is better than this.'

'You're right,' he said. 'I *am* better than this. I'm sorry. I'll make it up to you.'

'You really hurt me.'

His face crumpled. 'I didn't mean to.'

'*Never* do anything like that again.'

'I never will, I swear.'

'And don't lie to me.'

He ducked his head like a chastised schoolboy, picked up her hand and kissed it. 'I won't. Don't give the bank stuff another thought. What you saw was a convoluted chain of boring transactions, but honestly it's all legit. Incremental business being done with like-minded colleagues. You need to believe me, Joss. Bank statements don't tell the whole story. Trust me.'

'Do I have a choice?' she asked. And he shook his head, smiled, and kissed her.

In the back-office of St. Roslyn's only high street bank, Joss stared at the accounts spread across the table and chewed her top lip, remembering.

In the months that followed that terrible evening, she'd

worked hard to improve her financial awareness. But the potential of those treacherous columns to determine her fate, and the fate of her loved ones, still filled her with dread.

Her old school contemporary Lorcyn may have made it to Bank Manager, but she was taken aback to see he'd lost most of his hair in the process. She fixed her eyes on the bridge of his nose, fretting it would be just her luck if he caught her staring at his shiny pate and exacted revenge by not signing off on a loan. Anyway, she thought dismally, he might be thinking time hadn't been kind to her either.

'I'd like to help,' he assured her for the third time. 'But honestly, Joss, any advance of funds is a real risk to your parents and the business in the long term. They've already re-mortgaged, and interest rates are going up. I'm trying to strike a balance here.'

'I know,' she sighed.

'In terms of a repayment plan, there's very little margin to increase debt. I understand the urgency of upgrading the sewage arrangements and I'm minded to cover at least some of that outlay—'

'Thank you, Lorcyn.'

'—but it's a big old house. What if it needs a new roof next year? What if Premier Inns get planning permission and steal your customers? What about the growth of AirBnBs?'

'We have a market,' she said firmly. 'It's a stable demographic, affluent silver surfers, walkers, people who appreciate our history and location. I heard the council may be thinking about an arts centre – that would be an added attraction.'

'I get that,' he said, though he was pursing his lips. '*If* it happens. But your proposition is limited at the moment Joss, and your market may dwindle as people turn to more adventurous or better packaged holidays. You don't even offer evening meals. Wheal Blazey needs a strategy.'

'A strategy?'

'A business plan at least. A robust approach to ensuring your income covers your outgoings, all year round. Your costs are high.'

Maybe I should talk to Guy. Maybe we really should sell. Anything else seemed horrendously difficult. But the thought of her parents listlessly stirring endless cups of tea on the paved patio of a 'later-life' bungalow, surrounded by potted azaleas and garden-centre hanging baskets, sapped her spirits. And how would *she* fit into that? She wouldn't, and neither would Ollie. After all these years, after so much effort, for her parents it would be a slow death.

She finally left the meeting with a short-term increase to Wheal Blazey's overdraft facility – enough to keep them limping along until the end of the year. Sticking plaster, she thought glumly, when the underlying diagnosis frankly required major surgery. But better than nothing.

She called into the creamery to collect a top-up order of butter, milk and eggs, then lugged her bags the short distance to her mother's battered old Honda, specifically borrowed for this trip, which she'd parked on the quay.

From ten feet way, she noticed the pancake-flat front tyre.

'Oh *for goodness sake.*' She searched the sky for any sign of the mocking divinity thwarting her efforts at every turn. '*Really?*'

It was a relatively cool day. The shopping would be fine in the car for a while, she decided, while she contacted a garage for help. She flipped open her phone, then growled at the screen. Of course – no damn service. *Peachy.* To her shame, her eyes started to burn with tears.

'Need a hand?' The voice transformed her mood like a therapeutic slap.

McCalvey glanced from her face to the offending wheel and waved in the direction of the outlets further along the front. 'I was just…' He faltered, then smiled broadly as she pressed her hands together, raised her eyes to heaven and said, 'Thank you, Lord.'

Her relief was instantly followed, however, by a sense of squirming embarrassment. 'It's so pathetic, in this day and age… I've never had to change a wheel and I was going to call a garage but there's no signal…' *Bugger.* The weak-little-woman thing was turning her pink with shame. 'I've been used to a Lexus with run-flat tyres, everything all computerised, but I borrowed my mother's car today and I don't really—' *Stop gabbling, for God's sake.* His smile widened further and he arched an eyebrow as if he found this hugely entertaining. She rolled her eyes and heaved a sigh. 'Sorry. It's been one of those days.'

'Right.' He studied her for a minute, then moved to release the vehicle's tailgate. 'The thing about these old models,' he observed as his head disappeared under the lid, 'is they usually carry a spare. And a jack.' He yanked a hardboard cover out of the bay, bent to rummage inside, then hauled out a wheel. 'Bingo!'

'Weren't you on your way somewhere?' she asked as he kicked the jack into place and started pumping.

'Won't take long.'

She watched him in silence, fascinated by his casual competence, guilt mounting as she noticed the oil and evil-smelling grease blotching his hands. As he squatted to tighten the bolts, she heard the slightly muffled enquiry, 'So it's been one of those days, has it?'

'I've just come from the bank,' she told him. 'We have a few challenges at Wheal Blazey. I'm not sure they're surmountable.'

He stood to survey his handiwork, then packed the tools and useless wheel back into the boot. 'What kind of challenges?'

She shrugged. 'Apparently we're too dependent on a small

market. We're too seasonal. We don't have a restaurant. We don't have a *strategy*.'

He found a wad of paper in his jacket and wiped his hands. 'Nothing as simple as changing a wheel, then.'

'No. Even you can't help us with that.' She gave him a coy look. 'Though I'm beginning to think you're pretty good at rescuing people, one way or another.'

'You reckon?'

'You crew on the lifeboats. You brought my dad home. You persuaded me to let Ollie go sailing on Kara, which pulled him out of the doldrums. And now you've rescued *me*. Do you wear a T-shirt under that jacket with a big fat S on it?'

His eyes twinkled. 'Well, there's a phone box in town where I keep my cape, a pair of blue tights and red underpants, if that's enough of a clue. But I'm not one to boast.'

'Ha!'

His urchin grin made it impossible to stay gloomy. Despite her reservations about him – the maverick, impenetrable, evasive side that still irritated her – she couldn't say they were strangers any more. In town they'd probably keep bumping into each other, she mused, and it wouldn't feel uncomfortable now.

How *would* it feel exactly, though? Behind heavily defended mental walls, a tiny red flag began to flutter.

'Well, I'm done,' he said, pocketing the crumpled remains of paper towel. 'You'll need to check the pressure, when you find a garage.'

'You're a star,' she told him. 'I don't know how to thank you.'

He was still for a moment, his brow furrowed, evidently pondering the comment. Then he rubbed his nose with a grimy finger and said, 'Let me take you somewhere for lunch next week.'

'Lunch?'

'If you can get free one day when Ollie's at school. I can grab a couple of hours off. There's a café on the other side of the bay, only accessible by boat. The chef there – the owner – has some similar challenges. Might be interesting for both of you.'

So… he's helping me *network?* An odd mix of pleasure and disappointment tangled inside her.

'We can motor Kara there,' he added. 'It's only a short trip.'

'Oh… I don't know…'

'Lunch, that's all. Two hours. Go on, Mrs. Harris. Live dangerously.'

'I've never liked that phrase,' she sniffed. 'I'm a cautious type, as I'm sure you've realised.'

'Says the woman who sings Springsteen and plays air guitar in the middle of the ocean after two cans of wine,' he retorted. 'Cautious, my arse.'

She blushed at the memory, secretly tickled. *Might be interesting for both of you.* What was the worst that could happen?

'Well, OK,' she said. 'Thank you, Cal. I will.'

Good at rescuing people? *Jesus.* He watched her reverse out of the space and set off down the road. *If only she knew.*

But still. It was a cute thing for her to say.

He'd had a pint with Marty the previous evening, and Marty had nudged him when his glass was half empty and said, 'She's a looker, the woman you took sailing with her boy.'

He'd given his friend a non-committal grunt.

'But that lass who works with her – the redhead who looks like she wants to eat you up for dinner whenever she comes in the pub – she's a proper peach. Tegen, is it? If I weren't already spoken for—'

'Behave yourself.'

Marty had roared in mock exasperation. 'She's got it bad

for you, matey. You could be in there, no problem – you're like bloody catnip. But it's never that simple for you, is it?'

Nope. It never is. 'I wouldn't want to lead her on.' It was the truth. Late, maybe, but the truth.

'You're a sad case, McCalvey,' Marty had declared, raising his hands. 'I think the only thing that ever gets your pulses racing is that boat of yours. *Kara.*'

'Maybe. But at least I know where I am with her.' He'd poked Marty in the chest. 'And she doesn't come on at me like the Spanish inquisition.'

One thing he hadn't admitted, though. Since his outing with Joss, he'd thought about her more than he'd expected, wondering if he'd run into her again. Hoping he would. The woman was complicated: down on her luck, struggling a bit, damaged in some way. He recognised the signs. But there was a spark about her, under all the layers, that touched him. Realising it had begun to niggle like a stone in his shoe. He wasn't good with complicated.

As the car disappeared from view he glanced distractedly along the quay, trying to remind himself why he'd been there in the first place. The pharmacy, he remembered. He'd wanted something to help him sleep – pills or spray, maybe both – anything to get him through the nights when his brain took him into a stifling room where a child was crying in the dark.

TEN

'**Y**ou walk through the valley and get to a little lake with a kind of Monet bridge – *there,* see? I'll mark it up for you – then you're right by the beach.' Joss ran her finger down a wiggle of green within the enormous map the American couple had draped like a tablecloth over the desk. 'That's where the US infantry embarked for Omaha in 1944. It's an evocative place.'

'Oh my *goodness.*' The elderly wife gazed up at Joss, her eyes like moons.

'And you can swim there!'

That made them giggle. Over their heads, Joss caught Eva's eye. Jack's new carer had slipped quietly into the hallway to fetch a newspaper.

'I don't think we'll be swimming today, young lady,' the husband chuckled. 'But I do think we'll be hunting down one of your famous cream teas. Will they serve that in the café there?'

'Definitely. But you have to know the rules.'

'Jam first!' he shot back, delighted.

They took a minute to fold and refold their map, check pockets, fiddle with spectacles and re-read their entry tickets as the sound of crunching gravel beyond the front door heralded the arrival of their taxi. Joss watched them descend the steps and said, 'Lovely couple.'

Eva tilted her head. 'You're very good at this.'

'Oh I wouldn't say that. I just know Cornwall. The bits I loved as a child, anyway.'

'Well.' The older woman looked down at the newspaper. 'I gather things haven't been easy for you recently, Jocelyn. But you seem to be in the right place now.' She glanced up again, colouring slightly. 'I hope that's not too presumptuous of me.'

'*Joss*, please. It's fine. And… yes, I'm happy to be here. Though quite what the future holds is anyone's guess.' She made the comment lightly, but the ensuing silence gave her words a portentous heft.

'Your future, you mean?' Eva asked. 'Or Wheal Blazey's?'

An interesting question. It occurred to her the two things might be linked more closely than she'd thought. Would Wheal Blazey keep going if she moved on elsewhere? What if it didn't?

'I'm sure this fine house has a future,' Eva answered as if she'd spoken aloud. 'There's a spirit about the place, a character, something quite unique. You understand and cherish it, Jocelyn, that's obvious to me. You *embody* it.'

'Really?' It was a curious thing for Eva to say. But somewhere deep inside her, a little light came on. 'I love it, of course,' she admitted. 'It's been a huge, formative part of my life. But as a business it needs so much time, money, hard work and imagination…'

'If you give it those things,' Eva smiled, 'I know it will repay you in spades.'

Joss blinked in surprise, then slowly returned the smile. 'I think you must have been a very good nurse, Eva.'

In less than a week, in fact, the woman had proved to be a godsend; she was practical, discreet and intuitive. Jack seemed happy in her company, releasing Annie and Joss to schmooze their guests without any underpinning of anxious guilt. Annie had even booked herself a hair appointment and the first dental check-up she'd managed in eighteen months. And today – probably against her better judgment – Joss was escaping too. She was meeting McCalvey for the 'interesting lunch' he'd suggested the previous week.

Thinking about it put butterflies in her stomach.

'What about you?' she asked, distracting herself. 'You've been away from Cornwall a long time. Are you glad to be back?'

Eva nodded. 'It's my home. I knew I'd return eventually. And these mornings with Jack suit me very well.'

'I don't think I asked you why you left.'

'Oh – work, mainly. One or two stressful situations. Disagreements with my clinical masters.' Her expression darkened. 'I used to be quite – how shall I put it… '

'Forthright?' Joss offered.

Eva gave a short, mirthless laugh. 'Perhaps. Anyway – I decided I needed a change of scene. Better pay, different experiences. And the years flew by.' She rolled up the newspaper and tapped it against her palm. 'I'd better get back to your father. He may be hazy about personal things, but I've discovered he's a crossword wizard.'

Joss watched the carer head back to Jack's den. Eva seemed an intensely private person, sensible and wise, but there was history there. The past had left some kind of mark, that was obvious. Ah well, she thought. *Join the club.*

She looked at her watch. McCalvey was probably already on the quay, mooring Kara in readiness for what he'd said was a short trip. She wondered if he was feeling the way she was at that moment – wary, curious, maybe a bit shy. What would they talk about? Would they bore each other to death? Did he already regret asking her? *Don't overthink it*, she muttered aloud, and she reached for her bag.

The lunch spot – a dozen tables in a clearing rimmed by old roses and crimson fuchsias – was a ravishingly pretty surprise.

As it turned out, motoring Kara round the bay to the café's jetty was straightforward. They'd been able to step straight off the boat and saunter up through thick trees to where a handful of informed diners like themselves had arrived by sea. Woodsmoke pungent with garlic, seafood and roasting meat lured them closer, while a young man in chef's whites, frizzy-haired and whippet-thin, sped back and forth between huge grills set up at right-angles under a homespun willow canopy. As McCalvey claimed a table, the chef raised a hand and grinned in welcome.

'How do you know him?' asked Joss.

'Denzel? He has a boat.'

'Of course he does.'

Blackboards between tables advertised fresh crab, mackerel, mussels, rabbit and chicken, and a waitress circulated with drinks. The chef's sister, McCalvey explained. 'His partner threw in the towel six months ago.'

'Oh. Sorry to hear that.' Joss turned in a circle, appreciating the setting, then sat. 'Is that basically the kitchen? Two grills and a couple of fridges?'

'He works miracles with it,' McCalvey said. 'He'd like something more permanent, though. He doesn't own the land, the rent's high and about to go up, and he's started raiding his savings.'

'That must be hard. You did say he had some challenges.'

In the background, the rhythm of the tide was subtly hypnotic; slices of ocean glimmered between the trees, and the sun was like warm honey on her neck. With its gingham tablecloths, sparkling glasses and lush surrounding greenery, the place was idyllic. 'But what does he do when it rains?'

'That's one of them.'

She frowned in the chef's direction, thinking *If Lorcyn has reservations about Wheal Blazey, this place would give him apoplexy.*

'We should order,' McCalvey said. 'He'll have time to chat when service is finished.'

They ordered fresh crab dressed with cream and dill, a rainbow salad of foraged leaves, crusty bread and glasses of local wine.

'This is *gorgeous*,' said Joss. 'I'd never have known this place existed.'

McCalvey smiled. 'Nice to have an excuse to come. Makes a change from pasties and pies.'

'Is that what you live on?'

'A man has to survive.' He shrugged. 'And I'm a lousy cook.'

'Ever scrambled an egg?'

'Not intentionally.'

She laughed, but then felt stumped. He had a teenage daughter, she reminded herself – he must have been part of a domestic set-up once upon a time. Maybe he felt relaxed enough now to do some sharing. She swallowed some wine and braced herself.

'You didn't cook when Katie was little, then?'

'No.' The dark eyes that fastened themselves on hers were unreadable. Seconds ticked past. She was vaguely aware of dappled light among the trees, the lapping of waves on shingle below. *Is that all I'm getting?*

When he finally looked away, her eyes remained determinedly on his face, willing him to say more. She felt rebuffed and slightly adrift. *Moody bugger.* 'I don't mean to pry.'

At first he stared into the distance, as if he hadn't heard.

But then he grunted. 'I didn't do anything for Katie when she was little, to be honest. I was never really there.'

'Physically, you mean?' Joss went very still, sensing the creak of a reluctantly opening door. 'Or... emotionally?'

'Both, I guess. Playing happy families, when most of the time I just wanted to be somewhere else.' He toyed with his cutlery for a minute. 'Lisa – Katie's mother – used to call me an escape artist.'

'You must have been young, though.' Maybe that was a valid excuse. But then, what had Morwenna told her in the pub a few weeks back? *Always one eye on the door.*

'I wasn't what either of them thought they needed, that's for sure.' His tone was defensive, but the eyes fixed on hers once more were sad. There was something challenging in them too. *Is he warning me off?*

'Anyhow. No point dissecting the past – we are where we are. I'll get us more bread.' He rose abruptly from the table and set off to find the waitress.

Even if she'd able to formulate an effective follow-up question, his pre-emptive strike as he retook his seat – 'Tell me how Ollie's doing' – made it crystal clear the door had been slammed shut.

She outlined recent events at Ollie's school – his suspension for aggressive behaviour, albeit in response to provocation; her worry that he was still a long way from coming to terms with their changed circumstances. 'He's like phosphorus these days,' she sighed. 'Combustible. I have to watch for flash points.'

'So, what does he do to get out of his head? To relieve the pressure, I mean?'

It was Joss's turn to avert her eyes and push food round her plate. 'Not enough, really. He wants me nearby for understandable reasons, but I can't leave mum to run the place on her own... so he takes himself off to the beach, or goes for bike rides. They're lonely things to do.'

He frowned. 'I'd be glad to take him out on Kara again. But that wouldn't solve the lonely problem.'

She touched his arm. For just two seconds he covered her fingers with his own – a simple gesture of acknowledgement, the barest connection. But something jumped as if she'd brushed against an unearthed wire.

His gaze was steady as she pulled her hand away – a quizzical smile on his lips, new softness in his eyes. Joss grabbed her glass and took a large swig. 'I'll need to get more creative when the summer holidays arrive,' she said distractedly.

'You should talk to Marty,' he said. 'He knows most of the guys running courses and expeditions out of St. Roslyn – kayaking, windsurfing, coasteering. The chandlery's a meeting point, they all use his kit. He probably has brochures. Ollie might find something that appeals, pitched at kids his own age.'

Joss brightened. 'That's a great idea.'

'Want me to set something up? I'd be happy to come along, talk to Marty about options. I've seen first-hand what Ollie can handle.'

She shut her eyes for a second, breathing in the oxygen of hope. New friends, new interests, a proper coastal summer... the right activity for Ollie might make a huge difference to them both. A voice in her head whispered, *summer courses won't be cheap,* but she squashed it. Something would come along. She'd just have to make it work.

'That would be brilliant,' she said, and McCalvey nodded. *Good.*

The hour increasingly felt like a glorious stolen pleasure – an exquisite setting, good food, a beautiful day. McCalvey himself was turning out to be enjoyable – if slightly unnerving – company. She found herself taking covert glances at him, wondering what he was thinking, hoping he'd look at her again in that cryptically attentive way. And when he did – which she realised was often – she blushed in confusion, feeling oddly unbalanced. But pleased. He'd surprised her. He was thoughtful and positive; funny, intriguing and kind.

Actually – she silently confided to her empty glass – he was *lovely*.

As they waited for Denzel to get free, the conversation turned to Kara, her meticulous restoration, the dolphins, the weather, their shared tastes in music, the attractions and inconveniences of St. Roslyn in the summer months. 'Though you're planning to leave at some point, aren't you?' she ventured. 'Ollie said you wanted to sail Kara to the Med.'

'Maybe.' He spread his fingers on the table and looked at them. 'I did a few seasons in Turkey and Greece before I wound up here, moving yachts about for flotilla companies. Sometimes I wonder about making my way back there, once Kara's ready and I've saved enough money. Nice people, great climate, cheap beer. A simple life.'

Why this response irked her, she couldn't entirely explain. The idea of a laid-back, self-reliant existence, devoid of ambition or responsibility… it didn't feel *grown-up*. How could he detach himself so completely, simply take himself off? What about regular employment, housing, healthcare, security in his old age?

Bloody hell. I'm in danger of turning into a puritanical old cow. She was appalled at herself. There'd been times she'd hankered for escape too.

'There must be things you'd be sorry to leave behind, though? Places and people you'd miss?'

He refocused on the horizon. 'I suppose I try not to think that way.'

It took a full minute for her to notice that the chef had arrived at their table and pulled up a chair.

Introductions were made and compliments offered, which Denzel accepted with the good grace of someone who didn't need to be told. He was intense, fidgety, and passionate about food – as Joss quickly understood from his ardent deconstruction of her menu choices. His vision, he explained, was all to do with fuss-free dining that put great local produce centre stage. He'd imagined this spot would be a goldmine, but he'd been naïve. *To put it mildly*, he muttered. *Raving mad's more like it.* The place was as hard to reach for staff and suppliers as it was for customers; costs were going up; and he was losing trade to the burgeoning number of cheaper outlets in town.

Joss listened sympathetically. 'I think *our* guests are discriminating types, in the main,' she told him. 'Most of them are looking for something with character, something memorable. That's why they choose Wheal Blazey as a destination in the first place. Now that I know you're here, I'll recommend you.'

'I know Wheal Blazey.' Denzel's face lit up. 'The old mine captain's house. The location is fantastic.'

'That's been its main draw until now. We've never offered evening meals, but we probably should,' Joss sighed. 'It's obviously becoming a limitation. But it feels too difficult. We don't have the expertise or resources. Or the money to invest.'

'But you have the space?' He leaned forward.

Joss visualised the breakfast room. Beautiful flagstones, big bay windows, farmhouse-style tables arranged at generous intervals, views of the sea... She pictured herself topping up Guy Tremain's coffee a comfortable distance from other guests. 'Oh we definitely have the space,' she said. 'But—'

'So if you were open to *non*-residents, how many covers could you do?'

In her head she walked the floor, repositioning existing tables, imagining others. 'Fifty, at a push?'

'That's great!' he exclaimed. 'So with 100% mark-up on wine and food… you'd be looking at £2000 – £2500 per night in high season. Conservative estimate.'

'What? Crikey!' She stared at him.

'Obviously you'd need waitresses. And a bloody good chef.' The smile that crinkled his eyes was gap-toothed and enormous. 'Maybe we should talk.'

She laughed in his face then – an unintentional, nervous hiccup of a laugh – and shook her head. 'The thing is, Denzel…'

What was it though, the 'thing'? It perched on her shoulder, squawking like a cantankerous, pessimistic parrot. *It's my parents' place, I don't really know what I'm doing, I'm just a single mum helping out for a while, trying to get by…*

She glanced at McCalvey. He'd slouched backwards, hands behind his head, grinning in that beguiling schoolboy way she was becoming familiar with. *Pleased with yourself?* she flared at him mutely. *You suspected this might happen.*

But dear Lord. If they had someone like Denzel cooking for them… and they could make that kind of money…

'Oh for heaven's sake.' She frowned from one bright face to the other and groaned. 'Do you think we could get some more wine?'

By the time they'd shared another bottle and split the bill, Denzel's card was in her pocket. 'I could come up to Wheal Blazey, just for a look-see, if you wanted,' he offered. 'Maybe when we both have some breathing space at the end of the season. No pressure either way. Have a think.' He moved off to socialise with other customers, and McCalvey touched her wrist. 'I guess we should be getting back.'

She gathered her things and took a last look round. 'This place is very special. I could sit here all day.'

'I can't say I'm in any hurry to go either,' he murmured. She inclined her head and smiled, torn between the urge to tick him off and the temptation to give him a hug of thanks – a gesture her happily inebriated brain suggested might be both acceptable and appropriate. He'd put an opportunity in front of her, after all. He must have judged her *capable*. Heady stuff. But before she could act he'd risen to his feet, stretching out an arm to help her up.

She put her hand in his. 'Do you honestly think it could come to something? A partnership with Denzel?'

Briefly, his lips grazed her fingertips – sweetly old-fashioned, she thought – but his eyes were serious. 'If you want it to,' he said.

They wound their way back through the trees towards the boat. The copse was dense and shady, but the path was clear enough, worn away by decades of ascending feet. Even so, the gnarled old roots created multiple hazards – especially for visitors who'd enjoyed more than a few drinks. Half way down, Joss caught her toes in a knot of fibre and tipped forward onto the soft ground.

'Are you OK?' McCalvey reached down to pull her upright.

'Not concentrating, sorry.'

They faced each other uncertainly. She realised he wasn't letting go.

He studied her for a moment, a tentative smile migrating from his lips to his eyes. Within their black depths, embers were kindling. She understood the question he was wordlessly asking her – the question she'd been wanting him to ask for the last hour, to which there was only one satisfactory answer. *Yes.*

Yes. I would like you to kiss me.

But then she faltered.

I want this to happen. Don't I?

It had been such a long time.

Such a long time since that last night with Felix. The last physical contact. The final unravelling.

She swallowed as panic constricted her throat. *Kiss me, please,* she wanted to say. *Make it alright. Get me over this. Please.*

Too late. Memories flooded her brain like hornets exploding from a broken nest. Suddenly she felt nauseous – and afraid.

I can't.

McCalvey was drawing her towards him. She shut her eyes as his lips began to explore her face – the touch of them soft as air on her forehead, warm on the curve of her cheek, the tip of her nose, the edge of her mouth. A primitive force responded to him, *Let me lose myself in you, I want this to happen, make it alright,* as his hands moved to the back of her head. She felt the tug as his fingers threaded her hair, pulling her close.

In an instant she was back in the cold darkness of the flat, and London was shimmering below.

Everything was in shadow. Felix's face was in shadow – and her body was being crushed against the wall.

Don't.

She was gasping for breath.

She was fighting for her life.

McCalvey's physical strength, the heat emanating from him as he pressed himself against her, was engulfing, overwhelming. Her whole body shrank from his grasp in terror.

'*Don't!*'

She shook herself free and smacked him hard across the face.

Felix had stumbled across the threshold, late home, dishevelled and already drunk. She'd sunk most of a bottle of red herself as she waited in gathering darkness, sick with worry – wondering how to tell him about the visitors, fearing his reaction.

In truth, she'd been fearful for months.

She took a deep breath, watched him pour himself a scotch, then told him.

'*What* visitors?'

They'd arrived just after midday – three inspectors from the Fraud Response Unit of his firm. She'd shown them into his office. What else could she have done?

Felix howled and grabbed her arm. 'You *stupid bitch*! What did you say to them?'

'For God's sake. Get hold of yourself and keep your voice down. Ollie's asleep.'

'Don't come on all high and mighty with me,' he hissed. 'I need to know what you told them.'

'What *could* I tell them?' Tears like hot lances spiked her eyes. 'I have no idea what's going on. You don't talk to me.'

The officials had been civil but coldly determined, flowing into his private space like a tide, washing through every drawer and cabinet.

'They wanted to see bank statements.'

'*Fucking hell.*' Felix pushed her away and lurched through the door towards his desk. She heard papers being snatched up, crushed and thrown to the wall; the overturning of pens, trays and storage boxes. 'Where are all my client files? Where's my laptop?'

'They took everything, Felix.'

He walked back to her in silence. With a cool deliberation that put ice in her blood, he worked the fingers of one hand through her hair and pulled her close.

'You should have stopped them,' he said.

'*Stopped* them? Are you *joking*?'

Perversely, she wanted him to shout at her again. She wished they could have a purging, cataclysmic row, in which he would break down and finally admit the truth. Anything would be better than this terrible, ominous stillness – the hardness in his eyes. *I don't know this man any more,* she thought. Had she *ever* known him?

'Did they say what they were looking for?' He gave her head a small warning shake.

'Get *off* me, Felix. You're hammered. And no, they didn't – though I have a pretty good idea.'

'Oh you do, do you?'

'I'm not stupid.' Her father had privately aired his suspicions on their last visit home, when she'd shown him the transactions keeping her awake at night. 'It looks to me like you're taking backhanders and siphoning off profits from company accounts. Though you want me to believe it's all above board.'

'I see.' He smiled. The smile of a shark moving through its feeding grounds, she thought. 'And you've shared this fantastic theory with who?'

She hesitated just a second too long. Her father had incriminating information now, but he would never tell. Would he? And there'd been a few office socials where she'd yearned to do a bit of detective work – casually start a conversation with Felix's colleagues about deals, contracts and clients; winkle out any detail that might conceivably prove her wrong. But she'd stepped back from the brink.

'You've told someone,' Felix said.

'No.'

'I can see it in your eyes. You *wanted* this to happen. You want me to go down. Then you can walk away.'

'You're being ridiculous.'

'Ah. There it is. I'm ridiculous.' He twisted a hank of hair round his wrist, and she yelped. '*Stop it,* Felix. That hurts.'

'There's no point explaining anything to you, up there on your precious moral high ground. You think you're Little Miss Perfect, but you're just like everyone else. No imagination. No *loyalty*. But you took a vow, for better or worse. Love and obey, eh? I know you'd never throw it all away, everything I've given you. The life I've made for both of us. You'd have nothing without me. You'd *be* nothing.'

She stared at his contorted face, her own temper flaring. 'You're bloody nasty when you're drunk, Felix. And there'll be no *everything* once they work out what's been going on. Though if you come clean about it, show some remorse, try to explain—'

He threw his head back and laughed. 'Explain? Explain that I work my butt off in a world full of idiots? They know I'm better than any of them and they despise me for it. Just like you. You despise me too. Don't you?'

Tears had begun streaming down her cheeks. 'Felix, I've loved you for years. But now... now... '

I'm going to leave you. Realisation uncoiled within her like a waking giant.

Tomorrow I will take Ollie and I will leave.

He knew it. She watched his expression change – horror and disbelief streaking across his face like spilled paint; black terror leaching into the red of his rage.

'I'm not letting you go,' he said hoarsely. 'I know you still love me.'

'We need to talk, Felix, but not now. Not in the state you're in.'

'*Now.* Talk *now.*' It was the voice of a thwarted, petulant child. 'You think I'm a bastard and maybe I am. But you love me – in spite of everything. Tell me you love me. I *need* you, Joss, you know I do. If I didn't have you... there'd be no *point* to me. No point to anything.'

His agonised face was inches from hers. What could she say? Nothing that would pacify him. She could try to reassure him, sublimate herself, lie... but where would that get her – tomorrow, the next day, the day after that? As she stared into his bloodshot eyes, her revulsion was tempered by sorrow.

We'll never find our way back from this. But he twisted her hair again, angling his free arm like a vice around her neck.

'Show me you still love me.' He kissed her hard on the mouth. '*Show* me.'

As she writhed to escape his grip he slammed her against the wall, clawing at her like a wounded bear. She heard the fabric of her nightdress rip. Clutching the curtain to stabilise herself, she lost her footing and tore it down, pole and all. Felix took her weight as she fell, curling over her to press his lips to her mouth again before croaking, '*You won't leave me, ever. I dare you to leave me.*'

'*Stop it*, Felix. Think about Ollie. *Stop…*' But her plea was muffled – he'd flattened one hand across her face while the other opened his zip. His fingers clumsily jabbed her groin as he fumbled for her pants, then yanked them to her knees.

'Don't… *don't…!*'

She bit her lip as he forced himself into her, and tasted blood.

Pain made her dig her fingernails into her own wrists to stop herself screaming. He seemed determined to split her in half, break her open like an unripe fruit. A rough hand closed once more round her neck, tightening as she punched, scratched and pushed him backwards, but he had ten times her strength. Sweat poured from him as he rammed her, his animal grunts rising to a roar.

She twisted to meet his eyes and was shattered by what she saw there. Obsession, madness, misery… *God help us. God help him.* He was lost. However much he wanted to hurt her, he was fatally engulfed in the flames of his own hell. He couldn't own her, couldn't contain her any more. There'd be no more pretending, no more turning away. It was over. And he was punishing her for it.

No more. The phrase repeated in her head with every brutal thrust. *No more. No more.*

She was struggling for breath. Part of her longed to shut down, to black out, until at last she felt herself letting go. He was crazed enough to kill her – she knew that now. If she died, this would be the last thing she'd remember.

But something snapped her back to full consciousness.

The sound of an opening door.

'*Shit.*' McCalvey pressed a hand to his nose as blood trickled down his chin. 'You certainly pack a punch.'

'I'm so, so sorry,' she whispered. She found a tissue to dab at the injury, her fingers trembling uncontrollably as she touched him.

Shock and bewilderment burned in his eyes. 'I've been known to misjudge my timing once in a while, but that was a real corker.'

She was drawing raggedly painful breaths. Swaying on her feet, she realised she might be about to faint, as McCalvey grasped both her arms.

'Steady,' he said. 'Sit down, sit down here.' He guided her to a patch of grass where she was able to lower herself against a tree. 'I promise I won't touch you.'

For several minutes she focused on mastering her breathing, calming her thumping heart; then she glanced up, her eyes wet with distress. 'It's not you, Cal. I'm so, so sorry. It's honestly nothing to do with you.'

'OK.' He folded his arms, unconvinced. 'So, what's going on with you, Mrs. Harris? Talk to me.'

She took in his hurt expression, then looked miserably through the trees to where Kara's sleek hull was just visible, an intermittent flicker of green on blue. Gradually it dawned on her that she couldn't fudge things; she couldn't be untruthful to this man. She wanted him to know what had happened, she realised with astonishment. She wanted – needed him – to understand. And he *would* understand; she was suddenly sure of it.

So she told him. She described the fraud officers' visit and Felix's drunken rage – how terrified she'd felt that night, how powerless. The emotional devastation of his assault, so much worse than the physical battering. The final smashing-up of what she'd once thought was a good life. The searing *waste* of it. The annihilation of love.

'*Jesus.*' McCalvey dropped to his knees. 'If I'd known… Christ, Joss, I'd never have come on to you like that.'

'I'm so sorry,' she said again.

'A lot less sorry than me.'

They stared at each other for a long, uneasy minute. Then they got to their feet and picked their way down what remained of the path to the waiting boat.

Once he'd helped her take a seat in the cockpit, McCalvey dug into a locker for a blanket, tucking it solicitously round her knees. Then he squatted in front of her. 'What can I do? I'm an idiot.'

She heard the anguish in his voice and wished she could melt it away. 'You weren't to know, Cal.'

With a fervency that took her by surprise, she heard him growl. 'The past can be a merciless fucking bastard.'

'Yes, it can. But I'm the idiot here. Deluding myself, suppressing what I really felt and wanted, all those years.'

'No.' He closed his fingers over hers and gazed intently into her face. 'You were human and vulnerable, and you've been through hell. But look at you now – you've come through. You haven't let a horrible experience define you. You're strong.'

She managed a hesitant smile.

'Listen, Joss.' He cleared his throat. 'Chancing my luck with you back there – it was out of order, stupid and crass. I hope it hasn't spoiled things between us. Because – I'd like to see more of you. If you have the time and inclination, that is. Trust me, I'll be a model companion. No agenda, no expectations. I won't take advantage again.'

His wretched expression snagged her heart. 'Nothing's spoiled between us, Cal. I enjoy your company too.' Admitting it out loud felt good. Freeing, somehow. 'But you might need to be… patient with me. Until I get my head straight.'

'I understand,' he said. 'Of course I do.' He touched the side of his bruised nose and winced. 'I'll need time to stock up on medical supplies for our next few dates anyway.'

Her mortified choke of laughter finally put the smile back on his face.

ELEVEN

Mum seems good at the moment, like she's got more energy. She's been tarting up the website, and last night I heard her talking to Gran about doing dinners.

Gran got proper ratty. She says she's got enough on her plate without extra work.

I know Mum's trying to move on. But my head's a mess.

Yesterday I woke up and thought I smelled Dad's bacon omelettes. I was downstairs before I remembered.

She found me curled up on the floor.

Now she thinks I should do a course in the holidays. She says Cal put the idea into her head.

Why would she even talk to him about me?

It's none of his stupid business.

If Joss was alone on reception for an hour or two, she used the downtime to trawl through guest reviews. Effusive comments still seemed to outweigh any quibbles, but recently she'd begun to sense a tiny, niggling shift in the balance. At some point, when she could catch her mother in a receptive mood, she planned to talk strategy.

Today there was a post from a Scottish couple she remembered well. They were complimentary about the location, the ambience, Annie's buffet breakfasts... then, there it was: the *but*. 'Cleaning of bedroom below expectations – light bulbs in need of proper dusting, dead bee at back of wardrobe, old sweet wrapper in bedside drawer...'

Bugger. She exhaled sharply. Oversights like that were so important, so damning. But in theory so simple to avoid.

While she sat glowering at the screen, Annie appeared from the breakfast room, brushing away crumbs. 'Right – I'm off to see the tooth fairy,' she announced. 'Hopefully he'll leave a few molars.' She unhooked her jacket from a hall peg. 'What time do you need to leave?'

The iffy review, Joss decided, would have to wait. 'Meeting Cal in the chandlery at two.'

Annie sniffed. 'That's the fourth time you've seen that man since the day he changed the wheel.'

'Is it?' She cast about for a notepad, then scrabbled for a pen. 'I suppose it is.'

As if she needed reminding.

Three days after the visit to Denzel's restaurant, McCalvey had texted her – a rare event apparently, as his own phone was usually out of battery in a random drawer – to ask if she felt like watching a gig race from a vantage point above the harbour.

It had been a happy afternoon. He'd bought her a cider, checked every ten minutes that she was enjoying herself, and kept his distance.

Then a week ago he'd suggested they meet for brunch at a new café just off the high street. Useful for her to understand the local market, he'd said. They'd talked about the food, the clientele, the prices, the atmosphere… then he'd looked at his watch, paid the bill, smiled regretfully, and gone back to work.

Watching him go, she'd been surprised by the weight of her disappointment. As if somehow she'd been short-changed. As if he'd left too soon. *Ridiculous,* she scolded herself. She should have been relieved. In the last few weeks they'd become easy together. No agenda, no expectations – he'd promised her that. It was what she wanted, wasn't it?

'You like him,' Annie said.

Her fingers stilled above the keyboard. 'Cal? He's a good contact. Wants to be helpful, I think.' She didn't trust herself to meet her mother's eyes.

Annie shrugged on her jacket, then lingered a second or two before adding quietly, 'Be careful, darling.'

Joss looked up sharply at that. But her mother was already walking away.

Honestly. I'm not some witless babe-in-arms. Careful about what, exactly? Pursing her lips, she turned back to the screen.

Tegen and Bridget burst into the corridor moments later, dishevelled and pink from changing beds in the upstairs suites. 'Breaking for coffee,' Tegen said, flicking a casual glance in her direction as they passed by the desk. *Telling me, not asking permission,* Joss noted crossly. But she was just the owner's daughter, after all. Visiting for a while, as far as they knew. What authority did she have?

She watched their progress into the kitchen, chewing her lip. She had a feeling Tegen in particular could run rings around her mother, given half a chance. With her father's health deteriorating and Annie increasingly under pressure, things were slipping. The evidence was there.

She tapped her pen a dozen times against the monitor and took a deep breath. *Right.*

Outside the kitchen door, she paused to rehearse the

feedback she felt obliged to give. The hushed conversation reaching her ears was irritatingly relentless – a continuous exchange of whispers from inside the room. Tegen seemed to be holding forth while Bridget paraphrased and colluded, loyal sidekick that she was.

'So, what did he say?' she heard Bridget ask.

'Not much. Thanked me for the drink. I asked him how Katie was doing back in Bristol, we talked about work, then he went all quiet on me.'

Concealed in the hallway, Joss froze.

'But he already *told* you he likes you, didn't he?'

'Oh, he was nice enough. Polite. But not… you know…'

'Properly interested?'

'He looked embarrassed, to be honest. Like he wanted to forget that anything happened.'

'Knob. He won't have forgotten.'

'OK, maybe he was lonely and pissed that night. But he was all over me, Bridge. He *fucked* me, for God's sake.'

'So what are you going to do?'

'Wait, I guess. I know I made him feel good. Anyway, where's the competition? At some point he'll come back for more. I told him as much.'

Icy talons scraped at Joss's brain and heart until both almost stopped functioning. Silently, she retraced her steps until she arrived back at reception, where she flattened a palm against the wall, closed her eyes and drew several lungfuls of air.

Tegen? He told her he liked her? She made him feel good? *Shit.*

The violence of her own reaction was a shock. For a few seconds she felt crushed from above and below, pancaked into a trembling, useless, insignificant thing. Then her brain started working again.

Was she surprised? Not really.

Tegen might be young and gorgeous, but she was wilful – Joss knew that much. And Cal? He'd been lonely and drunk. She said he'd looked embarrassed – like he wanted to forget that anything had happened. He'd actually been *polite* to her.

Oh for God's sake. She smacked the wall and marched back to the kitchen. Both girls jumped as she filled the doorway. The talking stopped.

'I need you both to know,' she said evenly, 'that some of our guests have been less than impressed with cleaning standards. The Stewarts last week have just posted a review. Dusty light bulbs, insects in the wardrobe and a sweet wrapper in the bedside drawer. That's quite an off day in terms of attention to detail.'

Bridget looked stricken, but after a second's bug-eyed astonishment Tegen's expression hardened. 'Bloody old farts,' she said. 'Those two were gagging for something to complain about.'

Joss folded her arms. 'Tell me you don't think dead insects and sweet wrappers are acceptable, Tegen?'

'So? We missed a couple of things.'

'It may be a couple of things to you, but it's lost business for us,' Joss replied. 'They won't be coming back. And neither will anyone who reads that review.'

Tegen stuck out her chin. 'It's crazy busy at the moment,' she protested. 'We only just manage to get through the work in the hours we're paid for.'

'Are you paid for breaks?' Joss asked. She knew full well they were. 'You get fifteen minutes for coffee, right?' In all the time she'd been there, she'd never known them take less than half an hour.

'Recovery time,' Tegen said defensively. 'It takes a lot out of you, this job. If you understood everything we have to do… ' *But you don't* was the message, delivered with transparent contempt.

'Tell you what,' Joss said after a moment. 'How about I put a plan together. An hour-by-hour checklist if you like, that helps you cover everything in the time available. I'd be happy to follow you both around, develop a proper schedule and review it with you and Annie. To make sure nothing gets missed. Useful for newbies, apart from anything else.'

'We know our jobs!'

'But Tegen, how come guests find dust, insects and crumpled wrappers? Seems to me we could all be a bit more vigilant.' She smiled as sweetly as she could manage. 'That goes for me too.'

Tegen scowled. 'Won't happen again.'

'Thank you, Tegen. That's all I ask.' Joss reached to pat her arm. 'The thing is, our bills and your wages are paid for entirely by guests who deserve their rooms to be pleasant and clean. Old farts included.'

She swept into the hall, expecting to hear blustering indignation, anger, murmurs of disbelief at least. Instead – with an unfamiliar rush of amazement and satisfaction – she could have heard a pin drop.

Buoyed by adrenalin, she arrived at the chandlery much too early.

She glanced around, desperate for distraction, before remembering that *Wenna's Antiques* was a five-minute walk away along a parallel street. The opportunity to call in on her old schoolfriend – someone connected to McCalvey, though she told herself this wasn't important – seemed too good to miss.

The quirky little shop was cluttered in an artistically vibrant way that reflected its owner's taste, charming Joss from the moment she crossed the threshold to the sound of a ship's brass bell. Morwenna emerged from a back room and enveloped her in a hug. 'Joss! How are you doing? Want tea?'

She smiled and shook her head. 'Just wanted to say hallo, Wen. I haven't got long. It's fantastic in here! You always had an eye for lovely things.' Light from the leaded bay window bounced off art deco mirrors, pieces of sculpted glass, copper pots, ornamental slates and cabinets full of antique jewellery. 'How's business? Are you doing alright?'

'Oh, I get by,' Morwenna said. 'And I do love it. Discovering unusual bits and pieces, selling them on to good homes... It suits me fine. You know me, I'm a magpie. Addicted to the next shiny thing. Not like you – you're clever and serious.'

'Am I?'

'Always were.' Morwenna chuckled. 'Don't look like that, it's a compliment.'

The observation made her squirm. 'Fat lot of good it's done me,' she said.

'How do you mean?'

'Well, look at you. This shop is lovely. You're your own woman, independent, doing what you enjoy. I'm just scratching about, wondering what to do with my life.'

Morwenna frowned at her, though her eyes were kind. 'Don't be so hard on yourself, girlfriend,' she said. 'You've had terrible luck, but you've raised a son and now you're supporting your folks in their time of need. And you're not exactly over the hill. Something will come along.'

'You're a sweetheart.' In spite of her downbeat words, Joss felt her mood lighten.

'What are you up to today, then?' Morwenna asked.

She met her friend's uncomplicated gaze and resigned herself to declaring what had been on her mind every step of the way since she'd left the house. 'Actually, Wen... I'm meeting Cal in the chandlery in a minute.'

The tiniest beat preceded Morwenna's 'Oh yes?'

'He's helping me think about summer courses for Ollie.'

She caught the slight raising of an eyebrow. 'We've bumped into each other a few times. We're just, you know, friends.'

'Good on him. He'll be helpful.' Morwenna smiled and put a hand on Joss's arm. 'Are you worrying about what I'd think? Don't. I put that bright shiny thing down a long time ago. I've picked up a few others since then.'

Joss breathed out. 'My mother thinks I should be careful.'

There was a brief silence. Then Morwenna shook her head. 'Well, maybe it's time you gave yourself a break from being clever, serious and careful,' she smiled. 'Sometimes in life, you just have to hold your nose and jump.'

Had she *ever* thought like that? Not since she was small, probably. She nodded as her friend gave her arm an encouraging squeeze. 'Before you go, changing the subject... ' Morwenna moved towards a table draped in velvet at the centre of the shop. 'Have a look at these little treasures. One of my clients brought them in a few days ago. She's been sorting through a maiden aunt's belongings and thought they might generate some interest.'

Joss cast her eye over a collection of rather fine objects: a crystal paperweight; an old-fashioned cigarette holder with a singed, slightly buckled edge; a mottled fruit knife; several sets of earrings; a faux-pearl necklace; and a wonderful, iridescent dragonfly brooch. She picked up the brooch and rotated it between her fingertips. Delicate filigree wings had been expertly fitted to a gleaming thorax, a long, narrow body of shimmering blue-green steel. 'Oh I *love* this,' she exclaimed.

'Pretty, isn't it?' Morwenna said. 'A lot of the stuff it came with is fire-damaged, unfortunately, but this seems to have survived intact.'

'Fire damaged?'

'Afraid so. That's how the aunt died, apparently. Very sad. I haven't priced it up yet, but I'm sure I can do you a deal if you're interested.'

It was a lovely thing. Joss didn't have much spare cash…
but then, she hadn't treated herself for months. And today felt
special somehow. A day of surprises.

'Twenty pounds?' Morwenna suggested; then when Joss
grimaced, 'OK, fifteen.'

Deal done, she wrapped the piece in candy-striped paper
and tucked it into Joss's handbag. 'Nice doing business with
you,' she grinned. 'And give my best to Cal.'

Marty's knowledge of water sports organisations produced a
number of promising options. One group, 'The Coast Club',
offered a full day's tutored kayaking and coasteering rounded
off by a barbecue on the beach – the kind of thing any normal
boy would relish. And he *was* a normal boy, Joss reminded
herself. Somewhere beneath that distrustful, protective shell.

'It'd build your lad's confidence, a day like that,' Marty
said. 'Afterwards he could do something a bit more advanced.
Windsurfing or kitesurfing, maybe. If he's into sailing, he
might think about doing the competent crew certificate. Cal
could help him with that.'

'Sure. If he's up for it.' McCalvey looked at Joss. 'Enough
to be getting on with?'

'You've been brilliant,' she told Marty. 'Besides helping me
with ideas for Ollie, you've given me loads of information for
our guests.' The wry look he gave her prompted her to add,
'They're not *all* decrepit, you know.'

He chuckled and raised his hands in apology. 'Maybe you'll
shake the place up a bit.'

She glanced at McCalvey, who winked. *You never know.*

They emerged into bright sunshine. McCalvey checked his
watch, and said 'I've still got forty minutes.'

'Tea and cake at Little Roslyn?' she suggested. 'On me. The
least I can do.'

As they strolled along the quay, Joss was acutely conscious of his quietly attentive presence. She was close enough to take his arm – but something stopped her. How would he react if she did? How did she *want* him to react? She frowned at her feet.

'It must only be a week or two till school finishes for the summer,' McCalvey said.

'Ten days.'

'The first kayaking and coasteering day is that Saturday. I wonder if Ollie will go for it?'

She raised two sets of crossed fingers.

Once they'd found a table, Joss left him looking thoughtfully at the sea while she fetched tea and flapjacks from the kiosk. He seemed mesmerised by wave after wave of pristine, tumbling surf. She set the tray down and followed his gaze. 'This has always been one of my favourite places,' she said.

'You come here often, do you?' he asked, then groaned loudly at his own cliché.

'Actually I do. If I need to be on my own to think.'

They were quiet a moment, the peace of the little beach underlined by the hiss of breakers and wailing of far-off gulls. He nodded. 'I can see why.' Then he picked up his spoon, waved it in the air and said, 'So, if Ollie signs up for that Saturday – could you get free?'

'Probably.' Anticipation tightened her chest. 'Did you have something in mind?'

'If the weather's good, I think we should come here and surf.'

'*What*? Absolutely no way.'

All at once he was boyishly enthusiastic. 'I'll be fun. Then we can go back to my place and order pizza.'

'I've never been surfing.'

'No time like the present,' he said. 'You live in Cornwall now.'

Anticipation rapidly turned to dread. '*No,* Cal. I'm sorry. Just the thought of it—'

'You thought you wouldn't like sailing, but you were fine.' He cocked his head and grinned. 'Eventually.'

'That's different. I had a lifejacket and several feet of wooden boat between me and the briny.'

The eagerness in his eyes softened a little. 'I'll be with you,' he said. 'Nothing bad will happen. Trust me.'

Trust him? Two imaginary parrots started screeching in her ears – one urging her to go for it and admit that an unexpected day with him was hugely appealing; the other squawking *what are you doing with this guy?* He seemed a bit of a chancer, rough round the edges, a type she'd have steered well clear of in an earlier life…

But in spite of everything she knew about him – admittedly precious little – in his presence she felt confident. Significant. *Alive.*

'I don't have any kit,' she said.

'We'll hire it.'

'I'll be rubbish.'

'It doesn't matter.'

'Oh – *bloody Nora…*'

Scenting victory, he reached to grab her hand and managed to slop most of his remaining tea across the table, where it trickled towards her lap. '*Shit.* Sorry.'

Joss rolled her eyes and opened her bag on the table-top, delving for tissues. The movement shunted the stripey little bag to the top.

'Aha! You've been to Morwenna's,' he said.

'I have! And look – isn't this lovely?' She extracted the dragonfly brooch from the paper and twirled it to catch the light.

McCalvey's sharp intake of breath made her look up in alarm. He lurched backwards as if he'd been punched.

'What?' She gaped at him. He was staring at the ornament with disbelief and horror, all colour bleaching out of his face. 'Cal – What on earth's the matter?' She almost asked, *don't you like it?* but realised the question would be wildly off-beam. His reaction had nothing to do with the aesthetics of the little jewel – that was as obvious as it was incomprehensible.

'What is it? Have you seen it before? Did someone you know—'

'Stop, Joss, *stop.*' He pulled himself abruptly straight. 'It's nothing.'

'But—'

'I'm being stupid. It's a nice brooch.' Still he hadn't looked at her. She watched him pick up the tissues and dab at the remains of the tea. His hands were shaking.

'I won't wear it if—'

'Just *stop,* for God's sake.' Finally he fixed his eyes on hers. 'Sorry. I just had a weird moment. Forget it. We were talking about surfing—'

Oh no you don't. She re-wrapped the brooch and returned it to her bag. 'What kind of weird moment? You were totally spooked, don't fob me off.'

As he shook his head and turned away, the noise of his pager ripped through the air between them. Joss watched in frustration as he grabbed it from a jacket pocket, then heard him direct a furious expletive at the sea.

'I'm sorry,' he muttered as he rose to his feet. 'So sorry, Joss.'

'*Cal—*'

'It's fine. Everything's fine. We'll come back here and surf on that Saturday, OK?'

He bent to place the lightest of kisses on her forehead and hurried away, leaving her to contemplate his abandoned cake and the footprints receding in the sand.

TWELVE

To be fair, the Coast Club thing on Saturday does look pretty amazing.

Mum says she's got loads of stuff to do that day and I'll get bored.

So, OK. I'll go.

'I *knew* you'd be good at this.' Joss sat hunched on the borrowed soft-top, resting her chin between gritty knees as McCalvey stepped nimbly into the shallows. He grinned and tugged his own larger board out of the water. 'Not sulking, are we?'

'Sulking? *Moi*? Just because I've been battered by salty, rampaging wildebeest trying to drown me for the last two hours before they chuck me face down on the beach…'

'You're having a good time then?'

She scooped up a handful of sand and threw it at him.

'Come on,' he said. 'Let's go again. 'You're so nearly there.'

She gave him a dark look, which made him laugh. Damp sand coated her hired wetsuit and her hair clung in crusty ribbons, though the sun was lush on her cheeks. *I must look like a beached walrus,* she grumbled to herself. *And he's like a seal, totally in his element.*

But he'd been as good as his word: patient and watchful – respecting her fear, working with it, giving her all the time she needed. Despite her protests, Little Roslyn was sheltered and its waves were gentle. As she dog-paddled out towards the breaks, he ensured she was never out of her depth. Whenever she slipped from the board his hands were round her waist within seconds, propelling her upwards before panic had a chance to grip. *'You're okay, I've got you, I'm right here.'* It was almost worth the indignity of a dozen wipe-outs to feel him take hold of her and hear that voice.

'I don't think I can walk,' she croaked. 'You may have to leave me here and come back for me in the morning.'

He held out his hand, brooking no argument, until she uncurled herself and finally, with a sigh, stood up.

Back in the water, he motioned her to lie on her stomach and scull towards the incoming sets. As before he stayed close, directing her, *'Watch for a good space between rollers… keep hold of that leash… toes on the rail… another two, we'll go after that…'*

'Right,' he said firmly, 'Up now!' and as the target breaker approached he grasped her board to steady it while she wobbled to her feet. *'Back foot by that knee… you're doing great… balance… use your arms…'*

She levered herself vertical as the board engaged with the fragmenting surf, her calves and thighs buckling with the strain, her eyes blurring. For several seconds she was propelled through air and spray towards the beach on what felt like the spine of a bolting animal. By the time the board put its nose into the sand her arms were flailing like windmills – but she was upright.

'There you go!' McCalvey exclaimed as he swept past and jumped into the water to help. '*That's* more like it.'

She beamed into his delighted face.

'Again,' he said. 'Let's go again – while you're on a roll.'

'*I can't,*' she gasped. 'Believe me – I've got nothing left. I've got jelly where I use to have legs. I don't think I can even walk up the beach.'

'Just once more?'

But they'd been in and out of the sea for much of the afternoon, and she was spent. Spreadeagled on the sand, she panted, 'You go again. I just want to die here.'

He knelt beside her, waited a few seconds, then accepted it was a lost cause. 'OK then. So now you know you can stand up. But we definitely need to get you back on it before the summer's over, or you'll backslide.'

'God, you're a tyrant.'

She clambered to her feet and looked down at herself. 'I am absolutely *caked*,' she moaned. 'I'm like a sand pie baked with double helpings of salt.'

'Let's go and clean up at my place then,' McCalvey suggested. 'I'll rinse out the wetsuits later.'

'Perfect.' She'd left a towel and a bag of dry clothes behind his door earlier in the day. 'Means I can sample your home-made jam and scones.'

'Hilarious. If you want to eat, you can get a pizza ordered.'

They trudged barefoot along the quay towards the harbour, the chandlery and McCalvey's apartment. It was still a beautiful day. He hadn't mentioned the brooch, and for the time being she'd chosen to store the topic in a mental holding bay. At some point she'd interrogate him – but not yet, she decided. Today the atmosphere between them was upbeat, even celebratory. She wasn't inclined to invite a spectre to the feast.

At the top of the steps, a scruffy black and white cat

was investigating the dried-up remains of a meal on a plastic plate she hadn't noticed before. 'You've got a moggy!' She crouched down and held out a hand, which the animal sniffed imperiously, then ignored.

'Ah. Actually, I haven't,' said McCalvey. 'He just uses me as a soup kitchen when pickings round the boats are a bit slim.' He bent to scratch the scabby head. 'Wilf – meet Joss.'

'Well, hallo Wilf.' Rebuffed once more, she straightened up. 'He looks a bit moth-eaten. Where does he live?'

'Moth-eaten? How *dare* you! Don't listen to her Wilf, she doesn't understand us nautical types.'

'Ha!' She glanced from the cat to the man. 'What makes him a nautical type, then?'

Wilf gave the empty plate a last once-over and accepted a few more scratches before slinking off down the steps.

McCalvey rummaged for his key. 'He belonged to one of the skippers,' he said, sombre for a moment. 'But the boat went down off the Scillies a couple of years ago.'

'*No.* That's terrible.'

'Oh, he does alright.' He shrugged. 'Wilf's a resilient old soldier. He's made a life for himself.'

She pressed his arm as she moved through the door.

Once inside, his eagerness to play host made her smile. 'There should be plenty of hot water for showers. You take the first one. Shall I put the kettle on? Or would you rather have wine? Or beer?'

Stepping into the spartan, half-tiled washroom, he rotated the handle to *on,* cupping a hand under the erratic jet to demonstrate. 'Pressure's crap, sorry. But the water's warm, and those should get the sand off.' He pointed to a collection of natural sponges on a shelf beside a twin-pack of unopened, decently up-market body soaps.

Joss perused each label in turn. 'Well, well,' she teased, ignoring the half-full supermarket-brand shower gel on its side in the shower tray. 'I'd never have guessed you were a ylang-ylang kind of guy.'

'They're for Katie, you cheeky mare. Thanks to her mother's burgeoning Latino romance, she'll be back in August. Which reminds me… she may be after a part-time job again in a few weeks. Could you use her?'

'Absolutely,' said Joss. 'She's a good worker.'

McCalvey nodded his thanks and took a step towards the door. 'I'll leave you to it then.' He paused as she groped behind her neck for the wetsuit fastener. 'Unless you want a hand?'

'A bit of help with this would be good.'

He freed the zip with chivalrous restraint, and she began to wriggle out of the clinging sleeves to reveal a demure blue one-piece, nervously selected that morning for its ample coverage.

'OK then?'

'Yes. Thanks.'

They hovered in the shared space for a moment, floundering on the outskirts of unfamiliar territory. He retreated a couple of feet. 'Right then.'

All at once she knew she didn't want him out of her sight. The day had been idyllic from the start – transformative, when she thought about it – and he'd acted the perfect gentleman for some time now. He'd *proved* himself to her, if anything needed proving.

'We could share the shower if you want,' she said impulsively, surprising herself as much as him. 'There's room for two. Saves water. We could rinse off the wetsuits at the same time, maybe?'

He glanced at the door. Then his eyes flicked warily to her face. 'Well, OK. Why not?'

They peeled each other out of the neoprene, emerging in their swimwear to kick the gummy fabric to one side. Then they took turns to stand beneath the flow of water, studiously polite.

McCalvey offered the shampoo, and she worked the fragrant lather into her hair, squeezing her eyes against the sting. She lifted her face to the showerhead to rinse away the last vestiges of salt and soap, then turned to hand him the container. The look on his face made her catch her breath.

There it was, as clear as day. His honest, helpless, anxious desire for her.

Something mighty shifted in her brain at that moment. Walls she'd painstakingly built over many months fractured and crumbled, as if a dark place buried deep at her core was being newly exposed to light.

How could I have pushed him away?

She felt exasperated with herself. Stupid. Thrilled.

What am I so afraid of?

The truth hit like a lightning strike, searing and intense. The journey ahead was inevitable. She'd been prevaricating, it was so clear now.

She wanted him too.

Even then, she heard a tremulous whisper in a far corner of her mind. *This is likely to be a rocky road. It might lead to a very bad place.* She quashed it with a defiant shake of her head. *It's a place I need to go.*

With her heart hammering, she reached to touch his cheek. Immediately, she felt him tense. 'Joss?'

Hold your nose and jump.

Trembling a little, she freed her arms from the straps of her swimsuit and rolled its fabric to her waist, below her breasts. Then she placed her hands either side of his face, daring him to keep his eyes on her, to read her correctly.

Bring me back to life. Want me. Be the one.

'*No*, Joss. What are you doing?'

'It's OK,' she said softly. 'It's alright.' Then, as he continued to hesitate, 'Please, Cal. *Please*.'

After what seemed like minutes, he selected a gel – jasmine, she discerned with approval – moistened a sponge, and traced a warm, soapy line left to right along her collarbone. She knew he was asking permission. Tipping her head back, she closed her eyes and waited.

She felt the sponge caress her shoulders and upper arms, then steadied herself as it travelled gently downwards, gliding over her breasts and stomach in cautious, circular movements. Water continued to ripple along the surface of her skin, but there were new sensations now – little explosions of pleasure as kisses dotted her throat, her breastbone, her belly, her hips. *Jesus, you're lovely*, she heard him murmur. *Look at you.*

Slowly, slowly, he rolled the swimsuit down below her stomach, her pelvis, her calves, until all she could do was step out of it. She could smell the ocean in his hair, taste the salt on his skin; he seemed to have brought the essence of his outdoor world into this tiny space, right into her mind, elemental and real. The sponge oozed liquid warmth over her thighs, her lower back, her backside; she bent to kiss the top of his head as he knelt, reverentially, to wash between her legs. And she realised she was whispering his name, over and over again.

Losing herself, she flattened a hand against the cubicle wall.

He turned off the water and reached for a towel. Wrapping it carefully around her, he tilted her face to meet his eyes. 'What am I going to do with you?'

Every atom of her body was charged. 'Oh, you must have some idea.'

His gaze was unblinking and serious, the muscles of his face taut as rock. 'This has to be right, Joss,' he said quietly. 'What happened with your husband… It needs to be a good experience for you. That's all that matters.'

'It will be.'

He stroked her wet hair but didn't move.

She kissed him on the lips – a lingering, encouraging kiss – and stepped back to regard his worried expression with tender bemusement. *Unbelievable. He's even more nervous than I am.* His unease was curiously childlike – intriguing and endearing at the same time.

'Be *sure*, Joss. Tell me what you want. Say it.'

'Well… now that you ask…' She tapped an index finger against her lips. 'I could *really* murder a Pepperoni. Maybe with a few dough balls on the side…'

It took two seconds for him to dissolve, at last, into laughter.

'So you find my seduction patter funny, do you?' He glared in mock offence as her smile widened. 'Well, you sassy bloody mare – I think this needs *serious* further discussion.'

Then he scooped up and carried her to his bed.

When the light outside had finally lost its glare and the colours of his bedroom were muted and delicate, Joss lay loosely wrapped in McCalvey's duvet, stretched alongside him in a state very close to bliss.

He was turned slightly away from her, but she could see and hear his quiet breathing. Her eyes roamed the contours of his back, the muscles of his burnished shoulders, the dark hair rippling into the nape of his neck. *He could do with a decent haircut*, she thought happily.

She felt astonished. Mad. Complete. *This amazing man is my lover now. How did I manage this? It's miraculous.*

He is miraculous.

Whatever the future held in store in the days and months ahead, she knew she'd treasure this time with him forever – lock it away in the part of her mind labelled *extremely precious: keep safe* – so she could retrieve the memory in darker times.

She squeezed her eyes shut, re-winding the last hours frame

by frame. The exquisite warmth, the substance of him, holding her so securely while his lips explored the whole landscape of her skin, eyes to toes… *Oh my God.* The recall made her take a huge, joyful inbreath. The stunning reality of his being *right there*, kneeling over her, naked and aroused. Heat had surged through every fibre of her body as she feasted her eyes on him, consumed by extremes of shyness and raw excitement. The expression on her face had made him smile – his sweet, mischievous, street-urchin smile.

She thought he was utterly beautiful.

And she replayed his voice, like gossamer against her cheek – '*Is that good? I'm not hurting you am I? Jesus, you're lovely. Tell me what you want me to do*' – while dust motes spiralled in the light from his window and gulls chuckled outside. She remembered his long, exultant sigh as she took him inside her for the first time; her own gasps, the pulse thumping in her throat, as he pushed deeper; the power she felt in his shoulders as her fingers gripped him; the curve of his spine within the girdle her legs made around his hips to press him down.

'*You are a revelation,*' he'd whispered.

'*You've revealed me,*' she'd whispered back.

She cried when he made her come – sobbing like a baby into the crook of his embracing arm. He lifted her chin to kiss the tears away.

Extracting herself from the covers, she wrapped herself in the discarded towel and tiptoed to the bathroom. She washed her hands, inhaling the sweet, musky fragrance, shivering as she recalled the tender play of his fingers. Then she flitted to the kitchen to find water.

Returning to the bed, she dropped to her knees in front of him, just to gaze at his face. *He looks at peace with himself,* she thought. *Hopefully it has something to do with me.* Suddenly she wondered if she'd really satisfied him. *God, I'm so out of practice.* With a prickle of anxiety, she pictured Tegen and Morwenna. Clearly that wasn't true for *him.*

For several long seconds she studied his profile – fine, strong features his baffling lack of interest in his own appearance couldn't disguise; the golden patina of his skin; the lips she'd so loved kissing – knowing she'd be desperate to remember every inch of him when, finally, she had to leave. *I'll learn,* she promised him silently. *I'll learn how to love you, Cal McCalvey, better than anyone else. Let it be me who understands you best; me you come to for everything you need, everything you could imagine.*

She couldn't resist smoothing a drift of hair away from his forehead.

Eyes still closed, he startled her with a grunt. 'When you've finished buggering about, woman, will you *please* get back into bed?'

Her laugh made him look up. His eyes, she noted with a rush of joy, had the depth and lustre of perfect expresso.

Climbing in beside him, she disposed of the towel and nestled against him under the duvet. He rolled onto his back then, creating space for her against his shoulder, letting her stroke the fine, dark, downy hair that flecked his chest, his abdomen, his groin. He closed a hand around hers. 'How long can you stay?'

The question had to come of course, but it was deflating. 'A while yet. You did promise me dinner, after all.'

His fingertips grazed her breasts in a languid movement that made her sigh with contentment, even as it re-lit a fire inside. 'Do you think you've done enough to deserve it?'

'Oh, is *that* what this was all about? My body in exchange for food?'

He grinned. 'Well, there's no such thing as a free lunch, as they say. *Ow!*' She'd poked him hard in the ribs.

But reality was beginning to extend its cold shadow into the room. 'Cal…? '

'Hmm?'

'Today, and beyond today – I don't want Ollie to know what's happened. I don't want him to suspect… to realise… there's something going on between us.' *Not yet,* she nearly added, but caution stopped her. One day, maybe. *If this lasts.*

'OK,' he said. 'But why not? Would he completely flip?'

'Possibly. I don't know. Things are still… confusing for him.'

He shrugged. 'If you think that's best, OK. I'm not sure I'd want Katie to know much about my love life either, to be fair. She thinks I'm enough of a reprobate already.' He gave a humourless laugh. 'And you're her boss, after all. Makes things a bit strange.'

They lost themselves in separate thought for a while. Then in a tone that suggested closure, he said, 'He's got lots of time, anyway, Joss. And so have you.'

She gave him a grateful smile. Wriggling closer, she examined his face as her fingers sketched slow circles downwards from the centre of his chest.

'So – it's time to tell me about *you* now,' she said.

'What about me?'

'Well, I understand your line of work, and I know you're Katie's dad – but that's it. What about your folks? Where did you spend your childhood, how did you come to live here? Who or what did that brooch remind you of the other day? I want to know all about what makes you who you are.'

'No, you don't.' He tapped her on the nose.

'Of *course* I do.'

'Why's it so important?'

Don't do this to me now, she thought, sitting up. *Not after this.* 'Because it's *you.* Because of *us,* because of... what's happened today. I want to know the whole you.' She prodded him again. 'I need to know what I'm dealing with here.'

'Honestly – this is all you need to know about me. Right here, right now. Today, this room, this moment. Nothing else matters. Trust me, Joss. *Nothing else matters.*' A change in his expression, a new sharpness in his tone, sucked oxygen out of the room.

She stared at him. *Don't put barriers up. Don't make me feel I don't know who you are.* 'Cal McCalvey,' she said firmly. 'We've only known each other a few weeks, and that's all I have of you – bits and pieces from these last few weeks. It's such a small part of your life.'

'Don't push it, Joss.'

The warning was terse and abrupt. Her stomach plummeted like a broken elevator, gathering speed on its descent to a gaping black hole. 'What's going *on* with you? Why won't you talk to me?'

'For Christ's sake.'

He threw the covers aside and manoeuvred himself above her, aligning hip to hip, breast to breast, his fingers in her hair. He kissed her forehead and each eyelid in turn – restless, agitated kisses; then traced the outline of her body shoulder to thigh, before parting her legs with his hand.

The electric intimacy of his fingers shocked her from bewilderment into pleasure.

'Do you want me to stop?' His lips skimmed hers. His breath on her neck was warm and rapid. 'Tell me always, *always,* if you want me to stop.'

She raised her face to his, desperate to be in contact with every part of him. 'No. *Don't stop.*'

'Tell me then,' he persisted, 'Isn't this enough for you?'

'Cal – *Oh God—*'

'Isn't this enough?'

The fierce entreaty in his voice was mystifying. She could hear that for him the question was urgent and real. But her hunger for him was a devastating, glorious thing, crushing everything else into sublime irrelevance. Arcing her back to accept him again, she could only whisper, *'Yes.'*

'Well then,' he said. 'I think we're done talking.' And his kisses stopped her mouth.

He lent her a shirt while they ate pizza in bed like a couple of enervated teenagers. From time to time he shifted plates and glasses out of the way, just so they could touch each other.

She ruffled his hair, ran teasing fingers down his bare torso and leaned in every few minutes for a kiss – looking, he thought, as if all her Christmases had come at once. Though he tried to channel an air of solicitous restraint, her tender encouragement was irresistible. With half an hour of the evening left, he slipped the shirt over her head, laid her across his pillows, and made love to her again.

When the time came for her to leave, he watched her dress in silence. Stunned by what had occurred, they became absurdly shy with each other. On the threshold she put her palm against his cheek, and he took her wrist and kissed it. Then he watched her descend the metal steps, heading home with a final wave.

Once she'd vanished from sight, he stood at his open door peering up at the darkening sky, listening to the sea.

Something unfamiliar lodged itself in his gut. He hadn't wanted her to leave.

Oh Christ.

Back inside, he went to the bathroom to splash cold water over his face. Closing his eyes and stooping over the basin, he relived the last few hours – the sensation of her skin beneath his fingertips; the catch of her breath as he kissed the space between her breasts, the hollow at the base of her neck, her mouth; the way she moved her hips when he entered her, opening herself up like a flower… God, he could still feel her, taste her, smell her…

He'd given her back something she'd forgotten, or thought was beyond repair. Knowing this was as intoxicating as it was disturbing.

What the fuck are you doing, McCalvey? This is not someone you want to hurt.

She'd had enough pain and loss in her life. Enough betrayal.

For as long as he could remember, responsibility for the happiness of others had oppressed him like a dragging weight: a burden he was always relieved, in the end, to put down. But this woman had unearthed something in him, something different. She made him feel… *hopeful.*

Maybe this was someone he could actually hold on to. Someone who'd help him make sense of what he'd been trying to escape from, all his adult life. For a second he felt a sweet rush of exhilaration. But he'd been at war with himself for too long.

I want to know the whole you, she'd said. But there *was* no whole him. If she dug into his past she'd only uncover a mess, a trail of destruction. And that *brooch…* the sight of it had disabled him, like kryptonite.

He opened his eyes and groaned. The person staring at him from the glass was not a person he liked, or even understood. As he turned his face away, an insidious, bitter voice took possession of his conscious mind. It was a voice he'd been listening to for years.

You don't deserve her, the voice rebuked him. *You're not worthy.*

She'll find out.

It's only a matter of time.

THIRTEEN

Balmy days and lustrous August evenings brought painters, ramblers and stargazers to St. Roslyn in increasing numbers. Wheal Blazey was fully booked until mid-September; money washing in at last began to cover the volume of cash flowing out. 'And we know the overdraft will get us a treatment plant,' Joss reminded her mother. Three quotations from water companies were waiting in Annie's in-tray for a final decision. 'So we're holding steady, just about.' *You could say the same about me.*

Most things in her world carried on as before – busy, predictable, unremarkable – yet every moment felt surreally fresh. She was like the proverbial swan, she thought – gliding serenely through the day while everything below the waterline paddled madly through raging torrents.

'I know you want to be positive, and I do appreciate it,' Annie sighed. 'But there'll be interest to pay, and the season's only another six weeks or so.'

'We'll get by. It'll work out.'

Annie eyed her beadily. 'You're unfathomably cheerful at the moment,' she said. 'Not to say distracted.'

'Am I?' Joss busied herself with the day's post to hide a blush. In the brittle silence that followed, she sensed her mother's appraising gaze; the expectation of a response. 'It's just that – well – Wheal Blazey has so much going for it, Mum. With a bit of imagination I'm sure it has the potential to—'

'Jocelyn, *please*! I don't have the energy. Big changes – like this restaurant idea of yours – need enormous focus and investment. I'll be a very old woman by the time that kind of outlay produces a reasonable return.'

'But when you think about it—'

'And what about *you*?' Annie shook her head, transmitting weary despair. 'It's all well and good you wanting to improve things here, darling – but don't forget how excited you were to go off to uni and experience city life. You're home now because of an appalling situation – but there may come a time, especially during our cold rainy winter, when you look around and think this is all very dull. And the reality is, if and when you move on…'

It was the closest her mother had come in months to saying, *we have decisions to make*. Joss stared blindly at the desk, trying to make sense of an upsurge of mixed emotions – anxiety for her parents' well-being; remorse at making smart-arse suggestions while her mother struggled to cope with the day-to-day; fear that Annie might actually have a point – *I did want a different life* – but also, a new sense of defiance. *Change will help us survive. I can change too.*

'What's brought this on?' she asked eventually.

Annie averted her eyes. 'I've been thinking about things recently, worrying about the future. And then, Guy was here last week and—'

'Ah.'

'He was just chatting, you know, about property values. It seems likely the council will get the money it needs for an arts centre, with studios and gallery space – even a small theatre, apparently. Something like that would be good news for house prices in St. Roslyn, he says.'

'And good news for local hospitality,' Joss countered. 'More visitors, with broader interests.'

'Well.' Annie brushed an invisible speck from her skirt. 'He's looking for land.'

'Mum! He's trying to soften you up.'

'He's always been a big fan of this house.'

'He's a big fan of what it might fetch on the open market.' Joss snorted and pushed her chair back. 'How much would he get in commission, I wonder?'

'I've no idea. And that's not really the point.' Annie shook her head, looking glum. 'I'm just trying to think about options, sweetheart. The need to feel that we're... *secure.*'

Through the window Joss frowned at the stately rhododendrons that had guarded her father's favourite bench for years. Behind them, plucky red fuchsias were cleaving their way through the boundary wall in search of light, while one lone gull soared obliviously overhead. She kicked off her shoes. The weathered flags beneath her feet were silky and warm. For a moment she visualised herself as a little girl again, dragging her precious blanket along the hall. Happy. Hopeful. Safe.

There's a spirit about the place. Something in the walls.

'Me too, Mum,' she said.

An odd wrinkle in the air vanished as Katie strode purposefully into reception. 'Sorry, I'm after brass cleaner.' She flashed a winning smile before ducking her vibrant pink head below the counter. 'Bridget says there might be a tin of it in the drawer here.'

'That's not where it's kept. What about the cleaning cupboard upstairs?'

'Nope. None there. I looked.'

'Hell's bells.' Annie snatched up a pen. 'I'll have to order some. What's it for?'

'Lamps in the guest lounge,' Katie said. 'But I can use salt and vinegar with a bit of elbow grease. Do you think anyone'll care if it smells like the local chippy for half an hour?' Her eyes twinkled, and Joss laughed. Then she looked away and busied herself with the post again.

She'd begun to feel acutely self-conscious when the teenager was nearby. She wanted Katie to like her, to respect her as a boss – not least because there was a good chance she'd be reporting back to the man occupying her thoughts every waking minute. And she couldn't look at Katie now without a *frisson* of guilty trepidation. Had the teenager cottoned on to the fact her dad sometimes sneaked into town for a surreptitious coffee? Did she suspect that his absence after dinner one evening to 'have a drink with a friend' might have had anything to do with herself?

She'd used Morwenna as her excuse on that occasion, but the lie made her deeply uncomfortable. Ollie had been grudging, and Annie coolly reserved, when she'd shrugged on her coat to go into town alone. She'd returned late, bright-eyed and a little breathless, to be intercepted by her mother asking, 'Everything alright?'

Yes, fine, she'd said. *It was nice to catch up.*

Even as those words left her mouth, she'd been thinking of McCalvey slipping the handbag from her shoulder to the footwell of his car before slowly unbuttoning her jacket; the way he'd smoothed a lock of hair behind her ear as he bent to kiss her neck.

It won't be forever, she'd persuaded herself. *We'll sort ourselves out. One way or another.*

Katie glanced between them and said, 'They sell brass cleaner in the chandlery. My Dad uses it on his boat. I'll pick some up on my way home if you like.'

'No, I'll go.' Joss stood up. 'Ollie's playing Scrabble with his grandad, and I could do with a couple of things from the market. Can I take your car, Mum?'

Annie's eyes narrowed just a little. 'You can,' she said. 'But be careful you don't get another flat tyre.'

Within seconds of hearing her knock on his door, McCalvey had her in his arms.

'It feels weird,' he said later, 'Katie being around in the evenings and Ollie off school for a few weeks. Skulking about because our offspring might think we're… *misbehaving*.' He was holding her at the waist, eyeing her reflection in his bathroom mirror as she tried to brush order back into her hair. 'Not that I have any problem with misbehaviour, you understand.'

'Misbehaviour? God, *look* at me!' She pointed the hairbrush at the glass. Hot pink patches were as vivid as paint across both cheeks. 'How can I make myself *not* look like someone who's been misbehaving with her dark, mysterious lover against his kitchen cabinets for the last half hour?'

He nuzzled the back of her neck. 'I'm afraid you'll just have to brazen it out.'

She sighed, thinking of her mother's despondency contrasted with her own joy.

'Anyway.' He combed hair away from her face with gentle fingers. 'I've had an idea which might make things easier in the short term.'

'Oh?'

'We could use Kara. She's out on a swinging mooring right now, but I could bring her into Mussel Cove for a while, just below Wheal Blazey. It's a place your dad knows well actually – a natural jetty, sheltered from the elements. The weather's likely to change before summer's out, so it's no bad thing if she has some extra protection.'

'What's in your mind?'

'She'll be accessible there. It'll be easy to take her out, maybe anchor off shore for an hour or two.' He kissed the top of her head. 'Or even just meet where she's moored. Katie's used to me sailing at weekends and the odd evening, and she never wants to come with me. I wish she did, to be honest.' For a brief second, Joss saw his eyes cloud. 'And during the week I can probably take a long lunch now and then. That is… if you want me to.'

'*Of course* I want you to!' She made a face. 'As if you need to ask.'

'Well, let's hope we get some opportunities.'

She deliberated for a moment. 'Ollie will be made up if he knows Kara's close by though. He'll want to be down there with her all the time.'

'We'll work something out. I'll take him sailing again. I'll take you both.'

She caressed his cheek, and his hand closed around her fingers. 'Thank you, Cal. He'd love that.'

'So, why don't you suggest we fetch her next weekend? Tell him you bumped into me in town.'

'I will.'

She began to hunt for her jacket and bag, discarded earlier in haste. 'And now I really have to go. My alibi is calling. I'll see myself out.' A teasing finger poked his chest. 'You should probably tidy yourself up a bit before Katie gets home.' His tousled hair, untucked shirt and abandoned mug of coffee made her smile.

'Disruptive bloody woman,' he grumbled. But she caught the gleam in his eyes before he closed the door.

Pausing on the top step, she straightened her clothes, checked her purse, and breathed in the ocean's green, vitalizing smell. And then, as she descended towards ground level, she noticed the stranger.

Cocooned inside a fleece jacket despite the warmth of the day, a skinny, awkward-looking figure across the road was shifting from foot to foot, hands in his pockets, the upper part of his face concealed by a hood.

She stopped when she reached the tarmac. In London, she'd grown accustomed to steering wide half-circles around shady-looking characters loitering on street corners – even if they were just waiting harmlessly for a mate, opening time, or the offer of something interesting, if not necessarily legal, to do. But here in St. Roslyn? Furtive strangers were as rare as hen's teeth.

Aware he was being stared at, the figure looked up. The hood slipped back and she took a breath. A mottled strip of purple ran forehead to chin down one side of a pale face, disfiguring a good six inches of skin along the hairline. Her immediate reaction was one of pity – *poor guy, he must have had a horrible accident* – but she quickly found herself drawn to his penetrating blue eyes, a suggestion of steel within them that defied his scars. He peered intently at her for a moment, then glanced towards McCalvey's door. His scrutiny was unnerving. But she had her manners.

'Can I help you?'

The stranger hesitated. Late twenties, she guessed, a few years younger than herself. The unblemished side of his face was smooth and creamy – boyish, she thought. *He'd have been handsome once.* The observation made her sad.

'Is that your place?' he asked.

'No.' The sharpness of his question put her on her guard.

He fished a piece of paper from a jacket pocket and consulted it, evidently troubled. 'Do you mind me asking who *does* live here, then?'

'Are you looking for someone in particular?'

He gave a cryptic smile, squinted up at the apartment again, and shrugged. 'Don't worry about it,' he said. 'A childhood friend. If he lives anywhere round here, I'll come across him sooner or later. Can't guarantee he'll be pleased to see me though.'

She followed his gaze up the metal steps, visualising the man behind the door spooning himself fresh coffee, tidying his cushions, smiling as he tucked the shirt back into his jeans...

A childhood friend?

Don't let it be Cal.

She flared with sudden, inexplicably fierce protectiveness. Against what, she had no idea. But this visitor didn't seem like good news.

'It's just a rental property,' she said, waving vaguely at the steps.

'Yeah?'

She nodded. ''Fraid so.'

'Well. OK.' He pulled the hood forward, retracting his head like a disappointed tortoise. 'Sorry I bothered you.' And with a last upward glance, he shuffled away.

Joss stared after him, chewing her lip. Part of her wanted to give chase, tap him on the shoulder and ask, *Is it Cal McCalvey you're after? Please tell me what you know about him.* A stubborn, more fearful part was relieved she'd seen him off.

Since the lunch at Denzel's, every secret hour with McCalvey had lifted her spirits, nourished her, helped her rediscover the person she once was. A person she thought she'd lost. The relationship already felt almost unbearably precious. Fragile, too.

The past can be a merciless bastard. Those words had stuck in her brain – simultaneously compassionate, puzzling and scary. What had he meant? Did she *really* want to know?

Today, this moment... Nothing else matters. Wishful thinking. In her heart she knew it. Sooner or later, the world would crash through McCalvey's door.

But *please,* not yet. Not yet.

FOURTEEN

Kara's the coolest boat in the bay, 100%.

Mum doesn't need to come, but she says she likes us being together when it's not all about Wheal Blazey. And I'd rather be with her than doing stuff with a load of posers I don't know.

Dad would have had a real go at me for that.

He always moaned I was like a baby, hanging on to her apron strings. Telling me I should man up.

Well, cheers for that, Dad. I did. In the end, because of you, I did.

They put the mainsail up for the short journey from Kara's swinging mooring to the shelter of the cove, towing the little dinghy McCalvey had used to fetch them from the slipway to the boat. As a light breeze fanned them close, he started the engine and beckoned Ollie to the helm. 'Right, shipmate – keep her steady while I get the sail down.'

Joss shot him an anxious look but he raised a hand to signal, *No problem, I've got this.* He levered back the gears, letting the motor idle as Ollie scrambled to take his place.

'So you're going to point her into the wind,' McCalvey instructed him. 'You know how to do that?'

Ollie gripped the tiller and peered up to where the slim metal arrow above the huge mast was horizontally aligning itself. 'I need to get that arrow pointing straight ahead, then I'll know the wind is dead on the nose.'

McCalvey winked at Joss. 'Excellent. And what will happen to the sail when you do?'

'It'll go floppy because we'll lose the wind.'

'OK, good. Let me know when you think we're in position.'

Joss took in the ferocious concentration on her son's face as McCalvey stood by, arms folded, quietly monitoring the hull's displacement in relation to the jetty while keeping a watchful eye on how his helper was handling things.

In fact Ollie was doing well. Slipping across tranquil water, still a way off target, Kara was forgiving and responsive in his small, determined hands. He manoeuvred the yacht through a stately arc until the sail began to flutter, then shouted, 'I think now is good!'

'Fine – hold her there.' McCalvey moved forward to release the halyard and haul the canvas down. Job done, he pulled the kicking strap tight to stabilise the hefty boom.

'Now for the next challenge,' he said. 'I'm going to put the engine into first, and you're going to take us alongside the jetty, bow forward, OK? I'll fend off.'

Ollie nodded and licked his lips. Joss held her breath. This complicated boy of hers seemed to have grown a foot taller in the last twenty minutes, fed by the trust McCalvey was investing in him, the romance of steering this beautiful boat from open sea into the safe embrace of the little cove. Adrenalin had put colour in his cheeks. *He's found his happy place*, she smiled to herself. She noticed again how agile and organised McCalvey appeared in this domain, the skill with which he commanded every inch of his yacht; loved his pure, physical grace. Watching him with little jabs of pride, she remarked to herself, *Out here he has no issues. Out here, he is free.*

As they neared the jetty, he pulled half a dozen fenders from a cockpit locker and tied them along the starboard rail in less than a minute. Then just as she'd begun to flinch at the speed of their approach, he jumped down to slam the gears into neutral before reaching over the side to grasp the wall and hand-walk the hull to a controlled stop. Within seconds he'd slipped mooring lines into the old brass rings and cleated them off; then he was back to cut the engine. The hull settled like a nesting bird.

'That was *brilliant!*' Ollie turned to Joss, his face alight. 'I brought her in!'

'You were amazing!'

McCalvey put a hand on his shoulder. 'You did well,' he said. 'Though there's a bunch of stuff to do yet.'

'Like what?'

'A proper sailor would pack up the mainsail, get the dinghy up onto the foredeck, stow the lifejackets, tidy the lines…'

'I *am* a proper sailor,' Ollie protested. 'I can do all that.' He glued himself to McCalvey as together they wrapped the canvas, hauled Kara's tender out of the water, secured it on the bow with bungees, coiled multiple lengths of rope into neat Catherine wheels, and generally restored a sense of order.

McCalvey surveyed the cockpit and nodded approval. 'Good job, buddy. I think you'll do.' Then he stepped out of the boat and onto the jetty, offering a supportive hand as Joss tottered forward to disembark.

'Sorry – the legs have gone. It takes me ages to get my balance back.' She felt his fingers tighten around hers, remaining there for several unnecessary seconds until Ollie swung himself down to join them.

It was a gorgeous day. Joss gazed at the path winding up towards Wheal Blazey and filled her lungs. The fragrance of wild flowers, damp shingle and seaweed was intoxicating. 'We're *so lucky.*'

An idea was floating in her brain. She frowned, trying to land it. 'It makes me sad for what our guests might be missing,' she mused. 'An hour in a beautiful boat, sailing round the bay in the sunshine... just magical. The best way to see Cornwall. An experience they'd always remember.'

McCalvey inclined his head. 'What's going on in that grey matter of yours? I can hear cogs grinding.'

'You could offer trips on Kara!' She took hold of his arm. 'Take couples or small groups out at weekends. Paying customers. Nice accommodation just up the path there – this lovely cove – we could put a really appealing package together.'

'Are you propositioning me, madam?'

'Think about it, Cal. Up-market picnics from Wheal Blazey's kitchen for guests to take on board... Crab sandwiches and Cornish bubbly...What's not to like?'

He squinted at her. 'You're serious.'

'Maybe.'

Her smile faltered as he pursed his lips, reached for the guardrail, and tapped out a nervy rhythm with his fingers. His gaze travelled to the top of Kara's mighty mast; the untroubled sweep of sky. 'It's not really me, Joss,' he said quietly. 'If you're serious – then I'm sorry. It's not what I rebuilt Kara for.' Slowly, his eyes returned to hers. 'Being tied to a regular arrangement like that... I'd only let you down.'

Dammit. She should have known better. Polite conversation, health and safety, terms and conditions, feedback, timetables... it wasn't him. *Of course* it wasn't him.

'That's not to say it's a bad idea,' he added with a shrug. 'It's a pretty good one.'

As he spoke Ollie yanked the back of her sleeve – a gesture she knew meant *enough with the small talk – let's get home.*

'Well. Perhaps I'll let it simmer for a bit.' She put an arm around Ollie's shoulder. 'Do you want to come up to the house, Cal? Have a coffee?'

He shook his head, as she knew he would. 'I've got stuff to sort out,' he said. 'Now we're moored here I need to pack up anything that's not nailed down and take it back to my place, just to be safe. Another time. Thanks anyway.'

She pulled a face at Ollie's reproachful glare. Clearly her son had deemed the social invitation wildly out of order. Ollie examined the green hull prow to stern one last time before muttering, 'You don't want crowds of tourists going out on Kara at weekends anyway, Mum. She's too old and too special. People need to know what they're doing.'

'Spoken like a true sea dog.' McCalvey sounded amused and grateful. 'You'll be a cracking skipper one of these days, Ollie.'

Ollie smiled and looked at his feet as pink crescents blossomed around his ears.

'Right, squirt. Home for hot chocolate, I think.' Threading her arm through his, Joss guided him away. Just before she reached the path, she glanced behind her and saw McCalvey shake his head before hauling himself back on deck.

Back, she understood with a pang of regret, to solitary, uncomplicated peace.

Ollie buttonholed Katie as soon as the girls assembled in the kitchen for coffee.

'We've been sailing with your dad!'

Joss put a mug in front of him and glanced warily at McCalvey's daughter before turning to prepare her own drink.

'Yeah?'

'We brought Kara into Mussel Cove, just down the coast. I helmed most of the way.'

Joss cleared her throat, then met the teenager's eye. 'Your dad was so good about letting Ollie have a go. He's been very kind, ever since he found out he used to have lessons.'

Tegen and Bridget shared a look.

'I think he did tell me he'd be moving the boat this morning,' said Katie. Her gaze flicked from Joss to Ollie and back again. 'It's… nice he had a bit of company.' Something close to a smile crossed her lips. 'He knows it's not my thing.'

'Well, anyway.' Joss breezed past the staring girls to fetch biscuits. 'Do thank him again for us, Katie, when you see him.'

She sensed three pairs of eyes on her back.

'So, why did he want to bring his boat out here?' Tegen's voice was tight with affronted challenge.

Joss prayed that the heat intensifying under her skin wouldn't flame in her cheeks as she replied. 'I bumped into him in town, and he mentioned putting it somewhere more sheltered. He thinks the weather might change soon.'

Everyone looked towards the window, at the beautifully cloudless sky.

'When was this?'

As she tried to formulate a coolly polite version of *what business is it of yours?* Eva appeared in the doorway. Her cheerful 'Morning everyone!' and 'Please don't let me interrupt,' punctured the accumulating tension.

Joss greeted her with relief. 'Everything OK, Eva?'

'Yes – but can you find me a screwdriver, Jocelyn? Mrs. Livesey's gone outside with a man from the water company. I've been reorganising books for your father, and one of his shelves is wobbly.' She flapped a hand, minimising the problem. 'It's only a loose bracket.'

'We keep a toolkit under reception,' Joss said. 'I'll show you.'

As she led Eva into the hallway, Katie's unruffled, moderating voice filled the edgy silence behind her. 'I didn't know you were into sailing, Ollie. So how do you like Kara?' His eager response – 'Well she's pretty fast… but I think I'm getting the hang of her' – soothed her agitation. *Good on you, Katie.* Under those defended outer layers, there was a seam of kindness in the girl. *Like father, like daughter.*

She opened the drawer and gazed through the window into the garden while Eva searched for what she needed.

'I think this fellow will do.' Eva twirled a six-inch screwdriver in a shaft of light. 'It's got paint on it, though. I'll clean it first.'

Joss turned to see Eva scraping a fingernail along the stem. 'Paint?'

A few wine-red flakes detached themselves, randomly spotting the desktop's white blotter. She eyed them with puzzled interest, wondering where she'd seen that colour before. Nowhere in the house or its outbuildings she could think of. She lifted a fragment with a licked fingertip to inspect it more closely.

The same colour as Guy Tremain's car.

A coincidence, surely. But there was a metallic feel to the little shard; a sharp edge, a definite gloss. 'Can I see?'

In her palm the flat-bladed tool was surprisingly heavy, the tip still bearing tell-tale speckles from its previous use.

Mentally she rifled through scraps of information retained from that messy morning. The damage, Guy said, must have been inflicted at Roslyn Glynn, when he'd left the car unattended on the rough perimeter track.

The two things couldn't possibly be connected, could they? Ridiculous. Did she seriously imagine someone could have taken the thing out of the drawer, searched for and vandalised the car, then sneaked it back? Who, for goodness sake? A jealous guest? A vindictive member of their own team? Her *dad*?

No way. She tossed her head. Sooner or later she was bound to come across the object she couldn't place at the moment, a piece of hardware painted in that same colour.

She returned the screwdriver to Eva, who set off down the corridor just as Ollie arrived from the kitchen, endearingly windswept from their earlier outing. He hugged her as she tried to smoothe his hair. 'You're all salty,' she remarked. 'You should probably have a shower before lunch. And then, my little man, you need to start thinking about your school holiday projects for an hour or two.'

He grunted. 'Maybe later, when it's not so sunny.'

'I ought to help Gran with admin this afternoon,' she sighed. 'So you'll be at a loose end otherwise.'

He glanced across the counter, frowning at the chair she'd occupy while she updated reservations, responded to enquiries and wrestled with the balance sheet. The drawer below the desk was still open. She caught his expression as he noticed it – a stiffening of the jaw, a compression of the lips. He looked up at her with wide eyes. 'I could take a bike out again,' he said. 'Go to the beach, or into town for an hour.'

Apart from the toolbox, the drawer was home to tubes of glue, tape, string, padlocks and cycle shed keys. Joss had a memory of him foraging in it; she could hear herself nagging him to wear a helmet.

The image of Guy trembling with rage by his car's disfigured wing flashed in her head. McCalvey, she recalled, had been grimly sympathetic, asking about CCTV while she stood helplessly by, and Ollie...

Ollie... did *what* exactly?

She remembered him arriving just before Guy. He'd been upset at the state of his grandad. McCalvey's offer of an outing on Kara had cheered him a little – but then he'd detached himself the moment Guy began to vent.

I'll just put the bike back in the shed.

An abhorrent possibility occurred to her.

No. Absolutely not. Ollie wouldn't do such a thing. He could be moody and judgmental at times, but destructive? Violent? If he ever lashed out, it would be in response to serious provocation. That, she had good reason to know.

God Almighty, what kind of mother *was* she, to have entertained the idea even for a second?

'Are you alright, Mum?'

Trusting blue eyes anxiously interrogated hers. She gently thumbed his cheek. She was so, so lucky to have him.

'I'm always alright,' she smiled, 'so long as you are.'

He bumped his forehead against her chest and gazed up. 'We're a team, you and me,' he said. 'Forever. Just you and me.'

That night, Katie offered to make dinner.

McCalvey poured them each a glass of wine – he knew she regarded that as one small upside to the whole dubious arrangement – found a radio station with a reasonable playlist, and stood at his kitchen counter waiting for instructions while she diced ingredients for a stir-fry. At one point he picked a shitake mushroom out of the carton she'd brought home from a trendy deli he usually avoided, and sniffed it.

'*What?*' Her knife stilled in mid-air.

'Nothing! Just… interested.' Sheepishly, he dropped it back into the container.

'It's an Asian mushroom – and I got beansprouts, scallions and Bok choy. Very tasty and healthy.'

'Marvellous.' He couldn't resist teasing her with a look of bug-eyed panic over the rim of his glass.

She slapped his arm. '*Dad!* You can't survive on pasties and pies the whole time. And anyway, I'm slicing some pork and making a sauce, so you'll get your protein fix.'

The smile he returned was wide and genuine. He wanted to say *this is nice*, but suppressed the urge – it felt like too much of a risk. 'Can I help?'

'Here,' she said, sliding pork fillet towards him on a board. 'You can slice this for me – thinly, please.'

Her eyes skewered him as he set about the task. So many years, and they'd never spent this kind of time together. Almost affectionate. But he caught the face she pulled before turning back to her chopping with renewed concentration. He wondered whether in some weird way, moments like this made everything worse.

Suddenly she cocked her head. 'Listen – they're playing your song!'

'My song?'

It was Springsteen. *Hungry Heart.*

'An anthem for every guy who's ever deserted his family.' She fixed him with a mischievous look and started to sing along, jarringly out of tune.

His smile evaporated as she pressed on, relentlessly, to the end.

'A few bum notes in there,' he murmured. *In more ways than one.*

'It's you, though, Dad, isn't it? You're the original hungry heart.'

She was three weeks into her visit: just over half way. Recently he'd begun to suspect – hope, at least – that the terrain between them was becoming marginally less rocky, more habitable. He'd trodden on enough eggshells in her company, for Christ's sake. But it still felt too dangerously easy to slither into confrontation.

'I think Bruce would say we're *all* hungry for something,' he said levelly. 'Even you, Katie.'

'Hmph.' She breathed out sharply through her nose. 'Maybe

it's not the right analogy then. Hit and run driver might suit you better. Still getting away with it. Not taking responsibility.'

'Meaning what exactly?'

She wiped her hands on a tea towel, grabbed her glass and took an enormous gulp. 'Well I'd have to be deaf and blind not to clock that something happened between you and Tegen, for instance.'

'Oh for God's sake.' He blew air at the ceiling.

'See? Hit and run.'

'Katie—'

'And the sailing thing with Ollie and Jocelyn.' She waved her glass in his face, slopping wine onto the floorboards. 'Are you going to tell me it's all innocent? That you've taken Ollie under your wing out of the goodness of your heart, and his mum just comes along for the ride?'

He fixed his eyes on the worktop, stuck between a lie he knew she'd find pathetically inept and a truth too complex to articulate. But as he wrestled to shape some kind of response, he sensed her gradually deflate. 'I don't know why I'm being so schoolmarmy,' she grumbled. 'It has sod-all to do with me.'

In a way, that last remark let him off the hook. But instead of feeling reprieved, he felt numbed by it. *Dismissed.*

'It *is* to do with you, Katie. I'm your dad, after all. A shit one, admittedly.' That, at least, produced an acknowledging grunt. 'You're totally within your rights to have a go at me, but it's a plus in my book that you're registering interest. Better than being ignored.'

She gave him half a smile and cocked her head, wordlessly inviting him to say more. The look in her eyes – curious and shrewd – unnerved him slightly. She wouldn't allow him to diverge too far from the truth, he realised. Even though meaningful analysis about himself was something he took pains to avoid.

'She's a nice woman,' he said carefully. 'And she hasn't had it easy, you know? She lost her husband and she's grateful for a bit of support. Support for Ollie, more than anything.'

'So that's one mother and child you actually want to be around,' she said. 'Good for you.'

Fuck. The irony struck home with howitzer force. 'Jesus, Katie.' He grabbed the heavy pan, weighing it between his hands. 'What an idiot. I'm sorry. Do you want me to clout myself over the head with this?'

'That would help.'

They frowned at each other a long, silent moment until her wry smile and a resigned shrug helped ease the tension. In the space of ten minutes their fragile camaraderie had transitioned into something convoluted and wounding. His fault, he groaned inwardly. Par for the course. *Master of the total screw-up strikes again.* Disappointing anyone who got close to him was clearly in his DNA. 'Sometimes I wish I could turn the clock back, Katie,' he murmured.

'Yeah. Well.'

He saw her eyes fill before she looked away. A pain like heartburn gripped his chest.

'Ancient history,' she sniffed. 'I guess you had issues. People do. And I realise you were only two or three years older than I am now when you got mum pregnant. That's crazy. But still.'

'I was a mess, no excuses,' he said. 'I don't expect to be forgiven, Katie, or even understood.' He was starting to feel as raw as the pork slices in front of him. 'But... I'm honestly glad you're here.'

'I missed a lot of things, you know?'

'I know.' *Me too.*

She retrieved her glass and examined what was left of its contents, her brow creased and her bottom lip thrust out. In sorrow or anger? He wasn't sure which.

'So, why not come and stay with us in Bristol for a few days?' she asked him. 'I'll be going into sixth form next month – it's a pretty big change. Gateway to adulthood and all that. You could come back with me on the train, maybe? Be there to see me into the new term.'

'You're trying to be nice now. Wouldn't that seem a bit weird?'

'I don't do *nice*.' She glared at him. 'Loads of my friends have parents who've split up. They make the best of things, they contribute. It's normal life, Dad. You could show up for once. Be a regular guy.'

'I'd make your mum uncomfortable.'

'You're wrong. She'd be cool about it, she's very together. She did love you once, remember.'

Don't, he begged her silently.

'She made her peace with how things were between you a long time ago, Dad. She always knew you felt trapped. Anyway, she loves Alvaro now and they're happy. So it's all OK.'

He poked at the meat, his appetite fading fast. 'I don't know, Katie.'

The look she shot him was fierce. 'What would you rather be doing? Sitting here on your own night after night with a beer and a pasty? Is that your plan for the next twenty years?'

'*Stop.*'

Her challenges were scrambling his brain. What *would* he rather be doing? He paused, trying to summon an authentic, head-and-heart answer. Racing across the ocean on Kara, he mused – harnessing the wind, miles from any sight of land. Readying himself for the next lifeboat shout, pitting himself against the elements, saving lives. Sinking the odd pint with Marty after work. Savouring quiet evenings on his own. And stealing time with Joss.

His gaze drifted to the bedroom door, visualising Joss

cocooned there in his duvet. He wanted to hear her laugh again, hold her close and safe, forget everything else…

'You like to keep everything simple.' Katie broke into his thoughts. 'Banish the bad stuff, avoid anything awkward. But it's all a big lie, Dad. Nothing's simple with you.'

'You don't know me, Katie. You might think you do, but—'

'I know you have nightmares,' she said.

'What?'

'I've heard you. You call out in your sleep.'

He went very still. She leaned against the worktop, facing him with a *don't give me any nonsense* look.

'Only once or twice,' she continued a little more gently. 'But it scared the shit out of me, you sounded so scared. You kept saying *no,* and *please, no.* And calling out someone's name. Troy, maybe? Or Ty?'

Somewhere deep in his subconscious, the lid of Pandora's box cracked microscopically open. He gave the sofa-bed a rattled glance. 'Did I wake you up? Sorry. Damn bloody springs. They poke me in the backside at night.'

Impatience flashed in her eyes. 'I don't think it's the *bloody springs*. Something's eating at you. What is it?'

'Just an overactive brain, I guess. Too much healthy food in the last few weeks.'

'Bollocks.'

He turned away and closed his eyes. Murky, impressionistic images fogged his head as if she'd blown smoke in his face. Now that she'd made him think about it, he remembered an eerie sense of falling, then blindly running, struggling for breath. A locked room, an acrid smell, the desperate screaming of a small boy…and this time, a woman's voice, whispering in his ear.

Don't worry. I won't be gone long.

So close, *so close.* He'd woken with a start, looking round for her, panicking. But he was alone of course, clutching at his rumpled, clammy sheets in the empty dark.

He managed a weak smile. 'Go easy on the designer mushrooms Katie, or it might happen again.'

'You're not going to tell me, are you?'

'Nothing to tell.'

The room was suddenly oppressive. He opened the front door to stand by the metal rail, filling his lungs with the sweet night air and his head with the slow, familiar pulsing of the sea.

It took him a while to notice Katie's fingers interlacing themselves with his.

FIFTEEN

Grandad was almost like he used to be today. He couldn't believe me scoring maximum Scrabble points with 'Macaque'! He really laughed and told me I had Mum's brains. Then he said he hoped I'd have more luck with them than Mum, because she never got the chance to use hers.

When I asked him what he meant, he whispered it like a secret: that Dad boxed her in. He stopped her from being herself.

You said it Grandad.

But I'm here. And everything's different now.

It had been years since life had felt this close to perfect. Nestled against McCalvey as they lay at anchor, every receptor in Joss's body vibrated with the beating of his heart, the rise and fall of his chest, the strength of his arms as he swaddled her in the blanket he'd spread across Kara's cockpit floor. She imagined the yacht floating like a leaf, a single speck of green in the boundless blue. Beneath her, the nudging of a gentle current was wonderfully soothing. Above her, all she could see was sky.

'So what does Ollie think you're up to?' His fingers traced a lazy curve over her hips through the layer of wool.

'Post Office, bakery, then bookshop.' She wriggled closer, inhaling the musky warmth of his skin. 'Anyway, he has art homework to keep him busy.'

'Art? Seriously?'

'A sketch or collage evoking *movement*, apparently. He's thinking of using dolphins as his subject.'

'Good choice.'

'And he has a geography project and history essay to complete before term starts. Cornwall between the wars.'

'Yikes. In my day we were given a lump of wood and told to make something useful.'

She pinched his cheek – 'My word, you're so *manly*!' – and received a cocky *if the cap fits* grin in response.

Today he seemed at ease with himself. She decided to take a chance. 'So – what school did you go to?'

'A few, actually.' He rolled onto his back and blinked at the sun. 'None of them any good.' Then he sat up, dug down into the blanket, and produced the silk bra he'd helped her remove with comically appreciative delicacy half an hour earlier. 'I suppose you'll be wanting this back?' She swiped at it as he dangled it out of reach. 'Only, I thought I might hang it over the side for a bit. Catch a few shrimps. Tiddlers, obviously.'

'Cheeky bugger!'

He caught her as she lunged forward, cupping her breasts with warm hands as his mouth found hers.

They dressed in companionable silence – tinged, it seemed to Joss, with a shade of melancholy. The man was such a vital, physical, exasperating presence. At times she convinced herself she understood him; then at others he felt like a visiting friend

– delighting in her company, but never completely at home.

'I need to decide what we'll do at the end of the summer.' As she put the words out there, she wondered why. To test him, perhaps? Or maybe to test herself.

He stowed the anchor and returned to start the motor. 'You and Ollie, you mean?'

She nodded. 'I came back for breathing space. Time away from London, so I could think about the future. In my twenties I had visions of training as a teacher, but now I don't know. I honestly don't feel like the person I was then. Even the person I was a year ago.'

He glanced at her, then focused on the stretch of water between the boat and the cove. 'So what's changed?'

'I'm not entirely sure. But it's definitely to do with Wheal Blazey. Now that I've spent serious time back here, getting to know the business…' How great would it be, she thought, if he mapped it out for her, made sense of everything. *Tell me I have a future here, that you see a way forward.*

Tell me you want me to stay.

She watched him adjust the throttle before freeing the tiller. Satisfied Kara was ready to move, he relaxed back on the bench, folded one leg over the other and pointed the bow towards home.

'What do you think, Cal?'

He sniffed the air, still looking away from her. 'About the business?'

'I mean… whether it might be worth me staying on. Getting more involved.' *He knows damn well I'm not just talking about Wheal Blazey.*

There was a long pause while he checked the depth gauge, the current, their distance from the jetty. Finally his eyes settled on her face. 'You know what I think.'

She pursed her lips and waited.

'I think with the right help you could turn that place around. Make it your own.'

'Honestly?'

'No question. But the important thing is – you'd need to commit to it, Joss. No half measures, no compromises. If you can't give it a hundred percent—' he scrabbled a hand through his hair, '—then there's no point. You'll end up feeling... trapped.' She only just caught the mumbled postscript: 'Too easily done.'

Curiosity sparked inside her like a lit flare. Had he meant to throw her a bone of insight about himself? If so, the colour creeping into his face suggested he regretted it.

'It could give you real independence if it worked out, though,' he shrugged. 'Even fulfil you.'

'So what about *you*, Cal?' Though she knew she was hurtling towards a line he was unlikely to let her cross, she couldn't stop herself. 'When the summer's over...' *Will you just sail away?*

She left the sentence unfinished. And unanswered.

The trip back was quick, and mooring Kara straightforward. Joss wondered if he'd even heard the question as he nursed the hull to a standstill, cut the engine and secured the lines. But once he'd helped her step onto dry land, he took her face between his hands and fixed solemn eyes on hers. 'Playing *what if* is a mug's game, Joss. Hoping things will come right – bargaining on a happy outcome – it's never done me much good. Can't we just... roll with the way things are for a while?'

If it weren't for the sadness in his voice, the *want* she detected behind his troubled eyes, she might have balked at his casual cruelty. As it was, the ache his words generated was more for his sake than her own. She wished she had the nerve to ask, *What happened to you? Who or what taught you to be so distrustful?* Deflection and denial, she knew only too well, were learned behaviours. But instead, she held him by the waist and managed a smile.

'I'm still trying to figure you out, Cal Conundrum McCalvey.'

'I wouldn't waste your energy.'

Then he kissed her – a long, slow, tenderly insistent kiss – while she pressed her body hard against his, hugging him close.

Suddenly tense, he pulled away and looked up.

Joss followed his gaze towards a group of trees on the coast path, fifty yards from the jetty. In a gap between thick fronds and twisty stems, she glimpsed the movement of a white sleeve, an abrupt pushing back of glossy red hair. Wide eyes in a familiar face stared the two of them up and down, then turned away.

'*Tegen*,' she whispered.

'Ah.' He took her arm. 'Sod it. Someone was bound to work things out, sooner or later.'

'She'll tell Katie. She'll make a thing of it. She *saw* us, Cal. Oh *God*.'

'It's not the end of the world,' he said. But his face was dark.

Joss watched the figure ascend the path to Wheal Blazey, head down, moving fast. She had no idea what Tegen was likely to say or do; how she'd use this new information, the power it might give her. Would her mother get to hear about it? Would Ollie? Tears stung her eyes as she glanced back at McCalvey and wailed, 'She'll be so jealous. Dammit, she'll want to punish you. Punish both of us. She's been *waiting*, Cal. Waiting and wondering if she can... have you to herself again.'

He gaped at her for a frozen, silent moment. Then he narrowed his eyes at the retreating figure, clenching his jaw. 'Well now she knows.'

Joss shook her head. 'We've been careless.'

'Come on. What can she really say? She can gossip all she wants, but why should it matter? We're friends, right?' He winced at her mortified expression. 'OK, *more* than friends. Consenting adults, if you want to moralise about it. It's allowed. We're grown up. If anything, she'll make herself look childish if she inflates it into some kind of issue. It'll blow over.'

Blow over? She had a mad surge of hope he might add, *What are you so worried about? We're together – why go on hiding it?*

But he didn't.

In his eyes she detected irritation and impatience. 'You think we should pretend it hasn't happened,' she reproached him. 'Ignore it, and it'll disappear.'

He shrugged in response. *What else is there to say?*

'I hope you're right.' She frowned towards the trees.

Seconds later, she felt his hand gently grasp hers. 'I'll be here for a while anyway, making a couple of mods,' he said. 'I'm owed a few hours off the clock. The mainsheet keeps snagging, and there's a problem with—'

'*Cal.* I really have to go.' Avoiding his eyes, she extracted her fingers. 'I'll see you soon.' And she forced herself to walk away.

Inside Morwenna's shop, she dumped her bags and scanned the nearest cabinets, hungry for distraction.

'You look a bit out of sorts,' Morwenna said. 'What's up?'

She reached for an enamelled figurine and glowered at its merry red face. 'Oh… Complicated people. Bad timing. The way things slap you in the face – just when you think you have everything under control – telling you not to be so *bloody naïve.*'

'Ah.' The other woman raised an eyebrow. 'Let me guess.'

But how could she unpack the chaos in her brain? Where

would she even start? She'd lost her head to a man who frustrated every attempt she made to connect with anything important in his life, past or future. And today she'd let her guard down. There'd be a price to pay for the insanity of these last few weeks, of that she was bleakly certain – though as yet she didn't know what that price might be.

'Would tea help?'

'Maybe a quick one.' If she dallied long enough, she might not be back until Tegen's shift had finished.

She drifted between tables and shelves while Morwenna boiled the kettle and rinsed crockery in the stockroom, remembering how made up she'd been to find that dragonfly brooch. *Wretched thing.* So alluring on the surface, while potentially harbouring something unfathomable and disturbing deeper down. *Now* there's *a metaphor if ever I needed one*, she muttered to herself.

'Wenna, can you tell me more about that brooch I bought?' she called out. 'Or anything that came with it?'

Her friend reappeared with mugs. 'Jill Glover's auntie's stuff? Most of it's over there now.' Morwenna nodded towards a wooden table bearing a range of dishes and trays, and set down the tea close by.

'Jill Glover – that's the name of the person who brought them in?'

'It is,' said Morwenna. 'Nice lady. She's been donating pieces every now and then, ever since I opened the shop. Apparently she was given a box of her aunt's keepsakes years ago but forgot about it until she decided to put her house on the market and cleared the attic. Her aunt died in a fire, did I mention that?'

'You did.'

Joss bent over the display, examining every object, wordlessly entreating each one to offer up its history. She remembered the paperweight, the scorched cigarette holder and the fruit knife, but Morwenna had cleaned and priced up many more items since her earlier visit. She picked up a framed photograph faded to sepia, showing the frontage of a grand old manor house boasting small-paned windows above the granite columns of an imposing entranceway – not unlike Wheal Blazey in style, though very much bigger. Maybe that was why it looked strangely familiar. Or maybe she'd seen it before?

A much smaller photo, matchbox-sized, was displayed a few inches to the left: the headshot of a rather beautiful middle-aged woman, dark hair gathered loosely into a chignon over a lacy collar. Joss peered at it intently as Morwenna leaned over her shoulder. 'The tragic aunt, I believe,' she said.

'So, do you think the brooch was hers?'

'I think it's a fair bet. Striking, isn't she? God bless the poor unfortunate soul.'

Joss's imagination exploded with questions and possibilities – too many to properly grasp. None of them simple, logical or obvious.

In the right-hand corner of the table was a brass plaque, engraved and dated in copperplate. She stooped to read the words aloud. *Regional Winners, Under-16s First XI. Raven House.* The plaque was twenty-three years old.

'Raven House?' She turned back to the photo of the stately old manor. 'Raven House! Guy told me about this place. The building's been restored recently. It's all swanky apartments now.'

'Interesting.' Morwenna wiggled her eyebrows. 'Perhaps one of the residents will recognise it and make me an offer.'

Joss stared at the photo, her mind beginning to churn. On Guy's recommendation, she'd googled the place and discovered it had burned down. That might explain the aunt's appalling demise, the damaged items. But something else nagged at her

– something connected with the blurb she recalled from the website.

Under 16s First XI.

She stood abruptly upright. 'A *children's* home. Before it was rebuilt – Raven House was a *children's* home.'

'That does ring a faint bell.' Morwenna frowned at her friend's shocked expression, then examined the picture herself. 'I don't recall Jill mentioning it. Must have been a while ago.'

'Twenty years at least.' Joss touched the copperplate with her fingertips. All at once she felt uncomfortably hot, a little shaky. She had to be on her own, she decided; she needed space and time to absorb the significance of this discovery. And then, maybe she could get McCalvey on his own and ask him…

…ask him what?

'Sorry, Wen. Thanks for the tea – but I need to go.'

Morwenna stared as she recovered the mug. 'Are you OK, girlfriend? You've gone a bit weird on me.'

'No! I mean, *yes*! Sorry. I've just remembered something.' She grabbed her bags, waved apologetically, and headed for the door.

Different narratives buzzed like turbulent wasps in her brain as she hurried back to Wheal Blazey – so much so that it took several moments for her to register the ominously silent tableau that greeted her arrival in the kitchen.

Bridget and Katie stood side by side, white faced, eyes like headlamps on full beam. Her heart plummeted. 'Where's Tegen?' she asked.

'Gone home,' Bridget told her. 'She said she had a headache.'

'And my mother?'

The girls exchanged glances before Bridget added hesitantly, 'She went to see if Ollie was in his room.'

Joss set down her shopping. 'In his room? Is something wrong?'

A terrible pause preceded what Joss instinctively knew would be bad news. Katie broke the silence. 'He seemed a bit… upset,' she said.

Joss held her breath. 'Why?'

With rising apprehension she watched Katie plant her feet, steadying herself. A sassy, insightful, resilient girl, she thought. But maybe – fingers crossed – not wholly unsympathetic.

'Tegen said…' The teenager stopped to examine her nails.

'Said what exactly?'

With a quick *here we go* look at Bridget, Katie lifted her chin to meet Joss's eyes. 'That my dad was kissing you.'

'I see.' The blood in Joss's veins turned to ice. 'Anything else?'

'She said – her words, not mine, sorry – that you were all over each other. Like, the two of you needed to get a room.'

For God's sake. 'And Ollie heard this?'

Katie nodded. 'He had a sketch pad with him, he wanted to show your mum something he'd drawn, but then he ran off.'

Joss eyed the two of them in turn, though her cheeks felt hot and her vision was blurring. 'Well, thanks for your honesty.' *It's allowed*, she repeated to herself without much conviction. *We're grown-ups.* 'If you're done for the day, I'll see you both tomorrow.'

Bridget sidled out, but Katie lingered. The gaze she returned to Joss was steady, solemn and knowing. She shook her head with what looked like practised indifference.

'I told Ollie not to worry about it,' she said. 'I told him that my dad… well… that my dad's not into serious relationships. I said it was nothing, just a bit of fun, that it wouldn't last. I thought it might… reassure him.'

Joss gaped at her. 'What did he say?'

'He didn't say anything. But… I don't think he went to his room.'

'Where do you think he went?'

Tentacles of fear took chilling hold as Katie glanced towards the window.

'I think he went down to the boat.'

SIXTEEN

If he could, McCalvey would have stayed tinkering with Kara's fixtures and fittings the entire afternoon, padding up and down the warm boards of her deck in his bare feet, salt caking his hair, the sun on his face. Safely moored in the little cove, the hull rocked gently in a micro-landscape of crystalline water and sweet-smelling cliffs as the ocean whispered in the distance. Comforting to a restless spirit. His, at least.

His brain and body clung to physical echoes of Joss – her scent, her skin, the shape and texture of her, by now softly familiar to his touch. But when he shut his eyes to conjure her bright face, that same old admonishing voice muddied all the pleasure of it, hissing *where the hell do you think you're going with this?* like poison in his ear.

He was painfully aware that his history with women – especially when things got serious – wasn't pretty. And it spooked him that his daughter was only half a mile away, working for the woman who'd been in his arms for most of the last hour. Added to which, the Tegen thing was a real bugger…

Well what had he expected? He was an idiot.

Not much he could do about it now. He'd just have to wait for things to unravel. One way or another, they always did.

Preoccupied with the mainsail's temperamental cleat, he didn't hear footsteps – but gradually sensed a presence silently watching from the jetty. *Joss?* He swivelled to welcome her back, but instead found himself face to face with Ollie.

His unexpected visitor shattered the startled silence. 'What are you doing?'

'Not much, Ollie.' McCalvey shrugged and indicated the problem hardware. 'Sorting out a few jobs. Enjoying the peace. How about you?'

'I came to check,' Ollie said.

'Check what?'

'That you'd still be here.'

A challenge in the boy's tone prompted McCalvey to pull himself upright, inclining his head. 'Well, here I am. Did you want me for something?'

'You've been with my mum.'

'Sorry?'

The blue eyes drilling into his were fierce. 'I know she's been here with you. You've been meeting her. Meeting her on this boat.'

Oh Christ. Not now. McCalvey's smile faltered. For a moment they stared at each other like cats in disputed territory – shocked, wary, instinctively hostile. *What do I say? What does he know?* He took a step forward, attempting an expression of innocent curiosity.

'You've been wanting her to come here,' Ollie burst out, 'so you can *get* with her. It's why you brought Kara to this place. You planned it. That's all you really wanted – to shag my mum. It was never about the weather.' The accusation contorted his face into something wizened and ugly.

'*What?*'

'I've found you out.' Ollie was glowering now, his voice strained and hoarse. 'You want to get with her. You're trying to take advantage. You want her to have sex with you.'

'Ollie! For God's sake.' On the boy's lips the words were repugnant, grotesque. McCalvey flinched as if he'd taken a blow to the stomach.

'Well, it's true, isn't it?'

'Where on earth did you get that idea?' As if he didn't know. *Jesus wept.* He stepped forward and swung himself onto the jetty, words tumbling uselessly in his head. He needed to play for time.

'It's obvious now, obvious. I should have seen it. What a twat.' Ollie looked forlornly at his feet and shook his head. 'The girls – they all know. They all know what you're like. Tegen saw everything. And *I* know now.'

The girls? Katie? *Bloody hell.* 'What I'm like? Meaning what exactly?'

'I trusted you!' Ollie whimpered. His nose had started to run. 'I thought you were cool. But you're just like… just like…'

McCalvey raised a warning finger, his voice stern. 'You've been listening to nonsense, Ollie. Tegen's imagining things.' But the ashen-faced boy shrank from his hand.

'Katie says you don't do relationships. She says to you it's all just a bit of fun.'

'Katie has *no idea.*'

'So tell me it's not true,' Ollie demanded. 'Tell me you're not shagging my mum.'

McCalvey's mouth had completely dried. He ran his tongue along his lower lip, tasting acid. 'I'm not taking advantage, Ollie,' he said. The more graphic, specific charge would have to wait until the storm in his brain subsided.

'What *are* you doing, then?'

He inhaled, inwardly counting to ten. 'Well – I like her. I

like both of you,' he said. 'You know I do.'

'Don't treat me like a child. I've seen you look at her. I'm not a baby. You want to get with her. Everything makes sense now.'

'You're wrong, Ollie. Stop. It's not about that.'

'You don't respect her,' Ollie hissed. 'You don't care what she wants. You'll never make her happy.'

McCalvey was perplexed. '*Of course* I respect her. And believe me, if your mum didn't want—' He retreated in alarm as Ollie lurched towards him, arms flailing, his face crumpled with fury.

'Shut up, *shut up*. How do you know what my mum wants? You've got no right… You don't understand, you don't know what she's been through. What if she doesn't think she has any choice? If she's not strong enough? If she's not allowed to be—'

'Ollie?' With growing horror he watched Ollie choke up, the verbal assault dying in his throat as a convulsion bent him at the waist. 'Buddy?' He risked advancing closer, murmuring, '*Hey*', but the distraught boy jerked out of range.

This was beyond surreal. He felt disoriented, stupidly on the ropes. Surely he could overcome Ollie's anger with logic and a bit of goodwill? But he had a bad feeling Joss's son was way past listening to reason. Deep, dark waves of unhappiness were crashing towards him – a volatile ocean of misery, too treacherous to navigate safely. McCalvey's own defensive indignation leached away. He knew grief when he saw it.

'I try to make her happy when she's with me,' he ventured.

'Yeah. You think. But you're not really *with* her, are you? In the end, you'll just wreck everything. Everything will be crap all over again.'

'Ollie, calm down and listen to me.'

'Why? You'll only lie.'

'I won't lie to you, Ollie.'

'You will, you *will*. *This* is all a lie.' Ollie gestured wildly at the boat. 'Taking us sailing on Kara, as if you want to be nice. Sucking up to me, when it's all about *her* and getting what you want. Don't think I can't see it. And then when it suits you—'

'Ollie, surely you know I've been impressed at the way you—'

'–when it suits you and you've had your fun, you'll disappear. In the end, you'll just *leave*. Leave her in a mess.'

'Ollie—'

'Well, if you're going to leave, *leave now*. Before you really hurt my mum. Don't spin it out, don't make it any worse.'

They were both breathing heavily – Ollie hyperventilating, McCalvey unbalanced by the huge, scorching eyes, struggling to think. What could he say to put this boy at ease that was reassuringly and indisputably true? What could he *honestly* say?

'Don't treat me like an idiot,' Ollie challenged him. 'You're going to go eventually, aren't you?'

McCalvey grimaced and turned to stare at the distant horizon. *Am I?*

God help me, I don't know.

Fog thickened and swirled madly in his head, generating a pressure he couldn't deal with. A debilitating, familiar pressure.

How can I promise him I won't?

Ollie was pointing accusingly into the centre of his chest, his face chalk-white and his eyes wet. 'She loved my dad, but something happened... things changed. *He* changed. And he really hurt her. Maybe she thinks someone might replace him – but no-one ever will. She's not going through all that again. She has *me* now. I won't let it happen.'

'Ollie, I wouldn't... I'm really not...'

Not what? Words failed him. *Shit.* He cast around from side to side, then looked down, raking his hair, as if he'd somehow mislaid the script.

'Go away,' Ollie said. 'We need you to go away. Or I'll stop you. I'll stop you ever coming near her again. I'll make you disappear like I did my dad – you and your stupid boat.'

Like I did *my dad*? What kind of twisted psychodrama was playing out in the wretched lad's imagination? The boy was completely in crisis.

He shook his head. 'Ollie, this is all wrong. I know you and your mum have been through a nightmare, and I'm sorry. Believe me, I understand how you must be feeling—'

'*Fuck you*,' Ollie screamed, swiping tears away. 'Just *go*. Leave us alone.'

From the coast path, they heard a shout and simultaneously turned in alarm. '*Ollie!*' Joss was hurrying towards the cove as fast as the uneven track would allow.

The expression on Ollie's face became beseeching, bitter and desperate. Fearful too, McCalvey realised. *Lost.*

And then he fled.

McCalvey watched him veer to the right at the end of the jetty, away from Kara, away from his mother, escaping at speed in the direction of town. Towards Little Roslyn beach, he guessed. It came back to him like a hammer blow, crushingly vivid – the mental image of himself as a child, Ollie's age, raging in despair at the sea.

Poor little bugger.

'Cal?' Joss gripped his arm. The anguish in her eyes cut him like a knife. 'What did he say?'

'Well, thanks to Tegen, he knows there's something going on between us. I tried to play it down, but—' He frowned in the direction Ollie had taken and took a breath. 'Basically, he warned me off.'

'Oh *Cal.*'

'He thinks I'll hurt you, Joss.' Taking her hand in his, he stared down at their joined fingers. 'He wants to protect you.'

She pulled away. 'I need to go after him.'

Apprehension flooded him like nausea. 'I should warn you – he was having a real meltdown. It was a bit over the top.'

'Oh God, I'm so sorry. I worried he'd take it badly. He's... he's—'

'Troubled,' McCalvey answered for her. 'Beyond stressed. And Joss – he said something really strange.'

She stared at him for a moment before averting her eyes. That, he pondered, seemed strange too.

'He said he'd make me disappear *like he did his dad*. There's something in his head that seems – I don't know – distorted. Pretty dark. He wasn't interested in a discussion, that much was clear.' Her fretful, wide-eyed silence caused him to frown and lean closer, mirroring her unease. 'I didn't know what to say to him, Joss.'

'He'll come round,' she said. 'He *will*.'

Unconvinced, he shook his head.

'Meet me for coffee tomorrow.' Her tone was urgent, pleading. 'Please, Cal. Can you do that? I'll make it alright with him, I promise. And maybe… maybe I can try to explain things.'

'*Explain* things?' He looked at her askance, but nodded OK. Joss reached to squeeze his hand, braving a smile before spinning away down the jetty in search of her son.

McCalvey watched until she'd vanished, foreboding descending on him like a shroud. A feeling of utter helplessness – of being worse than useless faced with her distress – made him groan out loud. And something like guilt – like *shame* – began, treacherously, to gnaw.

He pulled himself back on deck, retrieved his tools, tidied and locked up, the prospect of another hour messing about on the boat having lost its appeal. Better to dump his stuff back at the apartment and head for the marina, he thought. *Keep busy. Keep out of everyone's way.*

Trudging home, his hand closed around the pager in his jacket pocket. Selfishly he'd have welcomed the distraction of a shout, the focus and exhilaration of ploughing through lumpy seas with spray in his face and salt chafing his skin – but the better part of him was glad the human activity massing on the water today was uneventful. With all its problems, setbacks and misunderstandings, life was precious.

Joss was a survivor, he told himself. Ollie was wrong. She had choices, she was resilient. She was kind, funny and thoughtful; and she made him feel...

Hardly conscious of it, he slowed his pace until he stopped altogether where the harbour ended, just yards from the chandlery and his apartment. Above him, seagulls cruised and heckled. Tethered boats rode the current like shoals of fish.

She made him feel...

Whole.

But they'd reached a crossroads. Something had to give. Maybe they'd meet for coffee in the morning and she'd amaze him by describing Ollie's change of heart. Or hers.

He'd given up trying to predict outcomes and consequences a long time ago. If there was a God, he ruminated, he was a fickle one. Whimsical and cruel. And possibly mad.

He hoicked his toolbox firmly under an arm and started to walk on.

'Mackie?'

A figure approached him from across the street – tall and slender, a man somewhat younger than himself, a fleece hood covering most of his head.

'It's you, isn't it? Mack?'

McCalvey's heart seemed to miss several beats, then jerk violently back into action at twice its accustomed rate. As he peered in the direction of the voice, thin fingers clawed the hoodie back to reveal a pale face and shining blue eyes. All along one side, from brow to jaw, McCalvey tracked the purple seam of corrugated flesh, and gasped.

'It's me. Tyler.'

Tyler? Though his tongue and lips tried to replicate the name, no sound emerged.

'I'm over from Canada. I have a partner now – Brett – and we're touring the west country. I've been trying so hard to find you. *Jesus,* Mackie, there's a lot I need to say. Is there somewhere we can talk?'

It was like being sucked off a cliff. He felt short of air, unsteady on his feet, desperate. 'Tyler?' he whispered at last, and the other man pointed to his face and nodded.

But someone else was drawing close.

'Dad!'

Katie had caught sight of him from the foot of the apartment steps and was coming towards him now, her features creased with worry, palms pressed together in apology. She failed to notice the other man, who quickly covered his head before retreating a few feet.

'Dad – I'm *so* sorry. Is everything alright?'

He shook himself. Her anxious presence galvanised and buoyed him. Lately he'd started to think of Katie as a rare pearl, inexplicably emerging from the tangled weed and detritus of his life. She was *his*. He owed her stability and protection.

It seemed suddenly important.

He faced the other man and shrugged. 'Sorry, buddy. I think you have the wrong guy.'

His inquisitor drew himself rigidly straight. 'Don't say that. It's you, Mack. I know it's you. Mackie. Aidan. Don't walk away.'

'Not me, I'm afraid,' McCalvey asserted, with a brief glance at Katie's startled expression. 'And I have to be somewhere with my daughter right now. I'm sorry. I'm not the man you're looking for. I hope you find him.'

He slipped his arm through Katie's, turning her firmly towards home. Though she eyed him with intense curiosity, she matched his stride and they moved rapidly away.

Ten steps on, he risked a backward glance. The hooded figure was sagging against the wall, shaking his head. But he looked up just in time to meet McCalvey's eyes; and in a voice loaded with regret, he called out, '*I hope you find him too.*'

SEVENTEEN

He knew she'd track him down – it was obvious from the contraction of his thin shoulders, the way his head drooped when she was fifteen feet way. Slouched against a lump of granite by a giant rockpool, his left knee was clutched hard to his chest while his right leg kept him braced, toes below the pool's surface, sand clinging to his jeans. Both trainers had been thrown with ferocious disregard several yards along the beach.

Despite her best intentions, emotion broke in her voice as she drew close. 'Oh, *Ollie*. What did you say to him?'

The eyes that confronted hers were red-rimmed. 'I had to let him know, Mum.'

'Let him know what?'

'That I'd sussed him. That I know what he's really like. He needs to leave you alone.'

For a few uncertain seconds she fixed her eyes on the tourists spreading their bright towels, patting table-tennis balls across lines drawn roughly in the sand, squealing as they splashed in the ice-cold shallows. A breeze whipped hair across her face. When she finally stepped forward to hug him, he stayed doggedly still. *Not shrugging me off, at least,* she consoled herself.

'He had to understand, Mum.'

'Ollie – you have no idea about him,' she said. 'No idea. Whatever made you act so wildly?'

'The girls said. And I've *seen* him. I'm not stupid.'

'Tell me. Tell me what you think they said.'

Despite the encouragement of her fingers beneath his chin he refused to meet her eyes. 'That he was... *all over you,*' he muttered. 'Kissing you and stuff. On *Kara.*'

'Tegen may have thought that, but she was miles away from the boat. She's a scandalmonger.'

'She wasn't making it up,' he countered, thrusting out his bottom lip. 'And Katie says he leads people on, he does what he likes and then he leaves.'

'That's not right, Ollie.'

'How do you *know?*'

She raised her eyes to the sky, inhaling deeply. Could she offer a rational answer? A way to make him see that the man they were talking about had sparked her back to life, made her feel good about herself, made her feel wanted again? *For heaven's sake.* It was impossible to explain to her twelve-year-old son the way she felt when McCalvey made love to her; how attentive he was to her needs and desires. So much so that at times she almost believed – beyond all reason – that he was fearful of disappointing her.

But she couldn't deny his evasiveness. A restlessness about him. A malaise buried deep that she'd chosen to ignore.

'I just do,' she said.

He kicked out in frustration. 'All he wants is to *get* with you. He'll spoil everything. For both of us.'

'He *won't,* Ollie.' She shook her head vehemently. 'Cal is a good guy.'

'So was Dad, once.'

The impact was electric. She recoiled from the anger distorting his flawless face. 'Ollie – *no*. Dear God, no. What happened with Dad – it will never happen again.'

He looked up at her properly for the first time. 'I remember the dinghy sailing we did,' he told her. 'Sundays when he'd make us breakfast. Holiday barbecues. Playing with him here, *here*, on this beach. He said he'd always be around, pointing me in the right direction. I used to think he was special, that he could do anything. You did too.'

Joss traced his cheek with her thumb, a chasm in her heart yawning wide. 'Yes, I did,' she murmured. 'But your Dad… he lost himself, Ollie. Over time, he just—'

'*Don't!*' He sagged in her arms as she pressed him against herself.

'It won't happen again,' she whispered. She kissed the top of his head. 'You don't have to worry.'

For a while they stood together in a fragile silence. Joss turned to look at the distant surf, the cheerful bodyboarders, parents and toddlers excavating moats around lopsided castles, while Ollie stared down at the rockpool. Then something caught his attention, and he wriggled free.

'A starfish!'

He scooped it out and held it towards her. A peace offering? she wondered. At least a distraction, thank God. The delicate rays were bleached out, spindly and stiff, the living creature long gone.

'It's just a skeleton,' he mumbled.

'Fascinating though. Still looks perfect. A lovely find, Ol.'

He was quiet a moment, stroking the rough surface with a fingertip. Joss checked her pockets for space. 'Maybe take it home for the bathroom windowsill?'

He scowled and threw it hard against the nearby rock as

if it had stung him. The frail structure broke up immediately, delicate tentacles disintegrating into gritty shards.

'Ugly dead thing,' he hissed. 'I hate it.'

'Ollie!'

She bent to retrieve the debris, readying herself to deliver a few sharp words. But the reprimand died in her throat as she registered the tears coursing down his cheeks.

'He'll *hurt you*,' he moaned.

'Oh sweetheart.' She gripped his shoulders. 'You've got this all wrong. There's so much you don't understand.'

'That's what *he'd* say. But you don't really know.' He wiped the back of a hand across his wet face. 'And I think I'm right.'

'No, Ollie, you're not.'

'You'll see,' he growled. Suddenly he seemed very calm, coldly sure of his ground. 'He's a liar and he doesn't mean what he says. You'll see.'

Cal is a good guy, she'd insisted. He'd never lied to her, as far as she could tell. But was that really so different from choosing what *not* to reveal?

If they could just get beyond this maddening ambush, she'd ask him what he knew about Raven House. Or at least the owner of that brooch. The spectre of Jill Glover's tragic aunt had begun to stalk her imagination like the protagonist of a gothic novel. *Rebecca* maybe – a mysterious beauty haunting lesser mortals trying to get on with their lives.

With Ollie finally asleep, she took a mug of strong coffee to her room, charged her phone, stacked her pillows, and began scouring the National Archive in pursuit of twenty-year-old news.

At last, in the early hours, the key words *Raven House* and *Glover* yielded a few nuggets of gold. Joss rubbed her sore eyes, scrolled through disinterred column inches, then scrolled again, heart thumping, as fragments reeled in her brain.

Cornish Guardian: September 1994

Erin Glover, sister of the Right Honourable Roderick Glover MP, has been confirmed as Residential Manager of Raven House Children's Home. Chairman of Trustees Loic Penrose welcomed the appointment, commending Ms. Glover's dedication and long experience in the social care sector.

West Briton: December 1998

Local businesses have this year donated an impressive 1.5 million pounds to Raven House Children's Home. Speaking at this year's annual Cornwall Enterprise dinner, Manager Erin Glover expressed thanks on behalf of the Board and outlined plans to further improve the property and extend its facilities.

Cornish Guardian: March 2001

Forty-five children and residential staff were evacuated from Raven House Children's Home at 7.00pm on Saturday when fire broke out in a heavily timbered wing. One fatality has been confirmed.

Police have yet to formerly identify the body, but it is believed to be that of the home's long-serving Manager, Erin Glover.

Western Morning News: March 2001

Tributes have been paid to Erin Glover, Manager of Raven House, who perished in the care home's devastating fire at the weekend.

In a statement issued by the Trustee Board, members have strongly refuted claims made by an unidentified whistle-blower in the weeks preceding the tragedy, that failings in pastoral care were putting children at risk.

'These malicious and unfounded allegations do Erin and her team a great disservice and sully the memory of a highly respected figure who did a great deal for her local community and the vulnerable youngsters in her charge.'

Moonlight from the open window was transforming the room's contours and furnishings into eerily attentive silhouettes. Joss sat for a moment, staring into shadow, before pulling open her bedside drawer. Her fingertips traced the outline of the slender dragonfly.

So you belonged to a remarkable woman, little thing. I wonder what secrets you've been keeping all these years. What dramas have you been part of?

Sooner or later, she promised herself, she'd find out.

In the sunless rear corner of a backstreet café, her heart jumped, as it always did, to see McCalvey strolling through the door, heading for her table.

He eyed her a little pensively before taking the opposite seat and asking, 'How are things at home?'

'A bit calmer, I think.'

Crikey, he looks rough. Rumpled, unshaven and hollow-eyed, she thought, as if he hadn't slept all night. *Though I'm a fine one to judge.*

They ordered coffee, both glancing at the clock as the waitress took their order, conscious they had to get back to work. While they waited for their drinks, they talked about the café's decor, the guests who'd departed from Wheal Blazey that morning, McCalvey's latest client, happily in receipt of a beautifully restored hull – anything and nothing.

This is ridiculous, she couldn't help fuming. They were grown-ups. They had a relationship, for God's sake – but a combination of Tegen's misplaced ardour and Ollie's distrust had all but shipwrecked them. *Surely it doesn't need to be this complicated.* She rehearsed the speech she'd put together during her walk into town: *We can sort things out, people just need to get used to it. Used to* us.

She smiled at him, mining tenuous reserves of positivity. 'So… any overnight thoughts?'

For just a second he matched her smile. Then he turned to look for the waitress.

'Cal?' He wasn't quite *with* her, she thought. 'How are you feeling about things? What do you think we should do?'

'Do?'

'I'm wondering, you know, whether we should be more open about how things are between us. You hate sneaking about, Cal, and so do I.'

He acknowledged the comment with a small nod, but didn't reply. It occurred to her his preoccupation with the whereabouts of their coffee might be a ploy.

'Maybe it's time we bit the bullet and told everyone.'

'I don't know, Joss.' He shuffled round to face her, not quite meeting her eyes. 'What about Ollie? You thought you might be able to make it alright with him, but after yesterday's encounter I'd have said that was nigh on impossible.'

It was her turn to frown at the servery while she gathered herself. 'He has his reasons,' she murmured.

'So what's going on with him? You said you'd try to explain.'

'It's just—' Joss chewed her bottom lip. 'There are things he can't forget. Images, noises… memories he has to deal with… '

He looked at her in unblinking silence as the waitress emerged from behind the counter to deliver two Americanos, which neither of them touched. Once she'd retreated, Joss swallowed hard and took a shaky breath. 'Before Felix died… that last night, the night I told you about… '

McCalvey sat back very slowly. Joss took in his parted lips, deep lines tightening a face leaching all colour, and knew she didn't need to complete the sentence.

'He was *there*,' he finished for her. 'Ollie saw what happened.' He tipped his head back, his eyes raking the ceiling. '*Jesus.*'

Joss laid a hand over his, but he seemed oblivious. 'It was only last November,' she said. 'So, you can see why he needs more time.'

'God knows what that must have done to him.' Dropping his head, he stared into her face. 'Fucking hell, Joss—'

'So, come with me. Please. Let's talk to him together.' She worked her fingers between his. 'I think it would help.'

He looked sick, she thought miserably. *As if I've speared him through the heart.* 'If both of us spoke to him, he might be reassured.'

He dragged his eyes away from her, towards the door.

'Cal?'

But he seemed mesmerised by the slab of daylight beyond the dismal gloom of the café. The detachment of his body language chilled and confounded her. *Don't withdraw from me now*, she wanted to rail at him. *We can deal with this. Look at me, engage with me.* Instead, she released his hand and addressed him in as steady a voice as she could manage.

'You won't talk about it. But I know that you understand loss.'

The eyes he turned back to her were dark with shock. She held his gaze for a long moment, watching him intently, sensing him transition from resistance to dismay, then to undeniable sadness. Profound, unreachable sadness. At last he gave her his full attention.

'Of course he needs time,' he said gruffly. 'But right now I can't believe that hearing any more from me won't make everything ten times worse.'

'I don't know what else to suggest.'

He picked the teaspoon out of his saucer and toyed with it for a few seconds. Then he replaced it, sat forward, and stretched a hand towards her across the table. 'Maybe there's no harm in leaving things to settle for a bit.'

'What do you mean, settle?' Despite the conciliatory gesture, she noticed he was finding it hard to look at her.

'I've actually been thinking... about taking a few days off.' He glanced up, checking her expression – which she kept studiedly neutral – then lowered his eyes again. 'Katie needs to get back to Bristol. The new term's coming up, a new school year. Sixth form. I thought I might go back on the train with her.'

'Oh?' The air around her began to thin.

'She tells me she likes the idea.' He shrugged. 'A bit of space might be helpful, Joss. In terms of letting things... cool off.'

He's been preparing this. Now he'd said it, she could see him relax.

'Just a few days, my lovely – a week, tops. Her mother's been saying for a long time I ought to visit, to kind of... normalise things between us, I guess.'

She blinked at him, mentally urging her rational, empathetic side to kick in, telling herself not to panic. For a few seconds more they sat in ruminative silence. Then a thread of logic began to weave itself into her brain, tamping down the fear his plan had provoked. *Of course he should go*, she scolded herself. *She's his daughter, he wants to be supportive.*

'That sounds... constructive,' she said at last.

His gratitude and relief were palpable. He rested his palm against her cheek, and for the first time that morning she saw the dark eyes soften. 'It probably *is* helpful timing, to be honest,' he said.

She nodded, but the press of moisture behind her eyes betrayed the agitation she was fighting hard to suppress.

'It'll be OK, Joss.' He leaned forward to stroke her hair. 'It'll be OK.'

It? What about *we?*

'Cal—' But what could she say? It made sense – the timing might be helpful. There was definitely a logic to it. *Don't overthink it,* she counselled herself.

'It'll be OK, Joss,' he said again. Then he picked up the bill and got to his feet.

They were having sex in the dark.

It was scary and disgusting. He was pushing and grunting like a mad pig. She didn't want it, she kept saying no.

I didn't know what to do.

I shouted at him to leave her alone. I punched his arm but he didn't stop. Mum was closing her eyes and moaning. So I picked up the candle lamp and I smacked him on the head. He keeled over and hit the floor.

I really thought I'd killed him. But when I went towards Mum he got up, all sweaty and groggy. Blood was coming from his hair. I don't think he knew where he was. And then he started to cry.

He kept saying I'm sorry, I'm sorry, that he'd fucked everything up. He tried to touch Mum's cheek but I pushed his hand away. Then he looked at me and said, I suppose you hate me too.

The words just burst out. YES I DO AND I WISH YOU WERE DEAD.

He didn't say anything else. He grabbed his head like it was going to explode. Then he stumbled away and the front door slammed.

But I didn't mean it. I didn't.

I just wanted him to leave her alone.

He was my dad.

EIGHTEEN

So now she knows everything I said was true.

She thought he'd only be gone a few days. But that was in August.

Tomorrow's the first day of October.

Lisa Donaldson had just finished icing a cake in her spotlessly white kitchen when McCalvey arrived at the back door. Thirty feet behind him, at the end of a gravelled path, the guest annexe – converted from an unwanted garage – was just visible behind a screen of tidy escallonias. He was their guinea pig, she'd told him; they were thinking of letting it as an Air Bnb.

'Hey you,' she said. 'You're late up. Did you sleep?'

'Kind of.'

'Tea?'

It was 0930, an overcast Saturday. Beyond the sash window, grey clouds hung like neglected washing. He eased himself gratefully into the chair she pulled back, and nodded. 'Tea would be great.'

She filled two mugs and fetched milk from the fridge. A straightforward, practical woman – still classically pretty, he thought, as he followed her movements: blonde, slim, blue-eyed. The looks he'd fallen for all those years ago when they first got messily drunk together in a Plymouth club. Now she was a cheerfully efficient homebody on evenings and weekends; and during the week, a senior legal secretary for a well-regarded firm in the city. Competent, conscientious, thoroughly dependable.

He studied her with a wistful smile. Lisa always just *got on with things*. For her, life wasn't complicated. Everything had a solution – you only had to apply common sense. Possibly why he'd been attracted to her in the first place. Probably why he'd found it impossible to stay.

She settled with him at the table. 'You look blown away,' she said.

He rubbed his eyes. 'Sorry. Need a shot of caffeine to make me human.'

'A shot?' she teased. 'Better get down to Starbucks and ask them to service the tanks.'

'Watch it, you.'

She grinned. 'Well it's the weekend now, Cal, you can relax a bit. You've been a star doing handyman jobs and running Katie around for me these last few weeks. It's been a big help.'

Glumly, he rotated the mug his hands. 'Not much compensation for being the invisible man all these years.'

She flicked fine hair over her shoulder and touched his wrist. 'Well, you're here *now*,' she said. 'And it's been good for Katie to see more of you. We're doing great, Katie and me, everything's worked out for us. You can see that.' Her eyes lingered on him with unfiltered curiosity. 'I'm not sure the same's true of you, though.'

'Oh, I'm OK.'

'Really? Is that why you've been hanging on here since the summer, moping about like a permanent wet weekend?'

He leaned back and stretched. 'I just needed a break.'

'Cal. Something's going on with you, I don't know what. You look so... unhappy.' She peered at him more closely. 'I've heard you walking around in the early hours. I know you're not sleeping.'

He shifted his gaze to the window. *God, how I wish I could sleep.* The recurring dream, the immersive personal horror-movie he'd never felt able to share with her, seemed to have intensified lately. It was scaring the hell out of him.

Sometimes when he closed his eyes – even during the day now – he could hear the same boy screaming, trapped in the same airless room, desperately pounding his fists against the walls. *I want to get out, I want to get out. Open the door. I can't breathe. I can't breathe.*

Then came the pleading. Terrible, abject pleading. *Please – let me go. Leave me alone.*

Make it stop.

Or was that a different boy?

Everything leaking into his midnight brain was a mess. A new voice had begun to percolate through the foul stew: *I'll make you disappear. You and your stupid boat.* And that woman... that woman was in his dreams again last night. Tall and solitary, pitch-black against a backdrop of blindingly fierce light. Her voice soft.

Don't worry. I won't be gone long.

He'd snapped into consciousness in the early hours, drenched with sweat, shaking and incoherent. Then he'd stumbled to the bathroom, where he'd shocked himself by vomiting into the basin.

He stared at the hand Lisa extended towards him. 'I'm fine,' he said. 'But I'm starting to think...'

She sipped her tea while he fought to order his thoughts.

'...that I shouldn't be imposing on you any longer.' He leaned back in the chair. 'You've got your own life here, you need to be moving things on with Alvaro. And by the way, he's been fantastic. I really like him.'

The dapper, gentle Italian had warmed to him, genuinely interested to finally meet Katie's father, confident in his own unbreakably solid relationship with her mother. They'd even spent a few evenings out drinking together, Alvaro declaring with admiration, 'You are a such a *fixer* of things, Cal! You have fixed Lisa's shelves and re-hung her doors and re-wired her lights – I can do *none* of these things.'

But that's just stuff, he'd replied. *Not people*. And Alvaro had laughed and bumped a fist against his shoulder.

'I think it's mutual,' Lisa said. She eyed him over the rim of her cup. 'So, what's next? Taking off for the Med in that boat of yours?'

He shrugged. 'That was the plan.' Six months ago, it had seemed like such a good one.

She put down her cup and looked at it for a moment. 'To be honest, Cal,' she said, 'you're much easier to be around than you used to be.'

'Yeah, right. Only because I don't have the energy to be my usual pain in the ass self.'

She pouted, inclining her head. 'You were never a pain in the ass. You were just—'

'Just...?'

The atmosphere was fractured by Katie, wriggling into the leather jacket she'd snatched from a hook in the hallway as she made a beeline through the kitchen for the biscuit tin. 'Just off to meet the girls for brunch,' she announced. 'Morning, Dad.'

'Morning, lovely.'

Their eyes connected briefly. It occurred to him that Katie had the same features as her mother – though maybe with more *edge*. He'd only recently noticed.

Clamping a piece of shortbread between her teeth, with impressive ventriloquial skills she managed to say, 'I'll be back for dinner, mum, see you later. Love you.'

McCalvey watched her hug her mother tight – a gesture so natural, so affectionately familiar, it brought a lump to his throat. She gave him a brief wave before she swept out. She'd spent less than a minute in the room.

He gazed after her, bereft.

'The tsunami that is Katie,' Lisa grinned. 'Sweet sixteen. Oh to have that stamina again.'

He sighed and turned back. 'You were saying something about me not being a pain in the ass?'

'Oh – I don't know, Cal.' She tossed her head. 'You were always so restless. Always wanting something different. We've talked about this a million times. I never really felt... I had *all* of you.'

'Well,' he murmured. 'I'm sorry I made you feel that way.'

She covered his hand with hers. 'It stopped mattering a long time ago,' she said. 'But we were good together for a while, weren't we?'

'We were.'

This is the family I nearly had, he reflected as he finished his tea. She had *nearly* been the right woman for him, the mother of his unique, rediscovered daughter – and this could *nearly* have been the perfect scenario: a pleasant house in an elegant, attractive city; secure jobs; nice car; garden, dog – a normal home.

Nearly. But not quite.

'I think I should sort myself out and leave you to it,' he said.

Her mood seemed to change as she stood to clear the crockery. For a moment she hovered at the window, staring into the garden; then she glanced over her shoulder and said, 'There's something I'd like to suggest.'

'Ah. Why do I suddenly have a sinking feeling?'

'Cal. I should tell you – Alvaro will probably move in permanently soon.'

'Well, that's great news,' he said. He meant it. 'I can see you make each other happy.'

'Yes, it's lovely of course. But he's not… Katie's dad.'

Now cautious, he asked, 'Where's this leading?'

'Al and I have been talking.' She returned to the table. 'Look. Having you here is absolutely fine. We have lots of space, and the annexe is yours for as long as you need it. We were thinking—' Her eyes on his were steady. 'There are some big, reputable boatbuilders along the docks here in the city, and they all seem to be getting huge orders. Bespoke stuff. Not just for the forces and the ferries, but one-offs for films and TV, beautiful replicas. Yachts and schooners, wood as well as fibre-glass. The sort of things you've always loved to work on.' She put a hand on his arm. 'I know you've never been ambitious. You've always said you just want to be left to yourself, restoring things. But you could get a great job here you know – a job that would allow you to do what you're good at. You're a craftsman, Cal. You take damaged things, and you make them lovely again.' She paused as a small, gratified smile briefly lightened his expression. 'And then, in time you could think about getting your own place, when you're ready. You'd be nearer to us. Nearer to Katie.'

He closed his eyes and pressed his lips together. He *really* needed notice of a proposition like this. Right now, all he could see rolling down the road ahead of him was tumbleweed. *Please don't tell me this could be a fresh start.*

But she pointed to where the local paper lay on a worktop and said, 'There are several ads in there anyway. No harm in looking, Cal. Think about it.'

Alone in bed at night, the temptation to replay, over and over, the sensation of his body against hers – the heft and warmth of him as his lips kindled little fires along her skin – was like self-harm: sweet, addictive torture. But if anything, mornings were worse.

Waking to another bright day and its routines – guests, bills, bookings, ordering – pitched Joss from a few seconds of oblivious energy into a chasm of despair. Weeks had crawled by, *weeks*. Another day not knowing he was close. Another day without any prospect of hearing his voice, reaching for his hand. God, it was desolating.

Get hold of yourself, the drawn face in her bathroom mirror reproached her as she cleaned her teeth and brushed her hair. *You have to get over this.*

You should have seen it coming.

She smiled and joked with the guests at breakfast – everyone relaxed and chatty in full holiday mode – attending to each day's tasks with unruffled efficiency. Her mask was perfect. She didn't understand how she managed it.

And then… there was Ollie.

A new term was under way. He'd diligently completed his summer projects and seemed determined to redeem himself. Homework was done without complaint, and the marks he brought home were consistently good. He'd even started referring to one or two classmates as 'friends'.

'I think we may be getting the old Ollie back,' Annie remarked one morning as they waved him off through the gate.

The old Ollie? She was finding it hard to recall that straightforward, optimistic boy.

With a sizable helping of maternal guilt, Joss was thankful the school holidays were over. He'd begun to follow her round more than ever, adapting his mood to hers. Sometimes he played the joker, reading something funny into a guest's comment, or reprising a sketch he'd seen on TV. At other times he acted like her self-appointed PA. Over the course of an hour he might present her with a battery of offers: *I'll find that invoice for*

you, Mum; I can do the stock check; I'll take Grandad his tray.
His watchful presence had become wearing, sometimes even oppressive. And his anxiety was drearily self-perpetuating. If her mask ever slipped, revealing the sadness behind her stoical front, he'd collapse into sepulchral gloom and fasten himself to her even more closely.

He seemed oddly like a compassionate victor in a battle she didn't know she'd joined. He'd been proved right about McCalvey – she had to accept it. But *dear God* how she wished he wasn't.

On a fittingly bleak Saturday, with emails checked, invoices filed and accounts updated, she found her mother in the kitchen and said, 'I think I need a walk.'

'Go ahead, love.' Annie patted her arm. 'You've been so preoccupied lately. If you feel up to it when you get back, perhaps we can do the financials over a cuppa. Review the balance sheet and think about how we'll get through the next quarter.'

'Fine,' Joss said without enthusiasm. Her gaze drifted to the window. In the distance, a sullen mist was gathering – just above where she guessed the shoreline would be converging with the sea in a blur of silver-grey. How they'd get through the next quarter? She hardly knew how to get through the next *hour.*

Her mother appraised her through narrowed eyes. 'Or... maybe we could open a cheeky Malbec?'

'Now you're talking.'

She unhooked her coat on the way to the door, inhaling deeply as she paused on the outside step to button up. The air was briny and sharp.

'Where are you going, Mum?' Like magic, Ollie materialized at her back.

'Just out for a bit, Ol. I won't be long.'

'I'll come with you!' He turned towards the hall cupboard where he kept his own jacket.

She closed her eyes and silently counted to ten. When she opened them again, she saw her mother had him gripped by the shoulders.

'Ollie,' Annie said. 'Let your mum go, for goodness sake! She just needs to do a couple of things, then she'll be right back. You can come and help me with today's post.'

Joss cast her a grateful look, and by the time Ollie had twisted back towards the door she was gone.

For a while she stood by the harbour wall, watching the breakers and the soaring gulls, trying to clear her mind. She took out her phone and scrolled through the numbers until she came to McCalvey's. Her eyes burned as she looked at it. *Go on,* an inner voice wheedled. *Call him. Do the reaching out.*

But of course there was no signal.

She shoved the phone back in her pocket with a rush of relief. One good thing about St. Roslyn's terrible network coverage – it stopped you making a complete idiot of yourself.

In a folder behind reception, she also knew where she could find Katie's home address. Too many times in the last month she'd hovered by that file, agonising over whether and how to make contact; the wisdom – or folly – of putting her emotional turmoil into words, hoping he'd do the same…

But something inside her had changed. She was tired of being the one reaching out. She was tired of the crushing consequences of giving unconditionally; of trusting in things, in people, only to have that trust ground to pieces underfoot. She was done beggaring herself.

It's his call.

She walked on past the bright patchwork of cafes and shops, increasing her pace with a defiant lift of her chin as she spotted tables and benches where his ghost still lingered. *This will pass*, she told herself. *Everything does. I won't be this sad forever.*

Ten minutes later, she reached the chandlery.

She hesitated a few seconds before climbing the steps to his apartment. The windows were shuttered; there was a distinct air of abandonment. But she needed... *something*. To pass some kind of test, maybe? To salute the end of a compelling drama, now the final curtain was down? *Something.*

She knocked, listening for an answer she knew wouldn't come.

What am I thinking?

Tucked against the wall was an old melamine dish, licked clean. She glared at it. *I bet he said a proper goodbye to the cat.*

She'd tormented herself enough. It was time to go home.

As she descended the steps, she recognised Marty. Clearly he'd seen her walk past the chandlery entrance and decided to intercept her.

'He's not there, Joss,' he said.

'I know, Marty. Or at least, I was wondering – when he might be back?' She searched her pockets for a tissue, blowing her nose to hide the wobble in her voice. 'He said he was taking Katie back to Bristol, ahead of the new term.'

Marty sighed. 'He told me that too.'

They gazed warily at each other.

'I don't suppose you know what his plans are?'

Marty seemed to deliberate before lowering himself onto the bottom step. He patted the space beside him, and she sat. He looked troubled, she thought.

'Well, he took himself off the lifeboat roster,' he said. 'And I found out a couple of weeks ago he's on indefinite leave from his job.'

'*Indefinite leave?*'

Marty frowned at his feet. 'Seems he needed to get away.'

When he glanced up, the horrified expression on her face made him grimace. 'Sorry, Joss.'

'You don't think he'll be back,' she said dully.

He straightened with a grunt, awkwardly sliding big red hands up and down his thighs. 'Cal's been a good mate,' he muttered eventually. 'But he's a bugger. He just doesn't... *deal* with things.'

This was humiliating, devastating. For a few seconds, she felt a rush of such incandescent hatred for McCalvey that she had to grab the stair rail to steady herself. *Why would he do this? What is it I'm not getting?*

Marty fixed his eyes on the tarmac, his brow furrowing into deep lines. As she studied him in profile, Joss realised he was as mystified as she was. '*Deal* with things?' she repeated. 'What do you mean? Was he worried about something?'

He shrugged. 'Nothing he'd ever talk to me about,' he said. 'But I can't help wondering. Something odd happened around the time he left. Some*one* odd, I should say. May just be a coincidence of course...'

Her eyes drilled into his. He'd been wanting to share this, she suddenly knew.

'There was a stranger.' He spoke slowly, enunciating every word as if each described a puzzle. 'Came into the shop a day or two after they left, Cal and his girl. Never seen him before. Poor bloke had a disfigurement, half his face was burned away. He asked me if I knew someone called McCalvey.'

Joss went very still.

'I told him I did, and he gave me something to pass on. An envelope. Said McCalvey wanted nothing to do with him, even though he was sure he'd recognised him just a few days before. I asked what business he had with him, and he told me they'd known each other as kids twenty-odd years ago. Said they lost contact when he moved abroad. To a new family. Which I thought was odd.'

'He gave you an envelope?'

Marty nodded.

'Have you still got it?'

He jerked his thumb upwards, indicating the apartment door. 'I didn't know Cal planned to be away this long,' he said, 'so I put it through his letterbox. As far as I could tell, it was just paper. Nothing sinister.'

'Did he say anything else?'

'Well, this is the real blinder, Joss. He said, *tell him it's from Tyler, he'll know who I am.* And then he said, *he saved me.*'

Hairs rose along the back of her neck. 'Saved him? What did he mean?'

'He wasn't being flippant. Honest to God, Joss, I could tell he meant exactly what he said. That Cal had saved him in some way. But then he buggered off.'

It had started to rain; a cold, clammy Cornish mizzle, weightless droplets settling like spiderwebs in her hair. Marty was examining her face as if he expected her to come up with a logical explanation for what he'd just revealed.

'I don't understand.' She shook her head. 'If this person, Tyler, was serious, then why on earth…?' There were too many questions. She ran a hand over her forehead, took a breath, and started again. 'Why *wouldn't* Cal want to acknowledge someone whose life he'd saved?'

Marty shrugged. 'Especially someone he'd been close to as a kid.'

They shared two more minutes of frozen silence before Marty pondered aloud, 'They could be related, I suppose. Part of a dysfunctional family. Cal's always been proper cagey about his background. Something bad could have happened to split them up.'

'Perhaps,' she murmured. But what if he *had* no family? What if neither of them had?

What if the previous owner of her jewelled brooch had filled a huge void in both their lives, once upon a time? And then perished in that terrible fire...

She clasped her head between her hands. She could theorise till the cows came home, but in truth she had nothing solid to offer Marty. Trying to make sense of McCalvey's behaviour was like shooting at a moving target in the dark.

'He should have stayed, Marty,' she said. There was no realistic chance of resolution now. No obvious way to move forward.

He should have trusted me.

But he'd chosen to abandon her. Sacrifice her. *Damn him.*

Marty looked at the sky and hauled himself upright. 'He'll be back at some point,' he said.

'You think so?'

'He'll come for Kara.'

Of course he will. Beautiful Kara. Moored in the cove, silently waiting. Joss felt her heart contract with a mixture of hope, trepidation, and grief.

'After all,' Marty added, 'she's the one thing in his life he wouldn't leave behind.'

Her stricken expression caused him to colour up. 'Oh hell, I'm sorry, Joss – I didn't mean—'

'It's OK, Marty.' She gave him a sad, forgiving smile. 'I know exactly what you mean.'

He offered his arm, and together they headed for the chandlery's entrance. 'You can wait inside till this passes over,' he suggested, but she pulled the belt of her coat more tightly round her waist and said, 'Thanks, but I should be getting back. Ollie's probably driving my mother mad.'

'I dare say the lad's missing his trips on the boat.'

She didn't reply.

'If you're not in a rush, I've got some more brochures here. Might interest him.' Briefly he disappeared to forage behind the shop's counter, returning with a set of leaflets she hadn't seen before. 'These are good. Day trips to spot marine wildlife – seals, dolphins, puffins. Basking sharks if you're lucky. Custombuilt boats, powerful enough to reach the Scillies if conditions are right. Individuals can join a mixed group – Ollie might like that – or you can hire a skipper for a whole day. That might be a good option for your punters. Next year, at least.'

'Next year?' She arched an eyebrow. A potential minefield. But she knew he was trying to lighten things up, and appreciated it. 'It's kind of you to think about us, Marty.'

'Let me know if you want help organising anything like that. I've got a bit of spare time. Agency rates – very reasonable.' He grinned, and her spirits lifted a little. 'Though I'm sure you'll be doing a roaring trade next season anyway, if you want an old codger's opinion. Cal would agree if he was here.'

'What makes you say that?'

Marty snorted as if she had no need to ask. He gestured at the view beyond the open door. 'Well, look at all that. Ocean on your doorstep, terrific scenery, a working port with bags of charm. We've just had our best year ever for tourists. Summers are getting longer and warmer – it's a fair bet next year will be a cracker. St. Roslyn's a grand place, Joss. And Wheal Blazey is a grand old house.'

'Oh, I don't know, Marty. It's such a competitive market.'

'Don't be daft. Where's your competition? Don't let anyone tell you you'll lose out to bog-standard hotel chains or overpriced self-catering.'

'But staying viable would be incredibly hard work.'

'Course it would. Ten percent imagination, ninety percent perspiration, isn't that what they say about all the best projects?'

This stopped her in her tracks. She scanned his pleasant, grizzled face, and realised she *did* want his opinion. Very much.

'There's a school of thought we should sell,' she confided. 'I think my mother's tempted. A land agent's been telling her how much we'd get for Wheal Blazey on the open market.'

'Yeah, well. You don't just get sharks in the sea,' he huffed. Finally, she laughed. 'Tell her to give you a couple of years. See what *you* can do with it. Wouldn't surprise me if you managed to double its value.'

She looked him hard in the eye, but his gaze was unwavering. 'Did you ever… talk to Cal about it?' she asked.

'I remember telling him I thought the place had real character.'

She held her breath. 'And what did he say?'

Marty grinned and cocked his head. 'He said he thought you did, too.'

Hallo, house.

She stopped at the gate, taking time to survey the noble old building. Roof slates glistened with wet; mottled stone walls shone like slabs of honeycomb. As her eyes lingered on the granite steps, she pictured the merchants, miners and local dignitaries who'd passed through the entrance doors in the course of the last two turbulent centuries.

So, what could you be for me? A liability? An opportunity? Salvation?

A break in the cloud allowed a shaft of light to strike the windows, causing them to glow as if the whole place were suddenly lit from within – radiant and glorious.

She shook her head in momentary disbelief. Then she smiled and nodded.

OK, then.

As she hung her coat in the hallway, she called out, 'Crack open that Malbec, Mum. I really need to talk to you.'

Annie was at the desk as Joss walked into reception. It took a minute for her to notice Tegen leaning on the counter facing her mother, part way through what she immediately sensed was a conversation of significance. The girl was proffering a handwritten letter. Both pairs of eyes swung in her direction: Annie's visibly harassed, and Tegen's – there was no mistaking it – *smug*.

'Darling – Tegen wants to hand in her notice.' Annie's voice was hoarse with worry. 'I've been trying to persuade her to stay, at least until the end of October. We're still taking bookings. Seems we'll be busy for a while yet.'

Joss approached her mother's chair. The curvy, doe-eyed girl smiled at her without warmth.

'What makes you want to leave us, Tegen?'

'They want bar staff and waitresses at the Ship.' Tegen flicked her luxuriant hair, pointedly casual. 'To be honest, the hours and pay are a lot better.'

Joss returned the cool smile, the day's emotion dissipating like a ship's wash. She felt herself grow icily calm.

'We need to talk about it of course, Jocelyn,' Annie said, 'but perhaps we can do something to make it worth Tegen's while to carry on for a few weeks – if you can just hold off making a decision for twenty-four hours, Tegen?'

'Well – I guess I *could* wait till tomorrow.' Tegen heaved a magnanimous sigh. 'I do like the work in the mornin's here, I like the variety. But I can't ignore an extra 50p an hour, Mrs. L.'

Annie nodded as if this logic was impeccable. She glanced hopefully at Joss.

'When would you plan to go?' asked Joss.

'Soon as my week's notice is up.'

Joss registered the challenge in the girl's eyes, inwardly remarking *face like an angel and thick as mince* with uncharacteristic spite. For the first time in a while, fate seemed to have dealt her a favourable hand.

'Don't worry, Tegen. We won't hold you back.' Pressing her mother's arm – *trust me* – she began trawling through the box reserved for business cards. Unhurriedly, she retrieved the details of St. Roslyn's largest recruitment agency, then paused as something else occurred to her. Delving further into the box, she pulled out a second card and laid it by the phone. It was Denzel's.

'We'll get onto the agency and let them know we have an opening,' she said. 'Maybe we could up the hours and enhance the whole package to attract someone flexible – someone who can offer telephone and admin skills as well. '

An affronted look vanished from Tegen's face a split second too late as Joss turned back to her with a smile.

'They're pretty good, the agency,' she said. 'I'm sure they'll find us someone reliable within the week. And as soon as they do, Tegen' – she reached across the desk to extract the letter from the girl's fingers – 'you can go.'

NINETEEN

'This is three Sundays running,' Katie said. 'If we're not careful it'll turn into a regular dad-daughter thing.'

'We'd best be careful then.'

They'd taken to walking Lisa's elderly retriever along the towpath to a breach in the bank where they could watch the dog's inept attempts to round up the ducks. As luck would have it, the route took in an attractive canal-facing pub, perfectly located for a pit-stop on a pleasant day.

McCalvey procured Katie a vodka and tonic – 'No need to tell your mum' – and settled with her on a bench beside the water.

'Cheers, Dad.' She saluted him with a clink of her glass against his. Then she fished out a slice of lemon, sucked it clean, smacked her lips, and said, 'So I'm guessing you'll have to go back to St. Roslyn at some point.'

'Well, all my stuff's there. And Kara, of course.'

She flicked the peel onto the grass. 'And then what?'

'*Then* what?'

'I mean – will you stay there?'

He fixed his eyes on the water, though he sensed hers scouring his face. 'I'm not really sure.'

'But you're not sorry you made this trip?'

That made him turn. 'God, Katie, it's taken me long enough to start behaving like a grown-up when it comes to you and your mum. So, no.'

She looked curiously at him for a moment. 'It did seem like you needed a break. I thought nothing would ever prize you away from your little nest – then suddenly you couldn't leave fast enough. Did something happen?'

He shook his head, retreating behind mental barricades.

'There was all that stupid stuff with Tegen and Ollie,' she persisted. 'Then that weirdo who accosted you on the quay—'

It was as if she'd poked him with a stick. 'It was just the right thing to do,' he snapped.

'Oh. Right. OK.'

Bugger. 'Sorry, my lovely. I didn't mean—'

'It's fine,' she sniffed. 'Don't mind me.'

He contemplated his beer for a while, conscious of her averted face. *Get your act together, McCalvey. You need to have this conversation.* Eventually he put his glass down, took a breath and said, 'I gather Alvaro will be moving in with your mum before long. Are you... alright with that?'

'Sure. She could have done a lot worse.' She shot him a sideways glance, which he ignored.

'He seems a solid kind of guy. Down to earth. Very... supportive.'

'Well he's a grown-up,' she said.

He winced at that. She was too smart to be patronised. 'Touché.'

When she cut her eyes at him, he risked an apologetic smile. 'My life's been a bit... complicated lately, Katie. I'm trying to juggle options in my head. Not very successfully, if I'm honest.'

She wriggled straighter and folded one leg over the other,

assessing him. *Like a sodding psychiatrist,* he thought. Though he'd wondered recently whether that was exactly what he needed. 'Did you bring a notebook?'

She rolled her eyes. 'Just tell me what you're trying to juggle.'

He bent to fuss the mucky dog, scratching behind her ears as she barked her delight and nosed between his legs. As she padded back to the water's edge, a narrowboat glided into view: wide-beamed, dark green, the name of the rental company picked out in gold letters. He watched it slip past, tuning in to the gentle chug of the engine while he checked the hull instinctively for signs of rust. From behind a dozen potted geraniums, a cheerful couple in lifejackets waved at him. It made him inexplicably depressed.

'*Dad!*'

He twisted towards her impatient face, resigning himself.

'Katie,' he began slowly. 'One thing I've been wanting to say – and I really need you to hear it – is that I'm sorry about not being here for you in the past.'

She frowned at him, her lips a thin line. He saw she wasn't going to make this easy.

'I know it's probably impossible to put that right.'

Her expression told him she was taking this as a statement of fact, not a question.

'Anyway. Your mum had a few thoughts the other day. She pointed me towards the classifieds.' He hesitated, looking down at his hands. 'It seems there's a demand for people with my skills in the dockyards here. So I started to wonder—' *Jesus, the look on her face could turn milk* – 'if maybe finding work locally – being nearer to you – might go some way to repairing the damage?'

The silence that followed unsettled them both. They sat for a few more moments gazing blindly at the river, the air around them full of waiting.

Finally she asked, 'But what is it *you* really want, Dad? That's what I can't understand.'

Her question wrong-footed him. He scratched his head, struggling for a mutually satisfying answer. But his hesitation was too long.

'I don't think you know,' she said. 'And I think that's a problem.'

'What do you mean?'

'I mean – what's it all about for you, Dad? How do you see your life shaping up from now on?'

He dropped his head, fragile clarity disintegrating.

'Because as I see it, you've never been able to hack any kind of domestic set-up, or stick to a routine other people can depend on. I'm not even sure you know what a meaningful relationship is.'

'Now hang on a minute, Katie, I don't think—'

'Mum's told me her big idea. She has this fantasy you can start all over again just down the road from us – get a steady job, be part of our extended family, leave Cornwall, forget about everything you had there. Well I don't buy it. I can't believe it's the right thing for you. But then, I don't know what you want.'

'What I want is to do what's best for—'

'And *don't* put this on me,' she interrupted, her voice rising sharply. 'It's a bit late to play the good dad now. I'm not a baby. I don't need you to make up for things that weren't right in the past and start making sacrifices.'

'But—'

'It's not my job to make you feel less guilty about things, Dad. Or less ashamed. Whatever the fuck it is you think you feel.'

'Watch your language, miss!' As soon as the command left his lips, he jerked his head back and groaned, appalled at its ridiculous irrelevance. But an instant later something cut through the havoc in his mind – something unexpectedly sweet. Her *laugh*.

He peered meekly up at her.

'*Honestly.*' Her lashes, he was shaken to notice, were loaded with tears. 'That's not to say I don't want a relationship with you, Dad,' she murmured. 'I *do.*'

His own eyes started to burn.

'But whatever you do, it has to be something you know you want. You have to know it in your heart, that's all I'm saying. Let everything else go. Because I think you spend most of your life running away from stuff. I can't work out why. I don't get what it is you're avoiding. But it's what you always do.'

A creature with razor-sharp talons seemed to be clawing at every vital organ of his upper body. He looked down at the grass, grimacing at the discarded lemon peel, its flesh stripped ruthlessly away. *She's doing the same to me.*

'Dad. I'm *worried* about you,' she said. 'Fitting in to the daily grind in a new town, a new job, miles away from the one place where I know you've been happy – it may be just another kind of running away.'

He inhaled, then slowly blew air through his lips. Five minutes earlier, he'd had the bones of a plan. But she'd unpicked it even before he'd had a chance to set it out.

'I decided this summer I could get really get fond of you, Dad. Don't freak out!' She'd seen his jaw suddenly clench. 'In spite of everything, I know that deep down, you're a good guy.'

'Oh God, Katie.'

She moved a little closer to address the face he'd turned away.

'I also think there are... other people... who might feel that way about you too. But the only thing you've ever been able to love back properly is *that bloody boat*. It's obvious to me you're in a real mess about what it is you want.'

He pressed his fingers hard into his eyes while she focused determinedly on the dog and gulped the last of her vodka.

At last he reached for one of her hands, gingerly stroked her fingers, and asked, 'Finished now?'

'Pretty much.'

'How long have you been rehearsing all that?'

'A while.' She turned with a look that demanded his attention – simultaneously apprehensive and defiant. 'There's something I've been wanting to say for weeks, Dad.'

'Go on. I think you've softened me up enough.'

'I want to say, for once in your life try sticking to something – *someone* – that can make you happy.' She paused a few more seconds, her features wrinkling as she searched for inspiration. 'Just stop avoiding things because you think they're complicated. Don't be so *afraid*. Stop running away. Even if the running is... to us.'

He held himself still, waiting for everything flailing about in his brain, heart and stomach to settle. Slowly, he bent to retrieve his pint. Then he shook his head and tutted. 'Bloody hell, daughter.'

She examined his face. 'So how are you feeling now, Dad? Are you OK?'

He sipped his beer and gazed across the flat silver-grey of the canal while he pondered the answer. On the opposite bank, a seagull bickered with a group of crows over the remains of someone's picnic, shreds of plastic sandwich-wrap just visible between the gravel and the tired grass. A jogger weaved through earnest pedestrians, and a loved-up couple strolled arm-in-arm towards a bench, lost in each other's eyes.

Most of the heaviness, he realised, had gone. It was as if someone had managed to push a wire brush into his skull through one ear and scrubbed away weeks of accumulated rubbish. How was he feeling? The answer astonished him. He felt... *relieved.*

He shook himself slightly and turned to face her. 'Where did you get that wise old head?'

She shrugged. 'Not from anyone I know. It's a mystery.' Then she leaned into him and in a quiet voice asked, 'Are we good, then?'

'We're good.'

'Does that mean I get another vodka and tonic?'

McCalvey tapped the end of her nose with a stern finger. 'I think you've pushed your luck far enough for one day, young lady.' And he planted a kiss in her pink hair.

'The man's like a terrier,' Annie grumbled as Denzel advanced into the kitchen ahead of them. 'Nose in every corner, all darting eyes and manic energy.'

Joss chuckled and slipped an arm through hers. 'Oh, great. So now I'm seeing him with a waggy tail and a moist pink tongue.'

'*Ew.*' Her mother was not to be mollified with humour.

But the observation was brilliantly appropriate, she thought. There was a puppyish enthusiasm about the way Denzel whirled through 360 degrees, then back again; the giant steps he took across the flagstone floor to measure distances; the delight in his voice as he checked the stores and read out the names of their local suppliers.

'You could fit an industrial dishwater here,' he said, his outstretched arms defining a specific section of wall. 'And there's plenty of room for a bain-marie. Then there's freezer space to think about—'

'Freezer space?' Annie's eyes were rabbit-in-headlights huge.

'Do you have much? I'm thinking fish, primarily. Hake, sole, mackerel – at the moment I'm having to work with daily deliveries, but here it would pay to order in volume. You're not at the mercy of seasonal shortages then. Makes economic sense – less waste.'

'We have a large domestic freezer,' she sniffed. 'We get by.'

There was a beat as Denzel exchanged glances with Joss, then visibly reined himself in. He drew a chair back from the kitchen table and stood behind it, inviting Annie to sit. She eyed him uncertainly and stayed where she was.

'They're just my first thoughts, of course,' he said. 'The immediate reactions of an annoyingly excitable chef. Don't let me rattle you, Mrs. Livesey.'

His apologetic smile was genuine and disarming. A second or two later, Annie smiled back.

'It's just that I'm an excitable chef – a good one, actually – who has to make a decision in the next few weeks on his current lease. It's not been too bad a year, I still have enough in the bank to finance another start-up. But what I really need,' and his right arm circled to take in the whole kitchen, 'are premises.'

'But where would the extra equipment come from?' Annie asked.

'Me,' he said.

'And who'd pay for it?'

'Also me. Possibly with a bit of help from the bank.'

'What about staff?'

Denzel lifted the chair and carried it over to her, then pulled out two more. 'We should probably all sit down, if you're interested in a serious conversation.'

Joss raised her eyebrows at her mother, then winked at Denzel as Annie straightened the hem of her cardigan, and sat.

'I'm not saying it's without risk.' He dropped into a chair himself and leaned forward, hands clasped in front of him. 'But I honestly believe it's low. If you can give me the space rent-free for three months and stand the energy costs, I can take care of stock, equipment and wages. Three months. I'll break even in that time. And when we move into profit – which we will over Christmas, I guarantee you – we'll share it.' He sat back and slapped his knees, hooking Annie with gleaming eyes. 'I'll make you money, Mrs. Livesey.'

Annie smoothed back her hair, then spent a moment fidgeting with her cuffs. The eyes she raised to Joss were intense and serious. 'I'd need you to take complete responsibility for this from Wheal Blazey's point of view, Jocelyn.'

'I know that, Mum.'

'Are you really sure you want to commit to it?'

Joss lifted her chin, took a deep breath, and glanced through the window. Summer was slipping away. A volatile sea breeze was snatching foliage from the garden borders and the air was full of movement. She turned back to her mother.

'A hundred per cent,' she said.

TWENTY

I got the art prize for my dolphins!!!

Mum says we'll do a meal and a movie tomorrow – first time in ages.

Maybe things are getting back to normal. Finally. The way we were. Before Cal.

School finished at midday on the Friday before half-term – early enough to get to Newquay for an afternoon showing of the latest 'daredevil pilot saves western civilisation' blockbuster. Joss booked tickets online and borrowed her mother's car. Ollie deserved a treat.

He was stepping up, she had to admit – trying to do the right thing by her and put her first, all the time she'd been heartsick, bewildered and resentful. For *weeks*, she declared to the mirror, she'd been a miserable cow. And it wasn't Ollie's fault – not really. It had taken her too long to accept the agonising truth: his intervention had only accelerated the inevitable.

But still. How amazing would it have been to share a bucket of popcorn in the back row with Cal, like ordinary lovers…

Stop it. You'll drive yourself mad.

The film itself was a pacey distraction. High on caffeine, surrounded by appreciative cinemagoers, she snuggled close to Ollie and surrendered to three hours of audio-visual stimulation. It had been so long since their forays as a family to Leicester Square or the IMAX at Waterloo. The memory of those trips could still produce a kick of pleasure.

'I *loved* it,' she told him as they made their way to the exit, and he grabbed her arm, grinned at her with eyes like beacons, and proclaimed, 'Me too!'

In the burger restaurant, she allowed herself a glass of red and relaxed back in her seat as he chattered. School was a lot better this term, he was keen to tell her, and there were a couple of boys he was thinking of inviting to Wheal Blazey if that was alright?

'Of course it's alright! And with a bit of luck they might get their dinner cooked by a proper chef before much longer.'

'So we're really going to have a restaurant?'

'That's the plan.'

'Good.' Ollie stabbed at his French fries and waved his loaded fork in the air. 'We'll be a proper hotel.'

Joss set down her glass. 'Are you alright with the whole idea, Ol? It means staying on in Cornwall. There'll be a lot of work involved in getting things up and running – sorting out equipment, suppliers, staff, updating the website, doing all the marketing and publicity…'

'I can help,' he said.

She smiled. 'With your new-found artistic flair, I suspect you can. And then, I'm sure there's more we can do to attract different types of guest. Families, walkers, art lovers. Surfers and sailors maybe. I'm thinking we could partner with a water sports provider. Marty at the chandlery has some good contacts.'

He swallowed the fries and looked hard at his plate.

'Are you *sure* you're OK with it, Ol?'

He thought for a minute, solemn. 'Because of Dad – because of money – I know you have to work,' he said. 'But this way, you don't have to go *out* to work. This way, when I come home in the afternoons, you'll be there.'

'Well, yes. But Ollie—' Her smile faltered. Lately she'd noticed a stippling of gravel in his voice – random fluctuations that made him cringe with embarrassment when he heard himself. And his Adam's apple was definitely becoming more prominent. Fleetingly she felt like berating the uncaring universe, *do you have to torment him with raging hormones on top of everything else?*

'As time goes on,' she said carefully, 'you'll want to do more of your own thing. You shouldn't feel tied to the hotel.' *Or to me.*

He looked up sharply. 'But I *want* to be part of it. You'll need me, if it's successful.'

'A couple more years and you'll be thinking about a career,' she ventured. 'You could be anything, Ol. An engineer, an architect, a businessman. There's a big wide world out there.'

'I'd like to stay close to the sea,' he said.

'The sea? OK.' She swirled wine around her glass. 'So, you could think about oceanography. Marine engineering. Conservation. Any of those would be fantastic choices. *My* dream—' it crystallised in her mind, beautifully clear '—is to make Wheal Blazey profitable enough to support you doing whatever in life you're most passionate about. Following your heart.'

Her tone seemed to galvanize him. He widened his blue eyes, little lines appearing across his forehead. 'Sounds like a good dream.'

She raised her glass. 'Here's to it.'

'But what about you?' he asked. 'Are you OK, Mum? Will you be happy at Wheal Blazey?'

She hesitated. 'I don't know, Ol. But sometimes… if you can't predict what the future holds, in life or love or anything else… I think you just have to hold your nose and jump.'

For a tiny, intriguing second, she saw what looked like sorrow darken his face. The air clotted with something complicated. Regret? *No point going there.* She pushed her plate away.

'Anyway. If all goes well, your Gran will be able to step back. Enjoy her garden, and spend more time with Grandad.'

His expression lightened. 'Will we keep Eva? I like her.'

'I hope so. If we can afford it.'

'I just realised something, Mum.' He clapped his hands theatrically to his face. 'Tom Cruise is almost as old as Gran!'

Caught mid-gulp, she spluttered wine into a hastily snatched-up serviette.

Driving home, they sang along to modern classics on Pirate radio, Ollie doing his best with Beyonce, Adele and Ed Sheeran while Joss accompanied Rick Astley, Fleetwood Mac and – *praise be* – Bowie at the top of her voice. Ollie watched her with pink-cheeked fascination, nodding approval whenever she glanced left to exclaim, '*Epic,*' or '*I love this,*' or simply, '*Yes!*'

Later, as she heated milk in a pan, he said, 'It's been a great night,' and she replied, 'It has.'

He unrolled the artwork he'd brought home from school, flattening it in place across the kitchen table with bits of crockery. Joss set down their mugs – hot chocolate for him, coffee for herself – and stood to absorb it.

Dominating the bottom right-hand corner, the dark green prow of an elegant hull cleaved its way through a turquoise ocean, its wash suggested by energetic spirals of white. Across the upper half, a dozen grey dolphins rose and dipped beside the boat – some showing a fin, others revealing a white underbelly or a chuckling open beak.

'This is really, really good, Ol.' She cleared her throat, trying to disperse the tightness in her chest.

'Don't look at it if it makes you sad,' he murmured.

She pressed moisture from her eyes. 'Being sad doesn't take away from the fact this is a terrific piece of work,' she said. 'Or the memory of that day as… pretty special.' She tilted her head to look at him. 'You thought that day was special too, didn't you?'

And there it was again, a shadow behind his eyes. He dropped his gaze to the picture, soundlessly moving his lips for a moment, then scrubbed irritably at his face. 'I did. I *did* think it was special.'

She held her arms out to him. Tucking him against the soft fabric of her sweater, she heard a muffled sentence. 'But I feel like I've got you back.'

'Got me back? Back from what?'

'From… someone else. From your best feelings being… for *someone else*.'

She lifted his chin. 'Ollie, that makes no sense. Feelings don't gets divvied out between people till they're used up. Taking from one person to give to another… that's so *not* how it works.' She shook her head. 'You can be a daft egg sometimes.'

'Well, that's how it felt,' he muttered. 'But it doesn't matter now. Not now that I've got you back.'

She left him asleep the following morning while she went to help on reception. Her mother relinquished the swivel chair with a grateful squeeze of her hand and said, 'If you're up for doing today's check-out, I'll put a breakfast tray together for your father. I thought I might get him into the garden for a bit, but it's not looking good.' Behind her through the window, clouds the colour of slate were spilling into the sky like breakers among rocks, and the air smelt of rain.

The departing couple – ruddy-faced, wax-jacketed hikers who'd spent a week exploring the coast with rucksacks, binoculars and pockets full of chocolate – took turns to wring Joss's hand. 'You have *such* a beautiful set-up here,' the wife gushed. 'We'll tell all our friends. And your breakfast room is lovely.'

'Have you thought about doing evening meals?' her husband asked. He sounded frustrated. 'If your restaurant opened for dinner, people wouldn't have to stay out in all weathers taking pot luck with the local hostelries. Some aren't bad – but some are just awful.'

'Watch this space.' Joss felt a glow when their expressions visibly brightened. 'We may surprise you.' *Note to self: check email addresses for brochure mailing list.*

'Well,' the wife said, 'this place is a treasure.' They heard the honking of the station taxi idling by the main door. 'And so are you, my dear.'

Joss watched them check their pockets for rail tickets and cash. A treasure? If that's what she was, she thought wryly, she was definitely in need of a good buff.

'Ready? Let me help you with your bags.'

Outside, the driver helped load the cases and the car pulled away across the gravel, arms waving from the rear windows as she lingered to watch them go.

In no hurry to do battle with the week's accounts, she tilted her face upwards to feel the vapour in the air caress her skin like a fine gauze. Her nose filled with scent – cut grass, old leaves and desiccated blooms – harbingers of winter's approach.

What would another year bring? Felix would have said she was deluded, unprepared, underequipped. Well, that might have been true twelve months ago – but things were different now. *She* was different.

She caught movement in her peripheral vision – a figure

approaching from the gate. She looked more closely, and froze.

She'd have recognised that slight swagger anywhere; the battered old jacket; thick hair corkscrewing even more than usual in the damp; skin still burnished from months of exposure to the elements. Within moments he'd stopped in front of her, dark eyes nervously interrogating hers, drawing her in with that familiar lopsided smile.

'Hallo, my lovely.'

Astonishment rooted her to the spot. If he'd moved to greet her with a hug, there was no way her muscles would have allowed her to reciprocate.

'Hallo, Cal.' Her voice sounded like someone else's – warily formal.

'You've not forgotten me, then?'

She stared at him, stuck in suspended animation, waiting for the emotional tsunami she knew would come. All these weeks… the desperate, uncomprehending days without him, all the lonely nights…

'I think you've got that the wrong way round,' she said.

She watched his smile evaporate. 'I'm so sorry, Joss. Truly sorry not to have been in touch. A couple of things happened before I left and…' He glanced at his feet. 'I made a crap judgement call.'

Too bloody right. She looked away from him, trying to focus on the trees, the drive, the sky, the horizon – anything to calm the stew of emotion boiling up inside. Nothing assured or boyish remained in the eyes boring into hers when she turned back. 'I'm sorry,' he repeated.

It was so hard to forgive. He'd brought joy into her shattered world, breathed life into parts of her she'd thought were long dead – then crashed her mindlessly into a wall.

She steadied herself. 'Why are you here, Cal?'

The question seemed to dismay him, as if the answer were

obvious. He shook his head and whispered, 'Oh, *Joss*,' as his hand reached for hers. 'I want to be here. We should talk. It's just that I needed time—'

'*Now* you want to talk?' Anger blasted through every nerve and bone. 'You disappear with no explanation, everyone telling me *that's what he always does?* Confirming to my son you're one more parasite who'll suck the life out of us both and walk away? I *begged* you to reassure him, to show some kind of commitment, but for you that was a step too far. Why should it be different now?'

Tears leached through her shallow armour from a deep inner well of blighted hope. She brushed them furiously away. The familiarity of his fingers on her wrist was overwhelming – the memory of his caresses unbearable. The sad, sombre eyes in front of her seemed to gather her up, melting her, *drowning* her. With superhuman effort, she forced herself to turn back towards the open door.

His voice was hoarse with distress. 'Joss, *wait*. I don't know if I can properly explain myself. God knows you've got reason enough not to trust me. But *shit* – at least give me a chance to try.'

She pulled her hand away and faced him with folded arms, steeling herself. He acknowledged the defensive posture with a small, rueful nod.

'I got back this morning,' he said. 'Dropped my bag and came straight here. There's a shedload of personal stuff I need to sort out – the job, the apartment, the boat – but I had to see you first. I wanted you to know, Joss—' he palmed hair back from his forehead and took a breath, '—how much I thought about you. How much I missed you.'

She felt herself sway a little. His words were a dopamine charge, an injection of euphoria. She'd *dreamed* of him saying those things. But an instant later, an inner voice made her withdraw again – a voice that had worn her to the point of exhaustion in the last hard weeks, but kept her sane. *He may not mean to, but he'll hurt you again. One day, Kara will take him away.*

Protect yourself. Let him go.

'Joss?' There was urgency in his tone now, rising anguish. 'Can we talk? Please?'

'I'm sorry, Cal. I've missed you too, missed you like hell. But—' She closed her eyes. Beneath her feet, a bleak, lonely fissure was yawning open. *He doesn't do long-term relationships. One day he'll sail away.*

She summoned the last of her courage. 'I think it would be best if we—'

'No!' He gripped her shoulders. '*No*, Joss. Don't say it.'

'I *can't*. I can't do this, Cal.' She gazed through a curtain of tears into his stricken face. 'I thought I knew you. I trusted you. But—'

'You *do* know me Joss. Better than anyone.'

She shook her head.

'We'll work it out,' he persisted. 'Let me talk to Ollie.'

A moth of hope fluttered among the ruins, a pinprick of light in the dark. *What if…?* She pressed her folded arms hard into her chest as if warding off the cold. In that second's hesitation, McCalvey reached out with both hands. 'Meet me on Kara,' he said. 'I'll be down there at two, if you can get free. There are things I ought to have shared with you, Joss. Please. Meet me. It's not too late.'

'I don't know, Cal.'

'*Please.*'

He put his arms around her and kissed her then – a kiss so full of longing, regret and desire her battered heart seemed to jettison its shackles and take to the air. Threading her fingers through his hair, she drank him in like a flower parched too long on waste ground, surprised at last by rain.

He lifted his head to scan her face. 'Two o'clock on Kara,' he repeated, and she nodded and sighed.

'I'll be there. But you have a *lot* of explaining to do, McCalvey.'

'Thank you, Joss.' He laid his palm against her cheek. 'And... I know.'

With a last brush of hands, she watched him set off for the walk back into town.

The air was cooling sharply; clouds were massing above Wheal Blazey, unfurling and rumbling towards the sea. As she scanned the darkening sky, fat drops of rain began to fall, splattering the steps and daubing her cheeks. She touched the side of her face, still warm from the press of his hand, the drumming of her heart vibrant in her fingertips.

The world had tilted on its axis.

By the end of today, she thought, *things will be clearer. And nothing will ever be the same.*

A strange animal noise and a rustle of leaves made her turn.

Ashen with horror, Ollie stood on the pathway to the house, staring. But when she called his name, he ducked around the corner and stumbled away.

TWENTY-ONE

Calling his name was useless. He'd fled, leaving her scraping damp hair back from her face while she scanned the empty space. *Damn.* Separately and together, she and McCalvey seemed destined to elevate bad timing into an art form.

She checked her watch. Nearly noon – two hours to go. So now she had another dilemma: chase after Ollie and attempt to diffuse his likely overreaction, or wait a bit in the hope he'd reason himself into a more objective frame of mind? *Good luck with that.*

She grunted in frustration, doubled back to the entrance and slumped down onto the top step, partially shielded from the drizzle by the slate porch roof. Even if she were to catch up with him, what would she say?

Cal's come back to apologise. We're meeting to talk, that's all.

Don't jump to conclusions.

It was just a kiss.

For God's sake – she was in enough turmoil as it was. Too enervated and apprehensive to deconstruct this turn of events with her son right now.

For a while she sat with her head in her hands, taking deep breaths, replaying the previous twenty minutes. The rain was increasing in intensity, and the visible landscape – garden, fields, clifftops, ocean – was beginning to blur. She hardly noticed. Despite the warning voice, an inner radiance had begun to spread into every fibre of her body. There was no mistaking the way McCalvey had kissed her – the look she'd seen in his eyes.

Sort things out with Cal first, then think about Ollie, she counselled herself. Surely that had to be the right order. Once Ollie knew McCalvey hadn't left for good, maybe there was a chance—

'Jocelyn?' Annie's voice cut in, 'What on earth are you doing out here in the rain? Come inside and talk to me.'

No more cloak-and-dagger, Joss resolved as she updated her mother over coffee in the lounge; subterfuge had become absurd. *We've been acting like idiots.*

For half an hour, Annie sat in round-eyed silence, sipping her drink without looking at it, periodically dabbing her face with tissues pulled from a box on the table.

'I've agreed to meet him at two o'clock on the boat,' Joss concluded. She sat back and waited, her bottom lip clamped between her teeth.

'So let me get this straight,' her mother said slowly. 'This man has been married before but abandoned Katie and her mother when she was a baby.'

'Yes.'

'He's been *intimate*, shall we say, with Tegen and Morwenna – doubtless among unknown others. He avoids telling you anything about his origins or family, but you think he may have spent time in a children's home, the manager of which – a woman you believe he must have been close to – died tragically in a fire more than twenty years ago.'

'Yes.'

'For the last few years he's been restoring a boat, planning to sail to Greece. And someone who knew him as a child recently came looking for him. After which he decided to disappear.'

'That more or less sums it up.'

Annie emitted a huge sigh. 'I think, my darling, you've had more than your fair share of damaged, untrustworthy men.'

'Cal's not cruel or immoral, not like Felix, Mum. He's just—' *Just what?* She frowned into her empty mug.

'And what if he decides he likes his freedom too much?' Annie asked. 'What if he leaves again – not next year perhaps, but the year after that?'

Joss looked up. As she met her mother's apprehensive gaze, the fog in her brain suddenly dispersed. Something clicked into place.

'I'll cope,' she said simply.

They both turned sharply as the sound of a scraped chair and a drawer being yanked open reached them from across the hall. 'There's someone in reception,' Annie exclaimed.

Joss got to her feet as rapid footsteps preceded the slamming of the entrance door. Tiny snakes of unease slithered along her spine. 'My guess is it's Ollie. He's probably looking for me. I need to go after him, Mum.' She touched her mother's arm.

Annie clasped her hand. 'Yes, talk to him.' Her eyes were wet, but she managed a cautious smile. 'If this is really what you want, sweetheart – if it's meant to be – sooner or later, I'm sure Ollie will come round.'

'Thanks, Mum. Wish me luck.'

But the cottage – her first port of call – was quiet. She climbed the stairs to Ollie's room. It was empty.

Returning to ground level, she glanced through the door into the kitchen. Something felt wrong. She moved towards the table – then stopped with a low moan of despair.

In front of her, the shredded remains of the dolphin picture littered half the tabletop and part of the floor below. 'Oh, *Ollie.*' She retrieved half a dozen fragments – a jagged rectangle of underbelly; a torn inch of eye; misshapen scraps of turquoise and grey. And crumpled under a chair, the skilful rendering of a dark green prow, ripped cleanly in two.

She grimaced at the mess, uncertain how to navigate forward. What had he been doing in reception while they talked? Eavesdropping? Maybe he was around there still, trying to decide whether to confront or avoid her. Retracing her steps to the main house, she crossed the entrance hall and returned to the desk. Its deep lower drawer gaped open; inside it, she saw the familiar collection of padlocks, keys and household tools.

Except… no screwdriver.

Item by item, she lined up the contents on the counter. Definitely no screwdriver.

She frowned through the window. A squall was threatening, but a worse storm was gathering inside her brain. She thought of Ollie's face, white with horror; the mutilated picture of what he'd once thought of as a brilliant day. Space in the drawer where the screwdriver should have been.

Guy's vandalised car.

All your best feelings being… for someone else.

She checked her watch again – less than an hour, and she'd need to head for the boat.

The boat! *Oh God.* A cold premonition sent her running from the house.

The limbs of rock giving Mussel Cove its protective horseshoe shape came into view as she descended, cursing herself for not grabbing a waterproof as rain soaked her dress, sluiced through her hair and lanced her eyes. Stones and clods of earth broke under her patent leather shoes, causing her to slide forward and nearly topple every few yards; but twenty feet above sea level she reached a treeless vantage point where the whole jetty was visible between sheltering cliffs. She stopped to peer down, and the breath caught in her throat.

Kara's dinghy was no longer strapped to the foredeck but bobbed expectantly on its painter at the stern. Steadily, the mainsail was rising.

'Cal?'

But the figure single-handedly hauling on the mainsheet, angling himself at forty-five degrees for maximum leverage, was Ollie.

She skidded the rest of the way. When her feet touched the jetty, she shouted his name. He didn't hear. She could see that his cheeks were red with exertion, his jaw set hard. As she pounded towards him, the noise of her heels on the wooden boards and shriek of 'Ollie! What are you doing?' finally made him turn. His look of fierce concentration collapsed into dismay.

'Go *away* Mum. Go back!'

Reaching the hull, she bent over to grip her knees and gasp for air. When she glanced up, she saw he'd cleated off the mainsheet and was freeing the tiller. 'Ollie – get off the boat!'

'Go away, Mum!' he hissed again. He lifted a flat palm towards her face, fingers splayed in warning. 'You shouldn't be here.'

She scanned her surroundings, willing McCalvey to appear above them on the track. No sign of him. The huge sail was flapping like a bird of prey, desperate to escape its leash. Beside her, its cover lay in a tumbled heap; half a dozen fenders had been flung haphazardly to shore.

'What's going on? Ollie, *get off the boat.*'

'*No*, Mum. I don't want you meeting him here. I'm taking Kara.'

'You're *what?*' She stared at him. 'Absolutely not. Get off the boat, Ollie – she's not yours to take.'

He shook his head and scurried from one end of the deck to the other, slipping the mooring lines. She watched in stunned disbelief, then dropped her eyes to the edge of the jetty. Between the hull and where she stood, four inches of sea were clearly visible – then a second later, six; then twelve. Kara was drifting away from her berth.

'Ollie – for God's sake. This is dangerous.'

From behind the tiller he glared back at her, his eyes enormous with a jolting combination of triumph and misery. It wasn't just rain guttering down his face, Joss realised. Though his cheeks were flushed with exertion, the rest of him was bone white.

Time seemed to stop, as did her heart and breath. A dire possibility chilled her to the core as Kara executed a graceful rotation. *If he heads out to sea, he might not make it back.*

She glanced round one last time, searching the path and cliffs. Within the cove, the wind was relatively contained, the sea moving in filigree ruffles – low-level, regular, theoretically manageable. Beyond it, the ocean was a foreign landscape of vast gunmetal grey. She shut her eyes, kicked off her shoes, and gave an involuntary whimper.

And then she jumped.

She hit the deck face-forward, her knees smacking the cockpit floor. She reached for a stanchion to pull herself upright as Ollie leapt towards her, aghast.

'*No, Mum!* Get back – *get off!*'

But Kara was already accelerating.

Caught out by a yaw to starboard, Ollie scrambled to reclaim control of the tiller and loosen the mainsheet. As the boat righted itself, Joss staggered to the mast and flung her arms around it, pressing herself against the sturdy timber. She squinted through the rain, wet hair clinging like paint. 'What the hell are you thinking? Stop this, Ollie! Turn us around.'

'*Mum*,' he rebuffed her, 'it's *OK*.'

'It's *not* OK. You need to turn Kara around, Ollie. You don't know what you're doing, you're not thinking straight. This is wrong. Take us back!'

In the seconds that ticked by while he hugged himself and frowned, Kara's canvas stabilised to a shallow crescent. Scooping up the wind, she began to heel.

'*Ollie!*' Joss tried again. She risked a backward glance; the safe little cove was rapidly receding. Air as opaque as broth thickened behind them, obscuring the route back, seemingly fed by the churning peaks and streamers of Kara's wake. Still clutching the mast, Joss surveyed the ocean in front of them through needles of spray; they were speeding into open water. She prayed to God her imagination was playing tricks – that the judders and thumps beneath her bare feet weren't increasing in frequency every second. Through eyes narrowed to slits she could just make out Chy Head in the distance, an imposing black slab breaking out from an expanse of what looked like boiling lead, the sky only marginally lighter. And the wind was gaining power, whipping her ears.

'We shouldn't be out here, Ollie,' she yelled. 'You're putting Kara at risk.'

Or, she suddenly thought, *maybe that's the point?*

He was studying the roiling sea, his expression grim, veins in his hands bulging with the physical strain of keeping the hull steady. Aiming, Joss understood with a surge of alarm, for Chy Head.

She glanced behind her at the dinghy – carefully tied, oars tucked securely into their central straps, ready for escape – and voiced a fearful insight: 'You want to hole her on the rocks. Is that the plan?'

He clawed at his hair before meeting her eyes. He'd started to look confounded, she thought – a little dazed. But she saw him nod.

'For God's sake, Ollie. Are you out of your mind? You *have* to take us back.'

'But *he'll* be there,' he whined.

By now Kara's progress was being hampered by wave turbulence. Her bow had started to dance in crude, circular movements as volumes of seawater battered and broke over each side of the hull. Joss could see the tiller pulling like a live animal under Ollie's rigid fingers, vibrating as the keel beneath the boat struggled for traction in a mass of lumpy unpredictability.

Little by little, Chy Head was growing ominously closer.

'Look at the water,' she pleaded with him. 'Look at the sky. It's getting worse. I'm frightened, Ollie.'

Something flashed in his eyes. Every muscle in his face tightened as he fixed her with a look of stern resolve. 'I'll look after you, Mum, please don't worry. I'll always look after you, you should know that.'

'How is this looking after me?'

He stiffened. 'You weren't meant to be here.' Suddenly he sounded like a petulant schoolboy – thwarted, defensive, upset. 'But it's OK, Mum. I can sail her. You need to get a lifejacket on, though, we both do. They're in the locker behind you.'

A sob rose in her throat. '*Shit*, Ollie. This is insane.'

'We'll be fine, Mum. Just get the lifejackets.' Was that a challenge she heard in his voice? Exasperation – she recognised the undertone only too well. She closed her eyes and shuddered.

He won't follow through on this, she told herself, *not Ollie. He's not stupid.* She had no choice but to hang on. She had to find a way to calm him down. But right now, most of all, she had to stay safe.

Clutching the rigging for stability, she pigeon-stepped her way across the lurching cockpit to the locker and heaved up the lid. Bending to look inside precipitated a fierce rush of nausea, foul liquid flooding her throat, nose and mouth.

'There's probably wet weather gear in there, Mum,' she heard Ollie shout.

She retched onto the deck. Her temples felt hot, but the rest of her, neck down, was seriously cold. As she stooped again to haul out the jackets she realised her hands were shaking violently. The locker was a deep, black hole smelling of oil and tar; she fought to stay on her feet and not collapse into it. Just before she let the lid slam back down, she cast her eyes among its contents, searching for something – anything – of potential use. Ropes, bungees, tarpaulin, oil cans… and a carefully separated pack of slim red cylinders.

She worked her way to the coach roof and thrust a jacket towards him, gasping, 'We need help, Ollie. We need rescue.'

He ignored her, pulling on the inflatable vest while he watched her do the same.

Gripping the mast again, she flattened one hand against the bulkhead and tried to lean into the boat's rolling motion. Ollie himself had started to look green. His temperature must be dropping fast, she thought – as was hers.

'Why are you doing this, Ollie?'

He shook his head. *You should know.*

'Ollie. *Why are you doing this?*' She had to shout to make herself heard above the capricious wind. 'What good will it do?'

He averted his eyes, his whole body rodded with cold steel. It was obvious he was being pushed·beyond his physical limits. Though they were making laborious progress across the bay, the sea was fighting him hard. Joss scanned the ocean on either side, terrified by its monumental emptiness. No other vessels had ventured out.

'You took the screwdriver,' she cried out. 'Is that in case you don't get her as far as the rocks?'

The face he turned towards her was haunted and bitter.

'Cal loves this boat,' she pressed on. 'You want to break her up, to hurt him.' Each word was propelled with agonised, painstaking care, despite her uncontrollable shivering.

'It's the only thing he cares about,' he shouted back, palming rainwater out of his eyes. 'He doesn't care about you. You think he does, but you're wrong.'

'He's done nothing to harm either of us, *nothing*.'

'He'll hurt you.'

'*No*, Ollie!' The wind was howling round them like a sick animal, and her voice was hoarse. 'He's a good man. He'd never harm me.'

'He's thinking of himself.'

She roared in protest. 'You think he's like your dad, Ollie. But he's not. Don't make that mistake.'

By now they were being lashed from above and below and Kara was pitching wildly. Ollie's whole bodyweight on the tiller made no difference – the wind and current were overwhelming. The world was totally black. Icy water slopped over her feet and her eyes burned with salt, but Joss fixed him with an unblinking, desperate gaze.

'*Don't look at me like that.*' He twisted away, covering his face.

In that moment she knew he was mentally no longer on the boat, no longer present. He was watching his father claw at her, witnessing her helpless panic; taking in the cruelty and destruction playing out right in front of him through the doorway of a familiar room.

'Cal's *not your dad*, Ollie!' she cried out again.

Something inside him burst. He screwed his eyes tight shut and howled into the storm like a beaten dog.

'Ollie. *Listen to me.* We need help. If you can't control Kara out here, we'll drown. Is that what you want? '

'But I can save you Mum.' His voice had weakened to a desolate screech. 'We don't need anyone else. We don't need *him.*'

All at once the wind dropped. Ten miraculous, deceptive seconds of peace followed. Joss glanced round uncertainly. Then suddenly the blast rekindled itself with far more aggression than before, targeting its assault from an entirely new direction. The canvas lost all power and started to drum against the mast with the noise of a thousand vicious wings. Unresponsive to the tiller, the hull stalled, then heaved to starboard and picked up the wind again. The boom swung free; the sail filled. Kara plunged forward.

Ollie scrambled to take control, but his hands were paralysed with cold, all strength gone. Kara was irretrievably beyond his competence. The gale seemed to be toying with them, beating a mad, capricious circle, blasting them with salt water every few seconds while sending the hull into a series of unstable loops. They were entering the orbit of the Head now – a long way from where the spit sloped down to an accessible little beach, much closer to a jagged necklace of rocks scattered along the edge, rising to meet them in the darkness.

Joss pivoted from the mast to his face. 'Ollie – shouldn't we get the sail down?' But he seemed stupefied.

'*Ollie!*'

She battled through walls of spray to where the mainsheet was cleated and gave the rope several sharp tugs. It didn't work. The wet fibres seared red marks into the flesh of her hands, and she retreated, grimacing, to the bulkhead.

'Let me do it!' Shaken from his torpor, Ollie abandoned the tiller and leapt to take her place, but the sheet had jammed. Still the sail continued to fill and empty itself with every strike of the savage wind, the rocking motion intensifying while Kara plunged on, swept up in the arms of the inbound current.

Joss groaned and hauled herself determinedly upright. She half climbed, half fell towards the cockpit locker and wrenched open the lid. Water streamed down her neck, her hair was a sodden paste. She was a terrified little girl again, somersaulting frantically in a lethal vortex, wrestling her way out of hell.

'Mum, sit down! What are you doing? You'll go overboard. *Please*, Mum, *sit down*.'

Her hand closed round a cylinder. She snatched it up, blindly trying to decipher the instructions, Ollie watching in panic as she fumbled for the tag.

'No, don't, Mum! I'll get us out of this!'

She jerked the tag as he lunged in desperation, violently knocking her sideways. Startled and unbalanced, she fell to the cockpit floor, yelling as her ankle cracked against wood.

'Mum! *No!* Mum!'

He threw himself beside her as a sudden, spectacular explosion temporarily blinded them to the carnage. Immobilised by shock, they stared into the illuminated mass of cloud boiling around the tip of Kara's mast, turning red, gold and then dazzlingly white above their heads. Seconds later, the blaze narrowed to an intense meteor-trail of light, streaking vertically into the turbulence.

'*Bring help. Please – bring help,*' she whispered. Her sore eyes tracked the flare's firework brilliance as it accelerated away, for just a second picking out the silhouette of the distant, unreachable coast.

Then the brilliance faded to smoke, abandoning them to the freezing dark.

TWENTY-TWO

So, what do I say?

He hadn't let himself think too deeply about it. He only knew that he had to get back to her – this kind, sensuous woman who'd taken a chance on him, despite her own barely-healed scars. She'd accepted him as he was – unreliable, irresponsible, barely at ease with his own life. At least until now. And what had he done? Run away.

Partly, he admitted to himself, he'd wanted to dodge a problem – the hostility of her son. But in truth he'd been trying to flee a ghost – the spectre of someone he used to be: someone barely human. Degenerate, unredeemable. Someone who filled him with fear and shame.

It's what you always do.

But maybe he hadn't run out of road this time. Not yet.

They'd been pleased to have him back at the marina, thank God. He'd even managed a couple of tricky repairs before heading for the cove, and they'd lent him the pick-up for the weekend. Weather aside, things looked promising. For once.

He stopped in a clifftop lay-by, grabbed his toolbox, and made his way in strengthening rain along the hundred yards of track that would lead him to the boat. Almost two o'clock now. Around the next curve, she'd be coming into view…

He froze.

Gone. Kara was *gone.*

His eyes scoured every inch of the jetty, the surrounding cliffs, the waves fragmenting onto rocks and shingle along the shoreline. Sure, the weather had turned, things were getting lively, but he knew he'd moored the boat securely and closed everything up before he left. There was no way she could have come adrift.

Then he saw the mainsail cover, crumpled at the side of the jetty. Fenders cast off in haste, one of them bobbing uselessly in the water. *Fucking hell.* The alarm bells in his head were angry and loud.

Reaching the mooring, he knelt to pick up a discarded line, turning it in his hand as if he could make it spill its secrets. Then he walked to the furthest edge and stared into the distance, mystified, looking for sail. *No-one in their right minds would take her out in this.* The motor would be useless anyway – he'd emptied the fuel tank as a precaution before he left.

He shut his eyes and took a breath. There were only two options – to call the coastguard, in case she'd been sighted or recovered at sea in his absence; and, failing that, to report her theft to the police.

Bewilderment and fury tightened their grip. He'd left the field radio and his own phone in the pick-up. Mind made up, he turned sharply to discover Jack Livesey eyeing him from the steps.

'Jack!'

Tentatively, the elderly man raised an arm. 'Are you looking for my grandson?'

'Ollie?' McCalvey hurried towards him. 'No – why?' Glancing along the path in the direction of Wheal Blazey, he noticed Annie approaching at a run, no doubt to retrieve her husband.

'She's a beauty, isn't she?' Jack smiled at the abandoned sail cover.

McCalvey looked back at Kara's empty berth. Something not fully grasped began to feed his anxiety. 'The boat, you mean? The boat that was here?'

'Kara, yes. Such a striking green,' Jack nodded. 'Beautifully restored. Did you do that?'

'Have you seen her recently, Jack?'

'Kara? Oh, a little while ago,' Jack replied. 'My grandson, Ollie, took her for a sail.'

'What?' McCalvey stopped breathing. 'In *this?*'

He pointed towards the horizon. Beyond the cove, breakers cascading like avalanches were distantly visible atop mountains of purple and black.

Worry lines deepened on Jack's face. He followed the direction of McCalvey's finger and started to shake his head in panic. 'She tried to stop him.'

McCalvey seized his wrist. 'Who? Joss? Tell me, Jack! *Tell me.*'

Jack stared wonderingly down at the hand gripping him. 'He went rushing through the door,' he said. 'I was sitting at my window. He's always got something in his head, that boy. He can be a handful, you know, but he means well. I thought I'd go after him. But my daughter beat me to it.'

'Where is she now, Joss?'

'Well, she's on the boat, of course. I came round the corner and saw he'd got the sail up. Then she just – jumped on.'

McCalvey held himself absolutely rigid for a second, his brain trying to absorb the reality of the nightmare unfolding in front of him. *No, not this. Please not this.*

Then adrenalin kicked in.

In a few strides he was back at the pick-up.

'Marty, it's me. *Yes, me.* Listen, Ollie and Joss are out on Kara – I know, I know mate, but don't ask, I'll explain later. We need the lifeboat, possibly the helicopter – call the coastguard, Marty, *do it now.*' Before he'd finished speaking he'd gunned the engine and was accelerating down the coast road towards the harbour.

As the ocean loomed to the right of his windscreen, he saw the flare launch itself into the sky – a lonely, galvanising slash of red in the malevolent dark.

No, no, no. His heart was pounding, the beat of it thunderous in his head and jaggedly painful in his chest. He snatched up the handset again.

'Marty – I'm two minutes away, just two minutes. Pull out my stuff, will you? I'm coming, I'm coming, only one minute now. For Christ's sake, Marty – *you have to get me onto that boat.*'

'*Mum!*'

Joss struggled to grip her son's soaking shoulders as he knelt beside her on the cockpit floor, his face an inch away. Her swollen ankle was on fire, her shivering rackingly intense. Every few seconds, relentless explosions of seawater drenched them both. Everything was out of control. A lethal alliance of wind and sea was tossing Kara like a champagne cork; she was bucking and swerving, bucking and swerving, the world spiralling madly around her as the sail above their heads billowed and collapsed like a giant lung, the tiller swinging in futile circles.

The end of the world. Wood, lines and rails snapping, the hull squealing like a mortally wounded beast.

Faced with the inevitable, Joss had begun to feel surreally calm.

We're going to drown. I've been sleepwalking into this. My son has put everything at risk, obsessed with keeping me safe. My poor, burdened son.

She fixed her eyes on his. For one apocalyptic moment, she felt she was looking right *into* him – comprehending his anguish, his catastrophic determination, his misery. The dangerous weight of his love for her. She wished she could carry it for him, lighten it, make everything finally come right.

Is this how it ends, then? Both of us doomed, on this beautiful boat?

Life was random. Love was perverse. The world was mad.

She closed her eyes. She was so cold, *so cold.* Disjointed images crowded her mind, echoes of faraway voices... Crimson rhododendrons by her father's favourite bench... Weathered flagstones under bare running feet...

There's a spirit about the place.

Felix's cool smile. *This is why you'd never make it as a businesswoman...*

Broken glass; slashes in a red car door. Cal's dark, shining eyes. *Look at you now – you've come through.*

She jerked back to full consciousness, grimacing into the black heart of the storm. *It can't end like this – Ollie fighting false predators, stressed out of his mind. Both of us travelling towards a cruel, pointless death.* Somehow she had to make her peace, help him open his heart to what was true and positive and good.

All he wanted to do was save me.

He needs to know I'm not afraid. Not lost, no-one's victim. Never again.

Kara continued to pitch for long, sickening minutes – a macabre rollercoaster, rising seawater saturating their clothes. Curled in the centre of the tumbling boat, Joss felt something release. 'Look at me, Ollie,' she said. 'Look at this, *look at us.*'

'I'm so sorry, Mum, I never meant to hurt you.' He was

whimpering pitifully, his face flayed and wrinkled like an old man's. 'I wanted to rescue you.'

'From another monster?'

He pressed himself against her, squirming in her arms while freezing water slapped and sucked at their clothes, their skin, their hair.

'Ollie – you wanted to take charge of me. You made it your mission, and it's led to this. Think about it, Ollie.'

His eyes widened in panic. Forcefully, he shook his head.

'Ollie, I love you. You've never needed to doubt it, never. Nothing will ever take that away. If we're going to die here, you have to know it. But remember that night, that night when something monstrous took over your dad?'

'*No!* I don't remember.' His headshaking became manic.

'You remember every second, I know you do.' She held him close, putting her mouth to his ear so her voice could prevail above the roar. 'A monster lived inside him because he was broken – not much more than a broken child. Money, family, love, success – it was never enough. In the early days he tried to fight it, but it ate him up. He lost himself to it.' She tried to hug him harder, but couldn't feel her arms. 'He loved me once, like you. But when the monster inside him needed feeding – he nearly destroyed me. Like this might destroy both of us tonight. You've put all your energy into making this happen, Ol. Even though it's the last thing you wanted. Even though I know you love me.'

'*No, Mum.*' He was gasping for breath. 'I wouldn't let you die.'

She flattened a hand against his heart. 'You've been struggling with your own monster for a while Ol, ever since Dad died.' Her voice was a rasp now, her throat desperately dry. 'It's been growing inside you, taking you over. But you don't have to let it. Please don't let it. *Don't be him.*'

She watched him swing his head violently back and forth; heard him wail as he raised his face to the storm.

'You can't rescue me from everyone, Ol. What happened with Dad was an aberration, a sickness. It will *never* happen again.'

Agonized, he reached to touch her streaming face.

'I did love your Dad,' she sighed, 'but he never let me be properly *me*. He controlled me – like you've been trying to control me ever since. Face it, Ollie.' She smiled sadly as his face contracted in distress. 'You can't keep me in a cage, protected from everything. That would have killed me in the end.' She managed to shuffle more upright, until she was level with his eyes. 'Can you understand that, Ollie?'

The head shaking stopped.

'And that man out there, who I guess is searching for us right now – he lets me be me. You need to do that too.'

Oddly, she'd begun to feel less cold. Little by little, the clamour of the storm was abating, the pain in her ankle less acute. If she could just finish telling him everything she needed to… maybe she could close her eyes for a while and rest. Only for a minute. She was so, so tired.

'You think wrecking Kara will make Cal go away. You want to break his heart. That's what you had in mind, isn't it?'

'I don't know any more, Mum.' He stared at her in unblinking anguish. '*I don't know.*'

'If you do,' she persisted, doggedly clinging to a strap on his lifejacket; 'If you succeed – you won't just be punishing Cal. You'll be punishing *me*.'

Her eyes never left him, though she felt increasingly sleepy and weak. In the background, something else trickled into her consciousness – above the unrelenting deluge, the whirr of rotor blades.

He wrapped his arms tightly round her neck. She kissed

his wet head. All she wanted was to lose herself to the inviting darkness. Soon, it would be over. If she could just close her eyes, she could gently slip away.

'Don't go to sleep Mum. Please, please, *don't go to sleep.'* She was dimly aware of him shaking her arms and pushing hair out of her eyes.

There'd been a conclusion of sorts; maybe a drawing of lines. She sensed it as a soothing torpor descended, surprisingly warm and calm. Perhaps the beginning of something too. 'If we get out of this,' she whispered, 'things will be different. I'll be different, and so will you. Better. I promise.'

'Joss! Open your eyes. *Look at me* for Christ's sake. Look at me and tell me you're OK.'

The shaking was suddenly more forceful, the voice urgent and different – but familiar. Sweetly, heart-wrenchingly familiar. If it was a dream, it promised to be a happy one. *If you'd just let me sleep…* She grumbled at the intervention, then found herself swimming back; back through the currents submerging her brain to a terrifying reality; crying out as pain resurged in her leg. Strong hands raised her to a stable sitting position and plucked Ollie from her neck. Above them, behind a streaming visor, brown eyes burned into hers.

Thank God – oh thank God. A sob broke from her blistered mouth.

'Hold still, Joss, stay as you are. We're right by the rocks. You're hypothermic, we need to get you into the helicopter. They'll winch you both up, but I need to get this under control first.'

'Ollie, he's here… Cal's here…We'll be alright… ' She felt an answering pressure on her arm.

McCalvey ripped a knife from its sheath within his storm jacket and sliced through the mainsheet. Immediately the canvas lost its tension and the mast rose with a groan, righting the boat to vertical for precious seconds. She saw him glance upwards. A powerful column of light was advancing through the roiling clouds, the throaty rumble and beat of huge rotors growing louder by the second.

He gave a thumbs-up to an invisible colleague further along the deck. Weaving past them towards the tiller, he shouted: 'Marty's fixing a tow.'

'I can help.' Ollie heaved himself groggily to his feet and stumbled forward, but McCalvey pressed him down, wordlessly looping a secure line around his wrist.

Something struck the hull. Joss felt a convulsion and heard wood shatter, then McCalvey curse. The nose began to point away as he forced the tiller through 180 degrees. Immediately she was confronted by a black mass to stern, rising from the breakers, desperately close. The outlying rocks of Chy Head were right beneath them.

Liberated from the sail's weight, Kara continued to roll as waves surged over each side, swamping them all again, again and again. On one steep downward plunge, Joss caught a flash of orange a hundred metres off – the all-weather lifeboat. The next descent revealed a boarding boat, linked to the ALB with a line. She realised the men must have entered the last formidable yards of mountainous water to reach them.

As she struggled to absorb the activity around her, a brilliant explosion of lightning split the sky overhead, followed almost instantly by a cannonade of thunder so loud and close it shook every bone in her body. The whole hull vibrated.

She heard the grotesque, amplified sound of splintering. At the same moment, she took in the look of dismay on McCalvey's face. She tracked his eyes. He was watching the mast.

It was breaking.

Right above her head, as shrouds snapped and unravelling sheets flailed in the mad wind, the gigantic spar tore free. The stricken timber spiralled, then advanced on her in slow motion like a cumbersome missile, its trajectory stately and lethal.

She covered her face, bracing herself.

In the four seconds it took for the beam to reach the deck, McCalvey abandoned the tiller to fling himself across her. She felt him stretch, thrusting his left arm to the side in a futile effort to ward off the blow. His body slammed lengthways against hers, crushing the breath from her lungs as the mighty pillar pounded him.

She heard him gasp her name. She heard Ollie scream.

'*Oh Jesus.*' Marty leapt down from the coach roof to manhandle the severed mast and useless boom from the deck. Joss pushed upwards with what little strength remained in her upper body as he gently pulled McCalvey away from her and carefully rolled him onto his back. The sight of his blood, spattered across her lifejacket and the front of her soaking dress, was a horror she would never forget.

He lay ominously still. Splinters of oak had penetrated his visor, lacerating the side of his face. One arm was twisted unnaturally at the shoulder; his right leg was distorted and limp. As Marty cradled his head, blood began to pool along the smashed edge of his helmet before dissipating into unrelenting rainwater. Forgetting her own injury, Joss dragged herself closer. *Oh God, dear God, let him be OK.* Marty was speaking in urgent tones to the helicopter's winchman. She clung to his arm, numb, watching his lips move without taking in a word.

'*Ollie.*' Marty looked up, suddenly fierce. 'I need you to do something. You have to help us now. You have to help Cal.'

Ollie got to his feet, still grasping the line, swaying like a bewildered drunk as the hull continued to pitch.

'We're going to get you into the helicopter, one by one – Cal first, then your mother, then you. They'll winch down a cradle with the paramedic and a stretcher. I need you to keep

Kara as steady as you can; try to point her away, against the current. The lifeboat can't tow with all of us on board, and she needs to be stable. She'll get movement from the wind, she'll be steerable even without sail. Can you do that?'

Gathering himself, Ollie nodded, *Yes*. He clambered to the tiller, planted himself behind it, and locked his eyes onto the dark shape in the sky looming larger every second, accompanied by thundering engine noise. A massive downdraft was already compressing the ocean surface as far as the eye could see.

As the hull bucked along a fragile invisible line, contained a little better by Ollie's renewed determination at the helm, the crewman descended, harnesses and equipment unfurling with him onto the deck. Joss held her breath, hand to her heart, as Marty helped him manoeuvre McCalvey into the cradle. Within seconds they were giving him gas and air while Marty rhythmically massaged his chest, exhorting him, *stay with me buddy, come on Cal, stay with me*. Distraught, she crawled nearer to slide her fingers inside his glove, pain and cold making her teeth clench. *Be OK, you have to be OK*. His hands felt like blocks of ice.

'Stand away, Joss,' Marty told her. 'You're next.'

Moments later he was helping her into a harness. 'I'll try to secure the boat,' he said. 'She's been holed though, we may not get her back in one piece. The chopper will take you direct to the hospital, the Royal in Truro. They've radioed ahead. I'll see you there.'

She ascended through a chaos of wind and rain, squinting through whorls of salt water to where Ollie stood grimly resolute at the tip of the heaving vessel. Her legs made contact with a platform as hands pulled her firmly into light; seconds later she was settled on a narrow bench wrapped in foil, ear defenders carefully placed to dampen the insistent throb. She registered urgent commands, a blur of orange overalls, clanking winches, pulsing monitors, needles flickering on dials. A hand on her shoulder. Kind words: *Steady now. Hang tight.* A plastic-spouted cup of sugary tea was pressed into her shaking hand.

Close by, a medic with his back to her was rigging up an IV drip. He was calling for oxygen, scissoring fabric, staunching blood – but she couldn't see the stretcher. No-one heard her cry *will he be alright?* Because her throat had seized, her voice wasn't working. She put her head in her hands, slumping forward just as Ollie was hauled to safety. A crewman grabbed him and wrapped him tight; then she pulled him close, rocking him in her arms as tears began to fall.

The crew were preparing to leave. Around her, harnesses were unbuckled and equipment stowed. In the seconds before the door was pulled shut, Joss turned sideways, craning her neck for a last look at the scene beneath them. Ollie shifted position to do the same.

Thirty metres below, the elegant almond shape of Kara's deck reared and squirmed like a rodeo horse. And in that moment, she was tipped sideways by a giant arc of water breaching a hidden fist of rock.

'*No!*' The gasp was Ollie's.

They saw Marty race to the bow, then retrieve the line that would drag him to the safety of the boarding boat as the hull cracked open behind him.

'No! *No!*' Ollie gasped again as firm hands pulled him further into the cabin.

'She's going.' The winchman shook his head. 'I'm sorry.'

A crewman grasped the door and slammed it shut as the helicopter dipped to circle home. But not before they'd witnessed Kara plunging, with slow, terrible dignity, into the sea's final, inescapable embrace.

TWENTY-THREE

After two sleepless nights in a hospital bed, Joss found she could walk – shuffle, at least – with a bit of support. The swelling round her ankle had subsided; nothing was broken, and a skilfully applied elastic bandage was doing its job. Her vital signs had returned to normal. She could go home.

Bag packed, she checked the number of The Royal's recommended taxi firm, having agreed with Annie that Ollie should stay close to Wheal Blazey in her absence. No long journeys, no more hospital – just rest, quiet, food, fresh air and space. Things were raw. There'd be time enough for talking later. And grief.

The Critical Care Unit was on the second floor. She knew it because she'd badgered the nurses for information. Someone had rung on her behalf, but the response had been maddeningly vague. *Yes, Mr. McCalvey was admitted on Saturday. Very poorly, awaiting scan results. Being monitored. No visitors without prior appointment.*

She tucked the taxi firm's number into a pocket and reached for the crutches by her bed.

The CCU was accessed via a shiny white corridor smelling, inevitably, of antiseptic and bland institutional food. She followed directions from the elevator, her progress occasionally punctuated by medical staff overtaking her in squeaky rubber-soled shoes. One last sign guided her round a left-hand corner, where the corridor ended at a nurses' station and waiting area.

A large man was in conversation with a staff nurse in blue. Both were standing by the desk – the controlled entry she'd have to negotiate, she realised with a sinking heart – and both glanced round as she approached. Suddenly overcome, she let out a shaky '*Oh,*' as she recognised Marty.

'Joss!'

He looked exhausted – rumpled and pale. He nodded his thanks to the nurse and waved Joss towards half a dozen plastic chairs ranged along the wall. She put down her crutches and sat.

'How are you doing?' he asked. She shook her head and shrugged. An impossible question.

'There's a vending machine over there.' He pointed at it.

'I'm fine, Marty. Please, just sit down and tell me how Cal is. Have you seen him?'

He lowered himself into the adjacent chair, paused for a second, then turned to face her.

'Briefly, from ten feet away. But that's it now, Joss. No visits for the next forty-eight hours. He's heavily sedated. Collapsed lung, broken ribs, shattered pelvis. If he's strong enough, they want him in surgery next week.'

'Oh my God.' She covered her face with her hands and howled. Her despair seemed to bounce off the walls and echo in the sterile, empty space.

Marty gave her knee an awkward pat. 'But he's alive,' he said quietly. 'And the good news is, the head injury's not that serious. Likely concussion, but nothing nasty like a clot... '

It was too much. She couldn't suppress the sobs that made her shoulders heave and tears leak through her fingers. A jolt against her chair told her Marty had stood up. She fumbled for a tissue and swabbed her face, fighting to regulate her breath; then just as she began to pull herself together, he appeared in front of her again, offering a plastic cup. 'Here,' he said. 'Tea.'

'Oh, *Marty*.' Everything she felt was contained in those two words: guilt, shock, desperation, sadness, hope – and now relief. She accepted the cup with a trembling hand.

'He'll pull through, Joss. He's a tough bugger.'

She nodded gratefully.

'Anyway,' he said, 'how's the boy?'

The boy. Not Ollie. She sipped her tea for a moment before responding. 'Physically? OK. Mentally? I don't know, Marty. He's quiet, very withdrawn. I guess he's… trying to come to terms with what he did.'

He glared down the corridor and grunted.

'They have a counsellor at his school,' she went on. 'I'm arranging sessions for him.'

'A counsellor?' Marty turned to stare at her, the look in his eyes speaking volumes. *He needs stringing up, not counselling.*

'I'm so sorry, Marty,' she whispered. 'I'd do anything – *anything* – to make things better. If only I could.' Tears started again. This time she let them fall. 'But I can't. I *can't.*'

'No.' He sighed and scratched his chin. 'But maybe you can save me a job in the next day or two.'

'What's that?'

He delved into a trouser pocket and pulled out a small bunch of keys. 'These are Cal's,' he told her. 'I just offered to go to his apartment to fetch him a change of clothes. He won't want to be messing about in a bloody hospital frock when they get him out of bed.'

'I'll go!' She almost snatched them out of his hand. 'Let me do it.'

'Fine. Well then.' He got to his feet again. 'Let's hope for the best.'

He hesitated a second, taking in the crutches. Then he frowned in the direction of the ward entrance, shook his head, and left her to her tea.

The impact of opening the apartment door days later was almost physical, as if everything she'd felt in that space was powerful enough to blow her over at any minute. It was – just as she remembered – pleasantly spartan and bright. She trailed a finger along the kitchen worktop, recalling half-drunk coffees and glasses of wine they'd been too consumed by each other to finish. In the tiny bathroom, she inhaled the scent of his shampoo and shower gel, the memory of his body making her weak at the knees. In the bedroom she sat – then stretched out – on his bed, closing her eyes as she hugged his duvet and wept.

Recovering eventually, she searched his simple drawers for T-shirts, pants, joggers and sweaters, folding them carefully into an overnight bag. Toothbrush, razor, comb, sponge… handling these intensely personal items brought another wave of tears.

What if he doesn't get properly better?

What if he can't – or won't – come home?

Bag eventually packed, she carried it to the door like a baby, cuddled in her arms. For now, it was all she had of him.

She scooped up the keys and took a last look round. There was post on his lounge table – he must have come home and temporarily put it to one side. The last thing he needed, she decided, was to wade through a pile of junk. But just in case…

She flicked through the meagre collection of leaflets, statements and bills. And then she saw it – a plain brown foolscap envelope. No stamp, no address. Just the name *McCalvey* scrawled in biro across the front.

She lowered herself onto the sofa, staring at it.

Tell him it's from Tyler. He'll know who I am.

None of her business, she told herself. Whatever this was, he hadn't wanted anything to do with it, or the scarred stranger who'd entrusted it to Marty.

But surely it was a signpost to his past.

Tentatively she picked it up, rotated it in her hands, then held it up to the light as if it might reveal itself without the need for stealth.

Perhaps she was being overly cautious, she debated with herself. It was only a bit of paper, after all. Possibly something that might interest him, if and when he felt better. And the troubling stranger had disappeared weeks ago. What harm could it do?

It's really *none of my business.*

Though when she thought about it… after everything they'd been through, the startling things she'd discovered, the conversations they'd never had…

Yes it damn well is.

She tore open the envelope and slipped its contents onto the tabletop.

For a few heart-in-mouth seconds she sat blinking at what looked like a school photograph – thirty or forty boys assembled in front of an imposing building she recognised immediately. A sheet of notepaper had slithered out with it, bearing a message scrawled in the handwriting she'd seen on the envelope. She pushed the photo momentarily aside, and read.

Mackie
I found this photo and thought you should have it. I'm marrying soon and clearing stuff out.

Chuck it if you want. But you know that place will always be part of us.

Sorry you weren't up for reconnecting. You look good though. A daughter, eh? I guess you've moved on, like I'm trying to do. Closure, I think they call it.

Anyway. After all these years, I just wanted to say thanks. I owe you.

Take care

Ty

She lowered the note and reached for the photograph.

He was there, in the middle of the back row. Dark-eyed, unsmiling, handsome even then. A well-groomed schoolboy, living at Raven House.

Oh, Cal.

Her eyes moved to his immediate left. The woman she now knew to be Erin Glover was smiling beside him, tall and imposingly elegant, the distinctive dragonfly brooch clearly visible on a lapel. She was resting a hand on his shoulder, a gesture that looked both comforting and familiar. Joss's eyes filled. Everything made sense. *They were close.*

Other adults, some not much older than the boys, were dotted around the group. She scanned the sea of faces, hungry to understand his environment, his friends, his *life*. At the edge of one row, a uniformed nurse had taken a position sideways-on, not quite facing the camera. Effacing herself?

Joss lifted the photo closer, scrutinising the figure with growing astonishment. The woman looked just like…

No. It can't be.

But the fine, bird-like face was unmistakeable.

It was Eva.

TWENTY-FOUR

'Eva – I need to talk to you.'

The older woman glanced up in surprise. 'Of course. Has something happened?'

Joss was trembling. She hadn't even taken off her coat. She'd tucked the photograph inside the lining for extra protection, and all the way home she'd felt it sliding against her ribs, giving off a charge that was almost electric.

Eva wrapped Jack's fingers around the TV remote. 'Three quiz programmes coming up back-to-back, Mr. Livesey,' she told him. 'We'll leave you in peace for a while and return with tea.' He nodded at the screen.

Joss led the way to the kitchen, where they wouldn't be disturbed. Check-outs had finished, changeovers were in hand, and Annie had taken Ollie into town to buy drawing paper. *Granny time,* she'd called it that morning – a chance to do her bit in terms of emotional repair. *There's a comfort in doing ordinary things – while we wait for the dust to settle.*

'Can I help with something? You look worried.' Eva took a seat on the opposite side of a breakfast table.

Joss cleared her throat. 'Eva. When we met... when we

interviewed you…' She pulled herself rigidly straight. 'You didn't tell us you worked at Raven House.'

For a moment Eva seemed genuinely bewildered. Then she pursed her lips and grunted. 'That was twenty years ago, Jocelyn. Maybe more.'

'What exactly did you do there?'

The bright eyes clouded. Eva placed her hands on the table-top and quietly examined them. 'I wasn't on the staff, if that's what you mean. I was a local community nurse. I attended the infirmary there twice a week – more if a boy had a particular medical issue.' Her expression had grown wary. 'Can I ask what's behind your question?'

Joss reached inside her coat and drew out the photograph, thumbing creases away as she flattened it between them. Eva leaned forward to scan it, and caught her breath.

For several long seconds, the silence in the room was absolute. Outside, gulls hectored each other in a dull grey sky; trees bordering the garden hissed in a fitful wind, and hikers' voices drifted towards them from the gate – but Eva appeared oblivious to anything but the images in front of her. A frown tightened her features as one hand stilled above the central group.

'Where did you get this?' she whispered. 'And… why show me *now*?'

Joss glanced from the photo to Eva and back again, disconcerted by the woman's obvious shock. She'd hoped simply to jog the carer's memory; gather more detail about her professional history in order to complete a jigsaw whose missing pieces had recently been driving her mad. But the path to clarity suddenly felt like quicksand.

'You didn't think to mention it before?'

God, that sounds pompous. Inwardly she groaned at herself. She needed Eva to open up. Questions were clamouring in her head, and her nerves were beginning to fray.

Eva moved her hands to her lap and began kneading her fingers. 'It was… a very difficult time for me, Jocelyn. Part of my life I've never wanted to revisit. Or talk about.'

'To do with Raven House?'

Eva nodded. She looked up again, her face white.

'I'm so sorry.' Joss stretched a hand across the table. 'I know that the Manager – Miss Glover – lost her life in that terrible fire. It must have been appalling for the boys, as well as her staff and family and—'

'Stop! *Please,* Jocelyn. *Stop.*'

Joss jerked backwards as if she'd been slapped.

With a peculiar guttural sound, Eva welled up. 'Oh, Eva!' Joss was mortified. 'I don't mean to rake up distressing memories. It's just that… I could really do with your help.' By now she was convinced Eva held the key to a door she'd been metaphorically pounding her fists against for months. 'I need to share something with you. I believe a man I know was… a child there.'

Eva went very still. 'Someone in this picture?'

'Yes.'

Joss bit her bottom lip. *This is it. This is where we get the drains up.* She watched Eva follow her finger as it moved over the sea of heads to that dark, unsmiling, arresting face. 'That boy,' she said.

Eva stared – first at Joss, then at the image. Seconds later, Joss heard her whisper one word. '*No.*'

She shuffled closer. 'Eva,' she said. 'I'm only interested in whatever you can tell me about this boy, Cal McCalvey. You *must* remember him. Trust me, I don't mean to upset you. I don't want to dig into parts of your life you've tried to bury. I don't care about the gaps in your CV. I just want to understand more about his background, his story.'

'McCalvey?' Eva looked stupefied. 'You say you *know* him? But—'

'He's a lifeboat volunteer, Eva.' Joss couldn't hold back a smile. 'The man who saved my life.'

There was a violent intake of breath. Eva's hands flew to her mouth. 'I don't believe it. Is this true?' Her eyes flashed with what seemed like wild hope. Joss wrapped her fingers around Eva's wrist and said, 'It's true.'

For a moment, the expression on Eva's face was one of pure joy. 'That's given me quite a jolt, Jocelyn, I must say.' She shook her head. 'And if what you're saying is true... It's rather wonderful.'

'So, you knew him well back then? Please Eva, tell me about him. I want to know *everything*.'

'Oh, Jocelyn...'

Eva turned back to the photo, but a shadow dimmed all the light in her face. Her fingers shook as she reached to touch the image again. Then she slumped back in her chair. 'I'm sorry, Jocelyn,' she groaned. 'I don't know if I can.'

'Eva – are you OK? Please, just take a minute. It's obviously bringing back a painful memory. I hadn't realised...' *What* hadn't she realised? 'You're making me anxious.'

'It was so long ago.' Eva refused to meet her eyes. 'Perhaps it's best to just... let things lie. Best for him I mean, not just for us.'

'What things? Eva – trust me, I would never do anything to put Cal, or you, in a difficult position. Please, *please* talk to me.' Her eyes devoured every furrow in the anguished face as if answers might emerge from them like invisible ink. After another bewilderingly long silence, Eva appeared to make a decision. Fixing her eyes on the hand still circling her wrist, she murmured, 'I *did* know him, Jocelyn, the boy McCalvey. In fact, you could say he cost me my job.'

'Sorry?'

Mystified, Joss watched the carer half stumble from her

chair to fetch a glass of water. Once she'd settled back in her seat, Eva rotated the drink between her hands, grimacing at it. 'You referred to him as Cal? That wasn't – isn't – the name he was known by.'

'No.' Stated aloud, it was obvious. Disquieting, all the same.

'We called him Mack, or sometimes Mackie. Short for *Mackerel*. Because his dad had skippered a trawler, and he could swim like a fish.'

Tyler's note confirmed this, of course. Joss nodded encouragement. 'He still loves the water.'

'He was a *perfect* boy. Smart, handsome, sporty.' Eva's sigh was despondent. 'He'd been in care a few years before I started at Raven. I was told his mother had been very young, just a teenager. She abandoned him when he was a baby. Then his father was lost at sea when he was only nine or ten.'

Joss swallowed hard.

'I attended the infirmary each week,' Eva went on. Her frown had grown noticeably more pronounced. 'Right from the start, I thought it was an odd place. You'd think a boys' home would be rowdy, lively, messy. But there was always something...' She hesitated.

'Something...?'

'Not *right*.' Eva took a gulp of water.

'What wasn't right? Please tell me.'

When she spoke again, Joss was startled to see the grey eyes blazing with something fierce and new. 'I began to wonder why *any* boy would need an escort, just to see a nurse,' Eva said. 'Why some of the older boys or staff members insisted on staying within earshot during the most routine treatments. Did they think anyone in my care would abscond? There was no logic to it. It started to worry me.'

'They wouldn't let children be alone with you?' Joss was perplexed. Had there been some kind of guardianship issue?

A protocol, or particularly draconian set of rules? As Eva was implying, that seemed like overkill.

'Of course, I dealt with plenty of ailments – infections, accidents and so on,' Eva continued. 'But over time I noticed other things. Marks that were never fully explained to my satisfaction. Once or twice I found myself looking into a child's face, thinking – *knowing* – that child was afraid.'

In the pit of Joss's stomach, something began to curdle like sour milk. 'So... you suspected bullying? Or... ' She felt herself turning to stone. '*Abuse?*'

'To my shame, I ignored it for a while.' Eva looked bleak. 'I told myself I was imagining things. Raven was highly respected and well-funded. Though I had my suspicions, the evidence was inconclusive. I was only dealing with a few boys, after all.'

'But what about... what about...'

'Mackie?'

Eva took a juddering breath. She dropped her head and traced his youthful outline with a forlorn, almost reverential tenderness as the question shrivelled to dust on Joss's lips.

'I saw him several times when I worked there, largely because of the contact sports he played,' she continued quietly. 'I treated sprains, a broken arm, injuries from the field. Even though he must have been a deeply unhappy child, he always came across as feisty and clever – a bit of a rogue. And there was a *kindness* to him. He looked out for the other boys, especially the younger ones, and they loved him. I was never so sure about the staff.' She took another swallow of water, set the glass down and stared at it. 'Then one day he did something to his back,' she said. 'I thought he might have slipped a disc. I was on my own with him for a couple of minutes when his escort was called to the phone, and I examined him more closely – though he clearly didn't want me to. What I saw brought everything to a head.'

'In what way?' Joss had all but stopped breathing. 'Eva – what did you see?'

Eva's expression darkened. 'Bruises.' Her voice clotted with emotion. 'Marks that in my judgement bore no relation to any kind of sports injury. And signs of other cruelty – cigarette burns, carpet burns, scratches from fingernails, human bites – things no one would have discovered without reason to undress him completely. Whoever was responsible had been careful.'

'No.' The room began to spin. '*No.*'

'I'm sorry, Jocelyn. I'm so sorry.'

Clutching her neck, Joss struggled to focus on the woman's bloodless face. 'But you spoke to him? You helped him?'

By now, Eva was looking haggard. Her cheeks were wet, her eyes haunted. 'He tried to blag his way out of it,' she answered. 'Talked about horseplay, pretended it was his own fault. *I give as good as I get* – I remember those exact words. But when he realised I intended to report what I'd seen, he panicked. He begged me not to. He told me other boys would be punished if I made trouble, that it would make things worse. He said he'd deny everything. And he pleaded with me to wait, because he said… he said… he had the power to make it stop.'

Joss clasped her head, fighting nausea. 'What did he mean? How could he possibly make it stop?"

Eva looked away. 'All I know for sure is that it *did* stop. After I spoke to him, it did stop.' A shudder convulsed her upper body, as if she'd ingested something unspeakably foul. 'But I reported what I'd seen to my Head of Practice anyway. He assured me he'd take it up with Raven's governing body and alert the child protection services.'

'So… it was followed up? Something was done?' Joss was bewildered. Nothing she'd read in any account of Raven House had hinted at this black episode in its history.

'If anything was ever done through official channels,' Eva muttered, 'I never knew about it.'

'But you said it stopped.'

'I was told it was being handled; that staff and boys had been interviewed and remedial action agreed. It was all kept very low key. Apparently my notes were passed on, but I was never consulted again.' The frustration in Eva's voice and eyes suggested long years of quietly smouldering outrage. 'Things seemed to return to normal, as far as I could tell. I tried to believe something positive had happened – that there'd been an intervention. But a few months later, I saw another boy in the infirmary, a smaller boy, Tyler – and I realised nothing had changed.'

'*Tyler?*'

Puzzle pieces clicked into place. The nervous young man waiting on the quayside, blond hair swept across a ribbon of discoloured skin. A valedictory note of thanks.

I owe you.

'Is Tyler in this picture, Eva?'

It took just two seconds for Eva to place her finger on a sweetly trusting young face. Smiley and hopeful – there he was, flawlessly pink-cheeked, a yard or two down the line from McCalvey.

'I went back to my Head of Practice,' Eva said. 'I demanded he pay attention, that he escalated the process. I told him if he didn't pursue it more forcefully, I'd go to the police myself.' She was seething now. 'Two weeks later, I was told my duties were changing. Raven had requested the services of a different nurse.'

'*What?*' Joss gripped her head harder, trying to stay focused despite this bombardment of deeply disturbing information. Still more fragments began to settle into a grimly coherent picture. 'I found an article that mentioned a whistle-blower,' she said. 'Was that you?'

'I'd hit a wall,' Eva said grimly. 'I didn't know what else to do. Erin Glover was a pillar of the community. She did a lot for charity, her brother was an MP. She had relationships with police at the highest level – and my Head of Practice, as it turned out, was a family friend. The governors marked me down as a troublemaker. A fantasist. So I had to be… *removed.*' She gave a cynical snort. 'I left a week before the place burned down.'

Joss's rage exploded like a grenade. 'But Miss Glover had a duty of care! She couldn't have known what was going on, or she'd have dealt with it. She must have been a mother figure to Cal and the younger boys. And you had hard evidence, Eva. Couldn't you have gone to her directly?' *Tell me something positive,* she felt like pleading. *Children were suffering, for God's sake. Cal was suffering. Tell me someone showed him a little humanity.*

'Miss Glover? A *mother* figure?' Eva gave a mirthless laugh. 'That's the worst part of it.'

'What do you mean?'

'Whenever I saw him after I submitted that first report, he was always accompanied. *By her.*'

'By Miss *Glover*?' Joss stared into the anguished face, baffled.

'She wouldn't let him out of her sight. I couldn't get anywhere near him.'

'But why did she feel the need to—' And then she stopped. Foreboding thickened inside her head like a toxic mist. If the most senior person in the place felt compelled to protect him, she *must* have been aware of an ongoing threat; something vicious and brutal she should have taken immediate action to crush. It made no sense that she'd routinely attach herself to one particular boy. Unless…

A blade of fear scythed through her. *No. There must be something I haven't understood.*

'What about the enquiry?' she asked. 'There was an inquest. After the fire.'

The look Eva gave her was bitter. 'Erin Glover's death was undeniably horrible. Recreational drug use was alluded to. Alcohol, the fact she smoked heavily. Habits that allegedly contributed to the tragedy. Rumours persisted for a while, but nothing was ever proved. She worked so hard, everyone said – surely she deserved a few creature comforts, like the rest of us? Staff went their separate ways, the children found new homes, here and abroad.' She pressed her fingers hard into her eyes. 'And Mackie never, ever, said a word. *Not one word.* Not to the police, not to social services, not to anyone involved with the inquest.'

'Perhaps he couldn't face talking about it. Perhaps at some level he felt too… involved. Responsible in some way. Or… *ashamed.*' The insight broke from her in a sob.

'Or else he suppressed it. Blocked it out.' Eva shook her head. 'Dissociation isn't an uncommon reaction to trauma. Especially in a child of that age.'

Joss stared again at the photo, her eyes blurring. 'So… how old *was* he?'

'Thirteen or so.'

Ollie's age.

'But he got out,' she wailed, desperate for a crumb of comfort. 'He saved at least one other boy – Tyler. He escaped, Eva. He survived.'

The carer nodded and bowed her head slightly. 'If he's the lifeboatman who rescued you, I'd say he's done more than survive. Though something did bother me for a long time after the inquest.'

'Tell me.'

Eva leaned across the table to coax Joss's trembling fingers into her own hand. 'The fire that night,' she said. 'Erin

Glover lost her life. It destroyed Raven. It changed everyone's fortunes. But Jocelyn... I've never been convinced it was an accident.'

TWENTY-FIVE

'Time to wake up. Come on, Cal, wake up. Open your eyes.'
That voice… soft, kind, familiar… He tried to climb towards it from the black depths of an unknown ocean, limbs flailing as he struggled to disentangle himself from the weed and slime that sucked him back down, hundreds of metres from the surface.

'Come on, Cal, try. Open your eyes. Everything's under control. You're in hospital now, you've had surgery, everything's fine. I'm right here beside you. You're safe.'

Safe?

It was a lie. The currents were relentless, overwhelming. He was in free fall towards the sea bed, too exhausted to fight; spiralling into the murky darkness of an abyss.

I'll never be safe.

As he sank into the shadows, images gradually began to resolve themselves – objects were taking shape now, looming closer; colours, smells and noises were becoming more distinct.

That boy. He's here. He's inside my head.
I'm looking through his eyes.
What can he see?

God help me. I know this place.

The waves part to reveal a heavy desk – walnut – with metal trays and stacked paperwork, a lamp, letters, photographs, a laptop, all tidied to one side. The room he's standing in smells of stale cigarettes, perfume, ink and brandy. He hears the click of a key and glances to his left, suddenly afraid.

She locks the door from the inside – a tall, striking woman in a well-cut suit, a dragonfly on her lapel – and pockets the key before approaching him. She points at the desk. When he looks again, he sees a brandy decanter and a crystal glass, full. Across the green baize runner is a line of white powder; next to that a straw.

'That's for you, pretty boy,' she says. 'To help you relax.'

When he shakes his head, she laughs.

He watches her dip two fingers into the brandy glass. Her nails are long and perfectly manicured, deep red. She extracts them and comes close, brushing the alcohol across his lips, left to right, forcing him to lick. Even that tiny dribble scours his throat and makes his eyes sting.

Then she leans forward, and kisses him.

'You know what to do,' she says softly. 'I've put a robe on the couch over there for you. I'm going to wash and change.' But she lingers a moment, inclining her head, taking him in with a slow smile that makes his stomach heave.

He lifts his chin and glares into her face. It's a gesture of defiance, though he's shrinking inside. She snorts, amused, then takes him by the neck and reaches for his fly. When he flinches she kisses him again, hard this time. Her tongue probes for his as her fingers tease his buttons open, one by one. 'Don't worry,' she murmurs, 'I won't be gone long. Dig out my cigarettes, will you, baby?'

He burns with shame, knowing what she expects him to do to her, knowing how she'll use her mouth and hands on him, even when he tries to push her away. Sometimes he moans, sometimes he pleads with her while it's happening. But he will never, ever, let himself cry.

And his shame is less than his fear. If he doesn't please her, he knows she'll hurt him. Worse than that – she'll let bad things happen to the others, the younger ones, the boys who aren't as strong as he is.

But tonight, something is different.

As she strolls away to her private bathroom, he hears a wail of distress. He recognises the voice – it's Tyler, whimpering in the corridor outside, *Let me go, please don't, I haven't done anything.* There's a muffled thump and then Lafferty, the biggest and meanest of her inner circle, starts taunting, *I'll give you something to do, you whiny little faggot.* A door slams.

What the *fuck*...?

Tyler's only eight. He's been here less than three months.

This can't be happening. It should have stopped.

He's supposed to be looking out for them, the younger ones. It's the role he's taken on because he's her favourite – the reason he's sold his soul and walked into hell.

She needs to call off her dogs. This wasn't the deal.

She gave me her word.

He can't, won't, be party to it. Not any more. Not if she's turning a blind eye again.

He hears her humming through the bathroom door. Rage grips him – rage, despair, fear, panic – and he grabs the glass and takes a good slug for courage.

It feels like his brain is melting. The alcohol is vile, but it fills him with heat. He glances at the open window. They're up on the first floor, but the walls outside are covered with twisty stems – he's escaped that way before. The next minute the decanter is in his hand and he's pouring the contents over the wool rug. *Jesus*, he hates that rug; he's been forced down onto it too many times, it must hold the permanent imprint of his body by now. Maybe others before him. He snatches the lighter from her desk, flips it open and kneels.

The flames catch faster that he could have imagined. There's a lot of wood, fabric and paper in this room, but he suspects the whole building is dried out and full of rotten, worm-eaten timber. The boys' quarters are in a different wing – out of harm's way, he reckons. Chances are he'll be brutally punished for this, but he doesn't care. This is the last time he will ever come to this room. *It stops tonight.*

'What have you done?' She's pounding towards him looking wild, half undressed in a lacy bra and slip. He realises he's seeing her through an intensifying pall of smoke. And now she's backing off, returning to the bathroom, probably to run the taps. But it's all happening too quickly. He knows she won't find a big enough container to do the job, there's no time. The crackling is rising to a roar, his eyes are beginning to stream, and he can hear the shrieking of a smoke alarm.

In three bounds he's at the window; then he drops to the ground, slowing his trajectory by clutching at thick knots of wisteria.

By the time he's stopped running fifty yards from the house, other boys and staff are spilling out of doorways and onto the lawn like frenzied ants. It's windy, and the speed with which the blaze catches and spreads is incredible. It's terrifying and thrilling. Windows in rooms adjacent to the one he's just jumped from are already full of flame. He can't believe it. *Did I do this? Oh shit…*

A boy he knows well grabs his arm and says, *Mackie, where were you? Do you know how it started?* He shrugs and looks beyond him at the growing line of boys, dozens of eyes glittering with reflected light, utterly transfixed. Some of them are laughing and whooping.

'Is everyone out?' he asks. Then he realises. He can't see Tyler.

'Lafferty dragged him to the boot room tonight,' the other boy tells him, his eyes huge with terror.

He should have known.

The boy is shouting his name, but he's running back into the house. The smoke is a hot, churning tide; it hits him like a punch as he battles up the stairs and along the corridor to what they call 'the boot room' – the tiny, lightless space where servants from another era stacked and polished leather for their wealthy masters. Now it's where recalcitrant boys are isolated for hours, before or after a beating. He knows it only too well. And he knows that the door bolts from the outside.

The landing is almost molten. Flaming debris drops from the ceiling as he ploughs on, his feet scorching and his throat and lungs filling with caustic gas. The lintels of the boot room door are glowing, and black smoke is spewing through the cracks, but he can hear screams. The bolt is so hot it flays the skin from his hands – it's impossible to grip – so he leans back and kicks it with all the violence he can summon. The act makes him double up and retch; he starts to cough, his airways desperate to expel the toxic dust before it chokes him. But Tyler bursts free.

Half the younger boy's face is black and his hair is burning. They clamp arms round each other and hurl themselves back down the corridor to the staircase, now just a tunnel of fire. Steps liquify beneath their feet as they descend to the door, timbers are splintering and crashing six feet behind them; but seconds later the entrance is miraculously there, and cold air blasts his face.

He glimpses a line of flashing blue lights and a dozen blurred figures rushing towards him before he collapses onto the grass, and Tyler is ripped from his arms.

A white vehicle is backing up. Seconds later, two strangers in green loom above him and a mask is pressed to his face. 'Take it easy, son,' a voice says. 'Concentrate on your breathing. You just did something completely mad. Mad, but incredibly brave. Good on you. You got your friend out. Everything's alright. You're both safe.'

Everything alright. Both safe.

The plastic over his mouth and nose is tight, but the air it delivers is sweet. His eyelids flicker. He's somewhere between the oblivion of sleep, and a new level of consciousness that feels suddenly shocking and raw. *Jesus fucking Christ,* his whole body hurts. There's a different face above him now, the face of a woman he knows. Hazel eyes, a maple-syrup cascade of hair...

His reaction is visceral. He swallows hard and tries to find his voice, his fingers clawing at what he now understands are bedsheets. When she takes his hand, he looks up and receives a euphoric smile. Her eyes are shining, her face is flooded with light.

'*Joss?*'

'Thank God.' She squeezes his wrist, then leans over to smooth hair back from his forehead with a warm, infinitely tender hand. 'I'm right here, and everything's going to be alright, Cal, you'll see. You're an amazing, impetuous idiot, and I'm only here now because of you. You and your incredible bravery.' She glows like early morning sunshine; everything about her is luminous, compassionate and good.

But he turns his face away. He's drowning in a pit of despair, unable to stop the tears as he tastes brandy in his mouth, the cloying lipstick kiss of a woman whose scent and voice and insistent fingers are nauseatingly familiar – and who he left behind half-naked in a locked room, to burn.

TWENTY-SIX

The logistics were *pants*, she complained to Denzel. Truro was fifty minutes away by car, and visiting times were strict. Even when she made it onto the ward, the precious hour often had to be shared with doctors completing their rounds, nurses delivering medicines, porters wheeling him away for scans, physio or follow-up treatment. Opportunities for private conversations – especially difficult ones – were vanishingly small.

Denzel glanced up from the bain-marie he was polishing with manic energy. 'So, how long's he been in there now?'

'Nearly four weeks.'

'Poor sod.' He pulled himself straight. 'Knowing Cal, he'll be sick to the teeth of endless TV soaps and hospital food.'

Joss sighed. 'Last time I was there, he told me he was suffering from pasty withdrawal.'

'Ha! Why am I not surprised? Is he doing OK though?'

'Getting there.' She frowned and started unpacking cutlery from a polystyrene box.

School routines, Wheal Blazey's multiple challenges, and her dependency on Annie's availability and public transport had limited her to a frustrating total of six visits. Sometimes McCalvey rallied in her presence, grumbling he was turning into 'ten percent water, ninety percent macaroni cheese'; that half his fellow occupants snored like warthogs through the night 'and that's just the women'; that his physiotherapist had 'all the empathy of Freddy Krueger'. He seemed to brighten a little if these rants made her laugh. But she knew he was being brave. On too many occasions he could hardly bring himself to speak.

A few days after his return to consciousness, she'd arrived to find the police, the coastguard and a marine agent at his bedside. Separated by thick dividing screens, she'd wrung her hands at the sound of their hushed interrogation, wondering how she could ever hope to atone for the ordeal they were making him relive. Later, she learned from Marty he'd told them Ollie had his permission to take out the boat; that it was a tragedy born of misguided enthusiasm, inexperience and freak weather – no malice intended.

She would never be able to thank him enough for that. But when she tried to tell him so, he closed his eyes and turned his face to the wall.

'He's so sad, Denzel,' she said.

He stopped polishing to touch her sleeve. 'Of course he is. It's a big deal, losing that boat. And he's not well, Joss. He'll be lying there with nothing else to do but think.'

Joss felt her eyes blur. That's what worried her the most.

'Next time you see him,' he said, returning to his task, 'tell him to come up here on his first day home. I'll make him a proper pasty for his tea. OK?'

'OK.'

They both looked round as Annie arrived in the doorway, pausing as she sized up the kitchen's transformation. 'My word,' she said. 'It feels like a military operation in here. And we've had three more bookings this morning. The website's doing its job.'

'*Visit Cornwall* are coming for a recce tomorrow afternoon,' Joss reminded her. 'Brochures are ready on the desk.'

'And still a month to go.' Denzel beamed. 'Booked your Caribbean holiday for next year yet, Mrs. L?'

She scoffed and flapped a hand at him, though she couldn't hide a smile. 'Anyway,' she said, catching Joss's eye, 'Guy Tremain's just driven up. I wondered if you might want to check him in and give him a little tour?'

'You've changed your car!' she exclaimed as he ascended the steps. He pecked her on the cheek and followed her gaze to the spanking new Porsche he'd parked a conspicuous distance from Annie's battered old saloon.

'Like it?'

'Well, yes of course. Who wouldn't? But you so loved your old MG.' She found she couldn't look at him. 'The day you brought it back with all those terrible scratches—'

'I was livid,' he said.

'I feel we were… responsible, Guy.'

'Why on *earth* would you feel responsible?'

Flames seared her face and neck. 'Well – you were our guest at the time, and… I should have been more vigilant… but Guy—'

'Don't be silly,' he interrupted cheerfully. 'Water under the bridge. I was insured, it got sorted, and I sold it a few weeks ago for more than I paid. Result! And speaking of happy financial outcomes, I understand there have been some interesting developments at Wheal Blazey since I was last here.'

She stood frozen for a moment, fearful and indecisive. Then she looked into his bright, untroubled face, and allowed herself to breathe out.

'Well, I don't think we'll be selling any time soon,' she told him.

'So I gather. My contacts at the Tourist Board are delighted and rather impressed with you. Investing in a restaurant, bagging a bloody good chef. And I see you've overhauled the website to broaden your appeal. You're a smart girl, Jocelyn Harris.' He raised an eyebrow. 'And I think you may have been even smarter than you realise.'

'Oh?' The knowing look in his eye made her deeply suspicious. 'What's that supposed to mean?'

He tapped the side of his nose. 'Is your mother around? Why don't I check in, then I'll share a bit of news with you both.'

Annie insisted on serving tea in the lounge once the usual formalities were completed, including fresh-baked scones that Denzel seemed able to produce in the time it took most people to assemble a cheese sandwich. Guy set down his empty plate with obvious satisfaction, then leaned forward, smiled at each of the women in turn, and said, 'Arts Centre!'

'Go on,' said Joss.

'The council have definitely got funding now. It won't be massive, but it'll be more than adequate for the community and its outlying parishes, enhancing tourism and attracting creative professionals. There'll be a gallery, a small outdoor theatre, studio space and some very select retail opportunities. Quite a boost for St. Roslyn.'

Annie put her hands together in prayerful thanks. 'Oh that's marvellous!' she said. 'It will put us on the map. Great for our local youngsters, too. I'm very pleased.'

Joss's spirits rose for the first time in weeks. 'We'll benefit from that, surely. As will everyone who works in hospitality round here.' She exchanged grins with her mother. 'I can't wait to tell Denzel. He'll be worked off his feet.'

Guy examined his well-kept nails. 'It's particularly good news for Wheal Blazey, actually,' he observed.

Joss narrowed her eyes at him. He looked like the cat

who'd got all the cream. An unpleasant possibility made her sit forward and scrutinize his face more carefully. 'Guy – are you here to negotiate?'

His smile never wavered. 'Yes,' he said.

'I see.' She pulled a face and sat back.

'The project will need land,' he continued. 'Reasonable access to town, ideally with a wonderful view.'

'Not *this* land,' Joss replied tersely. 'Wheal Blazey has a strategy now. You just told me you've seen what we're doing and you think it's smart.' She lifted her chin and folded her arms. 'Don't play games with us, Guy.'

'Ladies!' he objected, provoking Joss to emit an audible groan, 'that's the last thing I'd do. I *am* here to negotiate. But not with yourselves.'

They eyed him with wary confusion.

'I'm putting a deal together with your neighbour, Bill Finch,' he said at last. 'We're buying him out. I believe he's planning to retire – possibly to one of the larger houses down at Roslyn Glynn, or possibly out of county. At any rate, he'll be moving on. You heard it here first. But perhaps you'll be good enough to keep it under your hats for a week or two?'

In the silence that followed, tiny bubbles of joy began to sparkle and pop between Joss's ribs. She looked at Annie in stunned disbelief.

'So, in a couple of years we'll have expanded our business next door to a classy arts venue,' she summarised, 'without a cantankerous neighbour trying to stymie us every step of the way. I think that's what you're saying?'

His wide eyes parodied reproachful innocence. 'I couldn't possibly comment.'

'When will Ollie be home from school?' Annie asked in a faint voice.

'In half an hour,' said Joss.

'Well then.' Her mother stood up. 'I think we should ask Denzel to join us, and open the most expensive bottle of champagne we can find.'

By the time Ollie appeared at the main door, they'd managed to compose themselves. Denzel was cloistered in the kitchen, perched on a bar stool while he made calls to suppliers and catering assistants he'd previously employed who he felt would be a 'fit' with what they'd begun to envisage as a brand. Annie was checking bedrooms, and Joss was manning the desk.

Ollie took the hand she held out and smiled with the air of melancholy restraint she'd noticed about him ever since the storm.

'How was your day?' she asked.

'Good.'

'Counselling session at lunchtime?'

'Also good.'

She could see he meant it. He let her ruffle his hair, but took a step away to fetch his school bag and heave it onto the counter, digging into it for something. She regarded him wistfully, amazed at how tall he was growing, how wiry and lean his upper body seemed, though his movements were still self-conscious and gawky.

'I drew something for you,' he said.

From the depths of the bag he extracted a protective cardboard wallet. He laid it on the countertop in front of her, carefully opened it, and unfolded a sheet of A2.

Bending to scrutinise it, Joss murmured a delighted 'Oh!'

In soft shades of brown and grey he'd created a landscape instantly recognisable as the eastern edge of St. Roslyn. Prominent in the foreground was the curve of Little Roslyn Beach, complete with rockpools and café, two rough-hewn tables sketched so realistically she half expected to feel the texture of wood under her fingertips. The road from town curved upwards in a tapering arc towards their own house, solitary and majestic on the clifftop. Leaded windows looked out over a benign sea where tiny sails inclined under puffball clouds.

'I *love* this,' she exclaimed.

'Look, there's you and me.' He pointed out two impressionistic figures on the beach at the water's edge, feet in the shallows, waving at nothing in particular. The sun above the horizon, perhaps.

'They look happy,' she ventured.

'Well they're in a special place.'

She glanced up in surprise, those words more precious than gold. She touched his hand, then leaned forward again to absorb every pencil stroke, taking her time. 'Perhaps we can find a way to use this in our marketing material, Ol,' she said. 'It's so inviting and peaceful. A simple life, captured in one landscape. No traffic, no pressure, no stress.'

His fingertip grazed the smaller of the two figures. He pondered a moment, before adding in a quiet voice, 'And no monsters.'

'No.' A knot inside her seemed to work loose. 'No monsters. I think we've finally tamed them, you and me.'

She watched him gather up the artwork prior to heading off to change. 'Tell you what,' she said. 'I'll meet you at the café there tomorrow, after school. It'll probably be the last chance we get to have a paddle and a hot drink before winter sets in. I'll need to get back for 5.30 though – there's a journalist coming – but that still gives us plenty of time.'

'I'd like that,' he said.

Later, she replayed the exchange to Annie as they filed the day's correspondence and tidied the desk. 'I don't want to jinx it,' she said, 'but it honestly feels like today has moved all sorts of things further forward. The news about Bill Finch and the Arts centre, followed by the most constructive conversation I've had with Ollie in weeks…'

Annie pressed her shoulder. 'Don't fool yourself, love. You still have a mountain to climb – professionally and personally. But I agree. It does feel like progress.'

'I just wish… ' Half-formed words stuck in her throat.

'Call him,' said her mother.

'Sorry?'

'You wish you could share it all with Cal. So call the hospital, darling. If it's too difficult for them to get him to the phone, make an appointment for tomorrow. Take my car. You'll be there and back before school finishes.'

'Oh, *Mum*.' Her heart jumped. 'Are you sure you don't mind?'

Annie shook her head and smiled. 'Call him,' she said again.

Joss found the number, checked her watch and dialled, anticipation rising like a freed bird with every ring. To her relief, the familiar voice of the unit sister greeted her with genial efficiency. She could be there tomorrow at two o'clock, Joss explained, just for an hour, if that was manageable within their ward routines?

There was a brief, unsettling silence; then an exchange of puzzled voices muffled by the unmistakeable clamping of a hand over the receiver's mouthpiece.

Joss's skin prickled. 'Is everything alright?'

The line cleared and the nurse re-engaged. 'It's a good job you rang, Mrs. Harris. We wouldn't want you to have a wasted journey. Mr. McCalvey isn't here.'

'Not *there*?'

'He discharged himself earlier today – contrary to our advice, I should emphasise. His friend Marty came to pick him up. I'm afraid he's gone.'

TWENTY-SEVEN

Along the coast path, winter's breath was unmistakeable. Elderly hydrangeas and fuchsias were reduced to gaunt, disorderly lines of sculpture; hedges and trees had ejected their last russet flares onto the tired grass. Only a couple of well-wrapped walkers passed Joss on her way to the beach. Even the sea seemed exhausted.

She trudged down the coarse steps onto cold white sand. *Here I am again, ploughing on. Getting up in the morning, washing, eating, breathing. Shuffling forward, one step at a time.* It was like picking her way through the aftermath of a bomb.

Since her call to the ward the previous day, she'd lurched from bewilderment to white-hot anger, then abject despair. Discharging himself, disappearing with no explanation or message? That *hurt*. Now, as she watched tendrils of surf dissipating along the shoreline, she just felt hollowed out and numb.

She'd wanted so much to be strong for him. Even in the teeth of calamity and loss she'd clung tenaciously to hope, as if hope were a contagious thing – a gift she could transmit through a kind of osmosis to bring him relief; to salvage something from this God-awful trail of emotional wreckage. But in the end, she hadn't been enough. A light had gone out. She'd seen it in his eyes.

The rudimentary café was still operating at one end of the beach, tucked below cliffs matted with tussock grass, lichens and thrift, the colours of summer all leaching away. She bought tea and a pack of biscuits – more from a need to fidget than from non-existent hunger – and sat facing the sea while she waited for school to finish. She was early. But this windswept place suited her mood better than Wheal Blazey's increasingly frantic activity. And the look of powerless compassion on her mother's face.

The tide was ebbing. In front of her, the ocean rolled gently away towards Chy Head – part of her story now, whether she liked it or not. It got into people's blood, she reflected, this mesmerising body of water. She glared through eyes beginning to chafe with salt. The surface glittered with diamonds of light, painterly and serene – too flat for surfers today.

All at once, grief and rage caught her like a freak wave; she shook her fist at the tranquil expanse of silver-grey and shouted at it. '*Treacherous bastard!*'

'Mind if I join you?'

His voice stopped her breath. Clumsy with shock, she scrambled to her feet. 'Cal!'

'OK if I sit down?' He gestured at the sea. 'Only... I wouldn't like to interrupt anything.'

She gaped for a second, her heart and brain catching up with the reality of him being right in front of her. Then she pulled out a chair. 'What on earth are you doing? Yes, for goodness sake, *sit down*.' He'd armed himself with a cane, which he let fall to the ground as she reached for his sleeve. She was instantly, urgently, frightened for him. 'You shouldn't be out of hospital, you obstinate... Sit down here *now*, for goodness sake.'

'Don't *fuss*, woman.' He lowered himself gingerly into the offered chair and smiled, but the lines on his face were deep. She could see he was making an effort to ignore strident complaints from his body. 'It's fine. I'm fine. I need to be out here, I need to be walking and breathing the air. It's the only way I'm ever going to feel normal again.'

Reclaiming her own seat, she took a minute to study him. He'd lost weight – his thick winter jacket seemed ridiculously loose – and he was holding himself awkwardly. The damage to his face had faded, though one fine vertical scar was visible just below the hairline. She leaned closer, aware that the dark eyes she knew so well were sizing her up with obvious anxiety.

'I can see what you're thinking,' he said. 'You're wondering if I'm really Poldark, and I've been keeping it from you all this time. Or Harry Potter. One of the two. Whichever gets your pulses racing.' He managed half a smile.

Barely conscious of her actions, she let her fingertips graze his jawline, where a soft new beard concealed other healing scars. For the first time, she detected a few silver threads weaving themselves through the irredeemably messy hair. *If you only knew how much I've wanted to touch you again…*

'You're still a handsome specimen, whoever you are,' she said.

To her surprise and consternation he pulled away, beyond the reach of her fingers. 'Yeah, right,' he retorted, a little too late. 'All the girls tell me that when they want free pizza.' But his teasing fell flat. She knew he'd registered her expression.

With growing unease, she fastened her eyes on his. 'You came here to find me,' she said quietly.

'Yes.'

'There's something you want to say.'

He averted his eyes. 'Yes.'

She took a breath, sat back and erratically began to stir her tea, ignoring the fact it wasn't sugared. When he glanced at her again, his lips were a hard line, his eyes hooded and uncertain. At that moment he looked ten years older – desperately tired; helplessly diminished.

Whatever he's come to say, he looks pig-sick about it.

There were things she wanted to say to him, too. But she had to tread carefully. She needed to pick her moment. And *God*, she needed courage.

'I'll always be grateful to you for introducing Denzel,' she deflected. 'Another month and we'll have the restaurant open.'

Briefly, he looked nonplussed. Then he nodded. 'It's a good decision.'

'He wanted me to tell you that the day you left hospital he'd make you a proper pasty. To celebrate.'

'Oh, *Joss…*'

The crack of distress in his voice made her turn away. 'OK,' she murmured. 'OK.'

For a while neither of them spoke. Breakers continued to whisper along the beach; cackling gulls drifted overhead in a dull sky. At last he took her hand and placed it gently on the table-top, underneath both of his.

'Your tea's getting cold.'

She stared blindly at the mug and shook her head. 'I can't make it right, Cal. I'm so, so sorry. There's no way I can make what happened right.'

'Joss,' he responded. 'None of this was your fault.'

She raised her eyes, and saw that his were grave.

'Nothing that happened was your fault. Or even Ollie's really, not completely. There were too many things in play. Bad judgement calls all round. Mine included.'

'But what happened to you, and to Kara – your wonderful Kara – was just appalling. An unspeakable nightmare. And you nearly lost your life… '

'And so did you, and so did Ollie. But here we are.' He bent to grasp her other hand. 'I know that Ollie wanted to keep us apart, to stop you getting hurt again. Probably still does. I *get* it. I get that he wanted to drive me away before I had a chance to let you down. Punish me for being a threat.'

'How can you be so forgiving, Cal? When I think of—'

'I've *told you*,' he interrupted, '*I get it*.' His hands moved restlessly over hers. 'The thing is… I know what it's like, Joss. To want to escape reality. To find a safe place. Safe from… other people.'

The desolation in his eyes made her want to weep.

'If you love someone,' he went on, 'the chances are you'll lose them. And then, when you let yourself think you can trust another human being… they betray you. Annihilate you. Break you apart so you can never find the pieces of yourself again.'

'Oh, *Cal*.' She shuddered at the images his words evoked.

'The fear Ollie has, the animosity – I've been there, believe me. And if that's truly how he feels…' He examined their joined fingers for a moment. 'Then I don't think – I don't see how we can ever—'

'He'll survive this, Cal,' she said firmly. 'He'll find his way.'

'It's not just about Ollie.' He slumped back in the chair, releasing her hands. 'It's about *me*.'

'Meaning what?'

'Meaning… you deserve better.' He shook his head. 'I'm damaged goods, Joss. If you really knew me – knew everything about me – you'd understand.'

'Try me.'

He groaned and covered his face.

'It's time to trust me, Cal.' She leaned forward to take his wrist. 'If you walk away now, we both need to be clear why. You owe me that much. You say I don't really know you – well then, *talk* to me. Share your history, trust me with the truth. I may surprise you.'

He scrubbed his eyes with his free hand and looked at her, anguished and perplexed. 'My history? Jesus Christ, Joss. That's a place you don't want to go.'

'Whether you deal with it or not, the past is always there.' She tightened her grip. 'And in my experience, if you ignore it, it finds pretty toxic ways to make its presence felt.'

He tipped his head back, sucking air through his teeth, thinking hard. When he faced her again he had the abject look of a man bracing himself to free-fall from the edge of an abyss.

'I don't know where to start.'

'It doesn't matter,' she said. 'So long as you do.'

He eyed her for a moment, then gave a small nod. 'There are things I've never shared with anyone,' he began. 'Really tough things. You've always wanted to know my back story, Joss. But when I let myself think about it – it makes me sick, physically sick. Things that happened years ago. Things I've never… that I just can't seem to…'

He broke off and stared at the ocean, clearly struggling. *Hang in there,* she willed him. *Keep going. For both our sakes.*

'In the time we had together, Joss… if you'd had the slightest idea… '

She was close enough to sense his whole body trembling.

'I should have opened up more to you, I know that. My name, for starters.' He swallowed, wincing as if something painful had lodged in his throat. 'It's… not Cal. I guess that won't come as any big shock.' He rubbed his nose and sighed. 'It's *Aidan.* The name I was given at birth… it's Aidan McCalvey.'

She nodded. 'I know.'

'What do you mean, *you know?*'

'I have a mole,' she said softly. 'Eva Sibbert. Nurse Eva, as you'd have known her at Raven House. She remembers you very well.'

He recoiled as if she'd shot him.

'She looks after my dad now.'

What little colour he had bleached rapidly out of his face. 'But if you know Eva – If you've spoken to her about Raven House – then you must know—'

He held her gaze for a moment, rigid with shock, then seemed to collapse. Clutching his stomach, he curled forward at the waist, gasping for air like a stranded fish.

Joss leapt up to take him in her arms. He was seriously cold and shivering violently. She peeled off her own coat, tucked it around him as best she could, and said, 'Don't move – I'll get you a hot drink.'

From the servery she eyed him with apprehension, worried he'd either completely black out or stumble away. By the time she put a mug in his hand, however, he'd shuffled more upright, bracing himself with his elbows on the table-top while he laboured to control his breath. She took his hand and massaged it. 'It's alright, Cal. Breathe. Drink your tea.'

Liquid spilled from the shaking mug as he raised it to his lips. She held it while he took a sip, then helped him lower it to the table. Letting go, he raised desolate eyes to hers and grasped her wrist. 'I killed someone, Joss. Did Eva tell you that?'

She steadied herself. 'Not in so many words. But I think… she always suspected.'

'God knows I didn't mean to. I didn't plan it. I just wanted things – vile, terrible things – to stop. So I started a fire. To get away.' He tried to detach his hand from hers, but she held on determinedly, her heart breaking at the anguish contorting his face. 'You don't need this shit, Joss,' he told her, his voice a hoarse croak. 'You don't need my sordid, murderous bloody history to make your life any more complicated than it is.'

She waited until he'd recovered himself and his breathing had slowed. 'You were just a boy, Cal,' she said. 'Scared and vulnerable in abhorrent circumstances. That foul woman made your existence a living hell. And she's *still* doing it.' She rested her palm against his cheek, relief buoying her a little as she felt him lean into her hand. 'You once told me the past can be a bastard – *fucking merciless bastard* was the phrase I seem to remember – very apt – but you helped me believe it's possible to come through it and stay strong. To choose not to be defined by it. You can meet the past head on, Cal – confront it, deal with it, get professional support if that would help. Or you can choose to run.'

She'd profoundly unsettled him, she knew it as she searched his face. But shadows still lurked behind those wary eyes – persistent and insidious. Denial, she understood. And fear.

'I've lived with this so long.' He twisted away from her. 'Too long. It's a stain inside me, like the writing in a stick of rock. And the last thing you and Ollie need is—'

'Don't!' she reproached him. 'Don't make this all to do with Ollie and me. This is about *you,* Cal. *You* doing something about the demons that have been eating away at you for years. Don't run away from this again. It's not the answer. It's never been the answer.'

He hung his head, everything about his posture signalling defeat, exhaustion and racking sadness.

In the long, silent seconds it took Joss to scan every centimetre of his haunted face, she visualised how he'd leave her – the way his lips would brush against her forehead as he stroked her hair for the last time; his sorrowful backward glance; then a stiff, stubborn trudge across the beach to the spartan apartment where his bag was probably already packed.

She had no tools left in her armoury. Except one, perhaps. The nuclear option.

Hold your nose and jump.

'Run if you want, Cal,' she said. 'But I think you love me. And I—'

'Mum!'

Ollie's cheerful greeting ruptured the air from a few feet away. He was poring over something he'd found in the dunes, blissfully unaware that the atmosphere around his mother had turned electric. When he lifted his head and registered the man staring at her in wide-eyed astonishment, he stopped dead. His treasure slipped to the ground.

Joss turned in despair at the sound of his voice. She felt the spell unravel – her last roll of the dice, kicked into the sand.

'Ollie – you can see it's Cal,' she said faintly. 'Come and say hallo.' She beckoned him forward.

McCalvey heaved himself to his feet and stepped back from the table to create unobstructed space. He looked even more startled than her son did, Joss thought – though the darting panic in Ollie's eyes was acute.

'Hi, Ollie,' he murmured. He cleared his throat and fumbled with his jacket collar for a moment, evidently trying to refocus. 'I hoped I might see you. There are a couple of things it feels important to say.'

Rooted to the spot, Ollie glanced from McCalvey to his mother and shook his head, transparently terrified.

We must look like casualties of war, Joss thought despondently. *All three of us bleeding from open wounds.* 'Ollie,' she ventured. 'Maybe there are things you'd like to say to Cal too?'

More seconds ticked by while Ollie examined his feet and wiped his nose with the back of a hand. Then he took one tentative step forward.

'Cal... you – you saved my mum's life,' he stuttered. 'You saved both of us. I saw what you did. You were... really brave.'

At last he raised anguished eyes to McCalvey's. 'Thank you.'

'You're welcome.' McCalvey glanced briefly in Joss's direction before returning his gaze to her son. 'Come a bit closer, Ollie. I need you to listen to me now.'

Ollie's eyes were like dinner plates. Cautiously he advanced another yard.

'Ollie – it's important for you to be clear. I would never, *ever*, have lifted a finger against your mum. I truly wanted her to be happy.' He pressed his fists hard into his lower back and flinched, the discomfort of holding his position clearly nagging. 'But I understand your desire to protect her. I can relate to that, and I respect you for it. Just so you know. And I hope you can move on from this, Ollie. I hope you'll be OK.'

Ollie gawped as if he'd seriously misheard. 'But…' He cast his eyes about and scrabbled his hair.

'But what?'

Suddenly, floodgates burst wide open. '*Kara*,' Ollie wailed. Tears began to pour like rain down his cheeks. 'I wrecked Kara. She was so beautiful, the best boat ever, and it was all my fault she got wrecked. I'm sorry, I'm *so sorry*.' He ducked away from McCalvey's penetrating eyes, his chin pressed hard into his neck, arms knotted across his chest as if he could squash himself into invisibility. 'I don't know what to do. I can never make it up to you. It was mad and stupid. *I* was stupid. You must hate me for what I did. You'll never forgive me. You'll always hate me.'

In the overwrought silence that followed, the noise of crying gulls and tumbling breakers seemed amplified and peculiarly cruel. But McCalvey's voice, steady now, drew Ollie back.

'She *was* a beauty,' he nodded. 'That's true.' He let the words hang for a moment. Then he took a deep, slow breath. 'But I don't hate you, Ollie. I *get* you, though you can't see it right now. Maybe in another life we'd have been fine. Maybe

– if things had been different – you and I could have been friends.' He turned again to Joss, who in spite of the pain ravaging her heart managed to acknowledge his compassion with a smile.

'Anyway,' he added quietly. 'She was only a boat. There'll be others.'

Her jaw dropped. As she stared into his soft, sad eyes, she wondered what that remark had cost him. Suddenly she felt she'd known this man forever; that she understood everything about him she would ever need to know.

'Oh,' McCalvey said then, 'I nearly forgot. I have something for you.'

He dug into a jacket pocket, then held out a hand.

The brass casing of Kara's compass gleamed in his palm; the slender needle danced and shimmered as Ollie reached to take it. As his fingers curled around the exquisite little instrument, Joss heard his reverent *'Oh'*. He looked enquiringly at McCalvey, eyes shining as his thumb caressed the surface.

'Make sure you look after it,' McCalvey said. 'You can practice with it anywhere, so you're comfortable navigating with it later. On your own boat one day, with any luck.' He put a hand on Ollie's shoulder. 'Maybe you'll remember Kara, Abba, and a bunch of nosy dolphins when you do.' Stiffly, with an involuntary grunt, he bent to retrieve his cane.

'Are you *leaving*?'

McCalvey knocked the cane against the table-leg, dislodging gobbets of sand. He fussed with it another moment, shifting his weight from one foot to another, testing different positions as if trying to convince himself it was realistically of any use to him. Evidently sorted, he turned to fill his lungs with air and contemplate the horizon.

Joss waited for his parting words, her heart plummeting

like a fall of rock. But he continued to stand there, absolutely still. And then he looked at her.

She couldn't bear it. Disengaging from his eyes, she swivelled back to the undrunk tea, jettisoning cold liquid onto the beach, tidying spoons and crumpling paper napkins into the empty mugs. 'Cal thinks we'd be better off without him,' she said briskly, not looking up.

Ollie's face puckered. 'That's not true!' Too quick for her restraining arm, he launched himself at McCalvey.

'Ollie, *careful!*' Helplessly, Joss watched him thrust both arms inside McCalvey's half-open jacket to grab him around the waist. With an audible gasp, McCalvey staggered towards the table, only just keeping himself vertical, his cane rolling away.

'You mustn't leave, Cal!' Ollie implored. 'Not because of me. *Stay.* We need you to stay. *Please.*' Joss saw her son's shoulders straining as he pressed himself against McCalvey's chest, the agitated way his head wriggled from side to side, just before he started to cry again. 'We *are* friends,' he whimpered, 'We *are.* It's all my fault, everything's my fault, I'm sorry, I'm so sorry. I promise I'll help you build another boat. But I don't want you to go.'

For several bewildered seconds, McCalvey stared down at the boy half hidden in the folds of his clothes, thin arms hanging on with disproportionate strength, keeping him captive. Joss rose to intervene; then caught her breath as she saw McCalvey slowly lower his face into the fine fair hair, wrap his arms around the heaving shoulders, and hug Ollie tight.

'Cal – are you alright? Your cane—' She started towards it, but he cautioned her with a brief shake of his head. Ollie still had him gripped, though the sobs had lessened to a series of sniffles, hiccups and low moans.

For more than a minute, until Ollie was completely cried out, McCalvey held him close.

Joss moved nearer. She touched the sleeve of one encircling arm, and McCalvey looked up to meet her eyes again. He was desperately pale and drawn, battling obvious discomfort – but what startled her more were the tracks of tears that had nothing to do with salt or weather.

'It's probably too late,' she said. 'And I don't know what either of us can do about it… but someone here seems to think they've finally found a safe place.'

He loosened his hold on Ollie to grasp her hand. 'Maybe that makes two of us.'

The noise of gulls, wind and waves faded to nothing. Joy crept up on her silently, spreading through every cell and fibre like a balm. She closed her eyes.

The journey to this moment had been tortuous, volatile, desperately painful at times. *For each of us*, she thought. But here they were, standing together at the junction of something new. Was it worth it? Impossible to know. But it felt like all three of them were coming home.

'So, if I stay and find another boat, Ollie,' she heard McCalvey say, 'there'll be no solo helmsmanship until I've taught you how to manage the damn thing in rough conditions. I hope that's understood.'

'Understood.' Ollie grinned up at him.

'Be *sure*, Cal.' Joss put her free hand over his. 'Be sure you can commit to something that won't make you feel trapped.'

He raised an eyebrow. 'I've heard those words before somewhere.'

'Just… be sure what you really want.'

'What I want? Hmm.' He tapped a finger against his lips. 'Well, now that you ask… I could murder one of Denzel's pasties.'

'Oh for heaven's sake!'

And there it was at last – the teasing, irresistible, street-urchin smile.

'Does that mean Cal's coming up to the house?' Ollie asked.

She stooped to pinch his cheek. 'It looks that way,' she said. 'But we need to get a move on – I told you, I've organised a meeting.'

'You go on, Mum.' Ollie flapped a hand in the direction of the steps. 'I'll walk Cal up in a bit.'

She narrowed her eyes at him. *Did he really just say that?*

'Well, don't keep him out here too long.' She scooped up her bag. 'It's getting chilly.'

McCalvey leaned closer to Ollie and remarked in a conspiratorial whisper, 'Sassy bloody mare, your mum.'

She snorted. But the sound of Ollie trying to suppress an illicit giggle was delicious.

'Well then. If you'll excuse me, boys…'

She turned her gaze towards the cliff path and Wheal Blazey, half expecting the salt breeze to scoop her up and carry her all the way there, she felt so miraculously light. Though the ground beneath her feet had never felt more solid.

'We'll see you up there, Joss', she heard McCalvey say. 'Go. Wheal Blazey needs you. You've a cracking little business to run.'

ACKNOWLEDGEMENTS

Thanks are due to my brilliant mentors and readers: Becky Hunter – honest, forthright and hugely encouraging during the editing process; the responsive team at Jericho Writers; my amazing co-travellers on Curtis Brown's 3-month novel-writing journey – notably the very talented Georgina Sewell, Meera Shah and Cynthia Coleman; and my enthusiastic posse of early critics, Bernard MacDonagh, Jan Searle, Martine Millson, Colin and Niky Jux, Lynne Cornell. And where would I be without the insight and unfailing support of Lauren, Georgia and Alan Street – the three greatest treasures of my life? After long, moody months of scribbling I'm not sure I deserve you! But it's down to you that this story made it over the line.